This Hurts copyright © 2007 by Shaun Mathis & Aapri Books

5100 Lebanon Ave Suite 702

Philadelphia PA, 19131

www.aapribooks.com

Library of Congress Control Number: 2007906117

ISBN: 978-0-6151-5450-3

Cover & Back Design: Charity Leach

Cover Model: Chimere Mayo

Author: Shaun Mathis

Author Photo: Rochelle Morton

Printed in the United States of America

Aapri Books

My words, my story...

This book is dedicated to a number of people who are near and dear to my heart and is as follows.

My aunt Kiesha Fields for sparking the flame and feeding it oxygen these past six years. Thank you so much for everything you've ever done for me.

My mother Damita Mathis for simply being my mom, I love you so much.

My church family, Donald Williams, Renee' Williams, Toya, Crystal & Terrance for all the rides to church every Sunday, for the talks (Don) and for the overall love your family has shown me, I am forever thankful.

My big borthers Tracy Lee Graves & Benjamin Carter for inspiring me and looking out for me despite my anger and mood swings. Thanks for helping me grow up. I love ya'll.

To Billy Lucas for being a friend when I needed one the most. I wrote my second book with the pen you got me for Christmas.

My immensely talented circle of friends; Ronald *Jus Mula* Knight, Wes *Fai*r Hayward, James *Mook* Jamieson, Quincy *GQ* Griffin & Sean *The Bandit* Graves. My creativity would be nothing like it is today if it weren't for you all. Thank you all for your continued support & friendship.

Lastly to the apple of my eye; she knows who she is, thank you for just being you & accepting me, flaws and all. I love you.

For
Shaun, Chantall & Chanta

THIS HURTS

1

Pick up the phone and dial the damn number Syncere. My mind keeps telling my fingers to dial ten little digits but my fingers are being as disobedient as possible. The phone rang, once…twice…a third time. I was about to hang up when I heard her voice. Her soft, country filled warm sweet, sweet voice.

"Hello?" she said. I paused for a minute to allow my heart to beat again; I'd never heard such a sound so sweet that it gave my ears a toothache in at least not in two years.

"Hello?" she said again.

"Hey, Kendra?"

"Yeah, who's this?"

"It's, it's Syncere." The sudden silence was expected after what I did, I'm surprised she didn't hang up the phone.

"How did you get this number?" She asked.

"Mrs. Williams gave it to me. I kinda asked her for it." I said bashfully.

"Why'd you go and do that for?"

"Because I wanted to talk to you."

"Don't you think it's a little too late for that now? Why didn't you do that when you were running through the damn church with Jewa?" She'd brought up the time I was most ashamed at that I'd done. At the sound of that I tapped Evelyn on her head and signaled for her to stop sucking me off, my erection was completely gone.

Kendra, her mother and aunt caught me darting out of the old sanctuary with Jewa. They knew what we were doing; or rather they assumed what we were doing.

That day after church Jewa offered to suck my dick and we snuck into the old sanctuary to perform the act. When I looked at Jewa in the eyes all I saw was Kendra's face and I backed out. We were trying to sneak back out undetected, but we were spotted and the perception of what went down was already in the minds of her mother and aunt. I was trying not to get caught not doing something and it backfired on me.

"I apologize about that." I said as she laughed sarcastically.

"You apologize? You are much too late for that. You embarrassed the hell out of me in front of my momma, who thought the world of you. You made me look like a fool in front of the whole congregation…"

"How did I do that?"

"Word got back to Mrs. Pettiford and she told the pastor and he mentioned it the very next Sunday. The Sunday you conviently stopped coming to church. Everybody talked about it. Everybody stared at me, whispered about me behind my back and in my face. Do you know how I felt? I told my momma I wanted to stop going to church but she said that would make me look guilty. So I went. Week after week after week and heard people talk about me. Call me all types of fools, and dummies and no one said anything to Jewa. Everyone's focus was on me."

I didn't know what to say to that. The joy and excitement that filled my heart once I heard Kendra's voice is now replaced with the regret and shamefulness that I was able to block out for the past four years. But she stirred them back up and I can't help the way I feel right now, I deserve it. I should've felt like this four years ago maybe I wouldn't be doing what I am doing now. Well I'm going to keep my eye on the prize and make things right, I want the love of my life back. It is kind of hard to concentrate with Evelyn sitting next to me naked with her legs spread while she played with herself. Her moans grew a little louder each time especially when she took my hand and entered it into her warm wet pussy.

"Well I really don't know what to say. I really didn't mean to hurt you." I confessed.

"What, I didn't give you what you needed. I wasn't enough for you?"

"It's not that, I didn't do what you think I did. You have to believe me."

"So did you call me for a reason or just to continue a lie, because I think I know how this goes?" I'm not used to Kendra being so strong and so forward

She got quiet for a while, I got quiet for a while, it was just silence.

"Apology accepted. It's over and it's behind us now. So how have you been?" She said changing subjects.

We talked like we used to talk when we were fourteen and fifteen which pissed Evelyn off, she is not used to not being the center of my attention. While I spoke to Kendra time stood still and nothing else mattered not even the fact Evelyn was riding me backwards with her face buried in a pillow on the floor. I didn't jump right into the fact I wanted Kendra back, that'd be too early. Instead I concentrated on getting her to trust me again thus I didn't tell her I had a girlfriend because that would foil my plans. If I did that the option of us being together again would not even exist. She might think I was doing something wrong because I was calling her even though I had a girlfriend, that I'm fucking as we speak.

I didn't stop smiling, not until long after we hung up with each other agreeing that she would call me back tonight and Evelyn shook from her orgasm, mine hadn't come yet. My heart was at ease for once. Yes I currently have a girlfriend and I'm messing with two other girls to be exact but none of them could ever make me feel the way Kendra does. I didn't realize that until the shit hit the fan two years ago. I told my aunt when I first introduced Kendra to her that is the woman I am going to marry and I intend on keeping my word.

Today is already a great start. While Evelyn slept I went over to my closet and got out a real big box of memorabilia that I'd collected from past girlfriends over the years. I dug through it searching for one of Kendra's pictures, not just any picture but the one I think she is the most beautiful in. Found it! It is a picture of Kendra at her senior prom. She wore an all black dress and her hair braided, some of it was up and some of it draped down. In that picture her graham cracker brown skin and her flawless pearl white smile was perfection.

As I sat on the living room sofa my roommate Trevor came into the house. I got home from college a few weeks ago and Trevor was on the verge of getting evicted. So I moved in with him and helped him get caught up on the rent until he landed himself a new job. It actually worked out for me because my mom just moved to North Carolina a week after I got here and I really didn't know where I was going to stay this summer. All my family moved to N.C. but it's not a bad arrangement, its like being in the dorms. It's a one-bedroom apartment with a small kitchen and an even smaller bathroom. Hell I figure I can work for two months, save up some dough to get a car and go back to school in the fall. The only thing is this nigga was living in the dark ages before I got here. No T.V., no phone nothing, just an old rebuilt computer. I had to bring him into the twenty-first century.

"Yo remember that gas station we went to the other day?"

"Yeah."

"Well they called me in for an interview for this afternoon."

"Damn man, you already got two jobs. Turn it down so they can hire me." Trevor suggested.

"I would but I need a car, especially living in North Carolina. I only got two months and my one job don't give me a lot of hours and the camp really don't pay much I just do it cause I like it, so I need this gas station job."

"Aight but yo put in a good word for me."

"I got'chu." The sun was high today. This is the only time of year I like to be in Connecticut, summertime. Clear blue skies, a slight breeze and half dressed girls, it's a beautiful thing. The walk from Prospect Street to Watertown Ave is not far at all so I put on my headphones and went on my way.

The air conditioning felt good as I waited for the manager to interview me. Hired on the spot working third shift at Sunoco gas station. I never put a word in for Trevor, he is a grown ass man and if I could find three jobs then he could find one. My pager went off.

"May I use your phone?" I asked the cashier.

It's my boy Tracy. Tracy is one of the people I met and became friends with three years ago when I was in a foster home. Quincy, a member of Tracy's rap group, was the grandson of my foster mother who introduced me to Tracy.

"Thanks for the ride man." I said sitting in his hunter green Chrysler Sebring.

"No doubt, what you doing way over here?"

"I had an interview."

"Damn how many jobs you need?" We laughed. "Yo you 'posed to be home on summer break and doing some music, now you ain't gonna have time for anything. You're a Jamaican now." We laughed again.

"Nigga I don't work all day everyday. The camp is Monday through Friday til three, Finish Line is three maybe four times a week after three and the gas station is five days from ten to six. Shit this is third shift, I can write while I'm here." I explained.

"Aight dude, you going to work at the mall now?"

"Yeah."

"Yeah me too, yo we hookin up tonight. You mind if we go to ya house?"

"I don't care but it's gonna be tight."

"Ya roommate gonna be there?"

"Yeah, but he ain't nobody." We did our patent handshake and I left.

Althroughout my shift all I could think about is Kendra. I had butterflies in my stomach because I am looking at the clock every ten minutes until it is time to leave. Just then Evelyn walked in.

"Hey babe." She said as she greeted me with a hug as I gave her a kiss on the cheek before letting her go.

"What's good?"

"Nothing, where you going after work? She asked.

"Home, Tracy and everyone is comin' by tho'."

"Can I come?"

"Yeah, just be there when I get home, Trevor is going to be there."

"Ok."

I met Evelyn last year through my cousin Charm and at the time she was dating this dude named Launchpad. She was just getting out of the eighth grade and I thought she was cute but I was on my way to college and that didn't look legal. I don't know why I am dating her now, she's only sixteen and I'm eighteen but I like her. None of her friends know that we date and none of my friends know her real age. She knows how to act around my friends, mature but when we goof off she does also. She's not the type of girl to be all up in your business, she knows how to fall back and let me do me when we are around my friends. She acts like a woman.

Her body is crazy. Evelyn is a Trini girl, Trinidadian and black. Her ass is a perfect apple shape and is as firm as a tennis ball. Her breasts are no bigger than a handful but my motto is anything more than a mouthful is a waste. Her eyes are a perfect almond shape with a slight chink to them and when she smiles her cheekbones raise. I ran into her my second day back home and we've been kickin' it ever since, plus she braids my hair, for free. We have fun together and that is cool, she stays at my apartment real late sometimes because I kinda don't want her to go.

Tracy and I cruised to my apartment listening to the latest song recorded by Quincy, Wes and Jus.

"When did they do that?" I asked.

"Yesterday when you were at work. See man you be missin' out on sessions, you could'a been on this track, this shit hot!"

"Nigga there will be other ones."

"Aight dude. Yo Sunday you wanna come with me and Sondari to Smiles?" he asked.

"What about M.Dot?"

"Man she ain't gotta know, just don't say nothin' 'cause you know how you are. You can't hold water."

"Aight but if she find out you know she gonna beat that ass."

"Nigga she ain't doing shit, I run this."

"Yeah right, that's why you ain't tellin' her."

"Have you seen Sondari? I'm tryin' ta smash." Tracy added with a huge smile on his face.

"I feel you on that she is bad as hell. She Jamaican right?"

"Yeah son and she only here for the summer nigga. Her cousin hooked that up."

"I ain't ever seen no light skinned Jamaican girl before."

"I tried to tell you all Jamaican girls ain't midnight black." Tracy hopped on the phone to confirm the location of Quincy and the rest of my boys.

"Where they at?" I asked.

"Yo these niggas bullshittin'. Wes says he is too tired and Quincy ain't back from Saint Jos' yet."

"Fuck he doin' way up there for. That's way in West Hartford."

"Man he met some chick off line and he went up there to see her. I guess they hit it off."

12

"Ya'll niggas is always chasin' bitches." I claimed.

"Whatever dude, I bet ya girl is right upstairs ain't she?"

"Yep." He laughed. "But she is here and she gonna chill until I handle mines."

"Nigga you crazy, you eighteen years old and got ya own place, I would be fuckin' everything not just one chick." Tracy proclaimed

"What? I share a room wit Trevor."

"So get him a bitch too."

"Have you seen that nigga? He only twenty-three and he look like he forty. I ain't matchmaker. You commin' up or what?"

"What for? Ain't nobody comin'. Call Jus and tell him fuck it."

"Aight." I agreed.

I entered the apartment and found Evelyn sitting on my futon and Trevor on his flicking through the T.V. channels.
"What up." I nodded my head back to Trevor and flopped on the futon next to Evelyn who instantly threw her hands around me and kissed me softly on my lips.

"Hi." She whispered.

"Hi to you."

"Where is everyone?" she asked curiously.

"Oh, they ain't comin'."

"Why?"

"'Cause they bullshittin. Don't wanna talk about it. I need some eats." I signed

"I took the hamburger meat out of the freezer."

"Oh word, thanks babe." I kissed her cheek. "You want some pasta?"

"Yeah, you gonna cook for me?" she asked smiling.

"Yeah, I can do a little sumthin'." I said.

"Yo word, I been starvin' all day." Trevor interrupted. Evelyn and I looked at Trevor with a who-asked-you look but we both said nothing. "Did you get that job?"

"Oh yeah I meant to tell you, they hired me on tha spot. I'ma be workin' third shift startin' tomorrow."

"Did you say sumthin' about me?" he asked.

"Yeah I did."

"What'd they say?"

"They said they still have a few more spots open and they'll look over your app." I said from the kitchen knowing I was lying. Evelyn and I talked while I fried the meat and boiled the noodles. Occasionally she came up behind me and held my hand as I stirred the sauce. I would lean back and she would hold me close to her, both hands on my chest.

"You're a beast, so big." Evelyn blurted out as I smiled and stay attentive to the food. "Charmed is about to come on, I'll be in the living room." A few moments later I served Evelyn with a piping hot plate of ziti with bread. I sat beside her with my huge plate of food and ate in silence, starring at Charmed trying to catch what was going on. I could see Trevor out of the corner of my eye looking over at Evelyn and I eat and after he did that a couple of times he got up and went to the bathroom.

"Is there any more left?" Evelyn whispered when Trevor left the room.

"Nope I made your plate and took what was left." I said with a smirk on my face.

"That's messed up." She said laughing.

"No it ain't. I brought food so I could eat, I ain't about to feed no grown man." Just as I was done saying that Trevor came back and flopped back on his futon but this time he had a pissed off look on his face but I could care less.

It was eleven-thirty at night and Evelyn and I lay on my futon her on top of me. Her five-foot three frame wasn't heavy at all. We didn't say anything to each other we just starred into each other's eyes.

"Why aren't you saying anything?" she whispered trying not to wake Trevor up who is sound asleep across the room.

"I don't know, just thinkin'."

"I know what you want." She said smiling.

"And what do I want?"

"Hold on." Evelyn put her head under the covers and pulled down my Jordan shorts. Soon I felt her warm wet tongue going up and down on my man tool and it felt good. Her hand caressed by six-pack as I closed my eyes and took two hands full of her hair. The minutes felt like seconds as before long Evelyn was resurfacing.

"Why'd you stop?" I asked.

"I don't like the taste of cum. Do you have a condom?" she asked.

"You sure you want to do this?"

"Yeah, why you don't?"

"Na, I do but don't you have to get home soon?"

"My moms is never there, she always be at her boyfriends house then she go to work and goes right back to his house. I might see her twice a week."

"Oh ok, hand me my safe from under here." She did and I slid on the Trojan condom while she slowly and gently took off my shirt running her hands over my pecks then to my washboard abs. She is so gentle with everything as he helped me out of my boxers. Through the darkness I could see her looking seductively into my eyes making me more aroused than I was when she was going down on me; she is next. I took off her shirt and bra kissing on her perky b-cup nipples. She ahhed out of pleasure as I laid her down and unbuckled her belt with my teeth then took off her tight Rocawear jeans.

I separated her legs lifting them into the air; I put my face in between then and bit her lacey thong panties in the crotch area trying to pull them off. I could see the silhouette of her naked body though the moonlight that peered through the window beside us. Her body is flawless, not a blemish, not a childhood scar, nothing. I sat over her for a moment admiring God's work.

"Don't look at me." She said trying to cover up.

"Stop, you're gorgeous naked." She giggled and so did I. "Come here."

"Why?"

"Sit on my face." I saw her eyes widen.

"Sit on your face?" Now I could see the smile when she popped up and waited for me to lay back.

"Don't put all your weight on me." I warned.

"Ok." She whispered excitedly.

Evelyn positioned herself on her knees each of them on one side of me and slowly lowered herself onto my waiting face. I grabbed her thighs tight and stuck my tongue out and I tasted the sweet juices that flow out of her love nest. I dug my tongue deeper in her making wild circles while she began to ride my face. With every motion she got wet and I could feel her juices running down the side of my face. Her soft sensual ohhs and ahhs quickly turned into louder ones as we went faster.

"I want you in me." She managed to get out in between moans. "NOW!"

She lifted herself off my face and I licked my lips while she lowered herself onto my man tool and it fit like a glove. The feeling of being inside of Evelyn was beyond words as it feels like we were one. She started lifting herself and dropping back on me over and over again slowly as we caught a rhythm. At first it was slow, real slow as if she was controlling my joystick like playing an old arcade game. I thought to myself, *damn she knows what she is doing*.

"I want to ride you backwards." While keeping my stick in her she turned her body around with her ass facing me. She put both hands on my shins, arched her back and began dropping up and down again. I'd never had it like this before and I can't help looking at her lips around my stick going in and out of her. She kept her mouth on a pillow to muffle the sounds but to no avail. I'm not thinking about Trevor's sleep right now, he can kiss my ass.

"Now hit it from the back daddy." She purred. Hearing her call me daddy in that lustful voice did something to me because all of a sudden every time I went in and out of her it felt that much better. Again while keeping me submerged in her we switched positions. Her back was perfectly arched and her ass was up while I tried my best to smash it in and out as hard as I could and I felt my balls slapping against her outer walls. I don't know how long we had been going at it but I knew I didn't want to cum yet. I never want to cum because that is how good this feels. I looked into the darkness of the room and tried not to think about what I was doing but I couldn't fight the feeling of looking down, *oh what a beautiful sight*.

I got the feeling I was being watched so I looked over at Trevor's side of the room only to find him propped up on his pillow watching us. I thought I was embarrassed but in actuality I wasn't. It really didn't phase me; I just went back to what I was doing only I went harder. Then Evelyn let out the five words every guy wants to hear.

"I'm about to cum daddy. You gonna cum with me?" I palmed both ass cheeks and began smashing it harder than before. I saw her grab hold of the bar on the futon as if it was for dear life. Her body jerked twice and she released the bar and I knew what had happened. In my mind I'm celebrating because I made her cum first.

"Did you cum?" she asked panting.

"Na."

"Why not?"

"Because I didn't."

2

It felt good to have Evelyn lying on top of me not have to worry about her skating out in e the middle of the night. I caught a glimpse of the moon peaking through my window and I began to think what sex with Kendra would be like. During our relationship we didn't have the luxury of being along for more than ten minutes with each other. She lived thirty minutes away and neither one of us had a car so we only saw each other at church. To be honest after a while I only went to church so I could see her. I was into the church before I moved to North Carolina but she really got me into it. I could tell off the bat that she loved God and I knew that she was something worth holding onto. I knew that I had to get my act together so I even got baptized because of her. No she never asked me to but I knew that she got baptized when she was younger therefore I figured I had to do it as well.

Now that I think about it Kendra didn't call me tonight. If I remember correctly she is a woman of her word. But just like me she could be lying in the arms of some other dude. It's been two years and I would have to be naive to think she hasn't found some other guy by now. Who do I think I am that I can just call her up out of the blue like that? Nevertheless I am still going to go forth with getting her back. Inside no one makes me feel the way she does, I get a sense this is meant to be. I looked down at Evelyn who is sound asleep and thought of how wonderful she is. Despite the fact that she's young she really knows how to play her role as a girlfriend, not to mention the sex is something short of amazing. I looked around my shared apartment into the night and thought I want to get outta here and back to North Carolina. My eyes caught sight of Trevor who was now sitting on the edge of his bed fully dressed.

"Was she good?" he asked.

"Yeah."

"You think I can join in next time?"

"What? Na son, I don't get down like that and I doubt she does. Where you 'bout to go?"

"Out, I need some ass." He responded.

"Oh you got you a little chick somewhere."

"Na, all the hookers be right outside on Groove Street."

"Wow, you wilin'. Be careful man." I said chuckling.

"Yo, come with me?"

"And leave what I have laying here? Na, I'm good."

"Aight." That dude is crazy. I'll never get that desperate to the point I have to go out and pay for some ass, it ain't even that serious. I ran my fingers through Evelyn's hair and wondered if I was wrong for being with her in the first place. Not because of how young she is but because I know what my intentions are. I know that as soon as Kendra comes around and we are back on the terms we were two years ago the relationship Evelyn and I have will be nonexistent. I have the power to end it now and spare her feelings but chances are I won't. I have always been the type to want my cake and eat it too. Everyone says that it's not possible but I think differently because there is no reason why I can't. Right now I want to be with Kendra, who I love but I want someone who adores and makes me feel good and Evelyn does that. She wants to be with an older guy who can treat her well and show her new things, so it works out for both parties. I tussled with the idea a little more and decided to let things run it's course. I cut my thoughts short when I realized the moonlight was quickly turning into dawn.

Evelyn and I woke up and she passed on showering with me because she didn't have any clean clothes, instead she made up my bed and ironed my clothes for me. She lotion me down while staring at me seductively which is nice being pampered the way she does it and I think she enjoys it as much as I do.

"You beast." She would always say. She never took her eyes off me even while I threw on my Phat Farm jean shorts, sleeveless basketball shirt and my Nike Presto sneakers.

"What time you comin' home?" she asked

"Oh I start that new job at the gas station tonight it's from ten to six."

"You working at Finish Line after?"

"Na, just meet me here at five and sleep with me until it's time for me to go to work."

"Ok."

With my headphones on I power walked the six blocks to the North End Recreation Center where I am a camp counselor. It's my third year doing it; I've been doing it since my junior year in high school. I used to be a camper there when I was younger and the coordinator Margaret knew me since I was eleven and asked me to do it. It doesn't pay much, one hundred and eighty dollars a week but I love being around the kids. They remind me of the kids that adored Kendra and I at the church.

My group is a little more controllable because they are in the oldest age group, thirteen to fifteen. The boys try to act like they have more sense so the girls wouldn't think they were behaving immaturely, but I really have a great group of kids. Before I could relax India, a friend of mine from grade school who is also a counselor, came out of nowhere and punched me in the arm.
"What's good?" she asked

"Nothin'."

" Why you look like that?" she asked with a

"No reason, I'm just not feelin' right. Don't be hittin' me like that either, I might have to drop you."

"Please. You won't 'cause you can't. Syncere I'll beat that ass."

"Oh aight, we'll see." I would beat you up now but bitch ass Darius is coming this way.

"Andre you play too fuckin' much." Indian yelled. Just as India punched me in the arm when she came over Andrew did the same thing to her.

"Oh shut up." He said.

"Na it's too early for that shit. Don't nobody even like you like that. Make me fuck you up." India threatened.

"Aight. What's up Syn?" Andre waved. I just nodded because he and I aren't even on it like that. I just have the feeling I'ma have to fuck him up before the summer is over. He one of those dudes that'll fuck with people and when someone fucks with him he wants to get all serious and fight. So to spare his face I'ma keep my distance from him.

Just then I started coughing uncontrollably for no reason and I can't stop. The coughing continued even after it brought me to my knees. By that time I know everyone is looking at me but all I could see is black spots and it felt like someone is taking a rake to my throat. It hurt and it hurt badly, my lungs are on fire by this time. I tasted something in my throat and it was coming up fast. I put my hand over my mouth to stop it from spilling on the floor. I felt it on my hand and soon my coughing slowed until it completely stopped. I took my hand from my mouth and saw that my entire palm was red. Blood?

I looked around and soon realized that I'm on my back and Margaret, India, Andre and a few of the kids are standing over me but I can't hear anything. I see Margaret's lips moving but the sound is as if she's a block away.

"Syn! Syncere are you ok? Can you hear me? Ralph, call the ambulance!" she called.

"No, I'm good." I mumbled.

"No you need to see a doctor. I'ma call your mother."

"Stop, I'm fine." I leapt to my feet and everyone backed up. I feel tears running down my face so I wiped them with the back of my hand. "I'm a grown ass man, don't be callin' my mom for everything, I'm good."

"Are you sure?" She kept asking and I hate when people ask me the same question more than twice.

"Yeah, I'm a run to the bathroom, clean off and I'll be right back."

I am still short of breath as I walked to the bathroom. I stood over the sink for a while looking at the redness in my eyes trying to figure out what the hell just happened to me, my chest still hurts and my throat feels sore. My God this isn't a good way to start off the day. When I walked out most of the kids were back to their playful little worlds so that worked out perfectly for me because I really don't feel like explaining myself to eight-dozen kids. However, Margaret still has a concerned look on her face.

"You sure you don't need to go home?" she offered.

"Yeah, I'll just go to the doctor when I get off."

"Ok."

The day went on as usual. I played kick ball with kids on the basketball court and after that we all sat in the grass under a tree and read a book that one of my girls brought with her. Later as the kids ate I laid on the bleachers to rest a little when I saw Andre walking toward me.

"Yo, did you do a song about Nick's sister?" he asked standing over me.

"What?"

"Somebody told Patrice that you made a song about her and was callin' her all kinds of bitches and it got back to Nick."

"And?" I asked seemingly unaffected by his accusation.

"And Nick is pissed off, him and Darnell are supposed to be coming down here this afternoon to fuck you up." He reviled.

"Whatever, I ain't worried." I admitted while walking to the pay phone.

"Yo so you and Russ be down here at two-thirty. If these niggas wanna fight they gon' have to run me a heady. I just need ya'll to be there so I don't get jumped." I explained to Jus.

"You want me to call the Wolf Pak?"

"Na, them niggas don't fight."

"Aight." I hung up the phone pissed off now. Yeah I did a song about Patrice and now niggas wanna get they ass beat over it? I looked at the clock, one-seventeen, well I ain't gonna let it fuck up my day, I'ma go about my business.

"Yo Syn, you know Andre over there poppin' off at the mouth saying that him, Nick and Darnell are gonna jump you later." India warned.

"Andre said he was gonna jump me?"

"Yep."

"Na fuck that! He ain't gotta jump me, me and that motherfucka could fight right now."

"Whoa Syncere. You were sick this morning and you don't need to be fightin' nobody." India reminded stepping in front of me.

"Move India, this nigga sayin' he wanna jump me then let's get it." India stepped aside and I walked over to Andre. "Yo, come in the locker room." I demanded "For what?"

"Don't worry 'bout it, let's go." Before he could reply I turned and walked back across the gym. I knew he was following me because I can hear his size fourteen's thumping on the gym floor. We stood face to face for a while, him leaning on the sink me leaning up against the locker.

"So what'chu want?" he asked nervously.

"Don't fuckin' act stupid. What's all that shit you talkin' to India 'bout jumpin' me?"

"I…I ain't say that." He stuttered.

"Motherfucka don't lie. I saw ya bitch ass whispering to her a little while ago. You wanna fight me, let's go right here."

"Yo, I ain't say nothing. I'm just sayin', you wrote a song about my cousin."

"So what that got to do with you?"

"Nothin', I'm just sayin'…"

"Whatever, if you wanna do somethin' we can go right fuckin' now. We ain't gotta wait for ya fuckin' cousins."

"Na, ain't no beef." Andre said throwing up his hands. I looked him up and down for a minute before purposely brushing pass him calling his bluff. I could hear India scurry away from the door.

"Damn you a nosey broad."

"I was trying to hear but what happened?"

"He ain't doin' shit. Bitch ass." India laughed at my comment, which was loud enough for him to hear.

I waited for Jus and Russ to come down, three o'clock was approaching fast, but I still waited for Nick and Darnell. By four no one was there, so I left.

I don't claim to be no gangster but if a nigga wanna see me then we can do it. Damn right I wrote a song about Patrice. Before I left for college she was my girl up until the day before I ran into Evelyn. Shit was all fine and dandy when I was away. The letters came and the phone calls were full of I miss you's and what not but when I get home it was a different story. The night I get home, my sister Mone' told me there was a party at the Mason lodge on Bishop Street. I called Patrice to see if she wanted to go but she declined because she was going to stay home with her mom that night. At that point I told her I wasn't going to go either but after we hung up Mone' convinced me to go out and see the people I haven't seen all year, so I do.

I ran into this wanna be pastor Bryerson; we are cool because we used to work together at the Pride Cultural Center. He pulled me to the side starts telling me that while I was gone Patrice has been hanging out with this cat named Damien. I'm not the type to believe he say she says so I kept my cool even as Mone' tried to fuel up the situation. I used Bryserson's cell and called Patrice but her mother answered the phone. When I asked where her daughter was she replied,

"I thought she went out with you." Naturally I'm hot about it now but I'm really trying not to let this fuck up my night but before long guess who I see? Patrice…with the cat Damien walking together like it's a Sunday afternoon and their in the park somewhere. So I didn't spas out, she didn't see me so I

watch them for a little before leaving. The next day I called her out on it and she tried to hit me with that just a friend shit but I wasn't hearing it. That combined with the bullshit Trisha & Kendra pulled the last two months of school just had me upset so I wrote a song and let Patrice's friends hear it. I know birds talk and it got back to her but I really don't give a fuck. Don't lie to me, if you wanna be with someone else then be honest with your shit, the principal is what got me upset. It's ok though, she want to send her brother and cousin after me, it's nothing. I plenty of sisters that'll love to twist her ass up.

Tonight I get some much-needed relax. I don't have to work at Finish Line tonight and thank God because third shift job is kicking my ass. These jobs are kicking my ass so much that it is causing me to not be able to write putting me way behind on the CD that I'm involved in. I shouldn't be complaining though, the money I'm getting is great and I will be going car shopping real soon. I have a little more than a month left of summer vacation and things are right on track.

Kendra and I have been talking heavy since I first called her. She calls me almost every night even when Evelyn is here. I really don't care if Evelyn gets upset because I still talk to Kendra right there in front of her, sometimes even during sex. She doesn't say anything and it really wouldn't change anything if she did. I still haven't told Kendra that I am involved with anyone and I don't think I will because she doesn't have to know.

Trevor is out doing God knows what and I hope he found a job today because his rent is due and I'm not putting up that entire four-seventy-five all on my own again. As far as I know Evelyn went out skating with my cousin Charm so now I'm sitting at Trevor's rebuilt computer reading an email Kendra sent me. I get an overwhelming warm and fuzzy feeling in my stomach just thinking about her. It's so strong I can't begin to explain how it consumes my thoughts and my actions. You can't shoot the smile that I have on my face when I read her emails, hear her voice or play back last nights conversations in my head.

"Yo wussup?" Trevor just walked in carrying a medium sized brown paper bag. "Nothin'. You found a job today?" *Eww, I sounded like a fed up woman just now.* "Na, not yet."

"You know ya rent is due next week and I got my half so what you gonna do about yours?" He didn't answer just shrugged his shoulders.

"You talkin' to Kendra online?" Trevor asked changing the subject.

"Sendin' her back an email."

"Ya'll talk a lot, she know about you and Evelyn?"

"Nope and she don't need to."

"You smooth as hell. You be talkin' to that Kendra and Evelyn be layin' right on top of you. She don't be sayin' nothin'?"

"What can she say? I don't care. She just somethin' to fuck with until I go back to school. Once I hit North Carolina she gonna be a wrap anyway."

"So you just don't give a fuck about her huh?" he inquired.

"Na it's not that I mean she cool peoples and all but I want Kendra. So Evelyn is the appetizer, sometimes the meal takes a little longer to prepare na mean?"

"I feel you."

"Besides Evelyn is madd young." I added.

"She don't act like it."

"True statement and she sure don't fuck like it." He laughed throwing is head back and letting the world see his overbite.

"I need to get me a girl like that man. You gotta hook me up with one of your friends."

"I can try, I'll bring a few by to see who you like and I'll put in a word, but you gotta get a shoe and clothes game up."

"Yeah." He agreed.

"So what's up with you and Kendra? Why you so all crazy over her?"

"'Cause man. She…she just makes me feel alive inside. Like I can do anything in the fuckin' world. I mean just the mere thought of her puts a great feeling in my stomach. I can't think about her and not smile. It's…it's…I don't know. I can't fully put it into words. You know you're in love when you and only you can feel it."

"So I still can't figure out why you still messin' wit this chick if you love what's her name?"

"Kendra."

"Right, if you love Kendra then you shouldn't even mess wit this girl 'cause that's messed up. What if she finds out?"

"She won't. Check it. I don't even know what's going to happen. She could be with someone right now; she might not even want to be with me again. So I'm not going to put all my eggs in one basket. Evelyn can still be molded into what I need in case this doesn't work out."

"What if Evelyn finds out about you wanting to be with Kendra?"

"The only people that know are you and my boys. They won't <u>ever</u> betray me by telling her shit. So that only leaves you."

"Na, you know I ain't gonna say nothin'," I didn't respond. I just looked at him as he looked at me. I turned around back to the computer to reply to the email as Trevor turned on the television. Videos, all this guy watches is videos. Ginuwine's new video differences was on and I stopped typing as the hook came on. It said exactly how I feel about Kendra so I wrote the hook at the bottom of the email.

"Yo, yo. Syncere." I opened my eyes to see Trevor standing over me holding the phone. I must've drifted asleep.

"Hello."

"Hey." I woke up instantly sitting up on the futon.

"Hey, how you?"

"I'm fine. Did you mean what you wrote in that email?" she asked.

"What part?"

"The bottom part. When you said your life changed and I was that special one. Did you mean all that?"

"Yeah."

"Did you think of that yourself?"
"No that is a line from a song, but it put into words how I feel about you."

"You don't listen to the 911 song anymore?"

"No that song makes me cry every time I hear it." I admitted.

"Really! Why?" she asked

"'Cause when we dubbed that our song we were on the phone together in North Carolina, you remember?"

"Yeah."

"Yeah well we were breaking up during the part when he was saying "is this the type of love my grandma warned me out, we're in trouble" It was that day after church you brought Quamine there and I left the rose on your mother's car."

"Why'd you leave without saying good-bye? You moved back to Connecticut and I didn't even know."

"Because you came in and sat on the right side of the church, I was sitting on the left toward the back and I watched you sit next to him. I had to sit in the back of the church and watch you hold his hand, I had to watch you and him play with your aunts baby and worst of all I had to watch you smile at him and look at him the way you smiled and looked at me."

"Is that why you left?"

"Yeah. I left because I was feeling all kinds of anger and a lot of violent things were running through my mind. I figured if I felt that bad I didn't need to be in the house of the Lord so I left." I explained.

"But you never called."

"Ya'll look so happy together and I couldn't stand to see that. I didn't listen to a word the pastor said, all I was focused on were you and him and every moment I wanted to kill him."

I stopped talking because the thought of it was making me pissed off all over again. Kendra didn't say a word and neither did I. We both were probably trying to figure out what the other was thinking.

"Was that the only time you felt that way?"

"No I felt that way when you brought the nigga to my dorm, that really pissed me off, I remember thinking that you had some nerve."

"I told you I wanted you two to meet."

"Why would I want to meet the nigga my ex-girlfriend is dating? No man wants that."

"You both had a lot in common. Remember I told you he raps too."

"Kendra I don't care. I would never have you meet Trisha, those are just things you don't do."

"I wouldn't mind meeting her. I'm interested in knowing what you seen in us both."

"Who does that? I 've never heard of no mess like that."

"I'm just curious why you always went back to her whenever you and I broke up? I thought you don't date the same girl twice.

"I don't."

"But you dated her more than twice."

"And I dated you more than twice." I rebutted.

"So you love her too?"

"Not anymore."

"Well how can you love two people at the same time? I don't understand how you were able to do that."

"I loved you both at the same time but my love for you and her is different."

" So you do you still love her?"

"No."

"You said that too fast."

"Well I don't."

"Why?"

"Because she's not the girl for me, you are."

"How do you know I am the girl for you? It's been two years, I'm a different person now. I'm not sixteen anymore, I have matured."

"You're still the same girl I fell in love with."

"How do you know?"

"I just do."

"Tell me how." She pressed.

"I can't explain it. It's a feeling I can't escape or ignore."

"Do you have a girlfriend now?"

"No."

"Are you sure?"

"Yeah, why do you say it like that?" I asked trying not to sound guilty.

"'Cause I know you. You always have a girlfriend."

"Wow! Do you have a boyfriend?"

"No not anymore."

"What happened?"

"Don't wanna talk about it. So why don't you have one. I remember that when you got back to Connecticut for high school you'd write me all the time telling me about this one and that one."

"Na, right now I'm just chillin'. I'm working a lot so I can go back to North Carolina with a car so I'm not trapped on Saint Aug's campus all year again."

"I think I might do my senior year of high school in North Carolina."

"Why, what's wrong with New Hampshire?" I asked.

"I don't like it up here anymore. The white girls still treat me different because I'm one of the few black faces up here. They look at me and talk to me as if I don't know anything. It's just not comfortable."

"So don't run and give them that satisfaction."

"It's not about giving them satisfaction, I really miss my momma and family. She can't afford to come see me way up here you know she's not working."

"When you speak to her tell her I said hi."

"I will."

"So have you figured out where you want to go to college?" I asked hoping she'd say UNC.

"I am looking at a few places, why?"

"Cause I always used to tell you that I can see you at North Carolina Chapel Hill."

"Yeah you did. I was looking into that school."

"Well what other ones are you looking at?"

"Umm, just a few none real big. I'm not sure if I want to go to a big school."

"I see, you should still give UNC a look at, plus you will be closer to me."

"Syncere. Can I ask you a question?" she said softening her voice.

"Yeah, anything."

"Thanks. What do you want from me?"

"What do you mean?" I replied not knowing what to make of her question.

"What do you want? You call me up out of the blue and apologize. Now we talk and you send me sweet emails and now you're talking about being closer to me. So I'm just wondering what it is you want from me."

"Nothing. Just to talk to you. I miss the way we used to talk. You know that you are the only girl to keep me on the phone as long as you do? Remember how you would wake me up for school every morning? I miss that. You were the first voice I heard when I woke up and the last voice I heard when I went to sleep."

"I remember. I also remember you snoring on the phone a couple of times."

"Yeah right! I don't snore."

"Yes you do, and loud too. You would fall asleep on me all the time."

"Why didn't you hang up?" I asked.

"I did after a while, well once you started snoring. I could tell you were sleep because you would get really quiet and I could hear you breathe. You would still try to respond when I was talking but I always knew."

"And you never said anything."

"Nope."

"Thas wussup."

"What is?"

"Nothin' don't worry about it."

"Ok. Syncere do you have long distance on your phone because my calling card is running out of minutes. It doesn't seem like we've been talking for an hour does it?"

"Nope, it never does. Ok I'll call you right back." I hung up with Kendra feeling happier beyond explanation. I took a minute to stare into the darkness and envision her face, her smile and my heart got happy. I called her back and we spoke until we broke day.

"You're not tired?"

"Kinda but its too late now. I'm not gonna be worth shit today and I have to work all three of my jobs"

"I'm sorry I kept you up."

"Na, I kept me up but you're worth it."

"You're so sweet."

"Sometimes."

"Yeah, sometimes." She replied. "Syncere?"

"Yeah?"

"….never mind."

     I am running top speed with a five-pound book bag on my back. It's two fifty-three and Finish Line has me to be there at three o'clock. Margaret let's me leave at two forty-five so I'm not late but it's at least a half a mile away. The mall is buzzing with shoppers. It makes sense because it's Fourth of July weekend and everyone has to get an outfit for their cookouts and amusement park trips they'll be taking. Becky, my store manager, is talking to another employee when I ran past her and into the backroom. I dressed quickly, made sure my shirt was tucked in, name tag on and I darted for the sales floor clocking in at three o' five.

"Wow I thought you were getting chased by a dog the way you ran in here." Bekcy commented.

"I know I was trying not to be late. Can you please put me on after three-thirty? That way I can not pass out running in ninety degree weather trying to get here."

"No problem." She said laughing.

     Her lips kept moving but I couldn't hear a thing. My body kept growing increasingly hot and the left side of my chest has a sharp pain in it as if someone is sticking a thin needle into it. I lost my breath then collapsed to the floor and began coughing uncontrollably again. *What the fuck is going on?* Becky and Miguel are kneeling by my side yelling things I couldn't make out because the pain got more intense then…suddenly it stopped.

     I felt something running down my chin so I wiped it, blood again. Tears were running down my face and a bunch of people including mall security are now in my face.

"Syncere can you hear me." Becky yelled.

"Yeah." I uttered.

"You ok?"

"Yeah. I don't know what happened."

"Son do you need to go to the hospital?" Asked the husky security guard.

     "No, no I'm fine." They helped me to my feet and I saw that all activity in the store stopped. No customers were shopping; none of the other employees were running in and out of the backroom even people walking by the store stopped to get a glimpse of what was going on. I feel so embarrassed.

After a couple of minutes in the stockroom I came back out and was told that the whole ordeal that felt like forever only lasted about two minutes.

"I didn't know what to do. Do you have some kind of medical condition?" Becky asked.

"I don't think so. I'll go to the doctor on my day off." That was the same thing I told Margaret almost a month ago. This happens every now and again but I refuse to go to the hospital because it reminds me of death. Maybe it's the heat or maybe it's because I was running so hard and it was really hot outside. Whatever it is it cant be that serious.

The afternoon went without any more incidents into the evening. The store got extremely busy as Becky, Miguel, Maria, Daniel and I scrambled to help everyone while hitting all of our sales goals.

"Wussup Syncere?"

"Oh what's good Ash?"

"Chillin'. Is it true you datin' Evelyn?" Ashley blurted.

"NO! Who told you that?"

"She did. She said that ya'll been goin' out since you got home in June. She even said she fucked you and it was good too."

"Na, she wilin'. I ain't hit that. Now what guy would deny beatin' somethin' after the chick said it was good? Na, she be at my house every week 'cause she braids my hair but that's it."

"Well that is what she is tellin' everybody."

"Well you heard it from me, it ain't goin' down like that."

"Aight, I heard you. So wussup wit'cha discount on these?"

I can't believe Evelyn is telling everyone we go together. That makes me look bad because she's only fifteen and if that shit gets back to her moms I'm done. Even when she turns sixteen next month I'll be turning nineteen three months later and she knows everyone I knew in high school. Ok, what I need to do is get a chick my age, make it public before this Evelyn thing ruins my reputation.

3

"Yo you gotta work tonight?" Tracy asked while he drove me to my apartment.

"Na, why?"

"We gotta get up and write. Wes said he got a cousin in Atlanta that can probably get us signed so we gotta send her some material."

"With who? So so Def, I don't even like them niggas like that."

"Nigga a deal is a deal I don't care who its with. I'ma go with whoever get me outta Foot Locker." He said laughing lightly.

"Call everybody up and tell'em meet me at my house in an hour."

"You want me to drop you off now?"

"Yeah, Evelyn is at tha spot."

"Damn nigga, you goin' hard with that young chick ain't you? She got some friends?"

"Yeah but they around her age, nigga you three years older than me. That age difference is madd big."

"Nigga so."

"Wow!"

"See if we can run a train." Tracy suggested

"Na, I don't get down like that and neither does she. But tell me why Trevor asked the same fuckin' question the other night when I got done hittin' it."

" Get the fuck outta here! For real? But how you know she don't get down like that? Have you asked her?"

"'Cause she don't and even if she did I don't like to share."

"Damn dude you madd selfish. All tha ass I be hookin' you up with?"

"WHO?! You mean you be hookin' Wes up wit. Niggas don't ever call Syncere when they gettin' ass but ya'll niggas call me to do some destructive shit tho."

"Whatever man. Nobody told you to go out and get a third job at night. Shit you ain't never around, you mind as well be at college 'cause we still don't see you." Tracy said shrugging his shoulders.

"Well when I get a car like you I'll calm down until then I'm grindin'."

"You need to be grindin' on this music shit, fuck goin' back to school."

"Wow, na I'm good."

"You don't need a car anyway. Once you get one you gonna gain madd weight, that is what happened to me."

"Fuck outta here, you always Moby dick. Who tha fuck you foolin'?" I joked.

"Hear that, niggas always got jokes."

"So what's good with Sondari?" I changed subjects.

"Oh nigga I be chillin' wit her hard."

"You ain't smash yet?"

'Na, takin' my time. Plus every time I'm wit her the warden be callin' me. She went through my phone and every thing."

"How in the hell did she get your phone?" I asked already knowing the answer.

"Son, she be in my shit all the time. Madd stress when it comes to this girl."

"So why are you even wit her. Nobody likes her around, at all, and she be stressin' the hell out of you."

"I don't know dude, maybe 'cause I'm comfortable na mean?"

"Well if that is comfortable you can have it. Evelyn start actin' like that and it's a wrap."

"So what's good wit Kendra?" Tracy said smiling.

"We talkin' right now but I'm tryin' to get back in her good graces. The problem is we've never been in the same state or city with one another with access to each other na mean? So when she goes to college we'll both be in North Carolina and we'll become more accessible to one another. So for the summer I'ma bang out this chick and when I get back be with Kendra." I explained.

"You wild, be careful man. If you really feelin' this chick and I can tell you are, then don't let her know about Evelyn." Tracy warned.

"I'm way ahead of you, do you know who I am?"

I could smell food cooking as I opened the door and saw Trevor sitting on the edge of his futon. *Damn, does this nigga ever move from that spot?* Evelyn must've heard the door close because her little body darted from the kitchen before I could throw my keys down. She jumped on my waist, hugged me tight before giving me a long passionate kiss and I thought I love walking into this every night.

I can't lie. I love coming home and having Evelyn there, she plays her role as a girlfriend well for a young woman her age. She is dressed in tight blue jeans that looked like they are airbrushed on, topped with a white polo shirt that is unbuttoned down to the crease in her breasts while her big-hooped earrings swayed from side to side. We started at each other while as I held her up.

"Excuse me." A voice said from behind us. Evelyn and I looked at Trevor who is trying to see the television around us.

"Oh my god the food." As Evelyn ran back to the kitchen I threw some money in my fireproof safe and lay on the couch to unwind a little. I thought about checking my email to see if Kendra replied but I don't want to draw any attention to myself. I whispered to Trevor if Kendra had called, he replied no.

"Babe, I cooked." Evelyn announced proudly.

"I smell."

"Don't you want to take a shower before I feed you? I'll come in and…wash your back."

"I would but tha Pak is coming over so we can write a few tracks."

"Oh ok. Well we need to hurry up and eat before Tracy gets here, you know he always hungry."

"That is messed up." I said laughing. When it comes to Tracy we stay with the fat jokes, but it's all in good fun.

"Oh yo this came for you in the mail. How did they get this address?" I looked at the envelope Trevor handed me. Georgia State University Athletic Department? I read over the material basically stating they are offering me a full track scholarship if I attended in the fall, a much better offer than the partial scholarship Saint Augustine's College gives me.

"Wow! Babe read this." The expression on Evelyn's face isn't a pleasant one. She read or should I say skimmed over the information before flinging the letter back onto the futon. I ran in the kitchen and put my arms around her waist.

"Get back the grease is hot and I don't want it to pop you in the eye." She said trying to sound concerned.

"I'll be fine, what's wrong wit' chu?"

"Nothing."

"Evy?"

"I don't want you to leave." She said facing me.

'What? You know I'm in college, I have to leave."

"But why can't you go to a school up here? Why do you have to go so far? North Carolina is one thing, but Georgia?"

"I didn't even say if I was going to go or not." I said.

"You don't have to say it. I saw the excitement in your eyes. You're gonna leave me here with no one while you're off in college fucking madd pretty college girls and you're gonna forget all about me." She pouted as I kissed her cheek as soft as possible trying to make her feel better.

"Babe, I'm not going to forget about you. I will be home Christmas, Thanksgiving and all that."

"No you're not. You don't have any more family here remember? Your mom moved to North Carolina so you don't have a reason to come back. And not lie to my face sayin' you'll come back for me 'cause I may be young but I ain't dumb."

"Look, you got me for another month. And who knows, you can come visit me while I'm in school." I suggested.

"Yeah I will so I can let them bitches know who I be." We laughed about it as she fixed me a plate and got me out bottled water.

"We don't have no soda?" I asked.

"Soda is not good for you and I threw it out. You gotta stay in shape and by the way, when's the last time you ran?" Evelyn asked with her hands on her hips.

"A few days ago, I'll get back on my training schedule." Half way through dinner there was a knock at the door.

"They're here." Evelyn said taking out plates into the kitchen

"Are ya'll gonna be long?" Trevor asked before I opened the door.

"Why?"

"'Cause I wanna get some sleep, I'm tired."

"From what? It ain't like you worked today." I said letting my friends in.

"Tha Pak is in tha fuckin' buildin'." I did our patent handshake with Tracy, Wes, Jus and Q.

"Yo put this on." I took the CD from Jus and ignored the show Trevor is watching as I put the CD into the DVD player. The beat is knocking and before I knew it everyone had their pens and notebooks out. Evelyn sat in a chair in the doorway of the kitchen finishing up her dinner while she watched our heads move in a scaronized bobbing motion. My lines flowed out swiftly and easily when the phone interrupted me.

"Syn."

"Who is it?"

"Lawaya."

"Fuck she doin' callin' me and how'd she get this number?" I looked at Evelyn who was looking at me who was looking at Trevor. "Yo."

"Yo turn on MTV." She spat out then she hung up.

"Yo Syn what was that all about?" I didn't answer Q I just took the CD out turned the TV to MTV. A broadcast is airing about the death of Aaliyah. I looked around the room and saw everyone's mouth on the floor and their eyes glued to the television.

"Yo, ok she died what are all ya'll sad for? Get back to writin'." I said unaffected by the so-called tragedy.

"Nigga its Aaliyah." Tracy replied disgusted with my comment.

"So none of us knew the bitch, death is inevitable. Spit ya'll verses."

"How you gonna call a dead chick a bitch?" Wes asked shaking his head.

"The same way I would if she was alive."

"You mad insensitive." Tracy said

"So, ya'll niggas sad like ya'll knew her or her family or somthin'. Get over it, put the beat back on." I demanded as Tracy got me upset over the fact he was actually arguing over a broad he didn't even know. My creative juices started to flow and just as I felt them my pen moved and wrote: *My rap style is abstract, I wanna fly a plane and die in the same spot Aaliyah crashed at. I'd be a dangerous motherfucka if I ain't have rap, might wear a trench coat with a shottie in my knapsack.*

Once I recited my verse with those two bars the look on everyone's face is the same look they had while we watched the MTV broadcast. The only person to seem unaffected is Evelyn who clapped at the end.

"I'm not rappin' on the track if you use that line."

"Tracy you a bitch man."

"Na Syn you wilin', I agree wit Tracy." Quincy said.

"Me too." Wes cosigned.

"You too Jus? Tell these niggas it's just a couple of lines."

"Dame is gonna fuck you up."

"Fuck Dame Dash, I ain't worried about him and he ain't worried about me. The bitch is dead and no matter what I say the fact remains."

"Yo, that is some demonic shit to say. That is what I'm gonna call you all the time, Devil...Devil May Cry."

"Yo I'm hungry." Tracy said as the entire room erupted in laughter. "What's so fuckin' funny?"

"Nigga you always hungry." I added as everyone laughed more.

"Na seriously I'm hungry too, Denny's?" Quincy suggested.

"Oh hell yeah." Wes said in agreeance. Trevor woke up out of his sleep I guess because of all the commotion we are making as we gathered our things.

"Where ya'll ya'll goin'?"

"Denny's, you wanna roll?" Jus suggested.

"I ain't got no money."

"Oh, ok."

"Syn you can't spot him?"

"You spot him, fuck I look like a bank?"

"Yep, that nigga is the Devil."

Kendra didn't call tonight like I expected her to, then again I can't remember if I told her I would call her back or vice versa. I'll call her tomorrow while I'm at the gas station, in the meantime I'll chill with Evelyn and my boys. Evelyn and I rode in the car with Tracy, while Jus and Wes rode with Quincy.

"Yo where we goin', the highway is that way." I asked as Tracy turned down a residential street.

"Chill, I'm goin' to pick up Sondari."

"She up? It's like 2 a.m."

"Yeah I called her when ya'll was takin' forever to come downstairs."

Sondari is the whitest Jamaican girl I've ever seen. She is short and petite like Evelyn but her hair does down to the middle of her back. Her smile is as soft as her speaking voice but her complexion is that of President Bush.

"You think you can catch Quincy and them?" I challenged Tracy.

"Hell yeah, watch." Luckily Sondari lived not too far from the highway. Normally there are no cops out as we speed going east on I-84. Ten minutes later, while blasting my latest song "Who You", we spotted Quincy's white Toyota Camry.

"Cut Charlie's Angels?" Tracy looked at me and laughed.

"Yeah." He rolled down the driver, passenger side windows as well as his sunroof. We passed Quincy's car, cutting him off a little and when we were in front of them we stuck one hand out our window and the other hand out of the sunroof putting up our middle finger, we call that Charlie's Angels. With the wind in my face and Evelyn's laughter in my ear I pictured this same scenario with Kendra in the back seat. I looked at the passing moon and thought I've never been this happy in my life but I still feel incomplete. I mean I have great friends that are down for me, a pretty young thing in the back seat that is a ride or die chick for real but she's nothing in comparison to Kendra. My life is like an unfrosted cake and the only thing needed to make it sweeter is Kendra here with me. I really wished she would've called tonight, I would like to hear her voice. In high school her voice would be the last I heard at night and the first I heard in the morning.

"Yo, lemme use your phone."

"For what?" Tracy asked.

"Nigga just give me the damn phone." Tracy handed it to me and I dialed Kendra. To my disappointment I reached her voice mail and I left her a message saying I missed her and have a good night. I figure she'll get it in the morning and it would start her day off nice so I hung up feeling content with having Evelyn here. I pulled down the visor and saw at her smiling, bobbing her head to <u>my</u> music. She caught me looking at her and gave me a smile as I put the visor back up. She leaned forward and kissed me on the cheek and I feel really good now, almost completely happy. For a brief second not having Kendra here isn't an issue and I started to feel something in me, in my heart and I can't explain what it is. I shook it off just as we were pulling into Denny's.

We walked into Denny's seven deep being greeted by our favorite waitress Joyce."

"Wow you guys again, don't you's ever sleep?" In unison we said, NOPE! She shook her head and seated us. As usual the feast is big with everyone passing additional plates to try what someone else had and the conversations are full of jokes. The majority of the jokes are aimed at Tracy and his weight or his psychotic girlfriend how we call M.Dot. Once in a while I'll take a shot at Quincy since his weight isn't that far from Tracy's or a shot at Wes because of his height but it's all in good fun. Jus has the best jokes and once he gets started it's a wrap. The bill came and it's like one hundred and forty dollars.

"Aight ya'll know the deal, split it up evenly and everyone leave two dollars for the tip." Everyone did what Tracy told. No one moves unless he says so and it's always been like that. I really don't know why but he holds that kind of presence and leadership, I think it's a natural thing about him. I looked on the table and saw a shit load of ones laying on the table and decided to take them along with my half empty sundae glass and scurried outside with everyone else.

We all stood in the parking lot talking amongst each other when Jus pulled out his camcorder and instantly Wes jumped in front and started rapping. As soon as the rest of us heard and saw what was going on we formed a circle attentively listening to every bar anxiously awaiting our turn on the camera. I looked around at everyone's head bobbing as I spit a quick sixteen bars and Evelyn's face stuck out at me. I see a light in her eyes as she watched me and smiled a mile wide when I shot her a wink. I ended with a hot line and everyone cheered and Evelyn clapped and jumped up and down. The same feeling I had in the car I have now and I kinda like it.

"Hey guys!" Everyone stopped as the waitress from Denny's came over to us.

"Wussup?" answered Quincy.

"Hey you guys had a pretty big tab and we handled you well but I think we deserve something." I slid to the rear as I saw the confused look on everyone's face.

"We left like twenty dollars, what are you talking about?" Tracy asked.

"Guys there's nothing on the table." Quincy and Tracy both looked at me. I reluctantly reached into the front pocket on my cargo pants and pulled out the wad of ones and handed it to the waitress as she shot me a dirty look before thanking Tracy and Quincy.

"Syn you really wilin'."

"I told you, he's the Devil."

I hear my pager going off, or at least I think I do. I'm in mid sleep so I'm going to ignore it. I opened my eyes to see that it is still gray outside and it's not time for me to be getting up.

"Yo, yo." I woke up. Trevor said tapping me.

"Fuck you want?"

"Yo man you snoring."

"I don't givva fuck. You try workin' three jobs everyday and tell me if you're gonna snore. Back up before I lay your ass out." I warned.

"Whatever man." He said as he sucked his teeth. The audacity of this motherfucker to wake me up out of my sleep when I'm working and paying the fucking rent when he's not doing shit. I should knock him out just because of that. My pager went off again. Who in the hell is blowing me up? I looked at it, oh 919 area code, Kendra! I jumped up frantically searching for the phone that I discovered is under Trevor's futon.

"Hello."

"Hey did I wake you?"

"Umm no, I was in the shower." I lied.

"Ok, you want me to let you go?"

"Na I'm good, I air dry anyway. What's good?"

"I was up getting ready for class and I was thinking about you."

"I was thinking about you too, I called you last night when I went to Denny's with my boys."

"Late?"

"Yeah. We stay up a lot."

"Ok I see."

"So when are you coming to Connecticut to see me?"

"You want me to come and see you?" Kendra asked sounding surprised.

"Yeah, why you sound so surprised?"

"I don't know, I guess 'cause I kinda am."

"Oh, ok. So when you comin'?"

"I don't know if I can. I teach all week and even on Saturday's. After the program is over school starts right up."

"So when do you have time for fun?"

"I do sometimes."

"So how about if I come visit you?" I suggested.

"Syncere I'm in Virginia."

"So, I can come on the weekend and stay with you."

"I'm living with a family of one of my students, it's set up by the program."

"Ok, I can get a hotel and stay there if you will stay with me."

"Ok, when do you want to come?"

"I'ma check my schedule cause you know I have three jobs."

"Why are you working so much? Shouldn't you be having fun like you said I should be?"

"I want to go back to North Carolina with a car so I'ma work now and have fun driving."

"Oh. Can I ask you a question?" Kendra asked sounding soft again.

"Yeah, what is it?"

"Why are we still friends? I mean after everything that we've been through you know? I hurt you and you hurt me but we are still friends, why?"

"Because deep down we still care a lot about each other."

"You do?!"

"Yeah, I always have. And we're still friends because you allow it. I can call but you keep in contact."

"Ok, I care about you too Syn, you're a good friend." I hate hearing that Kendra looks at me as a "friend". I don't want to be her friend I want to be her boyfriend and ultimately the man she marries. I want to tell her how I feel but I think it's still too early because I'm still unclear about how she really feels about me. I mean she says that we are friends but I don't know if she feels as if we can be a couple again. I don't know how deep the hate, if any, runs. Most women wouldn't date a man that they assumed cheated on them. I know from experience that once a woman puts you in that "friend" category, it's a wrap and I can't allow Kendra to put me there.

"Why did you get so quiet?" she asked breaking the silence.

"No reason."

"You have something to say?"

"No."

"Yes you do. Will you please just tell me?" I hesitated for a minute. I tossed with the idea of telling Kendra that I love her and with telling her how I feel. Instead I took another route.

"I don't like it when you say that I am your friend."

"Why?"

"Because I don't look at you as a friend." I said.

"What do you look at me as?"

"My girlfriend. Even though we are not together I still think of you as my girlfriend."

"How can you do that if you date other girls?" she posed.

"Because in my mind because I know I want us to be together again down the line. Any chick I mess with now is just temporary until you and I can be a couple again."

"If you think that then it's unfair to the girls you date now."

"How you figure?"
"Well what if someone you are talking to you ends up really liking you and starts to fall for you?"

"Then that is her fault. Anyone I deal with knows that this is a only for right now type of thing so she should know not to put any emotion into what we have going."

"How can you say that? That's not the Syncere I know. I never thought you are capable of doing something like that. If that's the case why don't you be alone, that way you wouldn't be hurting anyone?" I stayed silent on the phone not really thinking anything. I rested my head on my left arm while looking at the sun poke it's way through my black curtains.

"Because I don't like not having a female in my life. If I want a hug from someone or spend time with someone then I am going to have just that." With that said Kendra is the one who is silent. I think I said too much but it's the truth, I don't like being alone. I mean I can be but only for a short period of time. I love the scent of a woman, I love the touch of a woman and most of all I just love the overall company of a woman. The feeling that I get when I am with a woman is different depending on the woman and how much I really like her. For instance when I began to be with Evelyn I didn't feel anything special, she was just the woman at the moment. Lately I've been feeling the same thing I was feeling for Kendra in the early stages of our relationship. The problem is I don't want to feel that way about her because those feelings are reserved for Kendra and only her. That is one of the reasons I deny my relationship with Evelyn to everyone else, it's the reason why I am somewhat distant from her at times. It's so I don't led her to believe that something will come out of this.

"Well Syn it sounds like you got it all under control so I'ma let you go."

"Did I upset you?"

"No."

"Then why are you hanging up with me?"

"Because I know that you have to get up and go to work, I just wanted to say hi that's all."

"I can talk for a minute more."

"No, I have to get ready as well. I'll email you when I have a break ok?"

"Well I won't get it until later tonight but it would be nice to get a message from you when I get in. I'll talk to you later."

"Bye." Kendra hung up before I could say good-bye back. It's something she always does but I think this time it was on purpose; maybe I struck a cord in her. I didn't mean to that is just the way it is.

Why is she even mad anyway, I am this way because I am saving myself for her, can't she see that? I could deal with not being with Kendra as long as it's known that we are a couple and until that happens I am going to do what I have to do to occupy my time.

Working these three jobs is killing me. 21 hours a day at least four times a week is leaving me with no time to enjoy my summer. I haven't spoken to my mom since she's left, I guess I'm still pissed off at her leaving and not telling me prior to getting here. She doesn't givva fuck because if she did she would have called to see if I was all right.

"Yo you work tomorrow?" Tracy asked when I got into the car.

"Na, I don't work here on Sunday's but I do have to go to the gas station tomorrow night tho why?"

"'Cause I need you not to be busy tomorrow 'cause we all meetin' up at Q's to record fuck ya head up. Fair said his cousin in Atlanta needs some music so she can pass it to the people at the label."

"We gonna give them that? That ain't no hit and we only got one shot at this fam so we gonna send them some hot shit."
"Well we puttin' a bunch of shit on a CD to give to her. You should send that Who You song, that shit is a hit."

"Yeah that song is hot but it's not a hit. What else is going on the CD?"

" A solo song from everyone, Bounce, End Game, and Faithful."

"I hate Faithful." I expressed.

"Whatever dude, everyone likes that song, that motherfucker is a hit. Tha beat hot, tha lyrics are sick plus Deyo is singing on it. Man that says radio play all over it. You the only one that don't like that song."

"I'm the only one who is being honest." I admitted.
"What don't you like about it Syn?"

"The rhymes sound elementary. The concept is hot and so is the hook, ya'll should try writing different verses."

"Nigga you crazy, you mad 'cause you ain't on it." My pager went off.

"Lemme see your phone."

"Nigga watch my minutes. Who you callin' anyway?"

"Evelyn."

"Oh wifey."

"Not even. What's good? Ok…ok…thas cool, come by when you are done. Aight."

"What was that all about?" Tracy asked when I hung up.

"Nothin'. She goin' bowlin' with my cousin Charm and she gonna be by later."

"Hear that. Cut you fallin' for that chick ain't 'chu?"

"Please, she just there to keep me company but I like havin' her around…but the sex! Oh my God!"

"Hear that, so what'chu gonna do for tha rest of tha night?"

"Ain't got no plans."
"Aight, go to tha movies with me and Sondari."

" I ain't gonna be nobody's third wheel."

"Nigga call up one of ya chicks, I know you got somebody you can hit up."

"You right, I'ma call up Stacy. Come scoop me in like an hour."

"Nigga you ain't gotta get all fresh and shit just get dressed. The movie starts in an hour so be ready in a half."

"Aight."

Stacy is looking good. Her hair is in braids and wrapped in a French bun in the back. Stacy and I have known each other since high school because I beat up her ex-boyfriend for hitting her and she's never forgotten it. Stacy's complexion is chestnut brown and has a smile as big as mine. She's a lot taller than Evelyn and she's slim just like I like them.

The girls introduced themselves as Tracy and I went on and on about music and plans for tomorrow. The fifteen-minute drive that seemed like five was over in no time. Unfortunately the Matrix 2 was corny as hell and I spent most of the movie day dreaming about Kendra and the lyrics to that Ginuwine song. Despite the fact Stacy's head is rested on my shoulder and her hand clenching mine I still can't escape the thoughts. I looked down at Stacy who looked up at me and suddenly Kendra's face appeared.

"What?" she whispered

"Nothin', I just wanna look at'chu."

"Aww, you're so sweet." Then she smiled at me and nothing but sheer joy filled my heart. I put my arm around her and held her tight for the rest of the movie. The night seemed to fly by because before I knew it we are in front of Stacy's house and that was when I realized it wasn't Kendra I was sitting next to. It wasn't Kendra's eyes I was staring in and my joy turned into disappointment.

"I'll walk you to the door." I said reluctantly.

"How about I stay with you tonight?"

"Na, my roommate freaks me out and I don't want you to be uncomfortable."

"It's ok, I don't mind."

"Thanks but I do. I'll all you tomorrow."

"Umm… ok. Good-night." I didn't reply. I stared straight ahead while Tracy waited until Stacy was in the house.

"Why you ain't have her come by man, you probably could'a smashed"

"Na."

"Ohh you thinkin' 'bout Evelyn huh?"

"Na, someone else."

"Damn dude stop lookin' so sad, you depressin' me."

"Oh leave him alone." Sondari said. "Only love can make a man look like that."

"Damn nigga you got it bad."

"Shut tha fuck up."

"Daaammnn, why you snappin' at me cut, I'm just fuckin' wit'chu."

"Whatever."

I stood on the top of the cracked concrete steps taking a deep breath of the warm night summer air. The stars were out in full effect tonight and I located the brightest one in the sky and said hi to my cousin Little Jeff who passed away seven years ago. Then I dragged myself up the one flight of stairs to my apartment that was relativity quiet assuming Trevor was asleep.

It is pitch black when I entered the apartment so I quickly closed the door so no one would be awaken by the light from the hallway. I found my way to my futon and saw that Evelyn sleep with the covers pulled up to her face. I gently sat on the edge trying not to wake her but to no avail.

"Hi baby. It's 'bout time you got home." She whispered but I didn't respond as I took off my shoes. Evelyn sat up and from the moonlight peering through my window I could see that she is naked, completely.

"No, let me do it." She whispered. Evelyn bent down in front of me taking off my shirt, then unbuttoning and sliding off my jeans until finally taking my man tool in her mouth.

I laid back and looked out the window at the upside moon while Evelyn's soft lips and warm tongue pleasured me. The sensation made me more and more erect with every time her head came up but I couldn't help my body being there and my mind elsewhere. I really don't know what I am thinking or want to be thinking I'm just thinking blank thoughts. Next thing I knew Evelyn is riding me and her left titti is in my mouth. Her moans bounced off the walls in the one bedroom apartment and I periodically looked to the other side of the room to see if Trevor is watching again. Evelyn came before I did with her body jerking and her pleasure lips tightening around my manhood. I felt her juices running down my shaft as she lay on my chest and I am still erected inside her. I gently placed my hands on her perfect apple bottom and caressed it gently thinking her skin is flawless and her body is a soft as velour. Evelyn's breathing became more and more heavy as she fell asleep so I wrapped both arms around her, whispered goodnight Kendra before closing my eyes.

A loud banging on the door is disturbing my sleep. I sat up out of startelment and I looked over and saw Trevor had done the same.

"Yo, who is that?"

"I don't know, look through the peep hole." Trevor tip toed to the door and looked though.

"Yo its two women like grown women."

"Two grown women? What they want?"

"Hell if I know."

"Lemme see." Evelyn is still fast asleep while I frantically searched for some shorts to put on. I peered through the peep hole and to my surprise it is Evelyn's mother and another woman who both have the mean face on."

"Oh shit. Evy? Evy?" I whispered as the banging continued.

"What." She grunted.

"Ya moms in here." Her eyes flew open like window shades as she jumped out of bed wrapped in my blanket. She inched toward the door to see what I saw and she let out a gasp.

"Fuck, what do we do?" she asked frightened.

"I don't know, how does she know where I live?"

"I don't know."

"Look go hide in the bathroom."

"Okay." I lay back down and covered myself with my sheet and told Trevor to look like he just woke up when he opened the door.

"Syncere here?" She asked. I saw Trevor move out from in front of the doorway to let them see me on the futon.

"Yeah?"

"Where's Evelyn?" she asked as I tried to I looked puzzled.

"I…I don't know. I haven't seen her since she did my hair the day before yesterday."

"You a fuckin' lie because Charm is sittin' in the car downstairs and she showed me this is where she dropped Evy off last night so where is my fuckin' daughter?"

"I don't know she didn't come here last night, I didn't even get in until late. She paged me but by the time I got it I thought it was too late to call your house." Evelyn's mother and the other woman looked at me, then looked at Trevor who is obviously avoiding eye contact with them and me. We all just stared at each other for a minute not saying anything.

"See, you playin' games. Okay, we 'gon see how smart you are when the fuckin' cops show up in this bitch." She stormed off and Trevor quickly shut the door behind them and Evelyn scurried out of the bathroom.

"Wow she's pissed."

"I thought you said she never comes home?" I asked.

"She doesn't. I haven't seen her in two weeks 'cause she's always at her boyfriends house."

"Why did you have Charm bring you here? Why didn't you get dropped off at your place and then walk over?"

I didn't feel like it, I was tired."

"Evy, no one is supposed to know about us, I can go to jail for fuckin' wit'chu. Ya moms just threaten to call tha police on me."

"I know, I'm sorry. I gotta go."

As Evelyn collected her things I noticed that her panties, jeans, shirt and jewelry were all right on the floor in front of my futon but her mother failed to see it. That could've made her come in the house and look around and she would've discovered her fifteen-year old daughter naked under a blanket hiding n my bathroom. Ten minutes later, fully dressed, Evelyn and I cautiously walked down the steps to the front door.

"I'ma go out first to see if anyone is still out there, then you come out." She agreed. I walked out onto the porch and acted as if I was checking my mailbox and when I saw that no one was out here I signaled for Evelyn to run out.

"I'ma call you later."

"Okay, but go straight home. What are you gonna tell ya moms?"

"I'ma tell her I stayed the night at Sophia's house."

"Ok, good." Evelyn leaned over to kiss me but I leaned back.

"What?"

"She might come back up the block."

4

Quincy stays with is grandmother in their two-bedroom condominium off of Scoot Road. He has so many CD's and records everywhere it's like a music archive in his room and his room is too damn small for all of that. Combine that with the fact we have myself, I. Dot, Jus, Wes, Q, and Tre all in the same room huddled around one microphone makes it a huge joke fest.

"Yo Syn when you leavin' man?" Jus asked while we took a break.

"In about three weeks why?"

"'Cause we need to get you on some more songs for the Elements album."

"Aight, I got a few more I'ma record a Haze's crib this week."

"Yo son, I don't even know why you goin' back down there. You need to stay here and do this music shit with us." Tracy interrupted.

"Yeah boy." Wes cosigned.

"I need to get my degree fam. I don't have the luxury of living at home to do this music shit like all of ya'll do. I would if I could."

"Nigga, you can go to school here, why you gotta go all the way to North Carolina?"

"I got a track scholarship so I went where the money was."

"Hear that." Quincy said.

I feel a little envious that all my boys still live at home while their mother's let them work toward the dream of being a rap star. My mother never understood why I spent hours listening to the same beat over and over again and why I was so excited to let her hear a song I had recorded. My boys just work and work on music and I wish I could do that. Or be like Jus who doesn't even have to work he just does music all the time or at his leisure.

"Well I tell you what. Ya'll hold it down when I'm gone and I'll keep my writin' game up and hopefully I won't have to finish college."

"I got'chu my dude. You remember what I wrote in the year book." Wes said as he gave me pound.

To be completely honest I never wanted to go to college in the first place. I only went because I knew my moms would kick me out when the summer of my graduating year was over and I really wasn't working to save any money so I would've been up shits creek. I've contemplated with the idea of quitting but I've never quit anything a day in my life, plus I don't want to be out here like half of my graduating class who is stuck working dead end jobs because they didn't go to college. The other reason why I am in school is because I know that if I want to be with Kendra I need to have some kind of higher education. I mean with her wanting to be a Supreme Court judge I can't be another typical man who sits at home and does nothing while my wife goes out and works. I have to be able to support us as well and bring in the same type of income.

I sat at the gas station staring at the clock, watching the little hand tick down the seconds. 1:31 am. It seems like the later it gets the slower time passes. I thought about the first place I would go once I get my car. First I'll drive all around Waterbury showing it off, then I'll get directions to Exeter Academy in New Hampshire and drive the three hour ride up there. I'll stop on the way and pick up a teddy bear and some roses then find out which dorm Kendra lives in and surprise her. I'll hug her tight and swing her around as she kisses me repeatedly.

We'll stare in each other's eyes and smile and talk about nothing. Just talk to hear each other's voice and enjoy our own company. She'll introduce me to all her friends and walk me pass all the guys that's been trying to make her their girlfriend. Then when it comes time for me to leave we'll prolong it with several hugs, many kisses and repeated good-byes. I'll drive back home with a big smile on my face, warmth in my heart and a head full of memories about that day and plans for my next visit, it'll be perfect.

When she comes back to North Carolina while she is on break I'll drive over to her place on Six Forks Road and we'll spend all our time together going to every flea market, poetry club and park in Raleigh. I wonder if she is thinking the same thing I am thinking, what she would do once she saw me again? We've never spent any time alone together. Once when I was still living with my aunt Keisha in North Carolina Kendra's mother and uncle came to meet my aunt and grandmother. We swam and played with my cousins in the pool while the adults traded stories about each other and us. After Kendra and I got out of the pool we sat under the basketball hoop, me in her legs, as we talked and she put dirt in my hair. Most of the time she kept her arms wrapped around me as I held hands and we just sat there, together. We didn't say much, we just thought what each other was thinking, thinking *this is nice*.

We were so wrapped up with each other that we didn't see my aunt and her mother walking up the stone path from the back yard. Once we realized they were coming toward us my aunt was locking the gate back and Kendra's mother was making her way across the court. I saw the look her mother shot her as we scurried to get up and act as if they didn't see what they really did. That day was special to the both of us and important as well. Why? I really don't know it's just how we both felt when we recapped the day over the phone. I don't know if she knows it or not but Kendra was my first real girlfriend and she showed me the type of love that fifteen and sixteen year olds only think they have. Our love was different because it was innocent and pure. I wasn't trying to fill her head with bullshit so I can fuck her and leave her. The feelings were genuine, strong and only God knows why that was, but I don't question it because God don't make mistakes.

I reached into my wallet and pulled out the only two pictures I have of Kendra. Two pictures she'd given me when we first started dating. One is of her in her green and yellow tracksuit. She is bending on one knee and her hair is in long braids and the other, my favorite, is a school picture of her in this white, purple and brown striped v-neck sweater and her natural hair combed down to her shoulders. Her smile in both pictures is pearly white and flawless, as if she is smiling only at me. I kissed them both before putting them back into my wallet.

Thinking of Kendra inspired me to write so I pulled out my black and white composition book and titled the poem S.K.A.N.D.E.L.E.S. (Seductive Kindness Accompanying Natural Delicate Elegance, Leaving Everyone Sprung) The words just flowed off my pen onto the white blue lined paper with ease and before I knew it I had written a sixteen bar poem. I recited it to myself and decided it can be a song and I searched frantically through my book bag for my beat CD. Just then the door rang and I looked up to see Tracy and Quincy walking in.

"CUT!!!" I hollered.

"What's up cut?" We did our W.O.L.F. Pak handshake before getting to the bases of their visit to me in the middle of the night. Both of them are dressed in blue jeans and white Air Force Ones. Quincy in a red and gray Academics shirt and Tracy in a white FUBU t-shirt.

"What'chall doin' here."

"Yo we on our way to Denny's."

"Damn word." I said disappointed.

"Yeah, we were stopping by to see if you wanted us to bring you back anything?"

"Who ya'll goin' with?"

"Everybody goin' except the devil."

"Hear that. I need this paper. I'm like two G's away from getting' my car."

"Do you even know who to drive?" Quincy started laughing.

"Oh you got jokes huh?"

"Na cut I'm just askin'."

"Yeah I can drive. I take my test next week"

"Aight, if you need to practice before your test let me know. I'll take you in my car."

"Yeah me too cut."

"Good lookin'."

"Yo you like doin' this?" Quincy asked.

"I mean I rather be sleep or hangin' out with ya'll but it gives me a lot of time to write since I don't have enough time during the day to get it done. I'm workin' on somethin' right now actually. I got a session at Haze's on Tuesday."

"Lemme hear what'chu got."

"Na cut you know I think it's bad luck for someone to hear my song with it's not done."

"Aight, we gotta go we still gotta go get Bruce, Wes and Jus."

"Damn Bruce comin' too?"

"Yeah cut, we told you everybody." Tracy confirmed.

"Yo, I'm not sayin' don't work because I see you really want a car but you only got three more weeks here man, have some fun wit'cha boys. Quit this shit" Quincy suggested.

"Well I'm pullin' in like five a week, a little more so I'ma have my car in two weeks. That leaves me with a week to chill. I'll quit this job and keep the Finish Line and day camp jobs."

"Aight dude. What'chu want to eat?"

"Oh, I want three waffles, chicken tenders and cheese sticks."

"Damn, you eat like a fat guy." We laughed about it as they left out the store. Just as they left the phone rang.

"Sunoco gas station."

"Syncere?"

"Yeah, who this?"

"Me, Evy silly. You don't know my voice by now?"

"Na, I just wasn't excepting it to be you that's all."

"What'chu doin'?"

"Writin', why?"

"Nothing. I couldn't sleep and I was thinking about you. It feels weird not having your big ass arms around me at night. Not to mention I'm horny as hell right now, I got moist when you picked up the phone." The sound of that gave me an instant hard on as I thought about how warm Evelyn's pleasure temple is.

"Really?"

"Yeah, when do you have a night off?"

"Tuesday?"

"That is too far away. I miss you. I need to see you."

"Well tomorrow I only work at the camp I don't have to go to Finish Line. So from three to nine I'll be home."

"Ok, I'll be there at five."

"Aight."

As I put my keys into the door I heard whispers and rustling from inside the apartment. I figured Trevor has the television on. As I walked in my black curtains and blinds are still shut and I saw a figure dart into the kitchen as Trevor stood up when I entered.

"Who the hell was that?"

"Nobody." He responded panting. I didn't believe him, not with all that sweat beading on his forehead and the awful smell of bad pussy in the air. I cautiously walked into the kitchen and found Lawaya huddled in between the stove and the refrigerator. I had to fight back two urges, one the urge to laugh and the other urge to throw up knowing that awful smell came from between her legs.

"What the hell are you hiding for?" I asked

"I don't know." She responded quivering.

"Whatever." I walked back into the living room and flopped on my futon after opening the window behind me.

"Trevor I have to go." Lawaya said coming out of the kitchen.

"Aight, I'll call you later."

"Ok." They didn't hug and they didn't kiss, she just left as if they'd just met each other.

"You fuckin' her?" I asked sooner than the door can close.

"Yeah."

"Her pussy stinks."

"I know right?" He laughed but I didn't. "Oh yo, you got some mail." Trevor handed me the big brown envelope. I read it and saw that it came from the athletic department of Saint Augustine's College. It contained my room and board assignment but more importantly my partial scholarship papers and my student loan papers as well as a deadline to send everything in, one week from now. The moment of truth is right here as I thought about the Georgia State offer I got three weeks ago. I have to fill these papers out and mail them within the next two days, what do I do? I need to talk to Kendra.

I turned on the prehistoric computer and saw she did in fact send me an email, which brighten up my day. I replied with a message of sweet nothings and outlining my dilemma about continuing going to school. As I was typing Trevor began to put his shoes on.

"You leavin'?"

"Yeah. Yo, you think when you leave you can put in a word for me at your gas station job?"

"Yeah, I'll try."

"Do they know you leavin?"

"Na."

"Aight, if you can do that for me that would be cool."

"I got'chu."

I wasn't in the shower more than ten minutes before I felt Evelyn's hands caressing my chest from behind. I turned around and faced her as she took my cloth out of my hands and began to wash my chest, my arms, my waist and below spending an extra few moments on my erect solider.

"Turn around." She whispered. As she washed my shoulders, my back and the rest of my body. I did the same to her in return and once we were both rinsed clean she leaned up against the shower wall with her left leg cocked on the edge of the tub and a lustful look in her eyes. I entered her wetness slowly and heard her gasp from pleasure. The shower beat on my back as Evelyn dug her nails into me and her pleasure moans bounced off the bathroom walls. Shortly after she let out a high-pitched noise and jerked a few times before getting off.

"You monster." She said as she tried to catch her breath. "Com'on, I'll lotion you down.

As Evelyn lotion me down I thought about what Kendra asked me a couple of weeks ago, how can I love her if I mess with other girls. Here I am counting down the days until I can see Kendra again and in the same breath I have Evelyn tending to my every need. Tracy constantly asks me why don't I just be with Evelyn since she is everything I personally want in a woman but she is not Kendra. There is no doubt that for her age Evelyn is a wonderful girlfriend but she is missing the very thing that Kendra has. I don't know what that missing puzzle piece is I just feel it when I am with Kendra and I don't feel it when I am with Evelyn.

The walk to work has me thinking about saying good-bye to Evelyn in a couple of weeks, but she's young and she'll get over it. A sudden feeling of not wanting to go to work came over me. I visualized the walk in my head and calculated how far I had to go and I really didn't feel like it tonight. Tracy's hunter green Chrysler Sebring speed passed me and at that rate I didn't think he saw me but I see him making a u-turn.

"Cut need a ride?"

"No, I'm just walking for my health." I jumped in the car relieved at the fact I don't have to walk to work.

"Goin' to the gas station right?"

"Yeah man."

"You sound like you don't want to go."

"Na I really don't, I hate that job."

"Cut, quit."

"Na I can't do that, I'm mad close to buyin' my car."

"Ain't it cheaper to buy a car down south, just do it there."

"I don't know. Where you headed?"

"Home, just came from Wes's house." We were at the gas station before I knew it and I sat in the passenger side of the car just staring at the entrance. Half of me wanted to stay in the car but the other half was saying fuck it.

"Aight dude, I'll holla."

"Yo man don't go you know you don't want to." Tracy tempted.
"Na I'ma go." I got out of the car and walked snail like into the gas station. There is a heavy set white guy behind the counter, one I haven't seen before.

"You must be Syncere." He said when I walked behind the counter.

"Who you?"

"I'm Roger. The station was brought by a new owner and he wants me to train you."

"Train me. I've been doing this job fine for the past two months. There is nothing to it, what do you need to train me on?"

"Look, I'm just following orders, you don't like it take it up with the new owner." I looked outside to see that Tracy hadn't pulled off yet.

"Tell him I quit." I got back into Tracy's car to see he was on the phone.

"What happened?"

"I quit."

"Hear that cut!"

"Syn, you want some more chicken?"

"Yeah a couple of more pieces." I. Do fixing everyone's plate as she usually did whenever we had a meeting at her house. She is a hell of a cook and Tracy made it imperative that she cooks for us whenever we are there. I. Dot is an ex-girlfriend of Tracy's who remained a good friend to him as well as the rest of the group. I. Dot is cute as hell. She extremely short towering at just five foot two with a short hair cut. She's big behind but small up front but her waist is damn near invisible, which makes it hard for me to believe she has a five year old. Tracy, Quincy, Wes, Jus and I congregated in the living room finding a spot on her floor or couch while we waited until each other was settled enough to talk about the matter at hand.

"Aight, look. I got a cousin named Shawyna who lives in the A who said that she got madd connections I the music industry. I sent her a demo of our songs, Faithful, Fuck ya head up, and the Elements album and she was like everybody she let hear it is feelin' it. She said that she can get us a four song demo package at a big time studio down there and then pass it on to her people. So what do ya'll say?" Everybody looked around at each other and we could see all of us had some type of questions but no one wanted to ask I guess of fear of sounding negative, so I sparked it off.

"How much is it gonna cost us? Big time studio means big time money."

"I don't know but I can get more details from her once I tell her what our decision is"

"When she want us down there?" Jus asked.

"In a couple of months. I figure we can get some more songs written and bring them down there with us so we don't waste any studio time writin'." We talked about it more and more over the course of an hour and half tossing back ideas, pros and cons and almost every possibility including moving. As much as I wanted to be apart of what was unfolding I just can't. I have a college career to finish plus I still need to be in North Carolina next year when Kendra starts UNC. It's not something I had planned, however, we've been working toward a record deal since I was a freshman in high school but in this business you only get one shot and this could be it.

Tracy and I sat outside my apartment in his car talking it over and he is persistent in convincing me not to go back to school.

"Look man this could be our shot, the shot we've been waiting for. We got niggas in Atlanta feelin' our shit, our shit. Your songs and my songs."

"Yeah but I'm trying to be in North Carolina and be with Kendra. That's the woman I'm going to marry and I'm tryin' to be with her, plus I got this scholarship to run. I'll be jeopardizing a lot over something that's not guaranteed. I don't know if I'll make the wrong decision."

"Nothing in life is guaranteed. You can go to school and get hurt and not be able to run anymore and then what? Look, it's only your sophomore year right? Just take the first semester off, do this music shit with us and if it don't work out go back to school in January."

"I'll talk it over with Kendra first." I said.

"Aight dude, but don't let a girl dictate what you do with your life. If you really want to go to school then go, but if you want to do music as bad as I know you do then do it. And if this chick is half the woman you say she is then she will understand."

I called Kendra to tell her about the Atlanta offer but I'm going to mention the idea of not going back to school for a semester just to see what she thinks about it. Once part of me wants her to be supportive of my dream but another part of me wants her to tell me to go to North Carolina so we can be together. Being the type of thoughtful young woman Kendra is I doubt she'll tell me to pass up my dream, she'll simply say ok if that is what you want to do. The biggest part is I don't want her to think I am backing out of wanting to be with her. All summer we've been talking about me going back to North Carolina to be there when she starts school and here I am about to tell her I may not be there.

"Guess what?" I asked Kendra.

"What?"

"Wes' cousin in Atlanta said that she knows some influential people in the record business and she might be able to get us a record deal."

"That's great, but what about school? Don't you go back next week?"

"Well after talking to Tracy and them I've decided to take this semester off and see what is going to happen with music."

"Are you serious? Why?"

"Well you know that music is my first passion and I only went to school because of you and the scholarship. But if I can get a deal I won't need school."

"So what are you going to do if it doesn't work out?"

"Go back. I'm only taking one semester off. If things don't look promising then I'll go back in January."

"Syn, when people take off a semester they never go back. It's hard to get back into the swing of things."

"I'm good, I got it all worked out."

"Will you guys have to move to Atlanta?" Kendra asked with curiosity in her voice.

"I don't think so but if we have to and it don't work out then I can go back to North Carolina. I've already talked to my coach and everything. He doesn't like it but he said I can keep my scholarship as long as I come back by January."

"And what if you don't make it back? What if it takes longer? Is it really worth the gamble?"

"Please, as fast as I am a college will pick me up. I led my school to the nationals this year so who wouldn't want me? Speak of it; I got an offer from Georgia State to run on a full scholarship none of that partial shit. It's amazing how the black college give me half the money but a white college is willing to give me a full ride." I added

"Ok Syncere, it seems like you've thought a lot about it. I'm happy for you."

"Thanks, it seems like things are coming together the way I always thought it would be. Either way, I'll be in North Carolina when you start UNC, believe me."

"Ok, are you still coming to visit me?"

"Oh, I didn't pass my driving test. The guy said I couldn't back in right and I made sharp left turns." I explained shamefully.

"So you're not coming?"

"I can't, I can try like take a bus up there if you can pick me up somehow."

"The bus station is twenty miles away and I don't have a car up here. Syncere I was really looking forward to seeing you this weekend."
"I know, as was I. Well how about you come down here this weekend? I can pay for everything."
"I can't, I have class on Saturday's until 6 o'clock."
"So come up that night and spend all day Sunday here and I'll send you back Sunday night."

"Syncere, that is a lot of traveling for not even a whole day, I was looking forward to spending the night with you."

"I know I was looking forward to the same thing. I don't know I can think of something, ok?"

"Yeah." Kendra said before hanging up the phone sounding less than enthusiastic about my academic decision.

5

The Saturday afternoon in August is still a very warm one as I walked home from the mall after working a 9 to 4 shift at the Finish Line. I am anticipating my return home in hopes of finding an email from Kendra and at the fact Evelyn is coming by later tonight. The routine is always the same, I walk in and Trevor is on the couch watching TV still unable to find a job and I flop on my futon to regain my energy from the walk. Just as I hoped there was an email from Kendra but it is a forward, which peaked my curiosity-I read on.

At the end of the email I'm 38 hot, pissed off to the up most degree humanly possible. If looks could kill Trevor would be dead ten times over. I looked at his pale skin and his fucked up hairline and wanted to choke the miserable life out of him, but I said nothing. I just picked up the phone and called Jus.

'Yo where you at son?"

"I just got in the house, what's good?"

"Yo meet me at the Pride."

"Damn Syn I just got in the house, can't it wait like an hour?"

"Na son, I need to talk to you now, meet me there in fifteen minutes."

"Why? What's wrong?"

"I'll explain it all to you when we meet up. 1."

"1."

I fought back the killer instinct wanting to beat the shit out of Trevor while I changed my password on the thirty-year-old computer. All the while Trevor said nothing, nothing at all and that made me even angrier. I gathered a few notebooks, threw them into my book bag and left the house slamming the door hard enough to make the whole building rattle.

This ungrateful motherfucka, I thought to myself. After everything I have done for him since I've been sharing that one bedroom efficiency apartment this is what he does to me? My anger fueled my walk because before I knew it I walked passed the pride and almost ran right into Jus. I just stared at him trying to catch my breath as I felt beads of sweat running down my forehead.

"What happened?" he asked.

"Yo, this nigga Trevor sent Kendra an email tellin' her that I'm fuckin' with Evelyn." I reveled.

"Oh shit! How you know he did that?"

"'Cause she forward the email to me and asked was it true."

"Yo thas fucked up. Ya'll beefin' or somethin'?"

"Not that I know of. But that ain't it. He had the audacity to tell her when she comes to visit for thanksgivin' she should come to see him and not me." Jus burst out into laughter and I didn't find the same amusement out of the situation.

"Yo son, tha shit ain't funny. I wanna go smash on this dude like right now." I said punching my palm with my fist.

"Where you gonna stay if you do that?"

"That's what I wanted to talk to you about. Yo the new semester starts in January and I was wonderin' if I could crash on ya couch until then? I mean I can help out with the rent and all that, plus I'm workin' three jobs so I'll hardly be there." I suggested not knowing what Jus' response would be.

"You know I got'chu, you like my moms other son anyway so yeah it's cool. When you wanna move in?"

"Soon, 'cause I wanna beat this niggas ass while I'm still pissed off."

"You gon' do it tonight?" Jus instigated.

"If I can move my shit out and into yours hell yeah."

"Aight, we gotta wait. I gotta call Rus and tell him to bring the camera so I can tape this shit. I heard you a beast in a fight but I neva seen you in one. This is gonna be funny."

I went back to the apartment and said nothing to Trevor as I packed up my clothes, DVD's, toiletries and other belongings. I occasionally looked over at Trevor who looked nervous as if he knew I knew something but wasn't really sure. Still I didn't make eye contact with him to make sure my blood stayed hot enough to hit him as soon as I saw the camera.

"You movin' out?" he asked, but I said nothing to his comment. I let Jus and Rus into the house and they began to take my things downstairs.

"You still gonna fight him?" Jus asked in the hallway.

"You damn right, as soon as all my shit is out,"

"Aight, Rus come back upstairs with the camera." Just as we turned to go back into the apartment Trevor came down with a handful of my things.

"Thought I'd help." He said as handed the box to Rus.

"Damn Syn, you can't fight'em after he helped you with ya shit." Jus said.

"Why the fuck not? You got the camera? Let's go." I walked up the stairs with every intention to take Trevor's head off. I haven't verbally spoken to Kendra about the situation but if Trevor's confession has undone all the work I've put into getting back into Kendra's good graces then I'ma be back to fuck him up again. Trevor is standing in the middle of the room when we all got back to the apartment. I looked around. No television, no phone, no computer desk, no type of modern entertainment. It's as if Trevor was back in the dark ages.

"You got everything?" Still I said nothing, just waited for Rus to poke his head into the apartment with the camera but until then I acted like I was making sure everything of mine was out of the apartment and Jus stood around waiting for me. Then I saw Rus but Trevor didn't and I took a violent left swing and caught Trevor right in his chin. His head flew back and he staggered. Before he can regain composure I followed with a right hook to the left side of his face, a left, another right and then an uppercut that sent him crashing to the cold apartment floor. I got on top of him punching him in his face three more times before Jus tried to pull me off.

"Aight Syn that's enough." I could barley make out what he was saying over his and Rus' laughter. Rus held both my arms trying to escort me out of the apartment while Jus continued to laugh behind us. I looked back at a bloody crying Trevor and felt nothing, no emotion or remorse. None at all.

I sat on my futon in Jus' front living room thinking whether or not I should call Kendra tonight or wait a while. I figured if I called her tonight and had a good lie she'd be more likely to believe me than if I waited a couple of days to come up with a better one. I decided to call so I made the slow journey down the three flights of stairs.

The moon is full and high in the sky illuminating my walk to the corner store. I looked for the brightest star in the sky that that is my deceased cousin Little Jeff and asked him to ask God to help me with this mess and to tell him to forgive me for beating Trevor's ass. Convinced he got my message I sprinted to the store and back.

I held the plastic phone card in one hand and the receiver in my trembling other hand. *Think of a good lie…think of a good lie….* I told myself over and over again; even after the numbers were dialed and the phone is ringing I still don't know what I am going to tell her when she questions me.

"Hello?"

"Hey it's me."

"Oh hey Syncere." I immediately knew she wasn't the same because all the enthusiasm that is normally in her voice when I call has diminished.

"Hey, what's wrong?"

"Did you get my email?"

"No. You emailed me today?" I said trying to sound surprised.

"Yeah."

"Oh I haven't checked it yet. I went to work and then I was moving."

"Moving? To Atlanta?"

"No! I moved in with Jus."

"Why?"

"Because Trevor is a dirty dude and he hasn't paid his half of the rent since I moved in, so I asked Jus if I could crash on his couch and his mom said it was ok."

"Syn can I ask you a question?" Kendra asked in her soft voice.

"No." I joked.

"Thanks… Are you messing with other girls?"

"No why would you ask me that. I thought we established that."

"Trevor sent me an email saying you are messing with a fifteen-year-old girl." Kendra revealed.

"He's smokin' crack. The girl he is talking about is the one that does my hair. She likes me and I guess he be pickin' up on that when she at the house. But messin' with her? Hell na." I continued.

"Are you sure?"

"I'm positive." Nothing was said on either end after that, I know I'm lying but I wonder if she knows? I surely hope not.

"Yo Syn I want you to come hear this beat." Jus said poking his head into the living room.

"Hold on I'm on the phone."

"Nigga who you talkin' to?"

"My girlfriend."

"Oh aight, tell her I said what up." Jus said.

"Aight."

"What did you just call me?" Kendra said breaking our silence.

"Huh?"

"Did you just call me your girlfriend?"

"Yeah…"

"I'm your girlfriend?" Kendra asked with a hint of excitement in her voice.

"Yeah, you didn't know?" I asked joking again. She broke into laughter and it is the sweetest sound in the world next to her voice.

"I don't recall you asking me."

"I asked you the night you fell asleep on the phone. I said did you hear me and you said yeah. Don't you remember?"

"Nope, you tryin' to trap me." At this point we are both laughing and that put ease to my mind and to my heart.

"Trap you? I already got you."

"Do you?" she teased.

"Yep. You <u>my</u> girlfriend."

"Say it again."

"My girlfriend."

"Again."

"My girlfriend. Kendra… you… my girlfriend."

"Good. I like the way that sounds." Words can' t express how happy I am right now, at the sound of Kendra's conformation all I could do is smile and smile big. I've been waiting to hear those words again for months now and they have finally been uttered.

"I love you Kendra." I said in a soft, sincere voice.

"I love you too."

"Do you really?"

"Yes really. Why would you doubt that?"

"I'm not doubting that, I just like the way that it sounds." I said.

"Copy cat. So now that you are at Jus' house what are we going to do about thanksgiving?"

"Oh got it covered. I'm renting a hotel room that has a kitchen so we can still cook."

"Syn I don't want you to spend a whole lot of money on me. I'll only be there for the weekend."

"No I got the room from a friend of mine that works at the hotel, I'll spend a lot of money on all the food I'm going to eat."

"Are you getting all fat on me now?"

"Yep, huge."

'Are you sure it's not going to be expensive? Because I can pay for the food…or something."

"Babe I'm sure. Do you need me to fly you down?"

"No the school pays for it remember?"

"Oh yeah."

"I'm coming down the day before thanksgiving. We don't go back to school until Monday so you think I can go back on Sunday night?"

"Aww damn. You have to go back?" I signed.

"You silly. How are you going to get me from the airport?"

"I already got it covered. I'll hold onto your birthday gift until you get here."

"You got me a gift? What is it?"

"I'm not telling you, it's a surprise." I teased.

"Syn you know I hate surprises." Kendra said in a stern voice.

"Ok. I got you hundred-dollar gift card to Barnes & Noble since you like to read and all. I really didn't know what else to get you."

"No that is perfect, thank you, thank you, thank you so very much. That is wonderful Syn. You are so thoughtful, see there I'ma keep you around for a while."

"Just a while? Why not forever?" I signed again.

"You wanna be with me forever? Why?"

"'Cause I do, that is how I've felt since I met you."

"Really?"

"Really."

"What do you want for your birthday?"

"Never thought about it. Lemme think… If I tell you do you promise I can have it?"

"If it doesn't cost too much, you know I don't work up here."

"It doesn't cost anything, maybe a couple of flower petals or so."

"Flower petals? Syncere what are you talking about?"

"For my birthday I want you on a silver platter surround by rose petals. I'll take the same think for Christmas and Valentine's Day. Matter fact if you give me that it can be my gift for every holiday." Kendra burst into a loud laughter that lasted minutes.

"You are a trip. What am I going to do with you?"

"Love me and hope I never leave."

"I think I can do that."

Kendra and I stayed on the phone until my twenty-dollar phone card said I have less than a minute to go. I promised to email her as she promised to respond, then we concluded with I love you's before hanging up. I never did hear the beat Jus wanted me to.

The mall is gradually growing dead as the night grew later and I thought about what I'm going to do tonight. I still have two hours until the mall officially closes and Becky has us all cleaning up now, I hope she says I can go home first because I get destructive when I have nothing to do.

"Yo cut?" I turned toward the front of the store to see Tracy with a trio of young women and Quincy on his cell phone following not far behind.

"What's good hamburgerler?" I joked as Tracy took back his hand.

"Niggas always got jokes. Yo this is Dorian, Q's girl." He introduced me to a light skinned girl with big cheeks in glasses. Since she is Quincy's girl I didn't bother examining her body, for what?

"Oh you tha one who be makin' him miss writin' and recordin' sessions huh?" She giggled.

"This is Porsche, my girl…for the evening." Tracy continued while I shook the hand a of yet another light skinned girl slightly taller than Dorian and a little more attractive.

"Hello."

"And this… is Nadege." Wow! Nadege. Nadege is a five foot six rich dark chocolate skinned Haitian girl. Her eyes are the perfect almond shape with high cheekbones and pass her shoulder hair. Instead of saying hi she flashed me a smile filled with flawless bright white teeth and everything inside of me went haywire.

"Cut lemme talk to you for a minute." I pulled Tracy into the back of the store.

"What's good?"

"Yo please tell me you brought Nadege here for me and she is not for Wes."
" Oh yeah. We figured the dark skinned one was more your steez."

"You thought right, so that's all me?"

"Yeah nigga but you better hop on that fast because her friends said madd dudes be tryin' to get at her. Plus she just broke up with her boyfriend."

"Oh thas what's good."

"You chillin' wit your young girl tonight?"

"Na, I really ain't got nothin' planned."

"Come with us to Saint Joe's."
"What's up there?"

"They are apart of some group that is tryin' to raise money for some activity at their school so they throwin' a party." Tracy explained.

"Son you know damn well I can't dance."

"Nigga so what. Ain't nobody say you had to dance, just talk to home chick."

"Aight."

"Na nigga don't say aight and you get there and you act all shy and shit. I know you son."

"Na dude I'm good. What time ya'll going up there because I gotta go home and get ready."

"Well Q is takin' them up there right now and I gotta ditch the warden so you got like two hours. That means go home and get dressed. Don't be takin' 80 hours like you do."

"Aight, 1."

"1." I looked at Tracy join Quincy and the rest of the girls and I took a look at Nadege one more time. I scanned her body up and down remembering every curve, the round buttocks, the thick legs her noticeable breasts. *Nice* I thought to myself. *Very nice.*

As I looked over myself one more time in Tracy's car mirror I feel confident in my appearance and I put on my cocky attitude.

"Cut remember don't be playin' that low key shit. She is not going to come to you, you gotta go to her."

"What's my name?"

"Na son & leave that devil shit here. She a real cool chick so don't let her see that demonic shit."

"Son I got'chu."

"Aight."

We walked in to a very dimly lit gymnasium after paying the ten-dollar cover to a plus-sized white girl standing at the door. Tracy and I searched the room for Quincy and the girls and I spotted Nadege with a bottle in her hand standing by a speaker.

"There they go." I yelled over the Fabalous & Nate Dogg song playing. I made my way over and as Nadege saw me she threw her arms around me with a smile saying hello. This is a surprise to me because I don't even know this girl but I must say I love the aggressiveness, and Tract said she wouldn't come to me.

"You not going to dance?" I'm hypnotized by her voice and the accent as she spoke closely to my ear. I looked into her eyes and there is this sparkle there as if her life is perfect and she is the happiest woman on earth. It's the same type of sparkle I have in my eye when I talk about or see Kendra.

"I don't dance."

"Oh com'on. So you just gonna stand here all night?"

"Or until you are ready to leave."

"I guess I'll have to dance on you then." She said winking.

Nadege turned around putting her nice ass into my pelvis and started to move her waist to the music. I looked around the room and saw Tracy with his arm around Porsche as she did the same thing Nadege is doing. When he saw me looking at him he looked down at Nadege backing it up and nodded his head and I nodded back.

The DJ put some reggae on and Nadege threw her hands up in the air letting out a little yell. She turned to me and as we stood face to face I started to move my hips to the rhythm. Her eyes grew big as she started to move in the same motion as I am. Before long we were dancing so close you didn't know where she ended and I began. I looked at the clock that said twelve-thirty and Usher's You Got It bad came on. "I love this song." Nadege confessed as she got as close as humanly possible as we danced as if no one else is in the room. I completely forgot I can't stay on beat for more than a few minutes but we held each other tight and just danced. I closed my eyes while Nadege's perfume entered my nostrils. Sweet just like she is. I kept my hands on top of her butt while she kept her arms wrapped around my neck and her head rested on my chest as our breaths matched each other's.

The music stopped and the lights came on but Nadege and I didn't budge an inch and I didn't want to either.

"Nadege let's go." Dorian said behind her. She lifted her head and looked me in the eye and smiled.

"That was nice." She whispered.

"Yeah."

"Where are you going now?"

"I don't know, Tracy drove."

"Come with me." She took me by the hand and led me threw everyone trying to exit the gym until we caught up to our friends.

"Cut you aight?" Tracy asked patting me on the back.

"Hold on a minute." I told Nadege as Tracy and I purposely fell behind everyone. "I'm good."

"Son I saw you over there, yea nigg!"

"I told you I got this. Where ya'll goin' now?"

"Q stayin' here wit his girl. I'm tryin' to get back to Porsche's room. Why? You wanna leave?"

"Hell no. I'm tryin' to get back into home girl's room."

"Hear that. You hooked already." He laughed.

"Na I wouldn't say all that. I just want some ass." I said nonchalantly.

"Well if Porsche let me in I'm staying tha night."

"It's cool 'cause I don't have to work at all tomorrow night."

"Bet."

Tracy and I caught up to the girls and Nadege locked fingers with mine as we engaged in conversation on the way to her room. Porsche stayed on another floor but Nadege and Dorian were right down the hall from each other.

"My room is junky so don't laugh." Nadege confessed.

"Aight." I started laughing before she could open the door.

"See you laughing already."

"Aight, aight. I'm good."

When she opened the door I prepared myself for the worst but it isn't junky at all. When she entered she scurried to get the clothes off the armchair and into her closet, which is junky.

"Have a seat…anywhere."

She cleaned up for about anther five minutes before finally standing in the middle of the floor taking a deep breath and I made sure my pager is on silent.

"You got it all?"

"Yeah I think so." We laughed. "So tell me about yourself."

"What do you want to know?"

"Anything. I already know you're cute but what's up here?" She said as she pointed to her head.

Nadege lay on her stomach at the foot of her bed while I sat across from her in the armchair spilling out the last nineteen years of my life purposely leaving out my escapades with Kendra and Evelyn. She listened attentively occasionally asking me to elaborate on certain stories as well as seemingly very interested in the fact I wrote and performed music. The look in her eyes is so genuine and honest and if the eyes are truly windows to the soul then her soul must be beautiful.

A moment went by without either of us saying anything. I knew by her body language she is growing tired and I must admit so am I. I wondered when Tracy or Quincy is going to knock on the door signaling it was time to go but the minutes turned into thirty. I really don't want to leave but I am not sure what kind of girl Nadege is. Is she the kind that puts out on the first date? Is she the traditional type? I don't know and I don't want to make the wrong move turning out to be some kind of psycho in her eyes and mess up potential ass that my boys are getting.

I must admit with a body like hers and that intoxicating Haitian accent has my hormones doing the Harlem shake.

"So you gonna sit over there all night." She asked looking down at her bed.

"Not all night, I don't know how much longer I can keep my eyes open."

"Well I'ma help you with that." Nadege slowly and seductively inched off her bed and placed two of her biggest assets on my lap. I fought the urge of my manhood rising to the occasion. She wrapped her pure chocolate brown arms around my neck and it feel as if I have a silk scarf on. I looked into her eyes and broke eye contact and looked at her again.

"What?" I asked.

"You shy?"

"No."

"Why aren't you kissing me?" Her question caught me by surprise but luckily my lips acted on command. Her tongue still has the faint taste of liquor on it as our lips pressed against each other and our tongues greeted one another.

Nadege's arms grew tighter around my neck as our kiss grew increasingly passionate and my fingers and palms introduced themselves to her ass. I felt her body relax and I tightened my grip on her backside and at that moment she broke our lip lock and my tongue explored her neck and her collarbone. I continued to go south running my tongue in between the top of her breasts then before I knew it Nadege is throwing her blouse onto her bed and I'm unsnapping her bra. Before I opened my mouth Nadege grabbed the back of my head and buried my face into her 38DD chest.

I lifted Nadege up gently placing her on her bed where we kissed and let our hands explore our half dressed bodies…then…as we looked each other in the eye both waiting for the sign from the other to proceed to the fourth level of play…we did nothing… absolutely nothing. I rested my head upon Nadege's balloon breasts and we let the synchronized sounds of our breath put us to sleep.

"Cut you hit that didn't you?" Tracy asked in the car while he and Quincy burst out in applauds.

"Na son I ain't do it." I reluctantly confessed.

"Nigga you lying'. We saw ya'll all hugged up at tha party. You see them titis?" Quincy asked.

"I saw'em." Tracy said.

" Not like I did. But don't get me wrong her body is on point like a muhfucka, ass and everything but she a classy broad and I wanted to be a gentleman… for once."

"What tha fuck?! The devil wants to be a gentleman? Cut you were supposed to hit that."

"Yeah I know. She was down for it too."

"What'chu mean?" Quincy turned around in the front seat with a perplexed look on his face. I walked Quincy and Tracy threw the details of last night and watched as their facial expressions changed from surprised to interest then to disappointment when I told them we just went to sleep.

"You crazy as hell. I would've hit that."

"Did you smash Porsche?"

"Na she was bullshittin' all night after a while I went to sleep." Quincy and I laughed.

"Seems like ain't nobody get no ass."

"No sir. I got some ass last night." Quincy raised his hand.

"Q please. You're supposed to that is your girl."

"Yeah, yeah she is."

"Cut you're in love." I teased.

"Na na na I'm not."

"Look at this dude on the phone already. Probably explaining to the M. Dot why he didn't call her back last night."
"Yo that was Wes, he said he got some info about his cousin from Atlanta.

While I stood in the taco bell line on my lunch break all I can think about is Nadege and how stupid I am for not waxing that ass two nights ago, I ignored Kendra and Evelyn's pages last night for nothing.

"Syncere." I hear a distant call of my name behind me. I turned around to locate the voice but I don't see anyone so I kept looking until the voice is right in front of me.

"Remember me?" she asked smiling.

"Of course I do. Navarda right?"

"Yeah you remember." Navarda and I hugged asking each other how we were doing. Navarda is a four foot six West Indian girl. We were in the same English class in high school where her other West Indian friend Keisha liked me. Navarda isn't gorgeous but she's ok looking. She has a nice little smile; high cheek bones a small chest and a nice little butt.

"What have you been doing?"

"Nothing just working."

"You didn't go to college?"

"No but I heard you did, I thought you went away?" she said trying recall.

"I did. I went to North Carolina, I was supposed to go back two months ago but I'm takin' a semester off." I explained.

"Oh ok."

"What's good with you?"

"Nothing. I'm just working at the hospital."

"Oh do you like it? How long have you been there?"

"About two years now. Hey do you have any kids?"

"Hell no. I'm too young for that."

"Oh I thought you and Dorcea would've had a bunch of kids together by now."

"Dorcea? Why you say that?"

"'Cause ya'll were all inseparable in high school. Keisha couldn't get you and neither could I."

"You! You didn't ever tell me you liked me."

"You couldn't tell? Every time Keisha was around you so was I."

"I thought you and her were close 'cause ya'll was from the same West Indian region."

"Well at first but we both liked you so you became the topic of discussion a lot." She revealed.

"Wow, that is a surprise to me." Navarda licked her lips and smirked a little, its like I can see the seduction in her eyes.

"So you workin' at Finish Line huh? So which girl do you have in your life now?" I thought about mentioning Kendra or even Evelyn but when I looked at Navarda's breast poking out of her tight boy shirt I decided to lie.

"Na I don't have one. I'm single."

"Really. Want my number?"

"I don't know do you want to give it to me?"

"If I didn't I wouldn't've asked. Here." I took my food from the Taco Bell cashier while Navarda used my other hand as a piece of paper.

"Aight, I got'chu."

"You will if you call me." Navarda stood on her tiptoes to kiss my cheek, softly.

I didn't think much about it or much about Navarda because I already had my mind made up about what was going to happen. I am going to fuck her and leave her alone. I could tell just by the way she came off me that she still likes me and will do anything to have me including fucking me on the first night. Tonight I'll call her and do what I do.

I settled on I. Dot's living room floor while she and Tracy were hugged up talking in the kitchen. I wrote in my composition notebook to a beat playing on the stereo as we waited for Wes, Jus and Quincy to come by.

"Cut you want some ziti?"

"Hell yeah I want some ziti, what else you makin I. Dot?" I. Dot and Tracy look like a married couple and I know he is way happier with her than when he is with M. Dot.

"Tha Pak is in the building!" Wes shouted upon entering through I. Dot's backdoor followed by Jus and Quincy as we all exchanged greeting with our signature handshake.

"Yo we gonna talk in a minute just wait for I. Dot to finish cookin' then we can eat and talk." Instructed Tracy.

"Whut'chu writin' cut?" Quincy asked me.

"This track Jus gave me. I ain't really write nothin' yet. I'm just tryin' to figure out what tha beat is sayin'."

"Oh aight."

Before long I. Dot and Tracy were serving everyone massive amounts a baked ziti and the only sound in the air-conditioned condo is forks scraping plates.

"Aight cut tell'em what ya cousin was sayin'."

"Aight, so ya'll know I been talkin to my cousin Shawyna right? Well I sent her the demo and she say she can get us a deal."

"Which songs did you send her?" I asked.

"Syn does it matter?"

"Yeah because I ain't on a lot of shit that ya'll got and every time ya'll send somethin' out I ain't never on it."

"Nigga stop workin tha graveyard shift and record some music. We all got one job why you need two and three?"

"Yo, yo yo." Wes interrupted. "I sent Faithful, Run Dat, and that slow song that you and Jus did a Haze's crib along with some other shit. Trust me she's heard everybody and she think we all hot, that's not an issue."

"Aight, you may continue." Everyone laughed.

"Basically she sayin' if we can come up with $500 collectively then she'll put up the other $500 for a four-song demo with studio time and production included and she says the producer is hot."

"We gonna have a demo full of down south beats? The south ain't even on it like that. All they music is trash."

"Yo Syn why you gotta be the one to go against everything. This is the break we wanted, this is why you didn't go back so school so I don't see what the problem is. Wes when can we get down there?" Quincy asked.

"She said the only time the producer can do it is in two weeks. November 12th-November 18th."

"Son my birthday is on the 15th." I interrupted again.

"Ok so we'll party in tha A." Suggested Jus.

Wes outlined the details with us all while we ate and I. Dot got us seconds and drink refills. The only objection to anyone going is Jus because she doesn't have the $100 for his share because he is in school and doesn't work. We all offered to put up his part but he also has school and he can't afford to miss a whole week. The idea sounded great, we've been doing most of the work on our own, making the beats, writing the songs, recording in run-down basements and in each other's houses so a professional studio in Atlanta sounds real exciting.

I want to call Kendra but the clock reads four twenty-seven a.m. and I would hate to wake her or her roommates up so I didn't call. Instead I found myself daydreaming about the demo going well and the group being offered a deal, us going platinum and me being able to provide Kendra with the type of life neither of us had. The thought of that made me feel really good inside and just then my pager went off. Evelyn, what is she doing up this late?

"Hey what's up?"

"Nothin', how have you been?"

"I'm straight how are you?"

"Why haven't you called me in a week and a half. You haven't called me ever since you moved in with Jus."

"I've just been real busy tryin to make enough money to buy the car and recordin' that's all."

"Ain't it time for your braids to come out?"

"Yeah, can you do them tomorrow night? I get out of work at 5 you can just meet me at the mall and we'll walk together."

"Ok. I miss sleeping with you. I haven't been getting much sleep the past few days…I miss you."

"I miss you too Evy. I'ma see you tomorrow but for now go to sleep."

"Ok, I love you." *What?!* I thought to myself. Did she just tell me she loves me? I am at a lose for words right now. If I don't say it she is going to be mad at me then if I do tell say I love her then I will not be able to shake her when it comes time.

"Good-night." I said instead.

"Bye." Tonight my mother invaded my thoughts. I miss her but I am still upset at how she put me out the night of my graduation and how she knew I was coming home for the summer yet neglected to inform me she was moving. If I'd known I would've stayed in N.C. and who knows I might be in the middle of my sophomore year right now.

The more I walked the more pissed off I became remembering when I was kicked out of school last year and my mom telling me I couldn't come back home. She basically left me to fend for myself and I guess this is what adulthood is all about. I'm nineteen years old working two jobs and sleeping on a futon in someone else's house-not the future I had for myself. Tracy, Quincy, Wes and Jus all still live at home with their mothers who are supportive of their musical aspirations and here I am walking in the middle of the night as if I'm a stray cat in New York City. Five months and I still haven't heard from my mother and I'm starting to feel as if she fails to realize she has a son. You'd think I am used to it because I only talked to her three times my entire freshman year of school but I'm not. How can a child get use to it? I love my mom but it's not like it use to be before she got together with Smitty. Eleven years I've been carrying around this hope she'd change but the resentment for her not changing is escalating.

I looked up at the sky and looked for the God I was taught about and asked him for help. I feel so alone and I don't feel like I belong anywhere. Tracy, Wes and Quincy are tighter than I am with either of them and I feel like a guest who's worn out his welcome in Jus' house. This can't be life, I feel like a squatter just one step away from being homeless. I have half of mind to take my money and say fuck the car, hop on a plane to Raleigh and be somewhat happy again. I really want to be in school and I wonder constantly if I am making the right decision by not returning. By pursuing a pipe dream of becoming a rapper over my education and moving around every single year, not to mention going in and out of Kendra's life has me feeling like I don't want to live like this.

I want to be in school and have Kendra in North Carolina just up the highway at Chapel Hill where I can hop in my car and drive to see her every weekend or whenever I get the urge hug her. If I could have that then I probably wouldn't be using girls like Evelyn and Navarda as temporarily girlfriends or pieces of ass. Deep down I know in my heart that what I am doing is not right but at the same time I want and crave a smile from Kendra, the touch of Kendra, a hug from Kendra and I can't have it at that very moment then I will get it from Evelyn, Navarda, Nadege or any other woman at my disposal.

6

Since I've moved in with Jus I don't see Evelyn as much as I used to and it's been three weeks since the last time she's done my hair and to be completely honest with myself I miss the hell out of her. I miss her being at my house when I come home from work and I miss the ass no, doubt about that.

It'll be three more weeks until Kendra will be here to spend thanksgiving with me but I don't know where we are going to have it. I promised her it'd be our first thanksgiving and not integration with Jus' family. More importantly she is going to be here for weekend and I can't leave her in Jus' house where she's confined to just the living room area where I sleep. I don't know what to do, all the hotels I've called are either booked up already or the prices are sky high because of the holiday. Now it makes me regrettable that I lied about having a friend that hooked me up with the room already. As much as I don't want to do it I think I'm going to have to tell her not to come but I don't want to hear the disappointment in her voice.

I don't want Kendra to think I am flaking out or it's because of another woman. Lord knows the things Trevor told her in the email may still be lingering in the back of her mind and that is the last thing I want her thinking. Some how I'm going to have to figure it out, I haven't seen Kendra in almost two years not since she brought Quami by my dorm so we could meet. To this day I still don't understand by she wanted us to meet. I only did it for her if it were any other chick I wouldn't have entertained the thought. Why would I want to meet the guy dating the girl I want to be with? That just doesn't make any sense.

On the flip side Nadege and I have been spending an awful lot of time together hence the reason Evelyn and I haven't. Nadege comes to Waterbury to pick me up and brings me back with her to her dorm or I'll catch a ride with Tracy or Quincy when they go to visit Porsche or Dorian. The first night I stayed with Nadege she was expecting me to be expecting sex and when I didn't push it she thought I was showing her the utmost respect, she even wrote me a note detailing how she felt about it. Word got back to Tracy and Quincy by their girlfriends but I didn't care. According to Dorian I scored major brownie points with Nadege, which is cool because now that I've gotten to know her over the past two weeks I really like her so sex isn't an issue.

I must admit that when I do see her in her volleyball shorts my cannon still rises and thoughts of how I'd feel inside her to play around in my mind. Why haven't we had sex yet? I really don't know, I know she knows that I want to but I'm going to let it be on her terms because to be perfectly honest I really just enjoy her company…the company of a woman.

Now Navarda is a different story, I just want to fuck simple and plain. I act as if I'm interested during our phone conversations but during that time I'm playing Grand Theft Auto with Jus or writing a verse or multi-tasking on something else. I make it a habit of not spending too much time on the phone with her just enough time to keep her interested but not to the point she thinks we are actually going to have a relationship, oh hell no. Truthfully I could've fucked Navarda the day she gave me her number but since I know that it's pretty much in the bag I'm not going to rush.

The sun was beating on my forehead as we drove down Franklin Rd. in Marietta Georgia. The sixteen-hour ride didn't feel as long as it sounded which I am grateful for.

"Cut where do ya cousin live?"

"She said some complex called Hampton Village."

"Hampton, hear that!" I shouted with excitement. I've never been below North Carolina before and Georgia is beautiful but where's all the fat asses I kept hearing so much about?

"Yo Shawyna said the key is under the mat and don't mess up anything." Tracy smacked his teeth.

"What cut? We are guests in her house."

"Na it ain't that, we grown men. We ain't gonna mess up nothin'.""

"Aight then thas what it is." Wes ended.

"Yo I'm tired I wanna lay down for a minute."

"Q you always tired. A tired muffin man." Tracy and Wes laughed.

"Shut up sass mo." Wes erupted in louder laughter, as did Tracy.

"Aight, I got'chu. Yo I wish we could ride around and check the A out."

"Why can't we?" Tracy asked.

"'Cause we don't know our way around here and I ain't tryin' to be lost in tha A."

"Nigg, I remember where I'm goin'. I could leave here today and not come back for thirty years and I'd still know my way around."

"Oh yeah you're right. I heard elephants have big memories." The car exploded with laughter again.

Shawyna made good on her promise by introducing us to this producer by the name of Tim who blinked every ten seconds when he talked to us. His studio is in an odd part of town thirty minutes away from Shawyna's house but his equipment is state of the art. When we arrived a day after he gave us the beats we chose to write to there was another southern rapper in the booth. This annoying beat was playing with children voices in the hook.

"To Tim, who's that?" Tracy asked over the thunderous music.

"Uh, uh that's Hit Man Sammy Sam. Yaw'll don't know who he is?" We all looked puzzled at the question. Tim went on to tell us that Hit Man Sammy Sam is a well-known Georgia rapper recording his new single Step-daddy. Tracy and I danced and mocked the song long enough for Shawyna to see and signal for us to stop. Tracy leaned over and whispered in my ear.

"Cut, this shit'll neva sell."

"I know, tell me about it." I agreed.

Shawyna insisted we write a hit, something that was sure to get us some serious radio play. Little does she know it isn't that easy, you can't force a hit because it's something that has to come natural doing what you already do best. For four days we hit the clubs, strip clubs and the downtown area for inspiration and to get a feel of what excites people down here. Late at night we all coped a squat on Shawyna's living room floor to write and bounce around ideas while Shawyna served us home cooked meals and peach soda. After the first day at the studio Shawyna and I got into a disagreement so for the remainder of the trip I've kept my distance because I can see early on Shawyna is a possessive, controlling little kid and if something doesn't go her way it's the highway. Despite her funny acting ways were walking away with four hot songs but in my opinion none of them are hits. But what should I care just as long as the label likes it and we sign on the dotted line? At least my passing up school and a scholarship will not be in vain.

"Alright, yaw'll get home safe and I'ma cawl yaw'll when I hear something." Shawyna said as we put the last bag in Quincy's trunk. Tracy, Wes and Quincy hugged Shawyna good-bye but I don't really feel like even touching her. Out of the corner of my eye I saw Wes signaling me to hug her so reluctantly I did but it was one of those fake hugs, the kind you give a relative you really don't know that well. We thanked her once again before piling into the car and driving off.

I am looking forward to returning home, I miss Nadege. I've used Quincy, Tracy's and Wes' cell phones over the course of the week we were in Atlanta to talk to Nadege and Kendra. I received a phone call from Kendra at midnight on November 15th to be the first to wish me a happy birthday just as I'd done ten days before and we talked for almost two hours. Nadege called me later on during the day when we were in the middle of a session but I spoke to her after my verse was done.

Just ten more days until Thanksgiving and I still don't know what I'm going to do about Kendra coming to visit. The weird feeling I get in my stomach when I talk to or think about her is here again and a smile came over my face. I often think about how it would be if we stayed in a hotel for the weekend of her visit doing everything I've always wanted to do with her. Falling asleep next to her and waking up to her radiant smile, gorgeous face in the morning and rushing home from work just because I know she's there. We both would be side by side in the kitchen cooking and cuddled in the bed watching TV and at night we'd make love to each other, for the first time.

No not having sex or fucking but making love. I chose to say making love because I do love that girl more than I can ever express and she'd ever know. The trip to Georgia put a little dent in my pockets and I'm more money away from paying for the hotel, maybe we can stay in the hotel for a day or two then stay at Jus'. I don't know if she'd go for that or not, I promised her something and I don't want to renigg on that promise. To anyone else I wouldn't care two shits but to Kendra it's different, her perception of me means the world therefore everything has to be right or not at all.

Nadege and Dorian met us at Quincy apartment on Scott Rd and I couldn't have come home to a better site than Nadege in a pair of tight blue jeans and a low cut black top exposing the crease in her breasts with a smile so bright a plane gets the glare. Nadege jumped into my arms and hugged me tight kissing me over and over again and it felt good to have been missed. Nadege has an early class in the morning so she only hung out for about an hour and as soon as I got to Jus' house I called up Navarda because I have no plans for the night.

"So how was Atlanta?" she asked.

"It was on point, tha A is hot."

"So what did you do for your birthday?"

"Wes and I celebrated ours together since we are only five days apart so Tracy and Quincy took us to this strip club called Blue Flame."

"A strip club? Really? Must've been nice."

"Yeah but I rather watch you take your cloths off."

"Is that a fact?" she asked curiously.

"Yep sure is, so where are you taking me for my birthday?"

"I want to take you to dinner."

"Where?"

"Where do you want to go?"

"Let's go to Ruby Tuesday in the mall." I suggested.

"Ok meet me there in an hour and wear something nice."

"I should be telling you that."

"If you're lucky I may wear a bow that you can take off later."

"Don't get my hopes up." Navarda laughed before saying good-bye. I didn't want to put on any of my good clothes like the ones I wear when I go out with Nadege so I just on a pair of blue jeans, white Air Force 1's and a white T-shirt. Nothing fancy.

Navarda is sitting on the bench outside of Ruby Tuesday when I turned the corner but stood up at the first site of me with a nice bright smile. Navarda is wearing a nice fitting pair of blue jeans and a skintight gray shirt putting her 36 B-cups on display that made me wanna skip dinner completely.

"Where's the bow?" I joked, she smiled.

"Underneath." She responded and we laughed again.

We talked all throughout dinner and I have to admit the conversation kept my interest. We started off sitting across the table from each other but by the end of our dinner we are sitting side by side hand in hand. I haven't spoken to Navarda since high school and even then it was on a hi and bye basis. We've never had any one on one time with each other like this and now that we have I have come to see that she is a really nice girl.

"So you wanna get out of here?" I asked pushing the ice cream away.

"Sure." Navarda paid I left the tip and we walked out arm and arm. The night is beautiful displaying a half moon and the wind blowing slightly makes it a clear November night as we walked off Union Street. Not knowing where we are going, I thought about bringing her back to Jus' apartment but I don't know how she'd feel about that. After another block of walking and a little thinking I thought what the hell.

"Hey I don't feel like walking around all night and I don't want the night to end so how about you come back to my place and watch a movie with me." I suggested.

"What are we going to watch?"

"I don't know but I have a bunch of DVD's."

"Ok."

I didn't bother to detail the living arrangement at Jus' house because I really could care less about her perception of me or of how I live. Nevertheless the three flight walk up the stairs didn't seem to bother her neither did Jus' little brother, sister and mother coming into the front room to meet her.

We watched Jason's Lyric, which is my favorite black love movie if that is what you want to call it. Navarda rested her head on my shoulder as we watched the movie with the rest of her body curled up on the futon. I want to kiss her so bad I can't concentrate on the movie, it's amazing what a little conversation can do to change your mind about a person. I kept looking down at her hoping she'd look back up at me making eye contact and after doing that three or four times we did make eye contact and at that instant we kissed passionately deep. From that point on the movie was none existent to us as we kissed over and over gain. I laid Navarda down on her back and kissed the top of her chest while my hand ran back and forth over her abed stomach.

"Wait, let me take it off." She whispered taking off her tight gray shirt. As I removed her bra her nipples hardened when exposed to the air and the moister of my tongue. While my tongue made my way away from her breasts to her stomach she started to tremble a little. I looked up and asked if she was ok and she moaned yes so I continued by unbuttoning her jeans. I pulled while she wiggled out and her thick pussy-poking out from under her gray thong underwear instantly aroused me. I wanted to tear her panties off and fuck her as hard as I could but I didn't. Instead I gently kissed her navel and waist and at the same time pulled down her panties. As I continued to kiss her stomach Navarda put her hand of top of my head trying to push it down in front of her mound but I resisted. I'm not going to eat her out as I only do that to very few women. Nadege I would consider it, Kendra…definitely.

I undressed and instructed Navarda to keep it quiet since the only thing dividing my room from Jus' siblings is a thin broken divider but that isn't going to stop me. I entered Navarda and she bit down on my shoulder to muffle her moan. I cradled her small frame close to mine as our pelvises met over and over again; each time we separated her juices came out of her and ran down my thighs. An hour later she lay on top me trying to catch her breath as the sweat on her shoulders glistened off the light from the television. I looked down at her and thought the sex was good but now I want her to leave. Ten minutes later she is dressed and I'm walking her downstairs. I came back to the futon disposed of the condom and called Kendra.

"Hello." she said in a groggy voice.

"Hey beautiful."

"Hi Syn. You haven't called me that since high school."

"I know but it doesn't mean that you aren't."

"Why are you up so late?" she asked.

"Late? It's only twelve thirty. I thought you'd be up."

"No I was asleep, I have a mid-term in the morning. I'm trying to finish all mine this week so I can come to see you."

"Oh ok I'll let you go."

"No I can talk to you for a little while. What's up?"

"Nothing I was just thinkin' about'chu and I wanted to hear your voice, that's all."

"Aww, Syn. I was thinking about you too a little while ago."

"Really? What about me? How dangerously handsome I am?"

"He hehe but no. I was thinking about what are you going to do when you first see me?"

"Hug you and swing you around and kiss you a thousand times."

"Ooh is that so? What are you going to do our first night together?" Kendra inquired.

"Can't tell you that yet, you'll just have to wait and see."

"Aww can't you tell me? Feed my imagination…pleeease."

"Ok, ok. Listen…."

"I'm waiting."

"Wait for a week." I burst out laughing.

"You're not fair."

"Life is not fair." I kept laughing.

"He hehe silly. What did you do tonight?"

"Oh nothing. I just went out to eat at Ruby Tuesdays and I came back home to watch a movie but I'm not sleepy."

"You went to eat by yourself?"

"Yeah. All my boys were busy with their girlfriends and I really wanted to go so I went by myself."

"Ok, what is a Ruby Tuesday?"

"It's kinda like a Golden Corral without the buffet. It's ok."

"Well you know if I were there I would've gone with you right?"

"Yes ma'am."

"He hehe, you sound funny when you say that…say it again."

"Yes ma'am."

"He hehe, you're so cute."

"I know I know."

"Syncere can I ask you a question?"

"Nope."

"Ok. Why do you love me?" Syncere hesitated for a moment and that got me a little worried because it is a question I was expecting him to answer on cue.

"Because I do."

"I know but why?"

"Babe, I can't tell you why."

"Why."

"I don't know it's hard to explain."

"Please try…for me."

"I love you because you are the first and last thing I think about when I wake up and before I go to sleep. Your face is the only face I see on any woman who looks at me and every time I talk to you I get a weird feeling in my stomach. I don't know it is a feeling I know is there so I just know. Why do you ask?"

"I just needed to know. Can I ask you another question?"

"What are you expecting out of me coming to Connecticut for Thanksgiving?"

"Nothing." I responded nonchalantly.

"Nothing?"

"Na, I'm just expecting us to be with each other and have a nice Thanksgiving."

"You know I'm not the fifteen anymore and I have grown up."

"I know I see. And I have grown up too."

"Wanna know something?"

"What?"

"I can put both legs behind my head."

"WOW! Can you really do that?" Kendra's comment caught me off guard as the extremely graphic sexual image flashed in my mind.

"He hehe yep and that is not all."

"Bet, we are definitely gonna try that out."

"Are you serious?" she asked sounding surprised.

"Hell yeah. I ain't know you knew tricks and shit like that."

"Don't get my hopes all up and when I get there you act shy." She warned.

"What? Shy? No ma'am. For real for real we are gonna try that out."

"Ok great!"

"Talkin' like that you got me wanna run to New Hampshire so we can do that right now. When you start talkin' like that?"

"What? I am a grown woman and I told you I'm not fifteen anymore."

"You sure ain't. Thanks for the visual"

"He hehe, anytime. So what are you going to do when you first see me?"

"Hug you and swing you around and kiss you a thousand times."

Kendra and I spent the next hour or so talking before she began to get tired and let out a trio of yawns.

"You yawned like four times, am I boring you that much." I asked.

"No. I hate to do it Syn but it's about that time. I have to get up really really early and if I want to do well on this exam I need to rest my brain. Thanks for calling I really needed to hear from you."

"You don't have to thank me, thanks for answering. I'll talk to you tomorrow."

"Ok."

"I love you."

"I love you too."

"Yo we gotta move to Atlanta." Wes announced when I walked into Olympia Sports where Quincy is the store manager and Wes is the assistant manager. My initial reaction was why but it soon changed to when.

"When?"

"The week after Thanksgiving."

"That's madd soon." I thought aloud.

"Well Shawyna said we need to be there ASAP because she got us into this showcase opening up for Ludacris."

"Luda? For real for real?"

"Hell yeah son. We just got done havin' a meetin' at I. Dot's house and the only person not goin' is Quincy."

"What? Why?"

"'Cause man. I can't just stop workin', I got bills."

"Nigga stop lyin' you don't wanna leave Dorian." Wes exposed.

"Cut, you stayin here for a girl?" I asked as Jus, Tracy and Wes laughed.

"Na on some real shit I got some things goin' on that I just can't pick up and leave right now. Not to leave and not have an actual deal, it's too risky."

"Dude take a chance, this is what we have been recordin' for. Jus ain't you in school? How you gonna move to Atlanta?"

"Man fuck school. I'm 'bout this music." He said proudly.

"Hear that!" Everyone but Quincy said in unison.

We stayed huddled around the car outside Jus' house as we talked out the details and how we are going to make the transition from Connecticut to Atlanta easy. We also weighed the pros and cons of moving. I personally have no objection to moving. I stayed out of school this semester for this and I'd stay out next semester if it meant getting closer to a deal. The best part for me being in Atlanta is being closer to North Carolina than I am now once Kendra starts to go to college. By that time I've would've gotten my license and brought a car and I'd be able to see her whenever I want to.

The only thing that sucks about moving now is that I've been getting close to Nadege and I would like to see how far this could go. It sounds kinda weird saying that and just a minute ago I talked about how I'd be more assessable to Kendra but I can't help how I feel and you can't help who you like. I wouldn't choose Nadege over Kendra in a million years but right now Nadege is the one who I am able to hug and kiss and go to sleep with when I want to. If Kendra were here Nadege wouldn't get the time of day but she's not and what am I to do? I crave the attention of a woman; it's what keeps me sleep at night.

Now that everyone knows I'm moving to Atlanta to pursue music plenty of haters and well wishers have been coming at me. The major problem I have now is shaking Navarda. She's been coming around Finish Line three to four times a day since I laid the pipe a week ago. Becky senses my aggravation when she walks into the store so she comes up and interrupts by saying that I have work to do. It's really beginning to get creepy to be honest. The other day she stopped in with a necklace she had made at the little kiosk outside our store. She had the artist write Syncere and Navarda forever with a heart in the middle on a piece of rice and she asked me to wear it. I looked at her as if she had three heads and I was kicking myself for fucking her in the first place. If I'd known she'd turn into a psycho stalker I would've stayed away from the gate.

"Syncere." I turned to the front of the store praying it isn't Navarda when I realized it is my god-sister Shanice.

"Hey hun." We greeted each other with a hug and a kiss on the cheek.

"Why are you being so mean to my friend?"

"Who is your friend?"

"Navarda." My heart dropped for a minute and I was hoping the loud music I've been listening to over the years has finally distorted my hearing because she couldn't have said Navarda.

"Navarda? Navarda who?" It couldn't be the same girl because there is a five-year age difference between the two girls so why on earth would they know each other?

"Navarda, little short girl you go out with."

"Go out with? Who said we go out?"

"She did."

"How do you even know her?"

"I met her last year at Crosby."

"Shanice she went to Wilby."

"She transferred when she had her son because Crosby has a day care."

"What son?"

"You didn't know she had a son?"

"Hell no. She never told me she had a son."

"Wow, I thought she did already." A lie. I found a way to get away from Navarda, I'll use the fact she didn't tell me she had a son, oh I'm going to spin this good.

"Na she didn't tell me."

"Well you need to talk to her because she's been calling me everyday for like a week and a half sayin how you fucked her and now you won't call her back or go out with her anywhere anymore.'
"What the fuck is she talkin' about. We only went out because she took me out for my birthday and we had sex…once, that's it. She is not my girl we never even went that far. She's psycho."

"Well you need to talk to her because she really likes you and she feels like she did something wrong."

"Why can't she see she was just a jump off?"

"That's wrong, I thought you were nicer than that Syn."

"Shanice, I'm not the same big eared little boy you and Nakea used to come visit."

"Just go talk to her, I think she is suicidal."

"You've got to be kiddin' me."

"Does it look like I'm playin'?" Shanice asked pointing at her face.

"Aight, aight. Becky, I'm takin' my fifteen."

   I walked to the food court where Navarda is sitting by herself eating a slice of pizza, her eyes got bright when she saw me walking over to her. I mentally got myself into asshole mode so I could be mean as possible.

"Hey." I said.

"Hi baby, sit down. Are you hungry? Want me to buy you something to eat?"

"No. Why didn't you tell me you had a baby?" Navarda let her pizza flop on her plate as she dropped her head assuming it was because she is caught out.

"What do you mean?"

"Oh now you're gonna try to lie to me? Shanice told me you have a son. When were you going to tell?"

"Eventually."

"Eventually? What kinda shit is that? And why did you tell her you are my girl?"

"I'm not?"

"No."

"I thought I was." She admitted.

"Why would you think that? I never said anything about you being my girl."

"I just thought because we had sex that I was your girl."

"No it was just sex."

"But you did it with so much feeling, I thought we connected."

"We did connect then I ejected that's it."

"Well why can't we be a couple?"

"I can't be with someone who didn't tell me she has a son and try to cover it up when I ask you about it."

"It isn't that."

"Na, I need a woman to be completely honest with me and you weren't. Now I don't know how I feel about you, I feel so betrayed. I can't fuck wit'chu."

"Syn just give me a chance." She pleaded.

"Na I'm good." I got up to leave and Navarda grabbed my arm and as I looked down at her I saw the tears begin to form under her eyes and I felt no sympathy at all and I liked it.

"Syncere talk to me please."

"I gotta get back to work. See you later." I turned my back to the tears rolling down Navarda's face and the sniffling in my ear. I feel a great sense of relief because I know I shook her off for good. When I got back to the store Shanice was looking at shoes on the women's side of the store.

"So...how did it go?" she asked.

"I broke it off. You might wanna go up there."

"Why?"

'She's cryin'."

"What did you say to her? I told you she is suicidal."

"Nothin'."

When I got back to Jus' house I just flopped on my futon and rested my legs from the twenty-minute walk home.

"Yo, Kendra has been callin' all day. Didn't she page you?" Jus asked.

"Yeah like 100 times."

"Why didn't you call her?"

"Because I don't know what to do? I've been saving my money for the car and for her hotel but all the hotels are booked and I have no where for her to stay."

"Son let her stay here." He suggested.

"No disrespect but she is not going to want to stay here, I know her she is not going to feel comfortable. She is going to feel like she is in the way and feel like she is confined to one room just like I feel."

"She can go into the kitchen and cook if she wants to just like you can."

"You don't get it. This is not my place and it's not familiar to her and it's not like I promised her. I'm not going to have this girl sharing a futon in a cold living room with me she deserves better than that." Jus started laughing.

"You just fucked a girl in there two weeks ago."

"I don't care about that broad, but Kendra is wifey. Us on a hard metal futon is not the way we are going to spend our first night let alone a weekend together."

"So you are just not going to answer her calls?"

"What else am I supposed to do?"

"You need to tell her what's goin' on. If she is the kinda girl you say she is she will understand and will be happy just to be with you."

"What tha fu...? No, no, no. Let me sit here and think."

"When is she supposed to be here?"

"Tomorrow. Her plane lands at eleven in the mornin'."

"How are you supposed to get her?"

"I was supposed to drive up there when I passed my driving test."

"But you failed."

"Duh." We heard Jus' room phone ring and after a short while he came back and my pager went off... it was Kendra again.'

"Good luck. I'm going to play Grand Theft, I almost got six stars."

"Aight."

I sat on my futon and thought long and hard at what to do about Kendra coming to visit. I know in my heart and mind that it would not be the perfect visit Kendra and I wanted it to be. I don't want her to see me vulnerable like this. I figure if I get through the night she'd catch a plane to North Carolina and I'll make up a lie about what happened and everything will be ok.

I spent Thanksgiving bouncing around from house to house taking food from every place I visited. All that day I wanted to call Kendra but I know she's probably upset at me so I decided to try to enjoy my Thanksgiving and wait a couple of days before I called her. Looking at Wes with his family, Tracy and Quincy with theirs make me a little jealous because I am not with mine.

The sun is going down and I find myself sitting on my futon staring at a television that isn't even on thinking blank thoughts. I desperately want to be with my family and I thought about the dinner my father's side holds every year at the Q Club on Pearl Street. I walked over in the chilly November air thinking of how great it would be to see people I hardly even know making a big fuss over me, Stewart's son.

Upon arrival I can see the lights on and the music pumping and I got excited when I got to the door.

"Who are you?" and older woman asked.

"I'm Syncere, Stewart's son." The tall thin man and heavyset woman looked at me with confused faces.

"Who?"

"Is Jimmy in there? Jimmy Welch? My family has had a Thanksgiving dinner here every year since I was a kid."

"No this is the Wilson/Henderson family."

"Are you sure?"

"Yeah we're pretty sure."

"Ok thank you."

I really feel like shit now and more than before I want to call Kendra because I need to hear her voice. On a day family is supposed to be together blessing food and sharing what we are all thankful for I am stuck walking aimlessly in the dark cold streets with no feeling of belonging anywhere. I haven't spoken to Evelyn in weeks so popping up on her is out of the question and I've pushed Navarda away with a vengeance and at this point I really don't want to go back to Jus' house alone.

"Hey sweetie what you doin'? Nadege asked.

"Nothin'. How's your Thanksgivin'?"

"Ok I guess. I'm in my dorm watching television."

"You didn't go to Norwalk to be with your family?"

"No, they went to Haiti to visit my grandma so I stayed here."

"Why didn't you page me?"

"I tried paging you all night last night."

"Oh that was you?"

"Yeah sweetie, who did you think it was?"

"I didn't know. I was really tired and I thought it was Tracy or one of my other friends asking me to go out." I lied.

"So how is your family?"

"I wouldn't know they are in North Carolina."

"Aww baby you spent Thanksgiving alone?"

"Not really. I spent it with everyone else's family earlier and now I am alone."

"Sweetie wanna come stay with me?"

"Yeah." I answered excitedly.

"I'm on my way."

"Alright beep me when you're gettin' off tha highway."

"Ok sweetie."

I don't know what made me call Nadege but I am glad I did. It's a forty-five minute drive from West Haven here that gives me enough time to go back to Jus' house, shower and pack an overnight bag. I thought to myself tonight is the night I'll make that move on Nadege and have sex with her, the thought got me aroused.

"Hey sweetie." Nadege greeted me before kissing me on the lips. Her hair is in a tight ponytail exposing her wide eyes and high cheekbones when she smiled. She wore a pair of blue sweat pants and a gray St. Joseph tee shirt that her breast looked as if they were about to break out of.

"Whas up?"

"Miss me?"

"Of course. How can I not?" Nadege smiled as she pulled off.

We stopped at Pizza Hut because I am done eating dry turkey and baked macaroni and cheese and she hadn't eaten all day. We spent the night cuddled in the bed watching movies that I had taken with me before I left Jus' house. I still have the desire to have sex with her but we are cuddled up close and she looks so comfortable. I don't want to kill the mood so we slept in each other arms and to me that is better than just having sex.

The next six days were pretty much a blur as we prepared to depart to Atlanta. We'd all stopped working two days ago and wrote and recorded a lot of music and said good-bye to all our friends. Now that I think about it I haven't made it around to call Kendra yet and she hasn't called me either. I really don't have time to talk or to argue with her because I know when I call that is exactly what we are going to do.

I have to buy an outfit for the last supper we are having tomorrow night at Jimmy's in New Haven. We've invited all our closest friends and family to share the last fest we'd have with them as us being non-famous. Nadege and I drove around New Haven and West Haven going from store to store trying to find something to wear and she was successful before I was. Eventually I found a brown and tan long sleeved Enyce shirt, a pair of navy blue jeans and a pair of chocolate Timberlands.

"So what's going to happen when you move to Atlanta?" she asked.

"What do you mean?"

"I mean with us."

"What do you want to happen? Will you start dating someone else?"

"I don't want to, will you?" she admitted.

"I strongly doubt it. I'm sure we'll be workin' a lot and any chicks that do try to holla at me will just be doin' it because they saw me on stage or somethin'. Besides, I don't think there is any women in Georgia remotely more attractive than you are." I complimented.

"You mean it?"

"Hell yeah! Why would I leave such a beautiful little thing like you to be scooped up by some other guy? You're all mine." Nadege smiled as we drove back to Jus' house so I can finish packing. The living room is a mess and the dinner is in an hour. Nadege helped me pack and we engaged in conversation then in hugging and kissing. Nadege sat on the love seat while I dressed just looking at me with her beautiful brown eyes. Looking at her she looks as if she is the happiest woman in the world just like I am everything she ever wanted or needed. This is the first time any woman has looked at me in a way that made me feel whole inside.

For a second I thought about Kendra and how it's been a week since Thanksgiving and it's been a week and three days since I actually talked to her. When I looked at Nadege again I was looking at Kendra. In my mind it is Kendra sitting across from me with her head rested on her fist smiling at me as if she is the happiest woman in the world, like I am all she ever wants or needs and it feels great.

"Baby…baby…baby…" I heard Nadege's seductive accent in my head and it broke me out of my trance.

"You have to get ready. Dorian just called, they want us to follow them."

"Aight."

A fleet of cars followed one another thirty minutes to New Haven. I've never been both excited and afraid of the future in my life. Twenty-seven of the nearest and dearest people in all our lives exchanged jokes, stories, plans and everything in between over the finest sea food in Connecticut. I had my new family, a gorgeous woman by my side so any problem I had going on disappeared. Kendra isn't an issue, not seeing my mother isn't an issue and not passing up my track scholarship is an issue. For once I'm living in the moment and loving it.

The celebration ended with the members of the group leaving with their significant others. Nadege and I chose to walk to the back of the restaurant where the ocean is and look at the moon light up the night sky. I held her from behind as she rested her head on my chest. I kissed her neck and cheek and we stood there for a little while purposely not sharing our thoughts with one another.

My thoughts were about how long would I have to swim to reach Kendra and what can I say to her for her not to hate me. I thought about asking Nadege if I could borrow her car so I can drive over to Evelyn's house and tell her that I really feel the same way about her as she does about me. But I'm too afraid to accept that feeling right now. I would also tell her how truly sorry I am for completely making her dead in my world two months ago. I then thought how could I love Kendra, love Evelyn and be falling for Nadege all at the same time? And why am I leaving these beautiful loving women behind with love and anger for me in their hearts? But I didn't act on either of my thoughts. Instead Nadege and I stand looking at the water and the waves like two love birds in a perfect world just like we are all we ever wanted or needed in one another.

7

"Hey Syn how is Atlanta?" Nadege asked me when she answered the phone.

"It sucks and I miss you so much."

"Aww baby I miss you too, why don't you come back here with me?"

"Because we are trying to do this music you know that."

"I know, so how is it going?"

"Not so good."

"Why?"

"Cause Shawyna is a bitch and we haven't don't any recording anywhere since we've been here. I'm starting to think she doesn't know what the hell she is doing. She doesn't even go with us to shows anymore. We do everything ourselves just like we were doing in Connecticut. Plus I'm tired of sleeping on the damn floor listening to Tracy snore."

"Oh my God! Baby come home." Nadege said again.

"Nadege I want to trust me I do but I have to pursue this. You are almost done with school and I left to do this so I have to see how it pans out. Plus I can't go back home, I have no where to live."

"Is there anything I can do?"

"Yeah, move to Atlanta." Nadege burst into laughter, which made me smile as well.

"How about I send you something to remind you of me." She suggested.

"Oh a naked picture…no I know some of your panties. Or how 'bout both?"

"No silly. I'm going to send you the blanket you like to cuddle with me in. I'll spray some of my perfume on it."
"We'll it's not a naked picture but I'll take it." I said jokingly.

"You are much too much. So have you met any girls at your shows? I know you must have tons of them wanting you already."

"Nope, no one likes me but you. I go to work, come home to write and hopefully do a show and that's all. For the most part we are stuck in the house because we don't know anyone. Tracy had a date with a ugly girl the other day though."

"Really? She was ugly?"

"Beyond ugly. I don't think he called her back though."

"So no dates for you?"

"Nope."

"You have always been so sweet and so respectful. How did I get so lucky?"
"I don't know but if you don't get down here soon one of these southern girls are gonna snatch me up."

"Ha, and if they do I'ma come down there and beat her ass."

"You ain't no fighter, but if that is what it takes to get you down here then come to mention it there are a few girls that live around us that keep throwing themselves at me and I feel really uncomfortable."

"Nice try. I know when you're playin' with me. You're so cute."

"Tell the truth woman." Nadege and I shared a gut-busting laugh and when I regained myself I found Tracy, Wes and Jus staring at me with strange faces.

"Nigga stop phone boning'." Tracy yelled.

"I hope you have a condom on your ear from all that love makin'." Wes cosigned.

"Damn son they comin' at'cha head." Jus said in my defense.
"Fuck all ya'll. Wes you was just on the phone with Anita for eighty hours so don't say shit." Tracy looked at Jus then to Wes.

"Cut he right. You was makin' madd love too."

"Yeah but this dude on the phone every five minutes. If it's not Nadege it's Rita."

"Shhh." I whispered while covering the phone.

"What did you say sweetie?" Nadege asked.

"Nothin'. That was Wes talkin' 'bout some girl he met."

"Nope, don't be lyin on tha kid."

"Babe hold on real quick."

"Look go with your friends and I will call you back tonight. Bye sweetie."

"Bye. Cut, why you tryin' to blow my spot like that?"

"She can't do shit you all the way down here. You mind as well get as much pussy as possible."

"So is that what you're goin' to do too?"

"No sir, I got a girl. You and Nadege ain't even dating technically so you can do what you want. And you are you been spendin' madd time with that chick you met at the Gap. What's her name again? Oh yeah Rita."

"Yo Syn you hit that yet?" Jus asked.

"Na I ain't hit yet but on the first night she did slob the knob. Other than that I just like the company and I think it goes both ways. I hate it here. We gotta be all crammed up in Shawyna's room to watch TV, sleep when she say sleep and I just feel like I can't be myself here."

"So you and her gettin' serious?" Tracy asked.

"What? Son I only known her for a month. She from New York so she madd cool and that's as far as it goes." I explained.

"She got a sister?"

"Yeah but I think her sister got a man."

"Damn!"

"What you damnin' for. You better hope M. Dot don't find out about ya date with the chick with chef pants." All four of us erupted in laughter at the remembrance of Tracy's first date with an Atlanta girl."

"Nigga neva mind M. Dot. What's good with you and Kendra?" I got real quiet and everyone is holding on to my next word.

"What you mean what's going on?" I acted dumb.

"I don't know dude. One minute you all in love and the next minute you spendin' madd time with Nadege before we left Connecticut and once we got here we don't hear anything about her. If anyone she should be the chick you phone bonin' wit." Tracy outlined.

"True statement but I don't think she wanna talk to me."

"Why?"

"I stood her up for Thanksgivin'." I confessed.

"Yo I thought I remember you sayin' she was supposed to come to Connecticut. She never came?" Wes asked surprised.

"Na."

'Why?"

"I didn't have no where to take her. I moved out of Trevor's place..."

"That dude frightens me." We all laughed at Tracy's comment.

"The hotels cost a grip for the weekend and if I'd done that I'd have no lot right now."

"Did you tell her that?" Jus asked knowing damn well I didn't.

"No."

"When was the last time you spoke to her?"

"This time two months ago."

"Two months! Son you wilin'. That was supposed to be wifey." Jus said.

"I know but I didn't want her to see me so vulnerable and unable to provide her with a place to stay for the weekend."

"Yo I told you she could've stayed at the crib."

"And do what Jus? Sleep on the futon? We were supposed to make love for the first time when she came down. I can't ask her to do that in someone's living room with kids in the next room."

"What? You fucked that short chick in the living room. Come to think of it, you fucked Evelyn while Trevor slept across the room, so what is the difference?"

"The difference is Navarda and Evelyn were just some bitches to bust a nut in. Kendra is like the perfect chick so everything that I do involving her has to be perfect."

"Yo I told you months ago. If she was really all that like you claim she is then she wouldn't've cared where ya'll slept as long as she was with you. Do you even know what she did during the time she was supposed to be in Connecticut?" Tracy asked.

"Na. Probably flew to North Carolina. Her school pays for her ticket so I'm sure she went home."

"Ok, ok, ok fuck all that. You haven't talked to her?"

"Na I figured she doesn't want to talk to me and if she did she would've been called me by now."

"Maybe you should try callin' her." Tracy suggested.

"Hold up why is everybody comin' down on me? Ya'll don't even know her and ya'll all comin' to her defense."

"Syn because that is fucked up. Check it. I didn't like o'girl with tha chef pants but out of respect and courtesy I took her out and had a good time anyway. So just 'cause something isn't perfect for you don't mean you shit on somebody and not even tell them."

"Yeah you right." I admitted

"Cut I know I'm right."

"Fuck you."

"Na nigga, you should've fucked Nadege." Tracy said lighting the conversation.

"Hold up Tre, he didn't hit that yet. Not even the night before we left? I got some good ass from Anita that night."

"Na I ain't smash."

"Wow! You crazy, I would've been up in that and done in two strokes."

"She just different. Nadege ain't one of these hoes I meet, fuck and leave'em. She special."

"Aww tha devils' in love." Tracy joked.

"Na son never that. I'm just sayin' that she's not the type of girl the shit on."

"And Kendra was."

"Yo fuck you Jus. You know damn well I was tryin' to protect her."

"Protect her from what?"

"Yeah Syn he right. What were you tryin' to protect Kendra from? Man up and admit that you wanted her to see you livin' all extravagant and shit didn't go the way you planned. Ain't nothin' wrong with that and if she didn't understand that then I would say to hell with her, but you didn't give her the chance. You actually did more damage by not sayin' shit." Tracy continued to explain.

"Fuck all ya'll, ya'll don't know me. Ya'll don't know what Kendra expects of me. She is a woman on the path to greatness and I'm a fuckin' screw up tryin' to be with a perfect girl, there is a lot of pressure to do right. I haven't done anything right a day in my life. I don't have an idea what right is."

"What do you think right is?"

"...Right is takin' my ass back to North Carolina so I could be with Kendra when she starts college like we originally planned, but...it's too late for that now." I said.

"Nigga if you wanna go to school then go to school and if you wanna be with Kendra then do that. Don't do this because you think we want you to. You need to do you and do what will be best for your life. You have to live for Syncere and not the Wolf Pak."

"No, I want to do this because this is what I want to do for the rest of my life, rap. I've invested too much time and effort into it. I don't wanna go to school and spend the rest of my life makin' some white guy rich. I made a choice and now I'ma stick with it."

"See, that's mannin' up. But you have invested a lot of time and effort with Kendra too right?"

"Yeah."

"Well you have to chose between what is more important. I know it's January now but you can apply to school for the summer and fall semesters and be in North Carolina when Kendra gets there and if shit in music jump off before then great and if it jumps off after you get back to school then you already know what it is." Jus assured me.

"Yeah homie, you remember what I wrote on the back of my prom picture. When I get on I got'chu." Wes added.

"I know. I'll think about it."

"Well think about it later we gotta get to that convention before we get there and there's 100 niggas there."

As expected every unknown artist in Atlanta is at the Sheraton Hotel tonight for the convention that is supposed to give everyone their big break and as usual Shawyna, our supposed manager is not in attendance with us. I looked around the room and looked at groups in matching outfits and individual people in corners practicing songs and dance steps while Tracy and Wes talked to Jus about a song idea.

"Eh man, what ya'll tawkin' 'bout?" Out of nowhere this country talking skinny guy poked his head in between our circle.

"What?" Tracy asked with his upper lip cocked.

"Na I ain't tryin' to be in yaw'll business but yaw'll niggas sound like yaw'll talkin' 'bout some real shit and I just want to be in the presence of creativity." Everyone looked at this guy as if he has three heads not really knowing what to say.

"So Jus, I'm 'bout to hit this muhfucka so follow."

"I got'chu Syn." Jus and I let the skinny guy into our circle strategically positioning me on the side of him and Jus in the back of him. As he talked to Tracy and Wes Jus kept looking for my signal but something is holding me back.

"Yo man, my name is Ben but my rap name is Fatal Mindstate."

"Fatal Mindstate? Where you from?" Wes asked.

"Mississippi." We laughed.

"They got rappers in Mississippi?"

"Yeah man, ain't you ever heard of David Banner?"

"Yeah and he sucks so ya'll don't really have a good track record when it comes to rappers. Spit sumthin'." I commanded.

Before Ben could get his first bar out the crowd that is huddled close in the lobby are now pushing each other to get into the room full of record executives. I lost site of Ben when the crowd started pushing because I'm trying to keep my boys in site all the while getting a seat. When we got in the room there were no record execs just a big screen projector and a tall white guy in the middle of the room and I knew that this "convention" is some bullshit. It is at this moment I am starting to grow tired of going from show to show and convention to convention all promising to put us in the eye of A&R's and producers. In two months all we've done is run around and perform at two clubs and we have gotten nowhere. Shawyna has managed to get us two auditions, one with So So Def & one with Outkast's label Aquemini but to no avail and the only explanation she's given us is they aren't the right companies.

Thirty minutes later a room full of artists stood once again in the lobby networking with one another. For a brief moment I thought we should be doing that but we weren't because I am just ready to go.

"Hey man, yaw'll got some time to tawlk?" That pestering cat from Mississippi is in our faces once again and getting on my nerves.

"Spit somethin'." I commanded again.

"Yo Syn chill." Tracy said.

"Naw'll man it's cool. Aight I'ma spit somethin' but I'm tellin' yaw'll it ain't that commercial shit that gets played on the radio. I hate commercial music man that shit ain't real hip-hop…"

"Look can you do it while we're still young? We really didn't need a synopsis." I said sarcastically.

"Okay, Okay." After Ben said the word yo ten times he began to unleash an arsenal of lyrical bars and after the fourth or fifth bar my guard dropped and I turned into a fan. I listened as attentively as I possibly could while ignoring everything else around me. *This cat is hot* I kept thinking to myself.

"Yo, on some real shit that was the hottest shit I've heard since I've been in Atlanta." I said giving Ben pound.

"Respect, respect. Now I gotta hear somethin'."

"Oh it's nothin'."

"Yo Syn let me get it." Tracy started rapping and his powerful deep voice caught the attention of nearby groups and a circle emerged around us as Wes, Jus and I took turns displaying our lyrical ability in front of the audience making me feel real confident. At the end the lobby erupted with applause and people swamped us wanting our contact information.

"Yo you live around here?" Wes asked.

"Naw'll man I stay in Decatur with my girl and her momma. Where yaw'll stay at?"

"Marietta. Yo come with us to tha car so we can get ya info." Ben obliged and he and I instantly engaged in conversation on the way to of the hotel. Tracy, Wes and Jus walked ahead of us while people still came up to us or walked by us saying "nice session or good shit".

"Yo Ben, we do this show every Thursday at the Celebrity Rock Café should stop by and check it out." I offered.

"Yo is it a talent show or is it a showcase? Cause I don't fuck wit talent shows 'cause the winner is already pre-determined."

"A little bit of both I think. Yo how 'bout we bring him to meet Shawyna?" Wes suggested. To be honest I am against the whole idea but they are going to do what they want to do anyway because according to them I am always the one who has something negative to say, I'm the devil.

"Yaw'll niggas got a manager man? See I knew when I saw'll yaw'll niggas that yaw'll was about yaw'll shit man. See that's what I need, real niggas doin' this shit seriously." Ben complimented.

"Yeah man we came all the way from Connecticut for music we doin' this shit the right way."

"Yeah we got a bad ass entertainment lawyer too. We just lookin' for a deal." Wes added.

"We'll my car right herre so I'll follow yaw'll niggas."

"Yo you mind if I ride wit'chu man?"

"Naw'll it's cool."

"Yo Syn let'em listen to our CD while ya'll follow."

"Aight."

I climbed into Ben's hunter green 2004 Ford coupe and popped in the CD as we sped off.

"Hello." I heard a woman's voice.

"Faith, I met some rappers from Kentucky…"

"Connecticut." I corrected.

"Connecticut and I'ma go meet they manager so I'ma be home a little late."

"Okay."

"Yo who tha fuck you talkin' too?"

"My girl."

"How?"

"I got a microphone right here and it plays in the whole car so I can have a convo hands free. In Mississippi it's illegal to drive and hold the phone so I got this installed."

"I ain't neva seen no shit like that before. Thas what's good."

"So where ya manager got her office at?"

"Office? We goin' to her house." I said shamefully.

"She doesn't mind us stoppin' by that late? I don't want her man to come out and try to fight us on some shit."

"Na man. We stay there too. She made us move down this muhfucka."

"Serious?"

"Hell yeah, so it's cool."

"So tell me about her man is she cool?"

"She can be sometimes but most of the time she a bitch. She thinks she is so fuckin' fine but personally I think she ugly as shit."

"For real man she ugly?"

"Yeah. The name of her company is Yellow Gurl Management 'cause she light skinned but she smoke and her front tooth is black. She just real unattractive."

"So what has she done for yaw'll so far?"

"We opened up for Ludacris at tha Dirty South Concert Series at the Bounce last month and we had two auditions with So So Def and Aquemini plus we do showcases and shit three or four times a week."

"Aight it sounds like she on her grind."

"Yeah." I don't know why I didn't tell Ben the ugly truth about Shawyna and what she is actually doing for us. I guess I am impressed at the fact he is impressed with what we are doing and it feels good to come off as someone who is perceived as being in a better position than another person. Ben and I chatted it up more as we drove from downtown Atlanta back to Marietta.

"Yaw'll shit sounds nice but yaw'll on some commercial shit. I told you I don't do that commercial shit."

"Well most of these songs I ain't even on and I don't even like'em. But that's tha kind of shit that gets played on the radio na mean?"

"Yeah I hear you but my music is gonna change all that. I'ma take this shit back to the essence of hip-hop. Metaphors, punch lines, concepts not all that dumb ass catchy shit they play on the radio all day like that Holla at a Playa bullshit." I listened to Ben express his utmost dislike for commercial music all the way to Shawyna's now dark complex.

"Yo cut you think she still up?" I asked getting out of Ben's car.

"I don't know we called in the car. Wes go in an see and we'll stay out here."

"Why I gotta go in?"

"Nigga she ya cousin." Wes went in the house and we stayed leaning on the car talking more with Ben.

"Yo B. what you think of the CD." Tracy asked.

"I mean man yaw'll niggas hot but like I told Syn I don't fuck wit commercial music. I cain't stand that shit man."

"That's what gets played."

"I know."

"Hey yo!" Wes signaled for us to come in the house and when we did Shawyna is sitting on one of her dining room chairs in her pink silk robe, black house shoes and smoking a cigarette. Immediately I am disgusted at her appearance because Tracy and them called first so she knew we were bringing by company.

Once she laid eyes on Ben I could tell she wasn't impressed and didn't want to hear what it was he had to say, nevertheless she let him spit a couple of bars while she sucking on her cancer sticks.

"Yo don't…you don't talk about other things?" Shawyna asked disgusted.

"Like what? Cars, hoes and money? No because I don't have none of that stuff. I don't rap, I do hip-hop."

"It's the same thing." She said.

"No, no it isn't. Hip-hop is what KRS-One and Eric B. & Rakim does when it was pure and all about showing what you can do off the top of the dome and not braggin' about how many cars and bitches you got. I talk about reality, my reality and the reality in the world. These nigga rep Connecticut I rep the planet earth."

"Ok, I mean you do what you do. That is not what we do. Good-night." Shawyna blew another puff of smoke before getting up and retreating back into her room. We all sat in the living room surprised at that just transpired and we really didn't know what to say. We all apologized to Ben over and over but he ensured us it isn't our fault but for some reason I feel really fucked up at the way Shawyna handled herself.

"Yo man yaw'll some cool muhfuckas but I ain't feelin' yaw'll manager. If yaw'll niggas wanna get up and colab or do sumthin' cawl me." Ben said as we walked him to his car.

"Aight drive safe." Tracy and Wes said heading back into the house.

"Yo lemme get'cha number."

"Tracy is it? Tracy got it."

"I know but I want it for my self. I'ma be real wit'chu, Shawyna is Wes' cousin and our manager and if she ain't feelin' you she ain't gonna want us to even fuck wit'chu. Tracy and Wes do whatever that broad says but I fucks wit'chu 'cause I can tell you a real ass nigga." Jus nodded his head in agreement.

"That's word man, I respect that." Ben jotted down his math and Jus stayed outside until we couldn't see Ben's taillights.

"Whut'chu think?" Jus asked me.

"I think tha nigga talented but I don't know what these niggas gonna say after Shawyna puts her two cents in."

"True statement. Let's go."

"Na I'ma go over to Rita's."

Rita stays in a complex right next to Shawyna's but hers is called Lincoln Suites. Normally I'd call but I don't want to go back in the house and hear Shawyna complain about it being too late for me to be on her phone and how I don't pay any bills in the house. Staying there is getting real old. I knocked on Rita's door three times before she opened it with the phone on her ear.

"Hi." She whispered. I didn't respond because I know she won't hear me. I met Rita last month while working at the Gap. We expected to get a record deal within days of us getting down here we that didn't think what if it didn't happen? I was the first to land a job but Wes and Tracy quickly scored one with Marshall's not too far from where I work.

Rita is a five foot five dark skinned girl from Harlem New York with shoulder length jet-black hair that I just love running my fingers through. She has high cheekbones that get even higher when she smiles and her breasts are at least a 36 double D. It's safe to say Rita's thick in all the right places except her ass but she makes up for it every where else. I guess that is why out of all the women that worked at the Gap she is the only one I clicked with; we click instantly on the first day and have been talking ever since.

The first night Rita invited me over to her and her older sister's apartment I was there so long they insisted I stay the night, so I slept on their living room. Rita played hard to get but as the night grew older Rita's face was eventually buried in my lap, her warm mouth and wild tongue showed my dick a good time. The next day we all woke up and her sister Tina cooked a serious breakfast consisting of pancakes, eggs, bacon, sausage and grits. Her cooking reminded me of my mother of whom I've spoken to for the first time last Sunday in months.

It is a usual night at the Bowe household, Tina has her eyes glued to the computer screen talkin' to God knows who and I'm sitting with the remote control in my hand waiting for Rita to get off the phone.

"What's good T?" I asked growing tired of just sitting there.

"Nutin'. How have you been Infinate?"

"Chillin."

"Your braids need to be redone. You should really let me put a perm in your hair because of how tender headed you are." She said while she examined my braids.

"I got a show Thursday night so can you do them tomorrow?"

"Why? So you can be lookin' all fine for them hoes in the club." Rita said moving her head from side to side."

"Well you can be cheering for me if you come to my show that I have been asking you to do for weeks."

"I'll think about it." She teased before giving me a hug.

"That is what you say every week and every week you never come."

"Do ya'll ever do the Gong Show at Café' Red Train?" Rita asked.

"What? Neva heard of it."

"Every Wednesday at Café' Red Train they have a Gong Show. It's like a talent show but it's like the Apollo except they don't boo you they just Gong you." She explained.

"We'll look into it. Thanks Tina."

"Does everyone call you Infinate?" Rita asked taking a seat next to me.

"Yeah."

"Why?"

"Because I don't like my real name."

"Why I think Syncere is cute. Who named you?"

"My dumb ass grandmother." I responded with an attitude. Rita lay in my lap as we talked most of the night like we do most other times. Yes Rita is very pretty but I'm not looking to make a relationship with her. The head is good so I'm really curious of how the pussy is so that is why I keep coming around. Yeah she cool and all but while I'm in the A I'm just focusing on fucking as many broads as possible. To be honest we enjoy each other's company I guess it's cool for me. Coming to Rita and Tina's house is an escape from Shawyna and my boys. My boys are my boys but I can only stand to be around them for so long. If I'm not at work, performing or writing a verse I am at Rita's as much as possible and neither Rita nor Tina seems to mind. Some days I don't even go to Shawyna's house after work, I get off the bus and go straight to Rita's. I think about having Rita's luscious lips wrapped around my shaft so much that I can hardly wait for the bus to come to a complete stop before I'm fighting to get off.

"Tina cooked if you are hungry?"

"Oh hell yeah. What'd she cook?"

"Fried chicken, mashed potatoes and some greens. And guess what?"

"What?"

"I baked the cookies." She announced excitedly.

"Did you take'm out halfway so they are softer?"

"No, that is raw dough and you are going to make yourself sick if you keep eating them like that."

"No I'm not. Oh I got a new job yesterday."

"You leavin' da Gap?"

"Yeah. I can't stand in the same spot and fold the same damn sweater everyday. It makes me wanna pull my damn braids out." I explained.

"So where is it?"

"At some print shop on Cobb Parkway. I start tomorrow."

"Thas cool, how much do they pay?"

"Trust me, a lot more than the Gap."

"Ok. So Mr. Infinate…"

"So Ms. Bowe…"

"Why haven't you made me ya girlfriend yet?" she asked while sending me a smile and getting closer to me.

"What kind of question is that? I'm just gettin' to know you na mean."

"I don't know what kind of question it is. What kind of answer is you just gettin' to know me? You can let me suck your dick but you can't make me ya girl?"

"Wow! I never made you do anything. That was all you, I mean I wasn't gonna stop you. But it's like this. A relationship is nothin' that should be jumped in and out of na mean? Yes we obviously have a physical connection but I wanna make sure we have that emotional connection as well. In order to do that I have to get to know you."

"How well do you have to know me to make me ya girl? What, I gotta fuck you and then you'll make me ya girl?" she belted obviously upset.

"What is this high school? Na I'm cool just as we are, you ain't gotta fuck me. Did I ever say that?"

"No. I'm just sayin'. I'm feelin' tha fuck outta you and I feel like you just here because I sucked ya dick the first night. I knew I shouldn't have done that shit."

"You blowin' this up for no reason. I ain't that type of dude to fuck a girl and drop her. I'm feelin' you too na mean? I just don't wanna rush into nothin'. We feelin' each other madd hard right now but what if we get in a relationship and find out that it was only a physical thing. Then we've wasted each other's time."

"Well just so you know I ain't fuckin' you until we make this official." She established.

"Aight." I agreed.

Rita says she's not going to fuck me now but I can see the lust in her eyes every time she says the word fuck. She licks her lips and looks down at my crotch and I see stars emerge in her pupils. I had to hit her with that I have to get to know you shit so I can keep myself open for other broads I'ma meet down the line. I'm only here to smash and get away from Shawyna with all her bullshit, nothing more and nothing less. Give me another couple of weeks and I'ma fuck Rita, she wants it…bad.

I got off the bus from my first day of work at the Print Shop and thought to myself this isn't what I came all the way to Atlanta for; I could work and ride the bus in Connecticut. The sun hasn't set completely yet so the sky is a color mixture of orange, violet and blues. As I look at it I think about how much Kendra loves sunrises and sunsets. Kendra. I haven't spoken a word to her since a week before Thanksgiving and I fight myself to pick up the phone every single day but to no avail. What can I possibly tell her to make things all right? I've done everything wrong to her except hit her or call her out her name yet she forgives me and gives our relationship another try. It's things like that when I know she truly loves me, so why am I dicking around with other chicks and dancing around calling her? It's the same reason why I didn't call her and tell her what was going on during Thanksgiving. I'm not settled and I can't call her until I can I'm back on my feet again. I mean what can a broke, college-dropout sleeping on someone's living room floor have to offer the most intelligent and perfect woman in the world? Exactly, nothing.

I think about being able to call Kendra, lay everything on the line and finally be the man I want to be; the type she needs, a man doing something constructive with his life. If I go back to school and get my degree no one can never say I didn't try because I did. I gave up everything to move down here on the promise of a deal and Shawyna hasn't delivered. I don't blame her entirely but she hasn't been the best manager as possible, I mean we wouldn't even be here if it wasn't for the promise she made. We barley have a steady income and our money has been running low for weeks now, luckily Wes' mom and M.Dot have sent money down for us to eat a number of times.

Things just aren't working out the way we all had envisioned and it's frustrating. I'd never thought in a million years that at age 18 I'd be out of school and sleeping on some strangers living room floor. I'm borderline homeless if you think about it and the fucked up thing is even if this doesn't work out Tracy, Wes & Jus can all go home. I have no home to go to unless I go back to college because I can't go back to live with my moms, so I have very limited options. Where is this God I've served and believed in all these years. I look down at the scripture I got tattooed on my left forearm before we moved down here silently reciting it to myself. *The times you saw one is when I carried you my son.* Well Lord how do I know if I'm being carried or not?

"Shawyna's here." Tracy shouted after peaking through the living room blinds." Everyone looked at each other as if our life is about to change, for the better or for the worst we don't know. Shawyna walked in with a pissed off look on her face and her clothes aren't exactly on right. I looked at everyone's confused faces confused as if they wanted to say something but they didn't so I did.

"So what happened?"

"Ya'll ain't signing with Aquemini." She said without breaking stride on the way to the bathroom.

"That's it?" I asked everyone. "That's it? What tha fuck is that? No explanation at all? This is some bullshit." I shouted standing up.

"Yo Syn chill man she gon' kick us out if you start spazin' out." Jus warned.

"Fuck this shit!" I left the house pissed off to the third degree and the only place I can think to go is to Rita's house. I miss the times when something went wrong I could call Kendra and she'd make light of the situation giving me great advice but I can't do that now. Right now the only way I can think is if I get some ass and release some of this anger.

"Who is it?"

"Infinate." Rita took extra long to answer the door.

"What's up?"

"Aint'chu gonna let me in?"

"I got company." She said without looking at me.

"And?"

"Ok." When I walked in some tall basketball size light skinned dude is sitting on Rita's couch with a smirk on his face.

"Syncere this is David. David, Syncere." She introduced.

"My name is Infinate." I corrected.

"Like I said this is Syncere." Rita said laughing as she went to sit beside David on the couch resuming the conversation that I interrupted.

"So it's like that?" I asked after being ignored for a couple of minutes.

"Like what?"

"You just gon' play me like I ain't standin' right here?"

"You can sit Syn don't act like you ain't been here before."

"Where's Tina?"

"She ain't here, she workin' late."

"Aight I'm out."

"Bye." She replied with a stank sound in her voice. Instead of walking back to Shawyna's house I walked down Franklin Road to blow off some steam. For some strange reason jealously fills my heart and the anger I have with Shawyna fused with the anger I now have for Rita caused me to begin sprinting down the street. So much shit is flowing through my mind and all I want it to do is stop. I'm tired of being pissed off, I'm tired of sleeping on the fucking floor, I'm tired of chasing a dream that someday will never come true. I want to go back to school and I want Kendra in my life, fuck it that's enough. I'm calling Kendra in the morning and I'm going to tell her the truth about what happened and if she accepts it great and if she doesn't…well it doesn't really make much of a difference. There really isn't anything left in my life to go wrong so if this does I'll just be at rock bottom. I'm calling my track coach and coming back to school this summer then I'ma call Aunti Luv and tell her everything and I hope she says I can stay with her until school resumes. I have it all worked out.

The thought of being back in North Carolina made an image of Kendra appear out of the sky and I stopped in my tracks. I looked into the sky at Kendra's face and she is as beautiful as the first day I saw her. In the sky her eyes are the brightest stars and her smile is the crest moon and I just stared aimlessly at the image I see. I remembered the day Kendra came by my aunt's house after church one Sunday so her mother and my aunt could meet. I lay in her lap while she played with my braids and we just talked for a while like we did on the phone and nothing else mattered to me, nothing else was more important. I felt tears running down my face but I didn't do a thing to stop them. I just blew her image a kiss and began to sprint back to Shawyna's.

8

It's been a hard two months since Shawyna kicked me out of her house. Wes chose to stay and Tracy left with me and I am forever grateful for him doing that. Ironically Ben was having problems with his girlfriend Faith and her mom so he was looking for a way out as well. So Tracy, Ben and I got a nice three bedroom apartment just two sub-divisions away from where Shawyna lives. I got a new job at the Olive Garden on Cobb Parkway and I am making a killing.

For the first time in months I have steady money flowing in my pockets and a comfortable home environment. Tracy and I are working so much to be able to eat and keep a roof over our head that music has been put to the back burner for a while until we get in the position to do it again. Tracy got a job with Footlocker, the same company he was with back in Connecticut as a manager and he is definitely happy as things are looking up for us.

Not bright enough for me to call Kendra, I'm still not at the stage where I can attempt a relationship with her. It's March and it's been four months since the last time I spoke her and with each passing day it feels like a year. I think about her constantly every time my eyes open and shut and numerous times in between. I think about her when a customer is running me back and forth at Johnny Rockets, I think about her when I am riding the bus home and I am thinking about her every time I see a happy couple walking down the street. I say to myself *that is going to me Kendra and I soon* and with those words I am able to press on.

I still go by Rita's house once every two weeks so Tina can do my hair but when I am there it is as if Rita and I never met. I still feel an immense amount of animosity toward Rita for what she did and I guess that is because deep down I like her and not just because she gives good head. It makes me no different, I have a chick named Melissa that I met in Best Buy just days after Nadege calling me and telling me that she got back together with her ex in my absence. Melissa is by far the smallest woman I've ever dated as she is only five foot even and weighs probably 100 pounds soaking wet. Yet and still she is very pretty, long black hair that is all hers, chestnut color eyes that are perfect circles and a smile that is as if God spent thirty days creating each tooth.

Every body part of Melissa is small, small breasts, small waist, small ass and hands but she's adorable. She lives about thirty minutes away in Kennesaw straight down Cobb Parkway and she either takes her mother's car down to see me or one of her friends brings her. I watch her from the living room sitting on one of our patio chairs on the balcony talking to Faith. We've been in our new apartment for less than a week so my room only consists of a pallet of blankets that I got from Wal-mart and a blue lounge chair but Melissa doesn't seem to mind at all.

"So you gonna talk to Faith all night or are you going to pay me some attention?" I asked walking outside.

"Come out here, sit next to me." Melissa offered.
"Goodnight girl."

"Nite nite Faith." She said as Faith tapped me on the shoulder before walking back into the house. I sat behind Melissa in the patio chair looking into the darkness of the night not saying a word to her. The side of my face pressed up against her cheek makes her skin feels oh so soft and I kept inhaling her intoxicating peach body spray.

"It's getting' kinda chilly, wanna go in?" I suggested.

"Yeah."

Taking Melissa by the hand I led her into my empty room and she sat on my lounge chair. I sat Indian style in front of her gazing into her eyes trying to figure out why I am so attracted to her. The moonlight peeked through the blinds in my room and formed over every curve on Melissa. The light bounced off her chestnut eyes and down her frontal illuminating her B-cup breasts and down her slim legs.

"I can't stay long." She said in a low disappointed voice.

"I know. I just wanna look at'chu."

"Stop." She said giggling. "Com'er." I sat in between her legs while she pulled me close to her mouth pushing her tongue into mine. The kiss turned passionate and her shirt came off then I helped her as she wiggled out of her jeans. Her body is a work of art just lying here in her pink thong and like the moonlight I wanted to be all over her flawless chocolate skin.

"What are you going to do with me now?" she asked as she tossed her thongs in my face. I replied by burying my face into her moist frontal lobe moving my tongue around wilder and using my tongue ring to make her released her arousing moans. I can't get enough of the taste and smell of peaches and as her nails dug into my shoulder the sensation makes me want to enter her but I waited.

Before long Melissa is literally tearing off my jeans to get to my endowment. She held it in her hands for a few seconds then starred me in my face and whispered,

"Wow! Put it in, put it in my pussy and fuck me." I love the forcefulness in her voice, it is extremely stimulating and I more than happily abided by her sexual command. Her mound is as small and as tight as her little body but she took it all. Melissa lay with her knees on the floor and her stomach on the lounge chair with her face buried in a pillow. I wrapped her hair around my forearm and held it firmly as I enjoyed her from behind. Occasionally I'd lift her head out of the pillow allowing her loud screams to bounce off my empty walls and echo in my ears. I think there is no better sound in the world than that of a woman moaning from the pleasure I am delivering.

I flipped her over into the missionary position and looked deep into her eyes and her face became one that is strangely familiar to me. It is a face whose beauty is unmatched by the early morning sunrises or the captivating image of a full moon. It's a face of a woman whom I've never seen naked in my life but have had pleasant dreams of what she'd look like. I starred at her slightly parted lips as the pleasure moans escaped her mouth and she grabbed my waist tightly before her body jerked for a couple of seconds and her breathing got more and more irregular. I watched the sweat run down her forehead, down her neck and chest and her body looks foreign to me, sexier than the naked body I laid eyes upon before this sexual engagement. I look up and see Kendra trying to catch her breath and as I smiled she smiled back.

"That was great Syn." She said in between breaths.

"It was everything I thought it'll be. I love you Kendra." I replied while resting my head on her sweaty stomach.

"Who the fuck is Kendra?"

I've been standing outside Rita's door for almost ten minutes before I decided to knock, hoping Rita isn't here while Tina does my hair. I'm tired of the awkward feelings I get and Rita makes it her business to sit in the living room the entire time looking at me as if she is waiting for me to say something to her.

"Who is it?"

"Infinate." I answered knowing who is on the other side of the door. It opened and Rita walked away as before I even entered the house.

"Ill be ready in a minute." Tina said as she is typing on her computer.

"Aight, how you?"

"Good and you?"

"I'm aight. Just a little tired."

"Workin'?"

"Yeah I got a new job at the Olive Garden."

"Really? I've always wanted to go there but I don't know how the food tastes. Is it good?"

"Yeah it's aight."

"Well maybe me and Rita might stop by one day." I reluctantly said ok as I took a seat on the floor picking my hair out waiting for her to finish. Rita sat in the love seat looking at me every few minutes and it is beginning to annoy me.

"Rita would you wash his hair for me please?" Tina asked.

"Na I already did it." I said as Rita smacked her teeth.

"Ok, let's go."

As I expected Rita starred at me and looked away then did it all over again but I didn't let that get to me. I just engaged in conversation with Tina, which seemed to piss Rita off more and I liked that.

"Here, thank you." I said to Tina handing her a twenty.

"What is this for?"

"For doing my hair."

"Since when do I make you pay me? I don't want that."

"I feel like I should."

"Tell you what. Put that back in your pocket and go talk to Rita."

"Who?" I played dumb.

"Oh don't act like that. I'm tired of ya'll tryin' to front like ya'll don't miss each other when it is painfully obvious otherwise."

"Na I'm good that it. I'll see you next week and thanks again."

"No!" Tina closed the door and made me sit back on the couch. "Riiiita!!! Com'er."

"Why you yellin'?" Rita said with an attitude sticking her head out of the bathroom.

"Ya'll talk." Tina demanded before she went in her room. Rita and I sat on opposite ends of the room, me in Tina's black leather computer chair and Rita in the love seat.

"So how you been?" Rita finally said after a series of huffs and puffs.

"How's ya boy?"

"Why you gotta take it there?"

"Makin' conversation. So are you expecting ya little boyfriend later on tonight because I'll gladly leave so you two can have some privacy."

"He's not my boyfriend Infinate."

"Oh now we're back to Infinate? Glad to see you remembered my name."

"That's not fair."

"What's not fair?"

"You don't want a girlfriend but I want a boyfriend. And yes I like the guy who was over here but he doesn't have what I want in a boyfriend and you do so I'm sorry." She apologized.

I swayed back and forth looking at Rita for any signs of deception but can't find any. Maybe she is telling the truth but I wonder more why I am so upset with her. I guess it is because I really do like her.

"Aight, it's dead." I said.

"Dead?"

"Yeah."

"Well can I have a hug?"

"Yeah." Rita and I hugged as if we haven't seen each other in years, the type of hug I long to give Kendra and the thought of Kendra remains me of the incident that happened with Melissa last week.

"Did you miss me?"

"Yeah...Of course I missed you Rita." We broke the hold on one another and sat together hugged up on the love seat.

"So what have you been up to?" before I could answer I checked my watch.

"Oh shit it's madd late and I gotta be to work at nine, I gotta go." I proceed to get up but Rita tightened the grip on my hand.

"No stay with me."

"Aight." I replied not putting up much of a fight. "Go get me a blanket please." Rita shook her head no and led me to her bedroom.

"Don't just stand there get undressed. You don't mind sleeping in your boxers do you?"

"Na just as long as you sleep in those." Rita looked at her blue panties and smiled.

"How about like this?" Rita revealed her naked body and my mind went blank. Something extremely powerful deep within me does not want to be here right now and just as I did last week I'm thinking only of Kendra. My subconscious can see Rita kissing my neck and chest but I can't feel a thing until she put me in her mouth and the sensation freed me of my trance. The feeling shot through every nerve in my body making it increasingly difficult for me to stand.

"Get in bed." Rita tuned off the light and her night-light made a very sexy silhouette of her shadow in the walls of her room.

"Gimmie a condom." I said. Rita pulled on out from her nightstand drawer, I reached for it.

"No let me do it." Rita put the condom in her mouth then submerged under the covers. Lying there during the oral display the sensation escaped my body and I starred at the glow in the dark stars placed all over the room, my mind drifting. *Why is this happening now?* I think of Kendra on the daily but up until last week it is never during sex. Lord knows I've been wanting to smash Rita from day one but now that day is here and I mind is else where.

I didn't feel when I entered Rita just her cold hands grabbing my chest while she road me like I was an untamed stallion. I'm slowly loosing my erection and I have to get it back somehow because I don't need the embarrassment of being a minuteman. I visualized Kendra's face on Rita's body and passion filled my heart. I pulled Kendra close to me and kissed her deep and hard while I firmly grabbed her buttocks and thrust as hard as I could.

She isn't as loud as she was last week as she tried to muffle her pleasure moans with short and feminine whimpers. I'm near climax when Kendra dug her teeth into my shoulder; I thrust vigorously into her bottomless wetland until I felt her river rush down my shaft and her teeth resurface out of my skin. She climbed off the top of me and exhaled a deep breath while fanning herself.

"If I knew it'll be like that I would've fucked you months ago." The comment made me turn on my side and look at her because my Kendra doesn't talk like that. I looked at Kendra who to my disappointment is Rita and it was Rita all along just as it had been Melissa last week. I rolled over and went to sleep, disappointed.

9

Sleeping the seven-hour bus ride then waking up in warm and sunny Raleigh North Carolina makes me feel really good about this visit. I've been working so hard trying to stay afloat with everything that I haven't been to visit my Aunt Dimpsey and cousins in a while. My aunt Rolanda greeted me outside the bus station and is driving me to her house where my aunt Dimpsey is on her way.

My Aunt Dimpsey greeted me with a big hug as I planted a kiss on her cheek the second she stepped foot out of the car.
"Hey nephew!"

"Hey Aunti. How's everything?"

"It's ok, how was your ride?"

"Long."

"Shit tell me about it. You need to hurry up and get your license."

"I know."

"So you gonna see Kendra since you here? I like her, do you and her still talk?"

"I haven't talked to her in a while. I think she is still in New Hampshire."

"She ain't home from school yet?" Dimpsey asked making me think... it is June! Kendra graduated already and she should be home.

"Oh she should be. Yeah I'ma call her."

"Aight, come see the house when you are done."

My heart is beating out of my chest as I held the phone in my hand trying to concentrate and dial the right numbers. I don't know where the nerve came from or why it came so suddenly but I think about hanging up. I've been thinking about Kendra for months and every time I have I've wanted to talk to her so bad. I almost forgot that I stood her up then vanished without a word but fuck it. What's the worst that can happen? Whatever it is I don't want to find out so I'm hanging up…

"Hello." She said so softly as my throat got dry and my mouth is so open that I think I just swallowed a fly.

"Hey."

"Who's this?"

"Syncere." The expected silence accrued and I'm thinking about hanging up again.

"Well I'm glad to see you are ok." She said after a while.

"Yeah. Congratulations."

"On what?"

"Didn't you graduate from Exeter?"

"Oh yeah, thanks."

"Guess where I am?" I asked sounding like a kid who can't keep a secret.

"North Carolina?" she guessed.

"Yeah."

"Really?"

"Yeah. I got here not too long ago."

"Where in North Carolina are you?"

"Raleigh?"

"I know you're in Raleigh but where in Raleigh?"

"I don't know, lemme ask my aunt. Aunti Lon where are we?"

"Cedar Road."

"Cedar Road." I repeated.

"I know where that is."

"For real? Are you close to me?"

"Yeah. Syncere can I ask you a question?"

"Anything." I responded bracing myself for the question I've been dreading to answer for almost a year.

"My family is throwing me a graduation party and I want to know if you would come?"

"You know I will. When is it?" I asked signing happy that she didn't asked what I expected her to.

"Today in a little while. Is that a problem?"

"Na, you comin' to get me?"

"Yeah. I'm on my way right now."

"Oh, ok that's what's up. Aight, I'll see you in a little bit."

"Alright."

I hung up the phone feeling great. I didn't expect on our first phone call in almost a year Kendra would be so…so cool with me calling. I expected her to be upset at me and ask me a bunch of questions as to why I stood her up for Thanksgiving but there was none of that. Her voice was as pleasant as it's always been and her North Carolina accent is like a familiar sweet melody to my ears.

Reality set in just now. She just invited me to a graduation party that her family is throwing and I know I am not on the best of terms due to what happened at the church. More importantly if Kendra told them about last Thanksgiving I may be walking into a big disappointment. Still I'm going to be optimistic about the situation, Kendra and I are back on speaking terms and I'm going to see her real soon. Nothing, not even the thoughts of her family chasing me back to Atlanta with pick forks and torches can dilute my mood.

I ran in the house and changed out of my traveling cloths putting on my navy blue Enyce jeans, my white and Carolina blue Enyce t-shirt with my pearly white Air Force 1's. I then checked my braids, my face and even brushed my teeth again just to be sure I am perfect…perfect for Kendra. I paced back and forth outside clenching my cell phone in my hand waiting for Kendra to call for directions or to tell me she is pulling in. I went over and over different things to do and say to her. Do I hug her like a lover or like a friend? Do I kiss her on the cheek or leave kissing out all together? Don't smile too big and don't act too excited to see her. I'm a nervous wreck when I see a hunter green Saturn coming directly toward me…its Kendra.

When she got out the car time stuck on the moment she stood looking at me. She is beautiful, the prettiest flower is green with envy right now. She wore her natural hair back in a ponytail showing off her sparkling chestnut brown eyes and her perfectly bronzed skin. She's wearing a regular white t-shirt, blue jeans and a pair of Nike running shoes. *I don't know what to do or to say.* For a minute we both starred at each other not knowing what to do. It's weird because we've known each other for the past four years yet it's almost as if we are strangers meeting for the first time on a blind date. I wonder what she is thinking and once I think about it she's probably wondering what I am thinking, damn she's beautiful.

"Hi." I said walking over to her still fighting with the decision to hug her.

"Hi Syncere. You ready to go?"

"Yea, lemme just tell my aunts. Can I get a hug?" She extended her arms and I gently wrapped mine around her trying to resist the urge to pick her up and swing her around over and over again. She smells great and at this moment I could die and go to hell with today would be the best day of my life. After a while my aunts came outside and Kendra and I let each other go.

"Hi Kendra! How have you been?" Dimpsey said extending her arms for a hug from Kendra.

"Hi Mrs. Dimpsey. How are you?"

"Girl I'm fine and don't start with that Mrs. Dimpsey mess, you call me Aunti."

"Ok." Kendra said smiling slightly.

"Ya'll about to leave?"

"Yeah. We'll be back a little later. How long you gonna be here?" I asked.

"I don't know. A couple of hours so if you comin' to my house be here before I leave. Matter if fact ya'll go have fun and I'll call you when I'm gettin' close to leavin'."

"Aight." I gave my Dimpsey a hug and she whispered.

"Be nice, I like her." I laughed.

"I like her too."

"Alright now."

While Kendra concentrated on the road I'm frantically searching for an icebreaker, something to say to spark up conversation.

"I see you got more tattoos." She finally said and I looked down at my forearms.

"Yeah, this one I got last December before we moved to Atlanta and these other two I got the day after the towers dropped."

"What do they say, I cain't look while I'm driving."

"This one says, the times you saw one it's when I carried you my son and the other two are in Chinese and they say independent and invincible."

"Oh so you did end up moving to Atlanta?"

"Yeah, last December."

"So why'd you get the biblical one done before you moved?"

"I figure since I'ma be in a place where I've never been and I have absolutely no family the only person I can turn to if things get rough is God." I explained.

"So you still go to church?"

"Na, I haven't been to church since I was at Saint Aug."

"So you only call on God when you are in trouble?"

"Na. The tat is there more of a reminder that even though I think so I'm really not alone na mean?"

"Ok. You know, Tausha and Erica are going to be at my party…"

"Ok…"

"Just thought you would want to know."

"Why?"

"I don't know." She said shrugging.

"So how have you been?"

"Fine I guess."

"Why just fine, why not wonderful?"

"I don't know."

"Ok. Where are you going to school? Please tell me you are going to UNC."

"Yeah…I'm going to UNC." When Kendra said that her eyes dropped and her mood went down a notch or two.

"You don't seem too enthusiastic about going. What's wrong?"

"Nothing. Why are you so happy I'm going to UNC?"

"I don't know. I just could always see you going there and I'm just happy for you that's all."

"Oh. Here we are."

We arrived at some kind of park area and up a head I can see the smoke from a grill and I hear people talking, children's laughter and music.

"Does your mom know I'm comin'?" I asked with fear in my voice.

"No. No one knows. She did ask about you a while ago though."

"Ok."

"You ready?"

"Oh yeah I'm good, let's get it." I said taking a deep breath.

"What does that mean."

"It means let's go basically."

"Oh."

Kendra and I walked side by side toward the parking area and my heart is beginning to pound so hard I could hear it even over the music. I don't want to appear nervous and I don't want to have another one of my coughing incidents happen, please. Kendra broke away from me to hug her guests and got congratulated by everyone. I just walked looking around for her mother so say hello. I found her sitting at a table with some other elderly people.

"Hi Ms. Lewis."

"Syncere. Hi, how have you been?" she asked pleasantly.

"I'm good, how have you been."

"Good, good. You came for Kendra's party?"

"Yes ma'am. She called me up and here I am."

"Well we're glad to have you. We have some food over there, are you hungry?"

"Not too much but I will eat before I leave."

"Syncere!!" A voice bellowed and a small body crashed into my waist.

"Hey Kim what's up?"

"Nothin'. What'chu doin' here?"

"I'm here for Kendra's party. What are you doin' here?" I teased.

"I'm her cousin I'm supposed to be here. Who told you about the party?"

"Oh I got my connections. I also heard you're goin' to high school huh?"

"No eighth grade, high school is next year. You in college?"

"I was but now I'm just takin' a break."

"Ooh you got tattoos? Can I see?" I showed Kim my tattoos and gave her the same explanation I'd given Kendra. "Did they hurt?" she asked cringing.

"Na I liked it."

"You liked it?"

"Yeah. It's like a rush goin' through ya whole body." I explained.

"Eww you got a tongue ring too?"

"Are you goin' to point out every little thing about me? You should be payin' that much attention to Kendra, this is her day remember?"

"You still like Kendra don't you?" she asked moving her eyebrows up and down.

"Why do you wanna know?"

" 'Cause I already know you do."

"How do you know that?"

"Because you wouldn't be here if you didn't."

"Is that so? Well I hope you are this smart in high school."

"Eighth grade, eight. You know the number 8."

"Ok, ok I got it." I said laughing.

"Tausha's right over there." Kim pointed to her sister who is sitting at a table with some other people her age. Wow, Tausha has gotten bigger since I saw her last which was in my dorm room my freshman year.

"So."

"You don't like Tausha?"

"Na she cool. I just don't see why you're makin' a big deal about her being over there.

"Com'on, come say hi."

"No Kim wait..." Before I was able to finish Kim dragged me over to the table where Erica, Tausha and some other people are sitting. I'm reluctant to go over there because I know Erica doesn't like me. She once told Kendra that I was a player so I had a hand in proving her accusations right with what happened at the church. I think

Tausha still holds some resentment for me because I broke up with her and feel in love with her cousin.

"Tausha look who's here."

"I saw him come in Kim. Hi Syncere." She said without looking up. Tausha is not attractive this size then again she's never really been attractive. She has packed on the pounds over the last four years but her weave filled head and bug eyes still remain. I think she tries too hard to be pretty as well as trying to hard using all the wrong products.

"What's good? What's good Erica?" Erica didn't look at me, she just casually threw her had up. Kim saw one of her other cousins and ran off leaving me standing at the foot of the table so I decided to take a seat. Everyone at the table is now quiet and I beginning to not like the silences so I started playing with my cell phone.

"So Syncere you came down here from Connecticut?" Tausha asked breaking the silence.

"Na, Atlanta."

"What'chu doin' down there?"

"Music."

"Oh you still rappin'." She giggled to Erica.

"A little."

"Yo man you play football?" a chunky dark skinned guy asked.

"Hell yeah, you got one?"

"Yeah."

"Syncere wait. You gotta go put money on Kendra's teddy bear over there." Kim informed.

"Ok." I see people pinning money on the life sized teddy bear sitting by Ms. Lewis. Walking over cautiously I pinned a hundred dollar bill on the teddy bear then slipped away undetected.

Chris, one of the males at the table tossed me the football and we threw it around in the empty field away from the other tables. Shortly the rest of the teens and young adults joined us then little ones followed. Before long the guest of honor joined us as well as we all ran around throwing the football, chasing one another. Occasionally I let the younger kids catch and tackle me to the ground. Every chance I get I'm looking at Kendra who looks like she is having the time of her life and that makes the time I'm having that much sweeter.

Kendra sat in her car with the door open and I stood on the outside talking while I waited for my aunt to come outside.

"Did you have fun today?" she asked.

"Yeah I had a lot of fun, thanks for inviting me. It was nice to see everyone and I still can't believe how big Kim and Taylor got."

"I know! I see them everyday and I still can't believe it."

"It was great seeing you too. I've missed you."

"Missed me? Why didn't you ever call me?"

"I don't know. Well I do know but it's a long story."

"Will you tell me please?"

"I will, I promise but don't want to get into it and my aunt comes out here and I have to leave."

"Will you call me and tell me later?"

"Yeah."

"Ok. Another question."

"Ok."

"Why do you still have that tongue ring in your mouth?"

"Why you don't like it?"

"No, what do you do with that thing?"

"Nothin'." I said smiling.

"Syncere, tell me…please."

"It's for sexual reasons so use your imagination."

"Yuck." Kendra shuttered at the thought and I laughed but the expression on her face is no joking one.

"Oh com'on it's not that bad."

"Maybe not to you but you will never kiss me with that thing in your mouth."

"You don't like kissing anyway remember? You said it's like swapin' spit."

"I don't like kissing all the time like most people do but I may want to kiss you one day and I don't want that tongue ring in my mouth after you've used that on God knows how many girls."

"You want me to take it out?" I offered.

"Yes."

"Really?"

"I really would like that very much." Without further discussion I unscrewed the bottom of the tongue ring and slid the bigger part out.

"Happy now?"

"Yes." She said smiling. For the next twenty minutes I listened to Kendra talk and every time she opens her mouth soul sounds ring in my head and my entire body and soul wants to dance to her rhythm. Every molecule in my body wants to wrap my arms around her and tell her how much I love her but I continue to fight the feeling. Instead a smile is on my face as we converse back and forth the way we use to do for hours on the phone back in high school.

"Hey."

"Hey Syn."

"What'chu doin' today?"

"I'm going by to see Kim but afterward I don't have anything planned. Why did you want to do something?"

"I mean I don't have anything planned, I would just like to see you today that's all."

"Ok, so what do you want to do?"

"I don't know this is your state."

"Don't act like this isn't your home too. You're from Connecticut but I know your heart is in North Carolina."

"Yeah because this is where you are."

"That's sweet Syn."

"It's the truth."

"You know what? I haven't been skating in a while, you wanna do that?" she said ignoring my comment.

"Sure, let's get it. I can't remember the last time I went skating."

"Do you know to skate or are you gonna try to hold on to me to keep you from falling?"

"Oh no that will be you. I know how to stay on two feet. It's ok, if you fall I won't laugh…until after I help you up."

"Same here. Ok so then it's settled. Is an hour too soon?"

"Not soon enough."

"He hehe. You silly. I'll see you then."

"Hold on do you remember how to get to my aunts house?"

"Couldn't forget it if I tried. Syncere, I'd been promising to take Kim and Taylor out for the longest so I hope you don't mind if they come with us."

"Oh na it' peace."

I can't feel better driving down the windy road away from my aunt's house this cloudless sunny June day in North Carolina. Kendra has the sunroof open, Taylor and Kim are in the back seat playing with one another and the woman of my dreams is on my side. Looking at Kendra then at Kim and Taylor I feel like a father going on an outing with his family. The whole picture gives me eyes into the type of future I want to have with Kendra.

The DJ called for couples only on the rink as he played Wyclef's 911.

"Wanna skate with me?"

"Sure. Taylor, you and Kim go stand to the side we'll be right back." Kendra accepted my hand as we made our way to the rink. We didn't talk while we skated, instead we looked and smiled at each other every couple seconds as well as waving to the girls when we passed them. I saw other couples skating with the guy in back with his arms around the female in front of him and other people skating face to face and it causing me to want to be in a more intimate position with Kendra, but it if this is as close as I'm going to get then I'm going to cherish these three and a half minutes.

"Are you ready to go?" she asked after the song.

"If you are?"

"Yeah. Let's get them something to eat and we'll drop them off so you can have me all to yourself."

"I like the sound of that." After we took the girls to dinner at Golden Corral and then back to Morrisville Kendra and I are now driving down a road somewhere in Raleigh.

"Do you want to go home now?" she asked.

"Only if you are tired of me."

"No. Then will you go some where with me?"

"Anywhere on God's green earth. Where we goin'?"

"A place I go sometimes to think."

"Ok." I didn't say anything but I really am tired. It's only a little after nine but for some reason my body feels extremely worn out but for Kendra I'd go weeks without sleep if it means being in her presence.

"Wanna get out or sit in the car?"

"It's a nice night, let's get out and go some where and sit." I said as we decided to walk over to a jungle Jim. A wonderful feeling swept my body as we lay under the stars on this warm cloudless night. I didn't imagine that this night would go as wonderful as it is right now.

"Syncere…" She said my name ever so softly.

"Yeah."

"Can I ask you a question?"

"Yeah."

"Why didn't you call?" It is the question I hoped she didn't ask but I am just being stupid if I believed she wouldn't ask it, so here goes nothing.

"Like a week before you were supposed to come so much shit was going wrong. You know I moved out of Trevor's apartment and I didn't want us to have to spend our first Thanksgiving with Jus and his family. My plan was take you to a hotel and put you up for that weekend. Let you meet and hang out with Amber or Tracy & Quincy's girlfriends while we were at work and then at night be with you in our hotel room or hanging out some where." I explained.

"So what happened so awful that we couldn't do that?"

"The hotels were dumb expensive and I couldn't afford to pay for it and I didn't have an alternate place to put you. I didn't want you to have to stay in Jus' house with his three siblings and sleep with me on a hard ass futon. I wanted us to finally have some alone time outside of seeing each other once a week at church or for a couple hours when you used to visit me at my dorm, like now. That whole weekend I wanted you and everything to be perfect."

"Syncere, how well do you know me?"

"Pretty well I guess."

"Then you should've known that I didn't need everything to be perfect. I was coming to Connecticut to be with you. Staying in a hotel or at Jus' house makes me no difference as long as we were together, that is all I wanted and I thought that was what you wanted."

"It was what I wanted. I just thought you deserved to have everything perfect. Perfect place to stay and a perfect Thanksgiving."

"Syncere I could've been with you in a shelter and it would've been a perfect Thanksgiving. Do you wanna know how I spent my Thanksgiving?" she asked getting up.

"In Morrisville with your family?"

"No. I spent it in New Hampshire with the family of one of my teachers. I spent my Thanksgiving with a bunch of white people that I didn't even know. I spent it worrying if you were ok. Syncere I am a simple girl and I don't need lavish hotels and perfect surroundings to be happy because I wasn't raised like that, ok?"

"Ok and I apologize. I had no idea you spent your Thanksgiving like that."

"I just wish you would've told me what was going on. I wasn't even upset I was just so worried something happened to you. I prayed for you every night."

"Thanks, I know you were. I thought about you all the time, even at the weirdest moments."

"So why after all these months do you decide to call me?"

"I don't know. I'll be lying if I said I don't think about you day in and day out. But so much shit went down when I moved to Atlanta and I wanted to be stable before I called you."

"Why."

"I don't know. I just didn't want to be callin' you with all the problems that I was havin' down here."

"But Syncere that is when we are supposed to be talking the most. Are you gonna shut me out and disappear every time something in your life goes wrong? I mean you do this a lot. In high school when you moved back to Connecticut, in college after you got kicked out your first semester and then Thanksgiving. You go months without calling me and then one day out of the blue my phone rings and its you. In that time so much has happened that you haven't told me. You need to talk to me, before anything we are friends right?"

"Yeah."

"So don't shut me out, talk to me."

"Yes ma'am. Did you miss me? I asked without looking at her fearing her response."

"Yeah, how could I not?"

"You know I love you right?"

"How do you know?"

"I just do."

"I love you too. So now what?" she asked after we hugged for five minutes.

"What do you mean?"

"I mean as far as us, what now?"

"What do you want?"

"You first." She insisted.

"I want you. I want us to have the relationship we have been trying to have since we were fifteen."

"Are you sure this is what you want? I mean really sure. I'm getting older and I don't want to go through all the stuff we already went through. I want you to be sure this is what you want before you say it."

"It is trust me." I assured.

"Okay, I can be a difficult woman to be with." She warned and I laughed.

"I think I can handle it. Is this what you want?"

"Yes. I thought about it a lot and realized that you are the man I would love to spend my life with. I know this is what I want and that is why I asked you if you are sure. I need to know you are serious before I put my heart into this again.

"Na I'm dead ass serious this is what I want. Can I tell you somethin'?"

"Yeah."

"Do you know why I went to college?"

"Because you wanted to run track professionally?"

"No, well kinda but no. Remember when we were datin' and I kept insistin' you go to UNC? I never thought I would go to college because I never had the desire to, until I met you. But when I moved back to Connecticut and you attend Exeter I remembered all the plans you had for your life I knew you are a girl with ambition. I realized to be with you I had to find my own ambition; I was seventeen when I made that choice. Do you know why I chose to go to school in North Carolina?"

"No, why?"

"Because deep down inside I know that you are the woman I am going to marry. I knew you were going to choose to go to school at UNC. I was setting us up to be together with me in Raleigh and you in Chapel Hill visiting each other every weekend and finally havin' a relationship with out thousands of miles between us. So when you ask me is this what I really want I can only think of all the nights we spent talkin', all the letters we've written each other and the funny feelin' I get in my stomach when I talk to you, think about you or even when I am next to you. I've never loved anyone like this before nor have I ever wanted to be with one woman so badly."

"Just because we want to be with each other doesn't mean we have to be."

"Well it's like I always said. I want to see you happy even if it's not with me."

I don't know what to make of Kendra's last comment. I want to hear her confirm our relationship status but instead I am left with a vague statement. Are we together or aren't we. I pondered the thought for a minute but let it go and just enjoyed being with Kendra right now even if tonight will be the last time I have her lying on my chest looking up at the stars.

There is so much more I want to tell her but I think it'll be over killing my feelings and I don't want to sound convincing. I'm not telling Kendra the reason I wanted everything to be perfect for Thanksgiving is I because in my eyes she is perfect and when she deals with me I want everything about me to be perfect in her eyes. When I look at Kendra I see no flaws, no signs of deception just nothing negative. She brings out the best in me and to me that is perfect and I can't help but to see her any other way. I know it sounds childish but it's the truth.

10

The whole bus ride there all I thought about was the time Kendra and I spent with each other and my heart feels better than it's ever felt in my life. No Kendra and I haven't established we are a couple but if I'm going to finally man up and be the man I've always wanted to be then it starts right now.

I remember the afternoon Kendra came over to my Aunti Dimpsey's house and my uncle Anthony was there. He'd never met Kendra but I introduced her as the woman I'm going to give my last name to and as God as my witness I'm going to make due on that. Tracy and Ben think I'm out of my mind to want to be with one woman at my age but love has no age limit and when it's real you know it, and this is real. This is as real as the sun that baths her body and the beat of her heart.

The sun shines brighter when I'm with Kendra; the sky is that much bluer and the worries of my life are millions of miles away. It's as if Kendra takes the burdens of my life and replaces them with pure bliss. She is a thorn less eternal rose that is admired by all but handled by few. This must be love that I'm feeling because everything I see and do now revolves around her. The more we talk the closer I feel we are getting to one another. I spend all day at the Olive Garden anticipating the night we talk on the phone. I think about the jokes we share and the topics we talk about and every day more and more I am convinced we are meant to be together.

Today is no different. It's been two weeks since I've come back from North Carolina as I'm standing at the server station waiting for my first table of the dinner crowd to be seated. I sipped on some sprite when a white girl about my height came over. I looked at her and remembered I'd seen her before. Her hair is pulled back into a bun showing off her plucked eyebrows and the faded freckles on her face. I'm trying my best to keep my eyes above her neck but her huge rack is just staring me in the face. Slim and cute.

"Hi." She greeted.

"Hi."

"Are you in Chianti too?"

"Yeah."

"Your first night on the floor?"

"Yeah. Jennifer is going to be watching me so I'm just hoping not to mess up too bad."

"Well I'm Syncere. I've been here for six months so if you need anything just lemme know."

"Syncere, so that is your name huh?"

"Yeah. Why do you say it like that?"

"I don't know if you remember but last week you brought the menus into the training room and I saw you. Me and the other girl I was sitting with thought you are cute so we named you braids because we didn't know your name." I laughed at the story and immediately I'm intrigued with this girl.

"Oh really. Braids huh? I've had a lot of nicknames but no one's ever called me braids. What is your name?"

"Oh I'm Diane. That day your braids were tight and every time we came in we always said I wonder if braids is here today. I've seen you while you worked a couple of times. Jennifer likes to use you as an example a lot."

"Oh really, ok that's what's up. So where you from?"

"Connecticut."

"Stop playin'. So am I, what part?"

"You're lying. I'm from Mystic." She said sounding astonished.

"Oh you from the ritzy part. I'm from Waterbury."

"No shit. I got people in Waterbury."

"What people?"

"You wouldn't now them, a bunch of white people. So how long you been down here?"

"Seven months."

"You go to school?"

"Na, I came down here to do music."

"Oh so you sing don't you?"

"I wish. But I rap."

"Why do you say you wish?"

"Because singers get all the ass."

"Rappers get ass too." She debated

"Yeah but you gotta have a deal for hoes to just throw tha panties at'chu. A singer can sing right here right now and the panties will just drop." I explained.

"I don't think you have any problems getting girls." Diane cocked her eyebrow and left when Ashley told her she had just been seated. I watched Diane go over to the table and am surprised that she has a black girl butt, instant hard-on.

Thoughts of sticking my solider into Diane's foreign territory invaded my mine and I'm trying with all my energy not to think that way. But once the thought is in my head it'll remain until I act on it. I thought about Kendra and my erection went down and I feel I'm back at normal. I between tables Diane and I talked and joked around which seemed to pass the night because I looked up to see I have one table left who is about to cash out.

"So how did you do tonight?" I asked while rolling silverware.

"I guess I did alright. I won't know who much I made in tips until I cash out."

"Do what I do. I keep my cash tips separated from the money I take from the guests so when I cash out I already have the amount I'm supposed to the managers then all I have to do is declare my credit card tips." I explained.

"How do you think you did?"

"I don't know about 2."

"Hundred?!"

"Yeah. I was covering some tables by the bar area too. When people get liquored up they tip big. The only thing I don't like about it is the cigarette smoke."

"You don't smoke?"

"Hell na, I'm an athlete and I try not to put anything harmful in my body. Why do you?"

"Yeah."

"You suck. You are too pretty to be smoking. Those things make your breath stink. Your boyfriend smokes too?"

"Why do you ask?"

"Because if he didn't he must not like kissing you if your breath smells like an ashtray all the time."

"Well I don't have a boyfriend."

"Looking?" I asked, not because I'm interested but to make conversation.

"Not really, I just want friends."

"I feel you."

"How about you?"

"Na, I don't like guys."

"Funny but I'm being serious. You with anyone? One of these big butt Georgia girls?"

"Not tied down if that is what you mean. I just want friends."

"Uh huh." Diane said smiling.

The night is still warm but humid as I waited for the bus. I glanced at my phone and see I have one missed call from Kendra and decided to wait until I got home to call her back.

"Hey you need a ride?" Looking over to my right I see Diane poking her head out of her gray Oldsmobile.

"Yeah cool."
"Com'on." I climbed into the back seat because another girl is sitting in the front. She is ugly. She's short, heavy and has her hair looked like I put my chest hair in a ponytail.

"Bianca this is braids, oops I mean Syncere."

"Nice to meet you." We both said at the same time.

"Where do you live Syncere?"

"Franklin Road."

"Oh so Bianca I have to drop you off first."

"So when you gonna let me hear you rap?" Diane asked as she put her emergency break on when we reached my building.

"You wanna hear me rap?"

"Yeah, rap right now." She said smiling and turning to face me.

"Oh so you gonna put me on the spot huh?"

"Yep. Let me see what you got."

"You want sumthin' mean or sumthin' nice?"

"Once of each."

"Oh you want two, that's askin' for a lot. I'ma have to charge you extra."

"I can afford it." Diane said sending me a wink." I recited two verses for her that ended with applause and the question everyone asks me, when am I going to get signed?

"Maybe we should exchange numbers so if we are working the same shift I can pick you up or if I'm off and it rains I can come get you." Diane suggested.

"Don't try to use that as an excuse you just want my number."

"Ok, ok you got me. So what, yeah I want your number and…?"

"If you wanna get up and chill just hit me up."
"I will."

I walked into my apartment asking myself why did I just give Diane my cell number? Then I thought she probably only took it down to be nice and I brushed off the thought. Since I came back from North Carolina my routine has been the same, I come in eat a little something, shower and then it's on the phone with Kendra.

"Damn son are you gonna be phone boning again all night?" Tracy asked.

"Why?"

"I wanna holla at'chu. You still ain't told us the whole story about you and Kendra. She wasn't mad at you for not callin'?"

"Yeah but I explained the situation to her and she accepted my apology. She did tell me that because of her not coming to Connecticut she had to spend Thanksgiving with one of her teachers. I felt really fucked up when she told me that. But our last night together we laid in a park staring at the stars."

"She crazy."

"What? How you figure that?"

"'Cause I would've been pissed off. I would've been like kick rocks nigga." He said laughing.

"Please, all the fucked up shit you do to M. Dot and she always takes you back. I don't do anything remotely that close to the disrespectful shit you do."

"Aight, so what's good wit ya'll then? You went to North Carolina now you come back and you cut all ya bitch off. I ain't seen or heard about Rita, Melissa or what's that grandma lady you was fuckin' wit?"

"Lisa."

"Yeah her. I ain't seen you wit nobody and you don't tell us shit. Everybody in the house thinks you're depressed and shit."

"Na man it's like this. I'm tryin' to get my life together and I seriously want to be with Kendra. So even though we ain't established as a couple yet I still cut the rest of them hoes off so I can get used to bein' alone in order be ready when Kendra says aight let's do it."

"That sounds like some bullshit but hey only you know what you're doin'. But how you know she gonna wanna be wit'chu again?"

"Because she told me she loves me and I'm the only guy she wants to be with. So I'm just givin' her time. I think she wants to be sure this is what I want just as bad as she want it na mean? Yo check it, she even made me take out my tongue ring because she doesn't wanna kiss me wit it in. Why would she make me take it out if she isn't plannin' on bein' wit me?"

"She just wanna see how far you gonna go wit her. I think you stupid."

"What! Who was the one sayin' I needed to stop fuckin' with Rita and Nadege and try to make shit right wit Kendra…you! So now I'm stupid? Fuck you!"

"I'm just sayin' you stupid 'cause you jumpin' through hoops and ya'll ain't even together. Nigga you still have freedom to fuck madd bitches. I know you wanna be wit this girl and all but I wouldn't've stop fuckin' until she made it official. Now you might be waitin' for somethin' that won't happen for months."

"So what. Kendra is worth it." I said in my defense.

"Really? So what happens if Nadege calls and says she wanna be wit'chu right this minute? What'chu gon' do?"

"For real for real Nadege can't stand in Kendra's shadow. Yeah I really really like Nadege and she could potentially be wifey but when put next to Kendra she falls short."

"What she got that Nadege don't?"

"There is something I see in Kendra that I don't see anyone else. I see her soul and it's beautiful. I see her heart and it's over flowin' wit love for me and everyone around her. She just makes me a better person. Just look overnight I stopped fuckin' wit everybody for her. She's the only person that can make me do the things I should do but don't want to na mean?" I continued.

"So why was you still fuckin' wit Evelyn and Nadege when you was home. I ain't tryin' to shit on you or make you feel bad I'm just tryin' to understand this sudden change in attitude. I don't think you're thinking rationally."

"Na I'm not takin' it like that and the change ain't sudden. The only reason, the only reason I was fuckin' with Evelyn and Nadege was opportunity and I crave the company of a woman. Evelyn was convient na mean? She was there when I got out of work and she did whatever I asked her not to mention she has the best pussy I've ever had in my life. Then Nadege reminded me of Kendra a little. She is smart and about somethin' na mean? I couldn't take Evelyn to Jimmy's or have the type of conversations wit her that I had with Nadege; we acted like adults and that was a turn on for me. Plus I loved hearin' Nadege talk 'cause that Haitian accent drives me bananas."

"You crazy dude. We in Atlanta! The land of phat assess and you wanna be tied down to one chick. When I was your age I didn't even have my own place. I was still stayin' in my moms place but I was still a hoe. I had bitches upon bitches all the time. You got ya own place with us and you should be havin' a hoe for us all every night."

"Why you ain't tellin' Wes that? Anita is all the way in Connecticut and he's faithful."

"I did tell Wes that. You and him should be bringin' a bang of bitches in the house everyday. We supposed to be havin' madd orgies and fuck fests." Tracy said proudly.

"Seriously that was never really me. I only mess wit a bunch of other women at the same time because all of them had qualities that I am lookin' for but not one of them had them all. Lisa has the car, nice fuckin' apartment but she's old and I can't fuck her. Melissa has the perfect body and the sex is good but she lives in Kennesaw wit her moms and she don't let her stay the night out. Then Rita has that New York attitude that I like but she flakey. None of them have any aspirations to do anything other than what they are doin', none of them have the humor I'm lookin' for or just any of the little things. Most importantly when I was messin' with Lisa, Rita or whomever I never woke up thinkin' about them. I only did that wit Kendra. Nigga when I fucked Melissa and Rita I thought I was makin' love to Kendra."

"Wow! That's crazy. Have you and ol' girl fucked?"

"Who me and Kendra? Na."

"Never?" Tracy asked again surprised.

"Na, we were never in the position for that to go down."

"Wow, so you bankin' all this on a chick you haven't even fucked yet?"

"What does that matter?"

"What If you wait for God knows how long and then I let's say it finally goes down and the sex is bad then what?"

"I don't think that is goin' to matter. I have been wit Kendra on and off since we were fifteen and my intentions were never just to fuck her. When we together that thought doesn't even enter my mind whereas if it is another chick that would be my main objective."

"Aight cut, I hope you know what you doin'. I still think you too young to be talkin' like this but I wish you luck. I do commend you on what you doin' as far as cuttin' all ya hoes off."

Tracy and I talked more on the subject with a lot of the things he said sticking in the back of my mind. I listened to it all ignoring anything negative. Tracy's love life is on the rocks just like mine so who is he to be giving advice? The minute we finished I shut myself in my room and called Kendra.

"So how was your day?" she asked.

"It was cool I made a total of three hundred and twenty dollars in tips today, I worked a double shift and handled two sections." I bragged.

"Why do you work so hard?"

"I need a car and I need money to go back to school with."

"You're going back to school!? When?"

"I don't know exactly when but I do know I want to go back. The more and more this music thing isn't workin' the more and more I need to think of somethin' else to do. And I can still do music while I'm in school 'cause I'll still be in Atlanta."

"Oh you're not coming back to North Carolina?"

"I want to I really do but I'm startin' to love Atlanta. Once I buy a car I would still be able t drive up and see you on the weekends or I can fly up na mean?"

"I guess."

"Are you mad at me?"

"No."

"Yes you are I hear it in your voice."

"I'm not mad Syncere."

"I know our plan is for us to both be in school in North Carolina but right now this is just a thought. I can't start in the fall but I can start in January so we'll see what happens."

"Ok. So what else is up?" she asked changing the subject.

"Nothin'. I want you to come down and visit me. Seeing you in North Carolina spoiled me. Now that we are old enough to decided to see each other whenever we want I want to take advantage of it."

"Really?"

"Yeah, why do you sound so surprised?"

"I don't know. So when would you like me to come?"

"Tomorrow." Kendra laughed and her laugh sounds like the melody to the perfect love song.

"You're silly. Seriously when?"

"As soon as you can get down here."

"Let me see. I can come July second through the fifth. The kids don't have school that Monday because of the holiday so I can fly back Monday night."

"Oh I forgot you were teachin'. Ok we can do three days."

"Why too long?"

"What? No not long enough. I was thinkin' like a week or more."

"Do you think you can put up with me that long?"

"Yeah, you're no problem."

"Syncere...I'm not the same little girl you met at Shiloh. I'm a young woman now."

"Yeah I noticed, so what does that have to do with anything?"

"Well we've never been around each other for more than a few hours and we both have changed so much. What if we get around each other and we realize we really don't love one another like we think we do?"

"I strongly doubt that will happen and if it does we will have to cross that bridge when we come to it. We have a great phone relationship because we were never in the position to see each other the way we wanted to but now we can and if we are goin' to be together we need to see each other as often as possible." I explained.

"You still want to be with me?"

"Yes ma'am."

"I love when you say that, say it again."

"Yes ma'am." Kendra laughed again and I love it.

"Ok how about I come down for that weekend and I'll come down before I start school."

"When is Summerbridge over?"

"August 5th but I don't start UNC until the 26th. I can come down the 10th and leave on the 24th. That gives me time to prepare for school and get all the things I need." She planned.

"Ok, cool."

"Syncere?"

"Yeah?"

"Now you know I love you and I really want to see you but I have to be honest when I say I must be crazy because of what happened last year."

"You know what? You have every right to be but I don't know what I can do or say to make you believe me but that is not goin' to happen again." I promised.

"What if something bad happens between now and then?"

"Then we will deal wit it together. Just like you said we would."

"Ok remember you said that."

"I will."

"Syncere…Can I tell you something?"

"Yeah."

"I'm giving you my heart again. After all the shit you've put me through I'm going to give myself to you so please do what you say you are going to do. I don't want to go through any bullshit with you. I don't want to get to Georgia and have to deal with a bunch of girls calling or claiming you. You have my heart again."

"Ok, I got'chu."

"I have a lesson plan to prepare for tomorrow so I'll call you later tonight and we can talk about the details of me coming."

"Ok."

"Te amo."

"What does that mean?"

"Look it up."

"Well what language is it."

"Spanish."

"Ok, I love you." I said.

"Bye."

Three more days, just three more days and Kendra will be here but the minutes are starting to feel like hours. In between tables I periodically check my cell phone to see what time it is or to see if Kendra has called. Every morning I send Kendra a text messages counting down the days until she is set to come. She thinks it's sweet but I do it so she knows I'm for real about her coming to visit me. I've been saving up a lot of money and using a lot to get things ready. I went to Wal-Mart yesterday to buy a new bedroom comforter set, the matching bathroom set, matching curtains and picture frames to put on the wall.

"Hey cut." Tracy said as I passed his room and he stuffed his mouth full of popcorn.

"What happened?" Choking on the thick cloud of smoke in our apartment.

"I was tryin' to make some popcorn and the pot caught on fire. I threw some water on it and the whole kitchen when up."
"You're a dumb ass. You don't throw water on a grease fire." I yelled.

"Damn sorry I ain't Martha Stewart fuck face."

"Well you gotta paint the kitchen before Kendra gets here. The whole fuckin thing is black."

"I'll get to it if I can get to it, I do gotta work. That shit ain't important right now." He said obviously not understanding the importance of this visit.

"It is to me. I already gotta do enough shit before she gets here and I don't wanna be fuckin' paintin' either."

"Aight, aight damn. But yo you should've seen Ben runnin' up and down the hallway screamin' GET OUT!! Fuckin' caveman." Tracy and I shared a laugh and I examined the kitchen one more time before going into my room.

I can't believe this shit. Here I am painting a fucking kitchen that I didn't fuck up and Tracy is out with Wes… scumbags. Kendra's flight comes in tonight at 10pm and its 8:30 and I have to get the kitchen finished before Tracy comes back with her.

"Cut you need some help?" Ben asked.

"Hell yeah, grab a brush and start over there."

"Oh I was just asking not offering."

"Fuck you."

"You missed a spot." I flung some paint at Ben but he darted out of the way before it could hit him.

I lay on my bed with all the lights out and vanilla scented candles lit on my nightstand and dresser as I waited for Kendra. I had it timed, if Kendra's flight lands at 10pm Tracy should've had her back here at 11:30, it's almost midnight.

"Cut where the fuck are ya'll?" I asked when calling Tracy.

"Calm down nigga we in traffic downtown. We'll be there as soon as we can get out of this."

"How does she look? Is she pretty?" I asked anxiously.

"Nigga I ain't answerin' that, this is your chick."

"Just tell me if she looks pretty."

"Yeah she does, aight you happy?"

"Thanks, now hurry the fuck up and get her here." The minutes are feeling like hours again as the anticipation of Kendra's arrival is suddenly making me tired.

"Syncere?" There is a knock at my door.

"Yo."

"Yeah man. Damn you got the room lookin' like ya'll 'bout to get down to fuckin' as soon as she gets in." Ben commented.

"Na it ain't even like that."

"You lyin' ass muhfucka. You know damn well you can't wait to fuck her."

"B. You think I flew her all the way down here for some ass? That's some shit you'd do."

"Probably." He said looking over at Faith whom he moved from Mississippi to be with.

"So ya'll ain't gonna fuck?"

"I don't know and I really don't care. I want to see her and that is as far as it goes. If we do then we do and if we don't then oh well."

"You dumb as hell, any chick I fly in I'm fuckin'."

"Keep on Faith is gonna fuck you up."

"Come in my room and listen to this song I'm workin' on."

"Na I'm waitin'."

"Nigga you'll hear the door when it opens so meet her in the hallway. Stop bein' a bitch."

"Fuck you. Let me hear the song."

I listened to Ben's song with one ear because the other ear is listening for the door.

"So what'chu think man, honestly. I know ya'll on that commercial shit."

"Na its hot, its hot."

"Man you ain't listen to it. Go ahead and wait for ya girl man and holla at me tomorrow. Peace."

"Aight." I walked back to my room and was surprised when I opened the door. There she is Kendra in the flesh. It's only been a month and a half since the last time I saw her but it feels like I just came home from doing a bid. She turned and looked at me and for a moment we starred at each other. I hadn't completely came all the way in the room yet and Kendra is still holding her bag. I wanted to grab and hug her but I didn't. I wanted to smile from ear to ear and tell the whole world how happy I am but I didn't.

"Gimmie ya bag so I can put it in the closet. I made space for you and you can have the top two drawers."

"Are these for me?"

"Yeah. I use to bring you flowers to church all the time so this shouldn't be any different."

"Thank you, they are beautiful. All this space for me? I'm only going to be here for the weekend."

"Yeah but I don't want you living out of a suitcase even if it is just for the weekend."

"Ok, I'll unpack in the morning. Nice room." She complimented. "You still have this picture."

"Yeah it's one of my favorite ones. I was so happy that day."

"I wasn't, not all day."

"I know."

"I never told you."

"You didn't have to. I could tell by the picture."

"How?"

"You see your face its content. You're not happy and not sad but you had a worry look in your eye."

"Do you want to know why?"

"Yeah."

"Remember when we were walking to your room and your roommate walked passed us? The shorter girl gave you a dirty look and she gave me a you-fucking-with-my-man type of look. I thought you were messing with her. That is why I pulled back when you started school."

" I didn't even know you picked up on that. Why didn't you tell me?"

"I was afraid you'd lie to me and I know how you are around women, you like the attention. Besides I was going back to Exeter and I didn't want to worry about you being faithful while I was gone. That's why I insisted we be friends." She explained.

"Well you don't have any worries now, that is all over. Give me a hug." We did and I don't want to let go. I got the feeling neither did she but reluctantly we did and for what seems like endless minutes we sat on opposite sides of the bed not saying anything to one another.

It feels funny. I've waited days and days for Kendra and now that I have her here in front of me and I'm a mute. I yawned twice and then she did once then we decided to go to sleep…on opposite sides of the bed.

11

I rolled over rested and happy that Kendra is next to me, Kendra? I opened my eyes to see the spot Kendra was in last night is now empty. I sat up and assumed she is in the bathroom, she was and she came back in the room quietly thinking I was still sleep.

"Oh yeah."

"Yeah. Did you sleep ok?" I asked shyly.

"Yeah. You snore loud." She said laughing.

"Oh my bad if I kept you up."

"No it didn't bother me once I was sleep but I knew you snored anyway."

"I never told you that so how do you know."

"Because you use to fall asleep on the phone all the time."

"No I didn't."

"Yes you did, don't even tell that lie."

"Okay, okay."

"Did you sleep ok?"

"I slept fine. I'm happy that you're here." I said.

"Really? I couldn't tell."

"Whut'chu mean?"

"I mean you didn't even touch me last night." I'm taken back my Kendra's comment. I desperately wanted to kiss her and make love to her last night but I didn't want to try and give Kendra the impression that all I wanted her down here for is sex.

"Wow my bad. I didn't...didn't...know." I stutter.

"You love me don't you?" she asked looking at me with sad eyes.

"Yeah."

"Don't you want to make love to me?"

"Of course I do."

"So what is the problem?"

"Nothing. I didn't want you to think that is all I wanted you to come down here for."

"Syncere if I would've gotten that impression I wouldn't be here."

"I feel you."

"So feel me." She said.

"Com'er."

"No you come here." Kendra sat in the middle of the bed and signaled for me to come to her. I gently positioned myself on the side of her as she took off my t-shirt. We kissed for the first time in almost two years and her lips are the sweetest things I've ever put my lips on, I'd almost forgotten how soft her they are. I took off my Enyce t-shirt that Kendra had slept in exposing her C cup breasts getting a little more excited than usual because this is Kendra and I've never seen her bare chest before.

Her breasts sit up nice and firm and her nipples perky. I kissed her neck as soft as possible before running my tongue down the crease of her breasts then taking each breast in my mouth. I looked up at Kendra who's head was tilted back as if she is watching the sky, only her eyes are closed and pleasure moans are quietly coming from her heavenly lips. I made my way down to her stomach and spent a moment or two licking her belly button occasionally running my tongue under the top of her shorts.

I sat up and placed each of Kendra's legs on my shoulders and pulled down her shorts.

"These are sexy as hell." I complimented.

"You like'em?" Kendra said looking down at her bright red French laced boy shorts.

"Hell yeah."

"Good, now take them off and put'em up there." She said pointing to my blinds.

"Yes ma'am."

"Say it again."

"Yes ma'am." I happily abided by the command as Kendra lifted herself up so I can slid them off. I wish I can stop time right now. Kendra looks exactly how I pictured her in my dreams for the past four years. A flawless body wearing nothing but a flawless smile. I proceeded to put my face between her legs but she stopped me.

"No, I don't want you to do that."

"Ok."

"Syncere?" she whispered.

"Yes."

"Do you have condoms?"

"Yeah."

"Get one please."

"We don't have to do this if you don't want to." I said holding the condom in my hand.

"You won't get mad at me?"

"Of course not. We'll do this when you're ready."

"I'm ready now. Don't be too rough."

"Ok."

I mounted Kendra and put the sexual part of me into the sexual part of her and it feels like lock and key, a prefect fit. I started slow by taking out every inch of me and driving it back in with a little force and sped up every time Kendra moaned faster, faster. The bed board beat the hell out of my wall and I am sure Ben and Faith hear us since his room is right next to mine but I don't care. Every time Kendra's hips meet mine it feels like heaven all over again as I keep telling myself not to cum yet. Kendra then climbed on top of me and rode me like she knew exactly how to bring me to ecstasy.

"Am I doing it right? Am I doing it right?" she managed to say in between moans.

"Yes." I whispered. I palmed Kendra's bubble ass firmly and pushed down has hard as I could while lifting myself to go deeper into Kendra's enchanted paradise. She's trying as hard as she can not to be too loud but I want her to stop fighting it so I pushed and pushed myself harder and harder into her pleasure walls until a loud scream let out; I smiled. Kendra's nails dug into my chest and the slight pains heighten the feeling I have throughout my body.

"Do you like it?" She kept asking and I kept whispering yes and with every yes Kendra went back and forth on my joystick like a pro.

"Bend over."

"You want it from the back?"

"Yeah."

"You want it, you want it, you want it? Tell me you want it." She said.

"I want it from the back." I said while smacking her ass twice.

Kendra arched her back perfectly, placing her pretty brown round ass in the air burying her face in my pillow was I planted my hands on her waist and inserted my key into her lock has hard as I could. I feel her pleasure juices run out of her and onto me every time my pelvis separated from her backside. I kept telling myself not to cum yet as I feel Kendra get wetter. I flipped Kendra over and put her legs behind her head and grinded slow…and…deep. In…and out…up…and down…side to side as slow and sensual as I know how. I took my time with every stroke putting everything I have into it. Not just the physical part of me but the emotional and spiritual part of me as well.

I've never put so much feeling onto having sex before but I realize I'm not fucking Kendra nor am I having sex with Kendra. I am making love to her. This feels so right, so sincere, and so natural.

"I'm coming. Oh my god I'm coming." Kendra said and then she didn't move at all. I let her legs down and I lay in between them kissing her sweaty neck as she tried to catch her breath as I smiled. I smiled because she looks so beautiful with the sun bouncing off her sweaty neck and chest and I smiled because I finally know what it means to make love to someone.

"Are you ok?" I asked her.

"Yes. Did you cum?"

"No."

"Why? I didn't do it right?"

"No baby you did it perfectly, trust me."

"But you didn't cum."

"So..."

"So I want you to cum."

"Ok make me cum."

"Take the condom off."

"Are you sure?"

"How many girls have you been with without a condom and don't lie to me?" she asked with a concerned look on her face.

"Just one."

"Did you love her?"

"Asia? Hell no."

"So why didn't you use a condom?"

"We'd been sleepin' together for a while and I was sure I was the only one just like she was sure she was the only one and that was back in high school."

"No girls in college."

"Hell no. I always used condoms in college. I don't trust too many people na mean?"

"Ok, take it off."

"Are you sure?"

"Are you telling the truth?"

"Yeah."

"So why do you keep asking me if I am sure?"

"I just want you to be comfortable... I don't like pullin' out." I confessed

"You can cum in me."

"For real?" she smiled at my response."

"Yes, I am on birth control."

"Aight." I didn't have to ask Kendra how many guys she's been with because I already know the answer and even if I am wrong my love for her doesn't need conformation.

"Lay down." Kendra slowly lowered her sex lips onto my love stick and her warm juices tinkled down my shaft. She started off slow snapping her back every time she pushed forward and each time she did that I nearly lost my mind from the pleasure. The natural feeling of the best of me in the best of her far exceeds making love with the condom on and ten minutes later Kendra gave me an orgasm.

"Did you like it?" She asked. I could only nod because my mouth is as dry as stale bread.

"That was amazing." I complimented.

"That feels really warm inside of me."

"What? My cum?"

"Yeah, it feels good. Do it again."

"Ok. Gimmie ten minutes."

Kendra and I lay in each other's arms in the nude drenched in our own nectar silent and satisfied. I wonder what she is thinking but she is probably wondering the same thing about me.

"Ok I'm ready." Kendra didn't respond and when I looked over I discovered her sleeping. Peacefully with somewhat a smile on her face. I kissed her forehead and feel asleep beside her. Beside my future wife.

Kendra and I dressed alike on our outing. I wore my blue Roca Wear shorts and white and blue Enyce t-shirt with my crisp white Air Force 1's that I'd brought just for Kendra's visit. Kendra had her hair corn rolled and put into a bun in the back and is dressed in her fitted white tank top and blue jeans and a pair of Reebok. Kendra expressed her like for my shoes so we stopped at Foot Locker in the Underground Mall.

"Syncere I can pay for them myself. I brought money with me." She said as I reached for my wallet.

"I know but I wanna buy them. Consider it a graduation present." I said.

"In a way you are buying them. I'm using the hundred dollars you gave me."

"When did I give you a hundred dollars?"

"Come on. I know it was you who put that hundred dollars on my teddy bear at my party. No one else in my family has the money to put that amount and even if they did they wouldn't give it to me." She explained.

"I don't know what you are talking about."

"Oh no. So I guess this 203 phone number is up there by coincidence?" she said pulling out the hundred-dollar bill and showing me the number.

"That is my grandmother's phone number I promise you."

"I thought you didn't give me this?"

"Ok you got me."

"Thank you by the way."

"You don't have to."

"Yes I do."

"Well you're not welcome."

"Yes I am." She said kissing me on the cheek.

"Want to find that tattoo parlor now?"

"Yeah."

Kendra and I have talked about getting tattoos on our ring fingers when I was in North Carolina so today we are getting them done. Para siempre, which means always and forever in Spanish will be tattooed completely around our finger like a wedding band.

"I can't tattoo them on your fingers." The skinny tattooist said after we explained the design.

"Why?" I asked.

"It's risky. We use our hands and fingers for everything, opening doors, cooking, scratching etc. You won't be able to let the tattoos heal properly and that can cause infections on your fingers."

"We understand that but that is where we want them. Can we sign a waiver or pay you extra?" I offered.

"Look, you two look like nice kids and its obvious you love each other so why don't you get them on a safer part of your body? Then I'll happily tattoo you."

"Thanks but no thanks. We'll find someone to do them for us." I said out of frustration.

"So what do you want to do babe?"

"I don't know what do you want to do?"

"I don't know. There is a big time tattoo parlor down Cobb Parkway by my house called Psycho Tattoo we can try them when we get back."

"Ok. What do you want to do in the meantime?" I looked around to get an idea for our next move.

"Let's get our picture taken." I suggested.

"Where?"

"Right over there."

"Dressed like this?"

"Like what? We are neat, clean and presentable."

"Ok, let's go."

As we rode home on the bus Kendra started drifting asleep and I stared at the beautiful picture we'd taken. I sat on a stool wrapping my arms around her while she sat in front of me placing her hands on top of mine. It turned out to be a great shot because I didn't smile to big but she smiled big enough, perfect. I reached for the cord when I saw Psycho Tattoo approaching but she's sound asleep now so we can wait until tomorrow. I held her in my arms until we reached my stop.

Once at the door we heard a bunch of commotion inside the house and when I opened the door all I heard was.

"CUT!!!!" Tracy's brother Sean is standing in our living room with his arms in the air and a big kool-aid smile on his face.

"What tha hell are you doing here?"

"Cut I came to visit my niggs. Gimmie some dap cut." We did our signature handshake and I gave Natalie a hug before introducing Kendra to everyone. Kendra sat on the couch and began cutting out the wallet pictures to give to everyone while Tracy, Wes, Sean and I told Ben a bunch of stories about our escapades in Connecticut. I sat back looking around the room and am over filled with joy. I finally have Kendra next to me, I have my boys all here with me and I don't have a worry in the world. I wish this weekend wouldn't end.

The house is filled with laughs and loud voices and the kitchen has an aroma of fried chicken, yams and macaroni. Sean is in the kitchen working his magic while the rest of us congregated in the living room with music and monopoly.

"So Kendra what are you and Syncere going to do tomorrow?" Faith asked.

"We are looking for a tattoo parlor that will tattoo our fingers." You can hear jaws drop in the living room and I think the chicken grease even stopped popping.

"Tattoo?" Tracy said breaking the silence.

"Yeah tattoo, on our ring fingers."

"Ya'll niggas crazy."

"Why we gotta be crazy?" I asked with a defensive attitude.

"Nothin' Syn, go ahead I forgot you in love." He mocked.

"When tha devil's in love, it makes him do some stupid stuff." Ben, Wes and Tracy began to sing. Sean laughed hard from the kitchen.

"What the hell is that?" Kendra asked getting upset.

"That's the Syncere song. This nigga the devil on records but a care bear when it comes to chicks." Wes explained.

"Yeah dude you was madd hard when I met you but ever since that night at the Waffle House I see that you got a soft spot for this girl." Ben cosigned.

"What is he talking about Syn?"

"You never told her?"

"Na it was nothin' to tell. You and I was havin' a man to man."

"Tell me." Kendra demanded.

"Na I was just tellin' him about you and how much I loved you."

"When was this?"

"This was months ago. Maybe the end of January."

"We weren't even talking then."

"So. We have to be talkin' for me to love you?" I asked.

"No."

"Ok, but that's all it was."

"Devil my ass." Ben said.

"Leave Syncere alone. I think it's cute he can express himself when he wants too. He ain't like you Wes and Tracy, ya'll assholes and hoes 24-7 and Ben you just bipolar all the time. I think it's cute. Ben let's go with them and get tattoos." Faith suggested.

"Fuck you!" The room erupted in laughter but when I look over I see Kendra isn't and I need to change the topic.

"So Sean where ya'll stayin' tonight? Ya'll stayin' here?"

"Na, Tracy got us a room at the Travelers Inn down the street."

"Wow, why did you put them in that hell hole?" I asked.

"It's fucked up?"

"Hell yeah its fucked up. That's a roach motel."

"No it ain't, stop exaggeratin'. It's not bad, plus they only gonna be sleepin'."

"Cut you gonna be pissed off in the mornin' trust me." Sean and Natalie gave Tracy a dirty look and all Tracy did was shrug his shoulders.

I lay on the edge of my bed staring at Kendra sit on the floor Indian style in front of my full length mirror painting her nails. It's day two and I'm still amazed at the fact she's here. Last night we made love again then we talked until the sun rose again before going to sleep. I've secretly been thanking God every chance I get for allowing Kendra and I to have a fresh start with our relationship. I know with all the dirt I've done in the past I probably don't deserve it but I'm grateful God saw fit for this to happen.

"Syncere?"

"Yeah."

"Remember when I said I don't want to have kids that I wanted to adopt children because there are so many out here without parents?"

"Yeah."

"Well I've been thinking and I want to have just one."

"By me?" I asked.

"Of course." She said smiling.

"Wow! Thas what's up. What made you change your mind?"

"You."

"What about me?"

"I thought about it and I want to spend the rest of my life with you and giving birth to your son is the ultimate way of displaying my love for you."

"A son! You wanna have a son?"

"Yeah. Think about it, a little Nature running around the house. I'll do his hair like yours and you'd dress him in Air Force 1's and Enyce then when he starts to talk he'll say, *yo moms* and *na mean* just like his father."

"You want to name him Nature? I was thinkin' Malachi."

"Where did you come up with that name?"

"There was a poet Ben and I saw at Club Apache back in February and I just liked the name. Malachi sounds strong and great but I like Nature as well and if you are willing to birth my son then you can name him. I'll love you and him the same." I leaned over to kiss Kendra her cheek and we started smiling at one another and I'm thinking I've never been this exultant before in my entire life.

Since the day Kendra and I began talking about a possible future with one another she has been adamant about not wanting to give birth to any children. Her heart is so big that she rather adopt children already born into the world who have been abandoned by their birth parents. Her logic is why bring another life into this world when there is an existing one waiting to be loved. The first time I heard it I didn't fully understand why she felt like that and I don't think I wanted to understand because my thoughts were concerned with the fact Kendra wouldn't have a child by me. It wasn't until I was in college that I realized what a magnificent person Kendra is to feel like that and it only made me want to be with her more. It gave me insight to what degree of woman I would be married to and it exhibits just what kind of mother she'd be and I'm truly blessed to be the man in her life.

Once men are ready to give up our wayward ways and settle down a woman like Kendra ideal to do that with. The great thing about this is I, at eighteen, am ready to settle and marry this woman now. All the months of us not talking and all the years of us fighting to get to the point we are now have been well worth the uphill battle and now that I have Kendra not even the Lord himself is going to be able to take her from me. I promised God if he delivered Kendra to me just once more I'd do right by her and this is proof that God listens. I will make due on my promise to the Lord, to Kendra and to myself.

There is nothing else on this earth that I want. I don't care if I never strike it big and become a rapper and I don't care if I never become filthy rich. With Kendra on my side and God on the other side I feel invincible and for the first time ever my life feels complete.

It's a dreary day as Kendra and I walked hand and in down Cobb Parkway to Psycho Tattoo but the weather can't descend our spirits. We walked in silence and I occasionally looked over at Kendra and I witnessed her head is hung a little low. I see the complexity on her face and I wonder what she is thinking about.

"Are you sure you want to get these tattoos?" I asked.

"Are you?" We stopped walking.

"Yeah I'm good."

"You seem so confident in us."

"What do you mean?"

"I mean I can't remember a time you've questioned if we were going to make it. Over the years you've been so optimistic about our relationship even in the mist of us going for months without talking, even after all the girls you've been with you always come back to me. Why?"

"I told you already I can't put it into words."

"Please try."

"I don't know. You know I've been with a bunch of girls since you've known me and all of them have something I'm looking for in what I think the perfect woman for me is but none of them have everything except you."
"So what do I have that none of them other girls do. What makes me different from Trisha?"

"You have every physical attribute I want in a woman from the shape of your eyes to the curve of your body. You have every intellectual quality I look for, you have aspirations of being a supreme court judge I mean it doesn't get any more aspiring than that. And your personality is perfect so all that combined with the way you make me feel and the way you affect my life is the reason I love you." I explained.

"We're so young. I'm just about to start my freshman year of college. What if the woman you're destined to be with is a woman you haven't met yet?"

"Then I don't want to meet her and I rather spend my life runnin' behind you. Do you think you are not the woman for me?"

"Sometimes." She confessed.

"Why?"

"I don't know. Maybe I'm just nervous. Don't mind me."

"Are you sure?"

"Yeah, come on let's do this." I took it like she said it, maybe she is nervous about this and I must admit that I am as well. I'm so nervous that I'm going to say or so something wrong that'll change the way Kendra looks at me that I am walking on eggshells around her. I don't curse when I'm talking to Tracy and them, I've thrown out all my porn movies before Kendra arrived because I'm trying to be the perfect guy for her.

We walked into the parlor to the sound of a woman screaming and the sound of the tattoo needle.

"Hi folks, welcome to Psycho Tattoo. What can we do for you today?"

"We want to get a tattoo."

"The both of you or just you sir?"

"Both of us."

"Ok, do you have an idea of what you want or would you like one of my artists draw you somethin'?"

"We know what we want. We want para siempre tattooed on our ring fingers."

"Lemme see your hand. Something like that is going to be very small to the point if I were trying to fit it all on your finger like a wedding band I'm assuming it wouldn't even be legible. Not to mention your girlfriends fingers are thinner than yours."

"What do you want to do babe? You want to get it tattooed somewhere else or just pick something different?"

"I really want it on our fingers. What if we break it up, you take the siempre and I take the para." She suggested.

"Can we do it like that sir?"

"Yeah but I do have to tell you it will take extra long for it to heal and it may cause infection because of how frequently you use your hands."

"I know, everyone had told us that."

"Excuse me." I slim white girl with piercing on her eyebrow, nose, lips and chin tapped Kendra on the shoulder.

"Yes."

"How long have you two been together?"

"Since we were fifteen." She answered.

"Is this your first tattoo?"

"For me yes but he has four already."

"When my boyfriend and I got matching tattoos we got our on our arm. Nothing big and unattractive but…well just take a look." The girl lifted her sleeve exposing her nearly covered tattooed arm and pointed out the tattoo her and her boyfriend had done. It was his name, Jared, wrapped around a heard. The whole tattoo couldn't've been larger than a half dollar.

"That is really nice." We both complimented.

"Thank you. So if you wanted to get that phrase done you can get in a different location."

Kendra and I flicked through eleven tattoo picture books trying to find a design that'll look right with the words para siempre but to no avail.

"Why don't we get each other's names put on our arm." I finally suggested.

"What if I don't want everyone to see it? Can we put'em somewhere that not everyone can see unless we show them?"

"Like where?"

"How about on our shoulders right here? Its only because I don't want to have to explain it to my momma or anyone else unless I want to."

"Ok we can put them there."

"Can we only to initials, like S.W.?"

"We can do that. How about it looks like this." I took a piece of paper and drew

Always, with the letters K.L. underneath it with a heart on the side.

"I like it." she said smiling.

"Do you?"

"Yes." Kendra said latching onto my arm.

"Ok let's get it. Sir we know what we want

 "Ok who wants to be brave and go first?"

"I'm good I have four so this doesn't scare me. Go first babe."

"Me?"

"Yeah."

"Don't make me get this done and you change your mind."

"What?" I said laughing. "You know what I'll go first just so you know I'm serious."

"No, no I'll go first." I looked on as the tattooist cleaned Kendra's shoulder and I was sure to watch him open a new needle.

"Ready?" he asked Kendra.

"Hold on." She turned to me. "Do you love me?"

"Yes, always have and I always will."

"You better not hurt me Syncere, you better not hurt me. Promise me you will not hurt me." She said as tears rolled down her pretty face.

"I promise."

"I love you too. Sorry sir but I'm ready now." She said smiling.

"Take a deep breath and relax."

"Syncere?"

"Yeah." I said in my groggy voice.

"Did I wake you?"

"No, you landed home safely?"

"Yeah I landed seven hours ago."

"Seven hours? Damn I was sleep that long?"

"Yeah I called you when I first got off the plane but you didn't answer. I figured you were tired because I kept you up so late last night, hehe he."

"Oh yeah, thanks for the memories. What's up?"

"I have something to tell you but you have to promise me you wont get mad."

"Ok."

"No promise me first."

"Ok, I promise. What's good?"

"I'm pregnant?"

"Huh? What?"

"I'm pregnant." Kendra repeated.

"Are you serious?"

"Yes. Are you upset with me?"

"What? Hell no. We're havin' a baby!!! Oh shit." I leapt to my feet and jumped up and down on my bed screaming *WE'RE HAVIN' A BABY!!!* I can hear Kendra laughing on the other end of the phone as I ran from Ben's room to Tracy's room to Wes in the living room screaming *WE'RE HAVIN' A BABY!!!* Then my phone rang.

My eyes flew open like window shades and I don't know where I am. I looked at my cell phone lying under me and Kendra's name read across the screen. Why do I have the sudden feeling of Déjà vu?

"Syncere?"

"Yeah." I said in a groggy voice.

"Did I wake you?"

"No. You landed safely?"

"Yes. I'm waiting at the baggage claim right now."

"Ok, what's up?"

"Syncere can I tell you something?"

"You're pregnant?" I said as I leapt to my feet.

"What? Pregnant? You know this is Kendra you're talking too."

"Yeah I know. You're pregnant right?"

"Syncere how can I be pregnant and I'm on birth control?"

"I don't know. It's possible."

"Are you ok? Did I put it on you that bad this morning?"

"Jokes? Did I put it on you that bad?"

"Maybe." She replied with a giggle.

"I just had the craziest dream then."

"Tell me about it."

"You know how you just called me? I answered the same and we said the exact same thing in my dream right up until the part you asked could you tell me somethin'."

"What did I tell you?"

"You told me you were pregnant."

"I did? Were you upset?"

"Na, that was the crazy part. I was beyond happy. I was jumpin' up and down on the bed screamin we're havin' a baby!!"

"You were happy? Syncere you are so sweet."

"I'm not just sayin' that but I really was happy, dumb happy at that. I mean neither one of us are ready to bring a child into this world but if you did get pregnant I'd be the happiest man alive and I'd handle my b.i. na mean?"

"Really? It makes me feel so good to hear that."

"Good, I want you to be happy. So what is really up?"

"Nothing. I just wanted to call to thank you for inviting me out to see you and for you to thank Tracy again for picking me up and dropping me off at the airport."

"I will."

"Well go back to sleep and I will call you later."

"Ok."

"Te amo."

"Hey, hey. I never found out what that means."

"It's I love you in Spanish."

"How do you say it? Tea amou?"

"No, you're so cute. Te amo. T-e A-m-o, Te amo."

"Got it, te amo?"

"Si papi. Don't take my panties down either" Kendra said. As I listen to her giggle I pictured her smiling that big smile in which she showed all her teeth and I smiled as well. I lay back in the bed thinking no more than four hours ago Kendra was lying right next to me with her head on my chest, less than two hours ago we were making sweet, passionate love and now she's 4oo miles away.

I looked over my headboard to the window where Kendra and I pinned up her bright red French laced boy shorts and I remembered the promise to never take them down. I took them down and smelled them surprised that they still had her pleasure scent on them. I thought about the first morning we made love and revisited the bath we'd taken together last night. Neither of us were subconscious of being naked in front of one another. I washed Kendra gently making sure I didn't miss an inch of her sculptured body as she did me in return.

Scented candles burned with Indian Aries' song *I See God In You* played in the little boom box on the toilet. Before bathing each other I lay in Kendra's lap while she stoked my head over and over as we spoke of our younger years.

"Remember when I put dirt in your hair?" she asked.

"Yeah. I remember what the hell is this girl thinkin'?" We laughed.

'I was thinking I can't believe this guy is letting me put dirt in his hair. You must've really liked me back then."

"Just as much as I do now."

"Really?"

"Yup." It bothers me sometimes when I express my feelings for Kendra and she asks "really?" as if she doesn't believe me. Kendra doesn't just come out and tells me things like she misses me or she loves me unless I say it. Should I care or should I be worried? Not really, I'm just being cautious. They say that whatever bad karma you put out into the universe it'll return to you ten fold. Well knowing that and also knowing all the women I've hurt over the years makes me petrified that karma will strike just as I'm starting my relationship with Kendra and she'll do to me what I've done to Keisha, Valarie, Evelyn and to people like Sherrica, Dorcea and Shana.

One thing is certain, I do love Kendra and I need her here with me in Georgia. I've never been in a serious long distance relationship before and I'm not sure how much longer I can resist the lip licking, eye-flirting I receive from Diane or the amount of beautiful women I meet and see on a daily basis. I've done very well cutting off Lisa, Melissa and Rita because I know what I am capable of. Eventually the need to receive attention from Kendra who is not here is going to take over and I'm going to run into the waiting arms of another woman. No Kendra won't know and no my boys won't dime me out but I will forever know. Even at the alter with Kendra I will know that while she was away at UNC obtaining her degree I was cheating on her with other women. That is unless I can persuade her to go to school in Georgia.

How do I go about doing this? For years I've insisted on Kendra attending UNC, not only because I'd be in school in North Carolina but also because I feel UNC is the best fit for her. But since I have fallen in love with Atlanta I have come to the conclusion this is where I want to be and if this is where I want to be this is where I want Kendra to be as well. We've never been in the same city and state for more than a week and we need to be together consistently in order for our relationship to flourish and to keep me on the straight and narrow. I need her here because I am not strong enough to do this alone. I took the bandage off my shoulder and looked down at the tattoo and whispered Always Kendra Lewis.

12

"Syncere you got company at the front door." Wes bellowed. I walked down the hallway and see Diane standing in the living room with a huge smile on her face. She is dressed in a blinding white blouse that is unbuttoned just above her breasts open enough to have a clear view of her d cups. She is also wearing her bright blonde hair low which is very long, which I've never seen it out of the French bun she keeps it in at work. Further examination of Diane I noticed her khaki tennis shirt and black punk boots. Black punk boots? What the hell?

"Hey."

"Hey handsome."

"What'chu doin' here?"

"I had the day off so I went to the Olive Garden to say hi but they told me you had the day off too. Why didn't you tell me?" I looked confused at Wes.

"I don't know. Didn't know I was supposed to."

"So what'chu doin'? Are you alone?" she asked.

"Na my boys are here. I'm in my room writin' a rhyme."

"Ooh can I hear?" I looked over a Wes again who shook his head with his thumb in his mouth.

"Huh yea, com'on. This is my boy Tre, Tre this is Diane."

"What the fuck? I mean hey how you doin'." Diane and I walked into my room and she instantly flopped on the edge of my bed.

"I love this pattern. I have the same one in my room. You got yours from Wal-Mart didn't you?"

"Uh, yeah."

"Yo Syn com'er for a minute would you?" I heard Tracy call from the living room.

"My boy callin' me. I'll be right back."

"Don't be long. By the way, can you bring me something to drink when you come back?"

"Aight. What'chu want?"

"Anything but water."

"Yo what's good?" Tracy and Wes are huddled in the living room with Ben.

"Yo who tha hell is that?"

"That is Diane."

"You got a white girl up in here?" Ben asked disgusted.

"Yo Ben don't start with that close minded racist shit. You are the Muslim not me."

"I use to be one I ain't one no more. This ain't nothin' to do with race but are you fuckin' her man?"

"Yo she just showed up. I know her from work, she gives me a ride home when we work the same shifts that's it."

"But why is she here?" Tracy asked.

"I don't know…to chill."

"Chill my ass, she wanna fuck."

"Fuck it, fuck her Syn. I don't even fuck wit white girls and she badass shit. You don't fuck her I will." Wes added.

"Ya'll think she cute?" All three of them nodded their heads.

"You see her titis dude?"

"How can I miss them? They were playin' peak-a-boo out her shirt." I said.

"What'chu gonna do?" Wes asked seemingly interested.

"I don't know."

"What about Kendra. Ya'll just got matchin' tattoos, don't tell me you gonna go through all that and turn around and fuck this chick."

"Yeah man Tre right. Ain't she comin' back in two weeks?"

"Yeah."

"Yo you been doin' madd good even before Kendra came down here so don't fuck up now. Kendra will be here before you know it." Convinced Tracy.

"Well since you ain't doin' nothin' wit her send her to my room."

"If you don't sit your country ass down. I ain't sendin' her to Faith's room. I'm tellin' you Faith gonna find out and fuck you up."

"Aww man Faith ain't gonna find out shit unless ya'll niggas behind my back snitchin'."

"We just gon' walk away from that comment." I got Diane a Sprite and walked back into the room to find her lying down completely in my bed and her black punk boots on the side of the bed. *Aww shit* I thought.

"This is comfortable. Lay down with me."

"Here is ya soda."

"Thanks, lay down with me." She commanded again taking the soda and putting it beside the bed." I looked at Diane laying on my bed with her blonde hair everywhere, open blouse with her breasts winking at me every five second. Not to mention her shirt looks like she hiked it up just enough for me to see her white panties.

I looked at the window where I still have Kendra's bright red French laced boy shorts hanging and repeated in my head *Think about Kendra, Think about Kendra*. It isn't helping and Diane just caught my pleasure tool rising from beneath my Jordan basketball shorts.

"So what's good?"

"I'm not tellin' you until you lay down with me." She said closing her eyes as if to go to sleep.

"Comfortable?" She didn't respond to my question only still acted as if she is sleep. I stood at the foot of my bed having a mental tug of war with the good in me and the bad in me. Diane lifted both her legs and planted her feet flat on my bed and I got an eye full of her pleasure lips that looked like her panties are getting moist. The bad in me won the battle and I lay beside Diane.

"Took you long enough. What were you thinkin' about?"

"Nothin'. So what's good?"

"Why do you keep askin' me that, like you don't want me here?"

"Na it's just a surprise that's all."

"Well just be happy I'm here."

"You should be happy you're here."

"Oh should I? So look, we flirt a lot at work and I see the way you look at me and I know you see the way I look at you so what are we gonna do about it?" I have a girlfriend. The words echoed in my head but they wouldn't exit my mouth. Diane opened her eyes and smacked me in the face.

"What the hell was that for?" I said jumping up.

"Answer me dammit."

"Yo for real for real don't come up in my house puttin' your hands on me."

"Oh yeah and what are you gonna do huh?" Diane jumped up on my bed and faced me. "You gonna hit me?" She said pushing my chest and smiling.

"Oh you wanna fight?"

"What? You can't beat me." She pushed me again and I pushed her back hard enough for her to land on her ass. She jumped up again this time off the bed and onto me. I stumbled back catching her then threw her back on the bed as she looked at me surprised.

"Didn't know I can do that did you?"

"Oh you think you strong huh?" Diane jumped on me again and when I went to throw her back on the bed she held on to my neck as to bring me down. I snatched my neck out of her grip but not before her nails scratched the hell out of me.

"Now you markin' me up? It's on and poppin' now." I jumped on Diane and delivered light slaps to her face and ribs as she violently slapped my face and head. I got hold of her wrists and pinned them down on the bed and we looked at each other out of breath and laughing.

"You didn't win. I'm just takin' a break." She said

"I got'chu arms, now what'chu gonna do?" Diane lifted her head and sank her teeth into my neck turning the bite into a kiss before she let me go. I am so turned on at it that I returned the gesture and the bad in me won the war. Diane and I tore at each other cloths until we are in our birthday suits.

"Lay back." Diane put her glossy lips and warm mouth on my erect dick and began sucking like she is trying to see how many licks it takes to get to the center of a tootsie pop. I watched as her head bobbed up and down in a rapid motion then I grabbed and held onto a hand full of her hair.

"Suck that dick D." She looked up at me with lustful eyes and a smirk on her face covered with her own saliva.

"Push my head down hard but don't cum in my mouth." I did as she wished and my toes felt as if they were going to break because they are curled so tight. I tapped Diane on the head signaling I'm about to cum and she kept sucking a few more moments before stopping.

"Damn D."

"You better not cum before you fuck me." She said. Diane's dominate demeanor turned me on in a way no woman has before.

"Wait lemme get a condom."

"You don't need one I'm on birth control."

"Na I do need one just hold on."

"No baby condoms dry me out besides I want to feel that dick all natural." She moaned while playing with her pleasure lips. Her fingers are soaking from her pleasure juices and occasionally she brought her fingers to her lips and licked them clean. I quickly put on a condom and fucked the shit out of Diane. I rammed my sex tool into her walls as hard as I could and did it even harder every time she cried out. I mounted her from the back with her hair wrapped around my hands and forearm while she kept a tight grip on my headboard and I pumped her from behind so hard it began to hurt my pelvis. An hour later I was shooting my pleasure juices all over her D cups while she wiped it off with and licked her fingers. She slept for about thirty minutes then she is leaving my house walking funny and I'm cursing myself. I cheated on Kendra.

I couldn't have been too mad at myself for fucking Diane the other day because I've allowed her back three times this week and we've done it each day she's been here, sometimes multiple times. She has a little routine she likes to do. I lead her to the room, she pushes me down on the bed, takes me in her mouth until the point of orgasm then begs me to fuck her from behind. She says she gets off better when I do it like that.

Fucking Diane has definitely showed me the difference between fucking, having sex and then making love. See Diane doesn't want to be my girlfriend so there are no feelings there, which makes what we are doing fucking. Kendra and I love each other and we explored each other's bodies on a physical and emotional level, which makes what we did making love. Either way you look at it I made a promise to God that if he'd given me a second chance with Kendra that I was going to do right by her so I am.

"You ready to go?" Diane asked me as I finished up my phone call with Kendra confirming what time she'd be flying in.

"Yeah, ok I'll see you tomorrow. Te amo."

"Who was that?" Diane asked.

"That was my girlfriend, she's coming down tomorrow."

"So where does that leave me?"

"What? You know I have a girlfriend."

"Yeah after you fucked me, that didn't seem to stop you did it?"

"You had a choice the second time and it didn't seem to stop you either."

"But I thought we were gonna hook up."

"We did, six times but if you thought I was gonna leave her for you then you were terribly mistaken."

"Really. So what if I pop up while your little girlfriend is here and tell her all the nasty shit we do, then what huh?"

"She wouldn't believe you."

"Oh I bet she would."

"I bet she wouldn't. You see I don't do her like I do you. I fuck you like the nasty slut you like to act like. Me and her don't do it like that."

"Oh so I'm a slut now. You weren't sayin' that when you was callin' out my name yesterday."

"I said you act like a slut just like when you're beggin' me to cum in your mouth. You tried to act all innocent the first time, oh don't cum in my mouth, but the second time I had to fuck you twice because you liked it so much. Don't play yaself. We are just fuckin and you know it."

"Syncere can I see you for a minute?" My boss Brian asked me interrupting Diane and my argument.

I noticed Brian has an envelope in his hand as he led me to a section of the restaurant where no patrons are.

"So what's up B?"

"This is a copy of a credit card slip from last Friday. Notice the tip amount is five dollars. Here is a copy of what you put in the computer, notice the tip amount says eight dollars. You put in too much."

"I see but that has to be an accident. That touch screen computer acts up all the time. How many times have I called you over because I entered the wrong order in. It happens to everyone, the five is right above the eight, I meant to hit five."

"I don't doubt the sincerity but this is a copy of the agreement you signed when you were first hired stating that if for any reason you over charge the guest it will result in automatic termination."

"You're firing me? Brian com'on. I work constantly and I'm good. You haven't gotten one complaint out of me in nine months. Vanessa is teaching me food expediting and Enoch is teaching me the bar so I can move up to assistant manger, com'on this was an accident. Three dollars, here I'll give it back its not that serious."

"But it is that serious you signed this and despite the fact you are one of my best I have to let you go just as I would any other server. I will however give you an excellent recommendation to anyone that calls just have them ask for me."

"This is fucked up. Can I like reapply in a month or something?"

"No, one year."

"A year. Man this is some bullshit. Aight if this is how it is then aight. You'll give me a good reference?"

"Sure I will."

"Aight man thanks." I shook Brian's hand before walking down the ramp.

"You ready?" I asked Diane as she smoked a cigarette.

"So you got fired?"

"Yeah."

"Don't call me for no ass when ya little girlfriend finds out ya broke ass ain't got a job no more. Take the fuckin' bus home I ain't wastin' my gas on you. Go to hell." She said flicking her cigarette on me as she walked to her car.

"Bitch." I yelled while throwing a rock that hit her back window. I wish it'd broken it.

I sat on the bus staring at my cell phone contemplating weather or not to call Kendra and tell her what happened. I counted my tips from today and added it with my money I have saved back home and I have a little over seven hundred dollars. Rent is due next week which leaves me with only a little over four. That should last me the two weeks Kendra is here and at least a month until the rent is due again, I have to find a job fast.

"Are you upset that you got fired?" Kendra asked.

"A little. I busted my ass in that place day in and day out." I explained

"I know you did work a lot. But maybe this is God's way of tellin' you to spend more time on your music you know?"

"I hear you but I need to get a job, I got bills you know. Tracy can call M.Dot and Wes can call his mom if they get in trouble but I don't have anyone."

"If you need anything you know you can ask me right?"

"Yeah but I'll be aight. I'ma stop at a couple of places on the way home."

"Where are you now?"

"On the bus."

"Do you not want me to come tomorrow?"

"No, no, no. I still want you to come. I'll be aight. I'll spend a couple of days with you and then I'll pound the pavement."
"Are you sure it's ok I still come."

"Yes babe its ok. I'll be fine, trust me."

"I'm sorry."

"Sorry about what? It's not you're fault. I got enough experience so I shouldn't have a problem findin' another job. I've never been without a job for more than a month so I'm good."

"Ok. I have some running around to do before I go to the airport. Remember I come in tomorrow morning at ten."

"Ok, M.Dot comes in at eleven thirty."

"Who?"

"Tracy's girlfriend."

"What's her name?"

"Michane but we call her M.Dot."

"Why?"

"Long story." I said laughing.

"You guys are weird."

"I know, I know."

The ride home on the bus seemed like an extra long one. I sounded so confident to Kendra about finding another job that I began worrying if it'll really be that easy. It took all of us a while to find decent paying jobs down here. Well since it's already late in the afternoon Friday I'll enjoy the weekend with Kendra and hit the street hard Monday.

"So Kendra did you like Atlanta when you came down last month?" M. Dot asked as we all drove from the airport.

"Oh yeah I loved it. This your first time down?"

"No, I came down when Tracy and Syncere first moved. I'm glad they ain't stayin' wit Wes' cousin no more."

"Who?"

"Shawyna, remember I told you she was our "manager" and she is the reason we moved down here."

"Oh yeah. So Michane do you plan on moving down here to be with Tracy?"

"Heck no. Well not right now I'm still in school but Tracy is comin' back home."

"What? Cut you ain't goin' no where right?" Tracy looked at me with the I-got-to-talk-to-you face through his mirror.

"Don't act stupid now we talked about this." M. Dot reminded. Tracy took a deep breath and put his head down for a second.

"Cut you know you like my little brother right? And it was a good try movin' down here to do this music shit but I could work for Foot Locket in Connecticut. I didn't come all the way to Atlanta to sell shoes I was already doin' that. I think it's time to go home."

"Go home to what? You have your mom and Sean and Wes has his mom but I'm goin' back to what? Livin' wit Jus again? I fuckin' hate Connecticut wit a passion and I'm not goin' back. I love Atlanta."

"I love Atlanta too but maybe we should just go back and regroup and come down here when we planned it better."

"What's gonna be so different about us bein' here now or us comin' back? We've come through the worst of it already, you workin', I'm workin', Wes is workin' and we good." I explained.

"I don't know man. We haven't done any new music since we moved into the new place. We ain't did no shows or nothin'. We were doin' so much more in Connecticut but here all we do is fuckin' work. The whole objective for comin' to this bitch was to get in a position where we wouldn't have to work. See what I'm sayin'?"

"I hear you but I ain't goin' back."

Kendra and M.Dot showered and change clothes and along with Wes we piled into the Sebring to head downtown to the World of Coca-Cola. It feels great to have all the important people in my life with me at one time. Kendra and M.Dot walked and talked together and seemed to be getting alone great which is a big relief from Tracy and I because M.Dot doesn't get along with females to well.

We hit up Dr. Jays after the world of coke with the nasty taste of the Beverly still in our throats because Tracy wanted to do a little shopping. The seven hundred dollars I have is burning a hole in my pocket and I don't know why I even brought all this money knowing damn well I can't spend it. I watched as Kendra looked at a few items in other stores and I wanted to pull out my wad and tell her to get what she wants.

"Syncere do you like this shirt?"

"Yeah it's real nice. Do you want it?"

"No, I don't need it."

"Pick ya size out."

"I can pay for it myself but I really don't need it, I really need some sneakers. You're not supposed to be spending money anyway." She reminded me.

"Why don't let me buy you things?"

"Because my momma told me to get the things I want on my own and don't depend on a guy for anything."

"I see where she is comin' from sort of. But I'm not just some guy tryin' to buy your affection or feelin's I'm ya boyfriend. Tell you what lemme buy ya sneakers for you."

"No, I already owe you two-hundred dollars from the money you sent me to fly down last month." Kendra reached into her back pocket and I grabbed her arm.

"That wasn't a loan. That was because I wanted you to come and see me and I didn't care how much it costs me, put that money back in your pocket."

"I need to pay you back." She insisted.

"Babe listen to me. No you don't, ok do this. Hold on to the money in case I need it next month ok. If I need it send it to me and if I don't it's yours to keep aight."

"Ok." Kendra smiled as she put her hand back in her back pocket and with her other hand she took hold of mine.

Back at home Kendra lay in my bed and I sat on her waist and thighs and caressed her stomach as I listened to her talk. It's as if we just picked up from where we left off from her last visit just like she'd never left in the first place. In the middle of Kendra's conversation my cell phone that is lying beside her. I looked over to see the name displayed on the screen, Diane. What the hell is she calling me for? I hope and pray she is not at my door because she only calls me when she is outside. I looked at Kendra who looked at me and I thought if I don't answer the phone Kendra will think I have something to hide and that can start an argument but on the flip side if I answer it and talk to Diane Kendra might think I'm disrespecting her.

"Hello."

"Hey, what'chu doin'?"

"Lying here with Kendra. What's good wit'chu?"

"Nothin'. I was gonna stop by but I'm glad I called first, I don't want to get you in trouble with your girlfriend."

"Na it would've been aight she ain't the jealous type like that."

"I just wanted to apologize for callin' you an asshole the other day and actin' like a young girl. I knew you had a girlfriend from the gate, I just thought our connection was more than just sex but I see your heart is else where."

"Na it's cool, you don't have to apologize. I haven't even thought about it since then, no biggie."

"Ok. Well since I won't see you at work anymore when your girl leaves I still wanna fuck you on the regular, can we still do that?"

"I don't know lemme think about it."

"What the fuck do you mean think about it?"

"Ill think about it." I repeated.

"Well I want you to think about it when you are explaining to your girlfriend why are a pair of blue panties in your room."

"What? Where?"

"Bye."

"Aight I'll holla at'chu later. Bye." I had to play it off so Kendra won't know something is going on. I thought for a minute, I don't remember Diane not putting on her panties the last time she was here then again I don't remember watching her getting dressed either. I wasn't out of the room except to get her something to drink so where could she have put them?

"Who was that?" Kendra asked.

"My friend Diane."

"Oh." Kendra's face has this look on it as if she know it is more to it than just Diane being my friend."

"What?"

"I told you I didn't want to deal with a bunch of girls calling you and coming by."

"She ain't even a girl like that, we just peoples from work. She's a white girl from Connecticut who just moved down here and we vibe at work. She even drove me home from a few times. That's all."

"So what did she apologize for?"

"The last time we worked together it was raining and she got off before me and didn't ask if I needed a ride home."

"So what do you have to think about?" Kendra asked another question without blinking.

"Huh?"

"You told her you'd think about it."

"Oh she heard about me gettin' fired and she asked was I goin' to try to work in another restaurant and I said I'll think about it."

"Ok, so why'd you sound so surprised?"

"She said our friend Precious got fired for the same thing and she's been workin' there for like three years, she got a little girl and shit so that is how she feeds her baby." That was the end of Kendra's questioning and I've told her three lies in a row without hesitation, not good Syncere.

"I'm sorry."

"For what?"

"Questioning you. I must sound like one of those insecure girlfriends huh?"

"Na you good. The only time you should worry about a phone call is if I don't answer the phone that is when you get suspicious. But my friends are just my friends you see I talked to her right in front of you and I said your name, it's nothin'.."

"Ok."

"So you don't want to move back to Connecticut?"

"Hell no, I hate it there."

"Why? Connecticut is your home."

"No home is where the heart is and my heart is in North Carolina."

"So when are you coming back?"

"I don't know if I want to, I want to stay in Georgia." I reveled.
"So what about all the things we talked about? Me at UNC and you at Saint Aug visiting each other on the weekends. Syncere, we do not have the money to be flying down here and to North Carolina every weekend."

"I know, I know. Look maybe you can come to school here."

"In Georgia?"

"Yeah. You got a scholarship to UNC right? Aren't those transferable or can't you apply for one to a school here?"

"I thought about going to Emory a few times because they have a decent program."

"You go to Emory and I'll go to Georgia State."

"You're gonna go back to school?"

"Yeah. I've always thought about doin' it and with the way things goin' here I need to be in school but I doubt if I'm goin' to be able to get a scholarship."

"Why?"

"It's been months since I've ran. I only run if the bus is passing me by, I can't remember the last time I stretched."

"So what are you going to do?"

"Probably apply for financial aid, you know loans and shit."

"You should apply for grants that way you won't have to pay them back."

"Yeah I'll look into it. So you'd really come to Georgia for me?"

"Yes. But would you be upset if I couldn't?"

"A little. I mean I like this, we're finally havin' a real relationship na mean? And in two weeks you're off to North Carolina and we have to work around you studying, midterms, finals…"

"Don't forget work study." She added.

"Damn. You're gonna have a full course load and then you'd need the weekends to study. Where if you were to go to school at Emory you can live here with me, we can take the bus downtown or when I get my car I drive you to class…"

"I have a car already remember."

"Right, see you can drive to class and I can drive to class then we can come back home and do the little things like help each other with our homework, talk you know just spend that quality time with one another. We need to see each other as often as we possibly can to give our relationship a fightin' chance na mean?"

"I agree with you all the way, it just might not be that easy. I would have to do at least a year at UNC since it is too late to change schools now. So if I do transfer it won't be until January of next year."

"I can wait that long but anything longer I don't know."

"What do you mean?"

"I mean I don't like bein' by myself for longs periods of time. I need my girlfriend with me. I need hugs, I need attention I need love na mean?"

"Syncere I need those things too. So you're saying if I don't transfer to Emory in a timely fashion you are going to find another girlfriend? Is that what you are saying?"

"I'm just sayin' I know how I get when I start missin' you."

"So why can't you wait just like I'm waiting? You think this is going to be easy for me too? Well it's not and I can't believe you're telling me you'll break up with me if I don't move down here."

"Kendra I'm not sayin' that."

"No! That is what you are saying! If you love me so much why can't you wait huh? I have your fucking name tattooed on my arm and now you tell me this?" Kendra and I are standing face to face with one another and I've never seen her so mad. Her chest is rising and falling with force and her eyes have anger, sadness and disappointment in them and I vowed never to have her look at me with such emotions.

"I do love you, I've loved you since I was fifteen years old and all I'm sayin' is now that I got a taste of how our relationship can be and I don't want to let'chu go. You're gonna be at UNC and I have to worry about guys and you bein' busy and a whole bunch of stuff."

"So why can't you wait? Weather it is six months or a year, why can't you wait just like I'm waiting?" I can't answer Kendra even as she searched my face for one.

"I'll try."

"You'll try? Unbelievable." She said as she pushed passed me and exited my room.

What am I supposed to tell Kendra? That deep beneath my persona of being over confident and arrogant I'm really insecure with myself? I'm jealous and afraid that she is going to go to UNC find some intellectual muhfucka or some hotshot football player and I'll be out of the picture. Do I tell her that I'm afraid all the skeletons in my closet are going to haunt me and make me reap what I soe? Or do I further tell her the truth, that I my dick has more control over my mind and I can only be faithful if she is here? What type of shit is that?

It's the truth but I can't tell Kendra the truth. If I do she may look at me for what I really am, a liar and a weak excuse for a man. Truth is I do love this girl, I love her like John 3:16, I'll die for her. So why can't I resist fucking with other women? I want the perfect woman, I have the perfect woman but I'm still playing Russian roulette knowing full well of the outcome. *GOD HELP ME!* Maybe after she settles down Kendra will think about it and see how much I do want to be with her. Maybe the thought of her loosing me can influence her decision. I know right now she thinks I don't love her and I'll easily run into the arms of another woman but once she thinks about what I said she won't see it like that.

I looked between my mattress, under my bed and my closets and dressers or Diane's blue panties and I can't find them anywhere. If I don't find them I won't have to worry about Kendra worrying about loosing me she'll leave me her damn self.

I sat in the living room with Ben, Tracy, Wes and our new neighbor Fahiem and listened to him talk about how many influential people he knows in the music business and how he can help up. Kendra, Faith and M. Dot walked from room to room talking and getting ready to have a ladies day out and after the argument Kendra and I had last night it'll do us some good to have some time apart. I want to take Kendra in the room to talk and smooth things out before she leaves but every time she sees me look at her she breaks eye contact or goes into the room.

I don't see why Kendra is so upset. I only want to express to her how much I want her to be here with me and ever since she's been visiting me it's been great. I see how much love and fun Ben and Faith have because they live together and I just want that same happiness. Ben is motivated by Faith and I know she doesn't know it but Kendra motivates me to better myself and my life, I just don't want to let her go.

"Syncere can you come into the room please?" I leapt off the couch at Kendra's request.

"What's good?"

"Are you going to be in the house all day?"

"Na, I got an appointment to get my hair dreaded and Ben and them are talkin' about goin' to some industry networkin' party with Fahiem tonight so we might do that."

"So you're leaving me with Faith and Michane all day?"

"Yeah, you're in good hands. Faith is cool and M.Dot seems to like you. If any goes wrong just call me on my cell and I'll come back home."

"Why are you going to that party tonight?"

"I don't know if I'm goin' yet but if I do it's to network with some people. I mean that's what Fahiem says, I guess I'll see if I go."

"I don't like him." She judged.

"You don't know him, you haven't even talked to him. Then again listenin' to him he sounds full of shit." I realized.

"So why are you considering going?"

"Just because I think he's bullshittin' doesn't mean he actually is. Plus Ben has been dealin' wit Fahiem since he moved in last month and I guess he's shown Ben some promise."

"Does this have anything to do with me?"

"What are you talkin' about?"

"Are you stayin' out because you are upset with me?"

"No, I have a hair appointment and then I might be goin' to a networkin' party. Not because I am mad at you but because you know what my dream is and you know what I came to Atlanta for."

"Ok Syncere if you say so."

"Kendra, I'm not mad at you. If I was mad I'll tell you that I'm mad but I'm gettin' mad at you thinkin' I'm mad. Wait, scratch that. Look I'm not mad at all, I've forgotten last night and I just want to move on and enjoy the rest of the time you're here ok?"

"OK."

"Where are ya'll goin'?"

"To the mall and I think out to lunch."

"You need money?"

"No."

"Ok, call me later or if you want me to come back home." I gave Kendra a kiss on the cheek and left the room. I sat back on the couch feeling a little better about Kendra and I just talking. I hope she realizes that I'm truly not upset and I hope she takes into heavy consideration going to school in Georgia.

"Syncere."

"Hey Faith what's wrong?"

"I'm callin' to tell you Kendra is mad at you."

"She's still mad at the argument we had last night?"

"No."

"Then what is she mad at now?"

"If you shut up I'll tell you. We were at lunch and she saw my sneakers and she asked me where did I get them. When I told her you gave them to me she's had an attitude ever since."

"Where are ya'll at now?"

"We still in the mall but she is using the bathroom, we are on our way home."

"Hold on I got Ben callin' me on the other line. What's good man I got Faith on the other line."

"What she doin' callin' you?"

"Be easy she tellin' me some shit about Kendra. What'chu want?"

"Yo man we 'bout to leave are you done yet?"

"Yeah I'm payin' the girl right now."

"Aight we comin' up there right now."

"Aight...Hello Faith? Aight, well ain't worried about it I'll talk to her about it when I get back. I'm in a good mood and I don't want to fuck my night but by arguin'."

"Oh yeah she's mad you're goin' to that party too."

"I asked her if it was alright and she told me yeah."

"Men are so stupid. Syncere it's her second day here and ya'll gonna spend all night at some party while she sits at home."

"But she got ya'll there."

"She ain't come here to see us, she came here to see you."

"Well I have to go because if I don't and we start arguin' about this stupid sneaker shit I'ma miss out on some shit tonight and I'ma be even more pissed off. So I'ma let her calm down, I'ma go with Ben and them to handle this and I'll deal with her when I get back."

"I think the best thing for you to do is come home and talk to her now because if you wait it'll just make it worse."

"Na I know her, I just gotta give her some time to herself. Hit me up later, thanks Diggs." Tracy, Ben and Wes picked me up and were dressed to kill for this so called industry networking party but for some strange reason I have a bad feeling about this, I have the feeling we are walking into a big disappointment. Kendra called twice while we were in the car but I ignored them both until Tracy said it would be best if I called her and not piss her off any further by not picking up when she called.

"Hey you called?"

"I called you twice, why weren't you picking up?"

"Because we were talkin', what's good? How was your day?"

"Why did you give Faith a pair of sneakers knowing that I need a new pair for school?"

"I told you I was goin' to buy yours before you left didn't I?"

"But why did you give Faith those shoes? You could've saved your money by just giving them to me!"

" I didn't give you them because they have been sittin' in my closet for like a month and I know you won't want them."

"How would you know? You didn't even ask me first."

"Kendra, look. We've arrive at the party and I don't wanna get into this right now so we'll talk about it when I get back ok?"

Click! Dial tone.

I walked into my room cautiously finding her sitting in my lounge chair reading a book. She looked up when I walked in, said a low hi as I returned the comment while taking off my shoes. It's too early to tell if she is still upset but we will see.

"How was the party?" she asked pleasantly.

"It was some bullshit, we left Ben there. It had nothing to do wit music." I groaned.

"Oh. Syncere… I apologize about earlier? She said softly.

"It's aight. Faith should'a told you why I gave her those sneakers instead of leaving you to think I just shitted on you."
"Why did you give them to her then? And why didn't you tell me?"

"They've been collecting dust for a month now since I couldn't find the receipt I didn't know what to do with them. So I gave them to Diggs." I explained.
"They are female sneakers Syncere, who were they for?"

"My friend from Saint Aug Sherrica. I was supposed to give them to her the last time I was in North Carolina but I never got up wit her."
"Was that the time you saw me?"

"Yea why?"

"So you came to North Carolina to see her?"
"Na, I went to North Carolina to see my family. It just so happens I saw her a month prior and we talked up until the last time I was there."
"So how'd she know you were coming the last time?"

"Like I said we were talkin' so she knew."
"Why didn't you call me? Did you call Trisha?"

"I did call you and yes I did call Trisha as well."

"Did you call her before or after you got to North Carolina?"

"Before, what's the point?"

"The point is why did you wait until you were in North Carolina to call me? If you loved me so much why was I the last person you called?"

"Oh my god! We weren't even talkin' and Trisha and I have been ever since I got down here. Okay, okay I saw Sherrica when Ben and I went to Saint Aug. It's not like I went there lookin' for her but we kinda bumped into each other. So you're upset that I didn't call you?"

"No, I'm upset because you only called me when you couldn't get in touch with the other two girls."

"How do you know?"

"Because you still have the shoes don't you? If they would've answered or if you would've seen them would you have called me?"

"Probably not. I didn't even know you were home from school; it didn't dawn on me until I actually got in North Carolina that you may be home from Exeter. I didn't know when you graduated. How you gonna get mad at me 'cause I may have not called you? You didn't call me."

"I'm not the one who left you stranded on Thanksgiving! Do you know what I did that weekend?"

"Yes you told me already." I mumbled.

"No I don't think you understand Syncere. I was with strangers when I could've been with my family who I hadn't seen in months. But no, I'm stuck in New Hampshire while you move up and down the east coast talking to Trisha and buying girls shoes. Is she the real reason you moved to Georgia?"

"Oh yeah Kendra. I'm secretly seein' Trisha and I just made all my boys move down here with me so I can pursue my relationship, oh yeah that's what it is. For your information Trisha goes to school at Winston Salem State and ok I brought a friend a pair of shoes so what is the big deal in that? She looked out for me while I was sick in college while you were out here playin' fuckin' house with Quami, bringin' the nigga by my fuckin' dorm and shit like I really wanted to meet him. You wanna talk about fucked up shit? Why did you invite me to church that Sunday but show up with Quami?

"So is that what this is all about, payback? You stood me up because you were upset about me and Quami?"

"No. I don't hold grudges like that especially with you so don't try to put words in my mouth. You're makin' a big fuckin' deal outta me givin' Faith a pair of sneakers that I brought for someone else. How would it look if I buy a pair of shoes for some other chick then I give them to you? How that look? So yeah I gave them to Faith and I didn't tell you because it ain't that serious." I explained trying not to raise my voice.

"You're right Syncere and I'm wrong, I apologize."

"It's not about bein' right and wrong. I'm just tryin' to make you realize that I didn't just give her sneakers because I wanted to. I don't want to give you something that was intended for another girl friend or not."

"Ok." I know Kendra is just saying ok to stop the conversation because she doesn't want to talk about it anymore, which pisses me off because she is not trying to hear what I have to say. She knows that I'm not going to change my mind about how I feel about the situation and she feels just as strong so in a way we are beating a dead horse. I undressed, brushed my teeth and went to sleep.

The sunlight pierced my eyes as I squinted and ducked under the covers and when I opened my eyes to see the left side of my bed is empty. I jumped out of bed to see a pair of black Enyce jeans and a matching black and gray shirt placed on top of it. *Where did this come from?* I thought and just as the words were silently rolling off my tongue Kendra entered the room eating a muffin.

"Mornin'." I greeted her still a little confused.

"Good morning Syncere. You like it?"

"Yeah. Where did you get this from?"

"A store in the mall when I was out with Faith and Michane the yesterday. It's my way of saying thank you for putting up with me."

"Thanks but you didn't have to buy me an outfit and I'm not puttin' up wit you, where did that come from?"

"I talked to Faith and she confirmed your store. I apologize for last night."

"Na its no biggie. Just know that I wouldn't do anything to hurt you and I'd never give to someone else before I give to you."

"Ok. And that is what pissed me off last night. I went out and spent my money, money that I really don't have and I brought you an outfit. Then I come to find out that you gave Faith a pair of shoes. I thought to myself I could've used that money. I overreacted." Kendra said dropping her head. I can't help but to laugh on the inside at the way she beats herself up when she feels like she's made a mistake.

"What'chu eatin'?"

"Blueberry muffin, want one?" she handed me a piece.

"This is good, you made these or did you go to Dunkin Donuts?"

"No I made them. I didn't use that Jiffy crap you have in the cabinet; I went to the store with Tracy and picked these up. Want another one?"

"Hell yeah."

Kendra and I sat silently on the bus as it rode down Powers Ferry Road. It is hot as hell today and the little vent on top of the bus only provided a slight breeze but only as it is in motion. Kendra has insisted on coming on my job hunt with me to offer support but I honestly don't want her here and the more and more I think about it the more and more it pisses me off. What is pissing me off more is the fact that I can't tell Kendra I don't want her here. I mean most men wish their girlfriends and wives support them in their time of despair but I am different.

I look at the scenario differently and I feel less of a man to have my girlfriend tagging along while I look for a job. Thoughts of waiting until Kendra leaves to look for a job creep into my mind as I stare out the window scanning every plaza for now hiring or help wanted signs. But the thoughts quickly vanish by the empty feel I have in my pockets. This is not the idea of spending time with Kendra that I had a week ago. I was supposed to go to my job at the Olive Garden and come home to the open arms of Kendra. She'd read to me the way she use then we'd have stimulating conversation, discuss our future together before making love. It was supposed to be the way I always dreamed it would be.

Instead we argue over stupid things and I can't even remember how they originated in the first place. To make matters worse we go to sleep without talking to each other some nights and we have awkward silences where we don't know what the other is thinking and that make me extremely uncomfortable. I can go months without talking to Kendra over the phone but I can't go five minutes without her conversation and smile in person and every minute feel like a month.

Kendra sat outside Houston's Restaurant while I went in and filled out an application and tried to talk to a manager in hopes of speeding up the hiring process. I can see her sitting on a ledge sweating while I sit at the bar in the air conditioned restaurant thinkin I just want to get her back home because she has no business following me around like a lost dog.

Nevertheless I'm trying my best to hide my outside bullshit and seem confident while I speak to the manager but to no avail. I know when I walked out those doors I didn't get the job, no the manger didn't say that directly but I heard it in his tone and my anger is only building. Outside Kendra said nothing to me and as I said nothing to her when I signaled with my head that we are leaving. We waited for the bus in silence and I'm growing angrier at the fact Kendra isn't saying anything to me. If she insisted on coming with me the least she can do is talk to me instead of acting like we're two strangers waiting on the same bus.

I whispered the Lord's prayer under my breath and asked God to take the anger I had in me and replace it with something good because I can only imagine the vibe I'm giving off to Kendra. Searching for a job reminds me of when we first moved to Georgia and we were staying with Shawyna then in that crummy motel because we didn't have any money. My only thought is I don't want to put us in the risk of getting evicted due to the fact I can't come up with my third of the rent.

I thought about going back to school in North Carolina but also thought I can get my big break here in Atlanta and sign that multi-platinum recording deal I've been dreaming about. This is a fucked up feeling, no money, no job, and thirty days away from being homeless again. My girlfriend won't talk to me, my mother abandoned me and I'm not doing any music.

"Syncere what are you doing? Syncere!"

I hear Kendra's faint voice behind me while walking aimlessly in the middle of the street escaping being hit by one of the speeding cars that passed. Fuck it, I should end it all now right? I turned around a looked at Kendra barley standing on the curb while she shouted my name over and over again. Her face filled with sadness, concern, fear and tears made me get all emotional and I began thinking about what I am actually doing. I didn't fight back the tears streaming down my face as I walked back over toward my crying girlfriend. I hugged her as if I'm on my way to the electric chair and I cried letting out everything I have bottled up and Kendra said nothing. She held me just as tight and let out some cries of her own and I'm thinking that I have a woman that is there for me and here I am for the second time in my life trying to kill myself and for what?

After almost a full night of convincing Just Faith and Kendra go Ben and I to go to the underground to see a damn psychic. At first she didn't tell me what we are going down here for. She tried to spin it by telling me she wants me to help her pick out a pair of running shoes. When I shot down her request the psychic thing slipped out.

"O' Syncere stop being so closed minded and com'on. Ben and I do this all the time." Faith said while I walk slower than a slug throughout the mall.

"Fuck it, I have a question anyway." I watched on as Ben obviously received good news from the braided psychic then Kendra and I watched Faith walk away with a smile and I'm thinking I really don't want to be here.

"You don't have to do this if you don't want to." Kendra said whispering to me.

"Na you want to so it's no biggie na mean? You believe in this shit?"

"I don't know."

"So why do you want to do it?"

"Just something to do. I've never done it before, it might be fun."

"Aight." I watched Kendra sit down at the table hesitating for a moment and I'm not sure of what is going on.

"Can you stand over there with Ben and Faith please?" She turned to ask me while shooing me away.

"You're not gonna let me hear?" I asked surprised.

"No, I don't want you to."

"Will you tell me later?"

"No."

"Why not?"

"Because. Let's make a deal, I wont tell you and you don't tell me ok?"

"Na I don't like that."

"Please? For me?" she pleaded until I reluctantly abided.

"Oh aight, that's what's up. Well I'm up." Kendra held my hand when tried to walk away but let it go after I asked her to tell me what is wrong a few times. Ben and Faith look so happy together as they discussed what the physic told them and I wish I could share that kind of joy with Kendra. She didn't say it but the psychic must not have told her what she wants to hear because the joy present in Ben and Faith is absent in Kendra.

"Is there anything specific you would like to know?"
"You tell me, you're the psychic remember?"

"You want to know if that young woman loves you don't you."

"Anyone could guess that." I responded unimpressed.

"You want to know if you will be with her forever…you want to know if she is right for you." She continued getting closer to my face widening her eyes.

"So."

"No."

"No what? I didn't even ask you anything." I snapped.

"She is not the woman for you. She will love you as you will love her but the relationship will last briefly and ultimately end in disaster. The woman for you is a woman not born of this country."

"Bullshit!" I said before stuffing five dollars in her cup then stomping away. What does she mean by last a brief time? Is this time our brief time? We have been fighting constantly with a week left and I don't want to leave with us not speaking to one another.

Hot water runs over my back and shoulders with so much force that it feels like a great heated massage and I need one after today. Letting the water run over my face for a while I continued to think about a future without Kendra which is a concept I thought about in her absence but I've never had to actually grasp that reality. What if that woman doesn't really know what she is talking about? I mean truthfully the only person to know what is to come is the Lord and nowhere in the Bible does it say God revels his plans to psychics.

If Kendra and I aren't going to be together it will be because we didn't do all we possibly could to build and save our relationship and not because some woman with bones for a necklace and nappy hair said we wouldn't. Do all we possibly could means me moving back to North Carolina. I want to bear witness to Kendra's every triumph and console her every defeat and not have to be hours away when she needs me the most and vice versa.

"You hungry?" I asked walking back into my room with a towel around my waist.

"No."

"You're not gonna eat?"

"No…Trisha called." She reveled less than happy about it.

"Where's my phone?"

"Here."

"You answered my phone?"

"No, I looked at the caller id to see who it was."

"Why?"

"Why are you still talking to her?"

"'Cause we are friends that's why."

"Really? Does your "friend" know I'm staying here with you right now?"

"Uh yeah." I said sarcastically. "That is why she still called. If I was doin' somethin' wit her I would've told her not to 'cause I assured her my girlfriend isn't the jealous type."

"Is that what you told all you're other girls like Diane? Call anyway so I don't look suspicious?" she continued slapping my phone out of my hand.

"What tha fuck is wit'chu?"

"Don't curse at me."

"I'm not cursin' at you I'm cursin' at tha situation. Why are you insisting I'm hidin' all these girls from you? Where is this comin' from?"

"You always have a bunch of girls ever since I've known you. I had to listen to all your stories about all your girls in Connecticut and hear it in your music and see freaking pictures everywhere so stop lying to me. You're still talking to Trisha, why didn't you tell me?"

"The same damn reason why you didn't tell me you were talkin' to Quami when I was at school. I don't see what the point is tellin' you every person or every girl I "talk" to and that's all I do I talk. We're friends, nothin' more. If it was somthin' more I would have them here and not you." I stressed.

"The big deal is I'm out here spending money on you trying to do everything I see Faith do for Ben and Michane do for Tracy trying to be this perfect girlfriend you make me out to be and you're talking to your ex."

"Kendra, I never asked you to buy me anything and I never said you have to be perfect. If I tell you Trisha and I are friends then that is what we are. But if you got a problem spendin' money on me then take the shit back because I don't want it. I never asked you to act like Faith and Michane, I fell in love with the way you treated me before you met Michane and Faith so what are you talkin' about?"

"You're talking to Trisha…"

"Would you get tha fuck off Trisha!!" I shouted.

"No because you're the one talking to her. I'm sitting around here stressing trying to figure out how I am going to move to Georgia so I can be with you because you can't stay faithful and I find out you're talking to other girls. Why do you disrespect me like that?"

"You want me to call Trisha back and tell her not to call me ever again? Want me to call all my female friends back home and tell them never to call me again? Is that what you want me to do then I will do it." I offered picking up the phone and dialing Trisha's number.

"Whatever do what you want."

"Whatever? It's whatever now? Aight." I slipped on my Iverson's and stormed out of the house.

"Syncere...Syncere wait...Syncere!!" she called for me but all I see is the entrance of the sub-division. Then what the psychic said replayed in my head making me turn around to run after her.

"Wait."

"What?"

"Why are you actin' like this?" I asked gently.

"Like what? Like a pissed off girlfriend? Well that is exactly what I am, a pissed off girlfriend."

"Kendra there is no other woman on this spinnin' earth that I want to be with. I don't want to be wit Diane and I don't want to be with Trisha. I want to be with Kendra Lewis."

"Yeah while I'm here. But what happens if I can't move to Georgia? Are you going to get tired of waiting and look for someone else?"

"I don't know. I don't wanna look for someone else but you never know who is going to come into your life, you said it yourself. Right not I want to only be with you and I have felt like this for as long as I can remember." I explained trying to throw in a little reverse psychology.

"You want to be with me right now but again, what happens in six months? Then what?" I didn't respond.

I'm sit ting up completely waiting for Kendra to tiptoe back into my room. In front of my door are her three bags she came down here with when it I realized that she's trying to leave. Leave like a thief in the night without telling me.

"What are you doing?" I startled her with my question.

"I'm leaving." She responded without emotion.

"Why every time we get in an argument you threaten to leave?"

"I'm not threatening I'm really leaving."

"So is that what we do now? We just walk out on one another when we don't see eye to eye? We've been fightin' to be together so long and now you were plannin' on walkin' out on me in the middle of the night when I was asleep? What are you runnin' from?" I challenged.

"Syncere I want to be with you so so badly but I can't live up to your expectations. I can't be the perfect girl you want me to be, I just don't know how to do that. When I try to help you get mad, when I don't help you get mad and when I don't do anything at all you get mad. It seems like you're always upset with me and I cant handle that. I'm just not the girl for you."

"Yes you are. Not every couple has a perfect relationship just look at Tracy and Michane. How many times have they argued since you've been here? Ben and Faith almost came to blows and they all still love each other." I explained.

"Syncere, you always have a way of talking me down and making me stay but it isn't going to work this time. I've made up my mind and the best thing for Kendra to do is just leave."

"Fine...fuck it then leave." I jumped out of bed taking my cell phone with me and the only person I can think to call is aunt Dimpsey.

"Syncere when you're done can I talk to you?" Kendra said inching from around the corner.

"Yeah." I said immediately getting off the phone.

"Syncere why do you put up with me?"

"What kind of question is that?"

"Can you just answer it for me please? I really need to know."

"I don't see it as puttin' up wit'chu but if you put it like that then I do it because I love you, unconditionally. I love you when we are makin' it, I love you when we are shoutin' at each other at the top of our lungs, I...love...you Kendra. The whole Kendra. The good, the bad, the uncertain, confused and everything." I explained being totally honest.

"How do you know?"

"I just do. It's the funny feelin' I get in the bottom of my stomach and the unbearable pain I feel when we aren't talkin' to each other. Please don't leave."

"Why? Why do you want me stay so bad."

"I just told you why."

"Tell me again." She said smiling at me as I smiled back before giving her a soft sensual kiss on the cheek. Then I got down on one knee in front of her loosening my shoestrings slipping off her sneakers and socks. She allowed me to unzip her hoodie pull her shirt off and I can't do anything but stare at her magnificent sculpture. Then I extended my hand and said,

"Come lay with me." She abided and we slept holding hands so tight that they grew sweaty and hurt a little but I love it.

13

"Syncere do you know a guy named Mulan?"

"Who? What type of name is that, Mulan? He from Connecticut?"

"No he's from Atlanta."

"No, why would I know him?" I asked curiously.

"Because he knows you."

"No he doesn't. The nigga might know of me but he don't know me. Where he say he know me from?"

"He said he saw you perform at some club called the Shark Bar?"

"Oh that's the show me and Ben did. How did I come up?"

"He saw your picture."

"How?" I said controlling my temper but I know where this is going.

"I keep it on my dresser."

"In your room?"

"Yeah."

"What tha fuck is a nigga doin' in your room Kendra?"

"I'm tutoring him."

"Kendra tha nigga needs a tutor already and classes haven't even started yet?"

"He just wants to get a jump on classes that's all. There is a lot of required reading. You know how it is the first couple weeks. No one wants to feel like they aren't up to speed with everyone else."

"Kendra, what did I tell you? The first three weeks of classes freshman women are targeted as being naive and stupid and every nigga you meet just wants to fuck you." I explained just as I explained before she left Atlanta two weeks ago.

"Syncere not every guy is like that."

"Maybe not but this nigga is, I know niggas man I'm tellin' you."

"Why would he try to get with me if he knows I have a boyfriend? I showed him my tattoo."

"Did you tell him I don't go to school there?"

"Yes, why?"

"Ok lemme tell you how niggas work, especially in college. Niggas look for smart looking girls like you for one. Then they make sure your boyfriend doesn't go to school and they wait. They will be ya "friend" and all that shit but what that really means is he's gonna stick around and be cool with you and give you someone to talk to but at the first sign of trouble with your boyfriend your "friend" starts to ease on in there and before you know it ya'll fuckin'." I outlined painting a picture that even Kendra can see despite her naïve notion that everyone is genuine.

"Syncere you know I'm not like that."

"Baby I trust you, I don't trust them muhfuckas in college. I'm not being paranoid I'm just tellin' you the truth. I've done it before, hell I was doin' it in high school. It's a waitin' game. A nigga will wait…and wait…and wait all semester. The longer a nigga waits depends on how much he is interested but I waited for girls to break up wit they boyfriends and I jumped on it. Just be careful please and if anything pops off wit this muhfucka you let me know."

"I know, I will. I do need something from you."

"What is it?"

"I need to borrow two hundred dollars for books. My scholarship doesn't cover then and I haven't started my work study yet."

"So use the two-hundred you owe me."

"But what about you? You haven't found a job yet."

"I'll get one. Are you excited about classes tomorrow?"

"Yeah. I'm a little nervous though. I start work study tomorrow and as soon as I get my first check I will send you the money back ok?"

" Yeah, but what are you nervous about? You'll do fine, you were born for this school."

"I know. I just really really wish you were here with me. You know if you were still at Saint Aug right now I'd drive to your school and spend the night with you. I miss sleeping with you and ever since I got back home sleeping without you feels a little strange. I sleep in your Enyce shirt every night and it still smells like you."

"Guess what?"

"What?"

"I still have your panties up."

"Syncere take those down. I didn't mean for you to actually leave them up."

"Na I'm keepin' them up there. I told you I'm gonna leave them up and I'ma leave them up."

"You're crazy."

"Yep crazy about'chu."

"Is that so?"

"Very much so. Listen I've been thinkin'."

"That's never good." She joked.

"Oh really? Na seriously. I thought about when I asked you to move to Georgia to be with me."

"What about it?"

"Well I figured since I pretty much talked and begged you into goin' to North Carolina I thought it is inconsiderate for me to ask you to transfer to Georgia and even worse get upset when you said it might not be possible."

"Ok. Where are you going with this?"

"I have decided I'm gonna move back to North Carolina in January, I've already made the preparations."

"Syncere is this what you really want to do?"

"I really want to be with you so if this is what I have to do then I will do it."

"Syncere, I appreciate you thinking of me but I just want you to make sure this is something you want. It's not just me you have to think about, you have to think about your education as well."

"I did and I figured I can get an education anywhere but you are only in one place so that is where I'm goin' to get my education."

"Ok, if that is what you want to do."

"It is. Why do you sound like you're not happy or you don't want me to come?"

"It's not that, like I said I just want you to make sure this is what you want and you're not doing it for me."

"Aight." I responded with mix feelings about her comments.

"What does that mean?"

"It means I understand what you are sayin'."

"And?"

"And I'm comin' anyway."

"Good."

"Good?"

"Yeah, I had to see if you were sincere."

"Why didn't you just ask me?"

"Because you never give me a direct answer. I have to act one way or trick you in order to get you to tell me how you really feel."

"No you don't."

"Yes I do, I know you Syncere."

"If you know me so well then what am I thinkin'?"

"I said I know you, I didn't say I'm a mind reader."

"Take a shot. What am I thinkin' right now?"

"You love me?"

"Maybe."

"Maybe? You better."

"I do."

"I know." She said.

The minute Tracy and I dropped Kendra off at the airport I hit the job search hard but to no avail. I went to almost every restaurant in Marietta and all said the same thing; they'll get back to me if something opens up. I cursed the dwarf of a manager Nima at the Finish Line in the Cumberland mall for promising me an assistant manager position then backing out when I moved down here. Reaching in my back pocket feeling nothing but a few measly dollars has me desperate to find work. I have a little less than two weeks to find a job and scrap this money up. I tried calling my aunt Dimpsey but she has my three cousins to take care of. Despite of the fact she said she'd call me before the week is out. Other than her promise I have nothing else to go on.

Every night Kendra and I spend talking on the phone I can only think about the nigga she had in her room and the jokes that Tracy, Wes and Ben make about me being stupid to believe Kendra won't

cheat on me. I've made so many girls cheat on their boyfriends when I was in school so what makes me think I am any exception. Kendra is an intelligent beautiful young woman to is easily likeable. Any guy with half a brain can see that she is something worth holing on to and that is what scares me the most. All her life people have separated Kendra her age because intellectually they weren't on her level but now she's in college where more than half the guys on campus are up to her speed. Let's not forget the fact she is dying to make friends, something she couldn't do at Exeter makes for a recipe that'll have me thinking about where she is, what she is doing and with who. Wow is this how this feels to worry if someone is going to run out on you? Is this the way Kendra felt when she witnessed Jewa and I sneaking out of the old sanctuary? Is this the way she felt when Trevor told her about Evelyn? Or is this the way she felt when I told her I can't be faithful without her here with me?

"Guess what?" Kendra said the minute I said hello.

"What?"

"I'm going out to a club with some friends tonight!"

"That's what's up, who?"

"Mulan and his friends." She answered as my blood begins to boil.

"Mulan...the football player that you are tutorin'? Why him?"

"Yeah, why do you sound like that?"

"Be careful. Remember what I told you about niggas and waitin'." I warned again.

"Did you talk to Tracy or Ben about when I told you about Mulan?"

"Of course I did why?"

"What did they say?"

"Nothin'."

"Did they really say nothin' or are you just saying that?"

"I'm just sayin' that."

"Then what did they say?"

"They are bias and close minded to the situation." I said dodging the answer.

"So why did you talk to them?"

"I was really talkin' to Faith because I know how Tracy and Ben would react but they butted in. It's just us in the house so I don't have too many options you know?"

"So what did they say?"

"Tracy and Ben said I'm stupid for trynna be wit'chu when I am here and you are there. They said that there are so many dudes in college and so much goes on that I don't know about."

"And what did Faith say?"

"Faith is the voice of reason. She said not to listen to the caveman Ben or Tracy and to trust you and I guess that's all I needed to hear." I said.

"Why did you need to hear it?"

"I just did. Uncertainly sets in sometimes. When I don't reach you on your cell or when I haven't heard from you all day you know? I know of some of those things I think you're doin' I only think about them because that's what I was doin' na mean? Do you trust me down while you're not here?"

"Yes. Do you trust me?"

"Of course I do."

"So why'd you ask me if I trusted you?"

"Because sometimes you just need to hear it na mean? Like I need to hear you miss me, I need to hear you love me and I also need to hear you trust me. When I'm feelin' jealous I look at our picture and your panties, ha ha, and I hear you sayin' those things in my head and it's enough to keep me goin' na mean?"

"Yeah."

"Just promise me one thing."

"Yes."

"Don't drink anything anyone gives you and make sure you watch the bartender make your drink."

"Ok."

I feel the warmth of Kendra's body in front of me. I inched getting as close as possible smelling her toasted vanilla body spray that is intoxicating to the point I'm getting turned on. I pressed my face against her oh so soft skin and smiled at the thought of her being here.

"Good mornin' babe." I said but got no answer. I kissed her on the cheek then opened my eyes to find myself clenching the hell out of my pillow. I sat up punching the pillow before throwing it against the wall out of frustration; *I can't do this* I whispered to myself. *Yes I can…no you can't…where is my phone* I thought.

While the phone rang I anticipated the sweet sound of Kendra's country voice but ended up punching my bed at the fact I reached her voice mail instead. It's eight o'clock in the morning so why isn't she answering her damn phone. *Class, she's in class Syncere* I told myself over and over trying to calm down and stop the flow of negative things rushing into my brain.

"I left my phone in my dorm last night because I knew I wouldn't have heard it anyway." She explained when I finally got her on the phone.

"So why didn't you call me this mornin'?"

"I over slept and was late for class. Tausha called and begged me to bring her up here so I did thinking it would do her some good to show her where she has the potential to go."

"So why didn't you call me when I called you two hours ago?"

"I was still with Tausha and you know she still hates you so I didn't want to throw it in her face that I was talking to you."

"Aight."

"Guess what I did manage to do today?"

"What?" I said sounding unenthusiastic.

"I got the entire football team to autograph a jersey for you. I was gonna mail it to you for your birthday but that's two months away and I couldn't wait to tell you."

"That shouldn't've been hard seeing as though you are tutorin' one of the players." I threw in her face.

"Don't say it like that."

"Like what?"

"Like you're suspicious or something."

"Do I have to be?"

"Syncere no, you know I would never do anything to hurt you. Mulan and I are just friends and he got his team to autograph the jersey because I asked him to."

"I don't like the football team. Get the basketball team to autograph a jersey for me."

"I don't know any of the players."

"Tutor one." I said sarcastically.

"Ok Syncere what is the problem? Are you upset with me?"

"Na, I just don't like you and this muhfucka spendin' so much time together. You tutor him, I don't like it but I'm aight wit it because it's for school. But as far as ya'll goin' out and him doin' favors for you I think he up to somethin'."

"How do you think that and you don't know him? I think you two should talk."

"Talk! What tha fuck I wanna talk to him for? And why are you defendin' him?"

"I'm not defending him. I just thought if ya'll talked you would feel a little better about me tutoring him."

"Just the mere fact that you asked me to talk to this nigga takes my uncomfortably level sky high right now. This is Quami all over again."

"Oh what is this? Are you doing dirt and now you're trying to justify it by lashing out on me? Is this your way of trying to push me away because it's been a month and a half and now you can't wait any longer? What did you find someone new?" She attacked.

"What...tha...fuck are you talkin' about? All I do is go to work and come home day in and day out every single day. And every day I wake up I mark off the fuckin' calendar as a countdown to when I'm gonna see you again. So don't sit there and try to pass your guilt onto me. You got some fuckin' nerve. Tell me the truth Kendra, do you like this dude?"

"No. I'm with you, I'm in love with you and unlike you I have the ability to like only one person at a time." Click!

For the next two weeks Kendra and I didn't dial each other's numbers and I would be a lie if I said I'm not thinking about her and Mulan. I threw myself into my job at the Green Papaya, a Vietnamese French Cuisine placed I started at almost a month ago. Dealing with the Kendra situation would be that much harder if I wasn't working because I'd be at home all day or riding the bus thinking about it. At least now I have some ease to my mind knowing I'm not going to get us all evicted. That leaving me to only have to think about Kendra when I am at home and nine o'clock rolls around without my phone ringing.

I can't help but to think I've pushed Kendra into the arms of another man by being jealous. This girl has done nothing but love me even after I've shitted on her twice and in return I'm accusing her of cheating. Still that little voice in the back of my mind is telling that Kendra is hiding something. I've had to endure her talking about Mulan every single time we spoke and quite frankly I'm annoyed. What man wants to listen to his significant other rant and rave about a guy she sees in a daily basis? Its things like that the reason I think the way I do. Call it paranoid but I know my girlfriend and she likes this guy. Being the wonderful woman that she is she's going to ignore how she feels inside because she thinks it's wrong. Call me crazy but I'd rather she come out and tell me so she can be happy but I feel like she's insulting my intelligence by denying it. Would it hurt? Hell yea, it'll hurt like hell. But I already told myself I want to see her happy even if its not with me.

Sitting on the bus looking out the window at the Atlanta skyline I thought of this past summer when Kendra was here, then my phone rang. A 919 area code and just like that everything went away.

"Hello." I said trying not to sound too enthusiastic.

"Syncere?"

"Yeah, how you been?"

"Good I guess. Are you still upset with me?" she asked in the softest voice possible.

"Why do you guess?"

"I don't know. I'm a little upset but it's nothing. How's the new job going?"

"Fine. Why are you upset?" I persisted.

"Nothing…"

"It's about Mulan isn't it?"

"Yeah but I don't want to talk about it. I haven't spoken to you in three weeks so what's up?"

"Kendra it sounds like you like this dude." I said getting frustrated all over again.

"What! No. I'm just upset that he ditched my tutoring session and when I went to his room to find out why I discover he is with some white girl."

"If you don't like him then why are you so mad at everything he does. I told you not to fuck wit'em no more. So he didn't show, fuck it. He's the one that's gonna fail not you so just charge it to the game."

"Do what?"

"It's a metaphor that means chalk it up you know? Let bygones be bygones."

"You just should've seen him laughing and giggling in each other's faces like they don't have a care in the world." She detailed. "Make me sick to my stomach.

"Kendra let it go, what do you care? You sound like a jealous girlfriend. Look, remember that day we went and got tattoos and you told me you can't help who you like?"

"Yeah."

"Well this is what it sounds like to me. It sounds like you like this dude but you are trying not too or you're just tellin' me you don't. Either way there is somethin' there that you feel and you are ignorin' it." I explained.

"So you're tellin' me I should date him?"

"Fuck no. All I'm sayin' is acknowledge somethin' is there and cut'em off. Be done with it. Or tell me that you don't want to be with me 'cause you like him. Spare someone's feelings."

"I can't."

"Fuck you mean you can't?"

"All I want is a friend."

"Kendra 40,000 students go to UNC and you can't let go of one? Lemme tell you somethin'. All these muhfuckas you see in college aren't doin' anything for you. They are not payin' your tuition, they are not takin' your tests and they certainly aren't givin' you ya degree so what is the big deal." I explained.

"You told me that college is thirty percent knowledge and seventy percent networking. Remember. Some of these people can get me what I need after college."

"Yeah I understand that but what is this nigga gonna get you after college? Season tickets to the Carolina Panthers home games? This sound like some bullshit."

"Why are you so upset?"

"Because. I'm sittin' here listening to you tell me how much you hate this guy, how he stands you up for sessions and in the same breath you're tellin' me you can't cut'em off? What type of shit is that?"

"I don't know."

"What do you mean you don't know?"

"I don't know."

"Call me tomorrow." I said out of aggravation.

"Don't hang up. I don't want to hang up like this."

"Like what?"

"You being mad at me."

"I'm not mad." I claimed.

"Yes you are, I can hear it in your voice."

"Na I'm good."

"I love you." She said out of left field.

"Love you too." I hung up the phone irritated at the fact we're having the same argument all over again. In the last three weeks nothing has changed except nonverbal conformation of what I already know.

"Syncere?" she said calling back.

"Yeah."

"Why didn't you say I love you?"

"I did."

"No you said love you but you didn't say I love you." She differentiated.

"Ok, I love you."

"But why'd you say love you instead of I love you."

"Kendra, I didn't think it would make a difference."

"Well does it." She snapped.

"What leavin' out the I? No."

"Ok."

"It doesn't."

"I said ok." She repeated.

"No you say it like you don't believe me."

"I do. Goodnight Syncere."

"I love you."

I didn't sleep much as the night drug on and on into the wee hours of the morning. I was starting to I feel closer to Kendra than we ever have been I now feel further than we've ever been. No matter what is going on every night at nine o'clock like clock work she rings my cell and we pick our conversations up from where we left off the night before. I think she feels a little animosity for me not making good on my promise of being in school when she started so I think this whole Mulan thing is her way of making me jealous. Reverse psychology like I tried on her when I said I don't know if I could stay faithful unless she in Georgia.

I never told her but every time we talk on the phone it feels like déjà vu. It feels like the day I first called her. The butterflies in my stomach and the sweat on my palms are still present even four years later. The sweetness in her voice makes my interior guard melt like candle wax the moment she opens her mouth. I missed talking to her so much after we broke up the first time that I'd play back every conversation we've ever had. *Damn I got it bad* I thought. Even with all that said I still listen to Kendra complain about Mulan this time without complaining because I'm trying really hard to understand where she is coming from. I desperately want to believe she doesn't like this dude but that little voice in the back of my mind tells me otherwise.

Like right now my mind is elsewhere while Kendra goes on and on about her and Tasha stealing Mulan's wallet and locking him out of his dorm. Not only do I have to worry about Kendra liking this guy now I have to worry about him hitting her or getting her beat up for what she's done

"Kendra why did you do that?" I asked sounding really agitated.

"Because he was with some other girl and he acted like I wasn't even there."

"So…"

"So that is disrespectful. Him and her all hugged up." She complained.

"Kendra I'ma ask you this again…do you like this nigga?"

"No! Why do you keep asking me that?"

"Because listen to you. Look at yourself. You sound like a jealous chick right now. You got upset 'cause he's with some other bitch so you steal his money, throw his wallet out the window and lock him out his room for the weekend. What are you doin'?"

"Tasha stole his money not me." She said dodging responsibility.

"It doesn't matter who did it, shit it's done now. What's to stop this nigga from comin' to ya dorm and beatin' ya ass for that? Huh? Then I'ma have to come to North Carolina and kill'em. Are you even thinkin' at all? I told you weeks ago to cut tha muhfucka off, do you want a friend that bad?"

"No."

"So what's the problem? Why can't you cut him off?"

"I don't know."

"I know why, because deep down inside you like him but you don't want to and more importantly you want him to only notice you! You buggin'. You don't know this nigga or nothin'. Now I gotta sit here all night and hope he don't put his fuckin' hands on you."

"Syncere he's not going to do anything." She said sounding confident and unworried.

"How you know? Ya'll cool like that?" What the fuck man?"

"Why are you getting so upset?"

"'Cause you actin' real stupid right now!"

"Don't call me stupid."

"I didn't. I called what you are doin' stupid. See this is why I want you here with me."

"What? What the hell does that mean this is why you want me there with you? So you can keep watch of me or is it because you need me there in order to stay faithful? Which one is it because I get confused?" she said lashing out.

"This has nothin' to do with me."

"Yes it does, it always does. No matter what I got going on you always find a way to switch it to you. Look I didn't call you for your I told you so's."

"Then why did you call me? To tell me you're mad at some guy but you don't like'em though right? You're just mad for no apparent reason. You like this dude, I know you and I hear it in your voice. I told you this shit was gonna happen months ago and I trusted when you said you don't like him."

"I DON'T!!!!!"

"Bullshit Kendra. If you didn't like'em you wouldn't be mad enough to do the shit you just did. When Faith pisses me off I just say fuck it and keep it movin' 'cause it don't effect me 'cause I don't like her like that. But when M.Dot is mad at Tracy she fucks shit up and that is how I know you like'em because you doin' that same psycho shit she does so stop lyin'." I begged.

"You sound like you want me to like'em."

"I don't want you to do shit but admit the shit. At least admit you're interested; just do anything but insult my intelligence by tellin' me you're not. I know I am only the second guy you've ever been with so naturally you are a little curious and I'm not mad at that..."

"I'm not insulting anything, you are trying to make something out of nothing."

"Me? Oh yeah like I woke up this morning and said I'ma pick a fight with you over a guy you don't like. You know what I'll call you tomorrow."

"No, you always do that. Don't just hang up, talk to me!"

"Talk to you about what Kendra? I've said all I have to say three times over and you still don't listen. So I don't have anything else to say."

"You're just mad at me because I didn't stay in Georgia. Say it."

"You're buggin'. Goodnight Kendra." I tossed Wes' two way onto the kitchen counter as she let out a long deep breath.

"I told you man. You can't trust bitches these days."

"She's not a bitch."

"You know what I'm sayin' tho." Just then his phone rang again but we both know who it is.

"Tell her I left." I instructed.

Hello?...Na Syncere not here Kendra he just left...I don't know, when he gets mad he runs so he might be gone for a while...aight."

"What she say?"

"She was cryin'. She said to tell you sorry and to please call her...I think you should."

"Fuck that."

"Hi Syn." Kendra uttered when she picked up the phone.

"What's good?"

"I was beginning to worry when two weeks hit."

"So why didn't you call me?"

"The night you hung up I called back and told Wes to tell you to call me so I assumed you would when you weren't upset anymore." She explained.

"He never told me. So you weren't gonna call me back unless I called you?"

"Like I said I thought you would call when you were ready."

"Umm. What are you doin'?"

"I just got finished studying. You just got home from work?"

"Yeah."

"How are things going?"

"They aight. The owner's husband is gettin' on my nerves but other than that I'm good. What happened wit'chu and Mulan?"

"What do you mean?"

"I mean did he wil' out on you for what you and Tausha did or did you go and apologize?"

"I apologized the next morning."

"Oh so he was able to get into his room?"

"Yeah but I didn't ask how."

"You still tutorin' him?"

"Yeah." She said after a long pause.

"You still ain't cut'em off I see."

"Syncere I'm fine. I don't need to do all that."

"You still don't know why you can't do you?"

"Is that what you called me for? To argue with me?"

"I called to see how my girlfriend is doin'."

"Oh so now I'm your girlfriend?"

"What does that mean? Are you sayin' you're not?"

"It means for the past two weeks I've been wondering if you met some big butt Atlanta girl and you didn't want to talk to me."

"I could've guess the same because I haven't heard from you in two weeks either."

"I don't like girls."

"You know what I mean."

"I do, but I'm not the one who hung up."

"I just don't like bein' lied to, I can get that shit out in the streets."

"I didn't lie. I told you how I felt."

"Whatever."

"Goodnight Syncere."

"Oh so now you're the one hangin' up?"

"I don't like when you say whatever to me and you know that. Plus I have a lot of homework I haven't even started yet so I have to go."

"Homework never stopped you before."

"I know but I am falling behind so I call you tomorrow?"

"Whatever."

Long days at work topped with sleepless nights make me moody and alienated from everyone else in the house. I hate to say it but I think that psychic may have been telling the truth about Kendra not being the woman for me. Still I need a little more proof if I'm going to just write Kendra off. We've been through too much and sacrificed a great deal to just throw in the towel now. Times like this I wish I have my mother to call so I can get advice and times like this I start to wonder if there is really a God up there. I looked down at my tattoo and whispered the words *Always K.L.* while remembering the summer that has passed. I wish I can go back to the morning Kendra and I explored each other's bodies and stop time just as we lay beside each other. I also wish I could relive her first visit over again cherishing all the little things. Watching her do her hair, staying up late putting together the two model cars and just falling asleep next to the woman of my dreams. I want to smell her toasted vanilla body spray or feel her cold feet on my legs not just once more but forever more.

"Hello?" I said trying not to sound sleep as the light from my cell phone blinds me.

"Syncere?" Kendra said.

"Hey I'm glad you called."

"Really?" she said sniffling.
"What's wrong...Kendra what's wrong?"

"You promise not to get mad at me?"

"Yeah I promise. Just tell me what's the matter."

"Mulan hit me."

"Mulan I'm going to call campus police if you don't LEAVE ME ALONE!!" I heard Kendra yelling from the other side of the door.

"It's Syncere, open tha fuckin' door!"

"Syncere?"

"Kendra open the door, is he still in there? Open the door." My blood had been on fire for the entire five-hour drive that Ben insisted on taking with me. I'm just as angry now as I was when I first got the call from Kendra. I didn't need to hear anything else after the words, *Mulan hit me* to make get in the car with Ben and do a hundred miles per hour. I didn't say anything to Tracy or Wes nor did Ben say anything to Faith, we just left. When Kendra opened the door I burst through and searched the apartment but he's not here.

"Where tha fuck is he?"

"What are you doing here Syncere? How did you know where I live?"

"Fuck all that, where is he?"

"He's in his room? Upstairs."

"What number? Kendra what number?" I repeated.

"619."

"Let's go B."

"Syncere it's alright, he made a mistake and he apologized for it. It's ok." She tried to explain we rode the elevator. Right now all I feel is rage and despite Kendra's lips moving I don't hear a sound. I only have one objective; take Mulan's fucking head off. Ben and I searched frantically for room 619 as my heart rate hit the speed of jackrabbits.

"Syncere here it is!" Ben shouted.

I kicked the until he opened it and when he showed his face I punched before he could even register what is going on. He stumbled back and I hit him again but this blow sent Mulan crashing to the floor hard enough to knock his football trophies to the ground.

"Syncere enough!" Kendra yelled but I ignored her. I continued to hit Mulan wildly with all the force my hundred and seventy-pound body could muster then when my arms got tired I stood up. I watched as his eyes went from side to side and the blood from his nose and eye dripped onto his white t-shirt but I'm not satisfied. *This motherfucker hit Kendra, so what are you gonna do about it?* I thought to myself. I pulled out my rusted black 9mm and put the edge of it right on Mulan's nose.

"You fucked up." I said. Then I pulled the trigger.

"Tha fuckin' gun wouldn't shoot...tha fuckin' gun wouldn't shoot. I'm pissed." I said to myself.

"I took the clip out." I heard Ben whisper.

"You did what?" I pulled Ben to his feet slamming him against the hard cold stonewall in our jail cell but not once did Ben try to fight me off.

"I saw the look in your eyes when we was drivin' up here and at first I thought you were just pissed off and was gonna turn around after a while. But when I started seeing signs for the campus your seriousness set in and I took the clip out because I knew you'd shoot him if you got the chance." He confessed.

"Fuck you." I said letting go of Ben's blue polo shirt.

"You're welcome."

"Fuck you!" I shouted.

That conversation played in my head over and over as I sat in the polished wooden chair awaiting to hear my verdict. I looked behind myself to see Tracy, Wes, and my aunt Keisha crossing their fingers and whispering not guilty, not guilty. I looked over at Mulan who is whispering something to his lawyer and I looked over on his side to see if I could see Kendra but she isn't here. She hasn't been here during the entire trial and for the last month I haven't heard a word from her. Not a thank you, not a sorry and probably not even a thought on her behalf.

It came out in testimony from friends of Mulan, he Kendra had an ongoing relationship and he hit her out of anger because she wouldn't break it off with me to be with him exclusively. I cursed Ben for taking the clip out and stopping me from killing Mulan but by him doing that saved my life. I've put my freedom and my life in jeopardy because the woman I promised God I would do right by got pimped slapped by a guy she persisted she didn't have feelings for. I turned around again and told Ben thank you as he nodded in return.

My lawyer, Uwonda, tried to dismiss the attempted murder charge because my gun wasn't loaded but she advised me to pled guilty to aggravated assault and having a firearm on a school ground. The advice was taken and the jury delivered a not guilty verdict on the attempted murder charge but I received the two guilty verdicts we knew I'd get. That lands me six years probation. I hugged Uwonda before jumping over the bench to join my friends and family. I hugged y aunt Dimpsey as if I'm never going to see her again then I stopped and stared at Ben.

"You ain't gotta say in man. You my nigga." He said opening his arms. I embraced Ben, not like the true friend that he is but like a brother thanking him repeatedly. I then looked at the courtroom ceiling about to thank God for the second chance he's given me but I changed my mind. Instead I saluted him with the middle finger leaving my faith in Chapel Hill North Carolina.

14

Everyday I shower I look at my left shoulder staring at the tattoo, the constant reminder of the commitment Kendra and I had made to each other only a few months ago. I smile at the memories and sometimes I can still feel her standing behind me washing off my back. Her pleasure moans still echo off the shower walls ringing in my ear reminding me of how blissfully happy she made me last summer. She stood by me even when I was out of work by coming with me on all my interviews and inquires.

I often think if the comments I made to her is the cause of why she started messing around with Mulan. I know sometimes I make blanket statements and Kendra takes them for how she hears them and I should've made myself clearer. I play back our conversations occasionally and I hear my statements as Kendra would've heard them and I begin to justify myself in my head but it's clearly too late for that. The part that sticks out most frequently is when I said I couldn't stay by myself for too long. To her that may mean that I am going to eventually start cheating but what I really mean is that I don't want to be away from her for a long period of time because I don't know what to do with myself. My probation forbids me to come within 1,000 feet of UNC's campus and I wouldn't know where to begin if Kendra actually answered one of my calls.

It disturbs me that she didn't come to the trail or call me after the verdict was delivered. I'm wondering if she really even cared about our relationship or if she was seeking revenge for what I did to her at Shiloh; that idea sounds like the more realistic one. What do I do now? I do what I always do to get over a woman, get on top of a new one but seriously I just want some me time.

Tracy keeps asking me why am I so big on being with "the one" instead of living the life of a typical nineteen-year-old guy with a bachelor pad and I keep telling him that's really not me. I only mess around with a bunch of women because not one of them had the qualities I am looking for in a future wifey. The only woman that possesses them all is Kendra and if I had it my way Kendra would've transferred last minute to Emory so we would be together. But instead of the paradise we both talked about with one another I look like a violent and deranged ex-boyfriend. Tracy was right and I didn't have to say it, yes I still love Kendra and I believe it's going to be that way for a long time. When you have a love for someone like I did for Kendra it's a love you just don't get over in a month regardless of the circumstances and right now it is what it is, I still love her.

Tracy made due on his word as he and Wes returned to Connecticut and I made good on mine by remaining in Georgia. I got my old job back at the Green Papaya and Ben and I down graded to a two-bedroom apartment. I often think of the night I almost killed Mulan and wondered knowing what I know now would I have still done what I did? I answer myself yes to my disappointment and I don't know why.

It's been a wild three months so with my twentieth birthday approaching I have a lot about Syncere I have to change. First thing is I meant when I left my faith of "God" in North Carolina. Every time I look down at my forearm I curse myself for getting the scripture tattooed on me.

Second fuck school. I knew at seventeen I didn't want to go to school but I only went to please Kendra. Well fuck her and fuck school. I'm too talented to be wasting my time in someone's classroom. I came to Atlanta to get a record deal and dammit that is what I'm going to do. Lastly fuck relationships. I have a new motto to follow now, fuck bitches and get money...exactly. Ben agrees with my idea because since the North Carolina incident he and Faith have fought non-stop causing Faith to moved in with Niki, a friend of hers.

A surprise waited in my mailbox when I opened it on my way in the house from work. A letter from Kendra, a thick letter at that. My childlike curiosity damn near made me break my neck trying to get into the house to open it. For the past month and a half I've waited for any sign of life from Kendra and now that I have it I am afraid to open the letter to read it.

The letter detailed her account of the Mulan situation and how she is furious that I've neglected our relationship. The seven-page letter also goes on to say how she is offended that she has my initials tattooed on her but she ultimately wants us to at least be friends. Friends? Friends my ass. According to her she is disappointed that I handled the situation so violently and now she is fearful to be in my presence. After reading the letter three time I am amazed that she hasn't accepted responsibility. She still hasn't grasped the fact that I did what I did for her. Either she hasn't understood her involvement or she doesn't want to, either way to hell with her.

I sat down all weekend trying to write a response to Kendra truly outlining how I feel. Her letter sounds as if she is the only one that has been distressed by this but more importantly she fails to realize I almost lost my life because of her. Instead of a letter I wrote a poem entitled "Words" and I published it on Poetry.com. Instead of sending Kendra a copy of the poem I purchased a blank post card and wrote "Words" on the back before mailing it.

"Happy birthday muhfucka." Ben said throwing down the Xbox controller in defeat. I glanced at his clock that read twelve o' six and I'm in shock Kendra's birthday was ten days ago and I still haven't called her but for the strangest reason she is the only person I want to hear from right now.

"Why I gotta be all that?" I asked.

"'Cause muhfucka. I can't seem to beat'cha ass in Madden no more man. I should've never taught you how to run."

"Yeah I know. See that, two hundred rushing yards with one player. Either I'm that good or you suck." I taunted.

"You only beat me by three muhfuckin' points, that's a field goal."

"Hey, three points or twenty, a win is a win."

"Hey man, can I tawlk to you about some real shit man?" he asked seriously.

"B, you my man hundred grand but if this is another one of your get rich quick multi-level marketing things I really don't have the energy to pretend like I'm listening."

"That's fucked up man. You really only pretend to be listening? See I thought you was my nigga, my brother."

"I am. I'm just fuckin' wit'chu when it comes to that. What you wanna talk about?"

"Na I'm pissed at'cha selfish ass."

"Nigga quit bitchin' and talk."

"I miss Faith man." I busted into the loudest laughter as possible.

"So call her then." I managed to say when I finished.

"I cain't man she so fuckin lazy man. That muhfucka don't wanna work ever since she found out she pregnant and she eatin' all these foods that she ain't supposed to be eatin' knowin' she got type 2 diabetes. I just cain't do it man, I cain't be responsible for her like that." He explained while shaking his head.

"You think she's doin' any better stayin' wit Niki?"

"Hell no and I know that bitch a hoe man. Probably got Faith around niggas all the time."

"Yo Diggs ain't even like that and you know it. I bet she misses you just as much as you miss her. But you a cave man so you don't know when to admit you're wrong."

"But I ain't."

"It don't matter. You got to find a way to talk to her without ya'll throwin' blows 'cause I'm tired of breakin' up fights."

"Chill, we ain't that bad."

"Shiiit. When I take a blow from you and her then that is bad."

"Well you should've never told her to break up with me."

"Yo B you my nigga na mean? But when you and ya girl start fist fighting maybe it's time to go. And you tryin' to throw me over the balcony ain't help the situation either. But I did see just how much you love her."

"Yeah man, I love that muhfucka."

"So get on the phone and call her. I'ma go watch the Shawshank Redemption."

"You need to watch the Count of Monte Cristo."

"If you like it then I know it's some dumb shit."

"Fuck you. If you like the Shawshank Redemption you'll love this shit."

"Lemme get it…matter fact just bring it to my room, my phone is ringin'." *Please let it be Kendra, please let it be Kendra, please let it be Kendra.*

"Happy birthday!!!"

"Thanks Trisha. What's good wit'chu?" I said trying to mask the disappointment in my voice. LaTrisha L. Joyner is the girl I dated before Kendra and the only other woman I've dated twice. She's a five foot seven dark skinned girl from Garner North Carolina by way of Greenville. Back in the day men would've called her a brick house because she is thick in all the right places. Her natural hair swings pass her shoulders, her smile is beyond radiant topped with her country accent and her laugh is the making of my ideal woman. Trisha and I keep a cool friendship as our relationships never ended badly. We are just two people attracted to the opposites of who we are but the feelings are the same but my feelings still run deep for Trisha, as I loved her once.

Trisha has known about Kendra since the beginning and vice versa. For a long time I would ping pong between the two because they are so identical yet individual when it comes to their personalities.

"I just got it from watching the game in the lobby with some girls on my floor." She said.

"Oh I was 'bout to say I'm surprised you still up."

"Yeah I know it is way passed my bed time."

"So what'chu get me for my birthday?"

"Shooot, nothin'."

"Nothin'. Damn that's how you do me? Come visit me then."

"What? Boy please, I'm in school."

"So come down this weekend."

"You gonna pay for it?"

"Yeah."

"You gonna fly to me Atlanta?"

"Take the bus."

"Oh no I only fly." She said.

"What? Do you know how much it costs to fly? Ok, ok answer me this. If I fly you down what am I gonna get?"

"Me duh!"

"You how?"

"What do you mean?"

"I mean let's finished what you couldn't finish at Fayetteville State."

"I knew that is what you wanted."

"Actually I want your virginity."

"Why do you want it so bad."

"'Cause you said I was your first love and for madd years I've never pressured you about sex. I respected you to the fullest when it came to that but now that image of you in those pink French cut boy shorts is embedded in my head. I think I have earned it."

"You know I want to wait until I get married." She reminded.

"But we were about to do it a two years ago so what is do different now."

"I don't know."

"So what's good then?"

"Do you still love me?" she asked.

"Of course. Once I love someone I will always love them no matter what. There is always gonna be something there no matter how much time passes in between phone calls and visits na mean?"

"Are you just sayin' that 'cause you wanna freak me?"

"Fuck, the word is fuck."

"Freak. You know I don't curse."

"There you go wit that church girl shit. I'll fly you down if you just say one curse word, just say fuck."

"Freak."

"I hate'chu."

"No you don't." She replied with a giggle.

"So you comin' or what?"

"Call me Friday."

"If I call you and you don't come I'ma be 38 hott."

"I don't speak slang."

"It'll take me all night to explain it to you but I can't 'cause I have another call."

"Ooh is it Kendra? Did you ask her to come visit too?"

"Oh please. Me and her ain't even on it like that."

"No? But I thought you loved her?"

"I did."

"But you just said once you love someone you always will because there is always something there. Isn't that what you just said?"

"Yeah but when I almost go to jail because of a lie then there are some exceptions to the rule."

"Whatever, I'll speak to you Friday."

"Aight...Hello?"

"Damn I was about to hang up." Another female voice said.

"My bad that was my sisters wishing me a happy birthday...who is this?"

"Damn you don't know my voice now? See I was gonna come over and give you a birthday present but since you don't know who I am now I'm not comin'." I heard Faith laughing in the background.

"Niki? What's good wit'chu?"

"Happy birthday sweetie."

"Thanks. Why is everyone still up tonight?"

"'Cause you and Ben just got finished playin' Madden and Faith and I were about to go out until Ben called. It took him long enough."

"So they patched shit up?"

"Yeah. I'm about to bring Faith over there and thought you'd might want some company on your birthday."

"That's wussup."

"Tell me somethin' first."

"Aight."

"Why'd you stop callin'?"

"'Cause you was just movin' too damn fast. By like the second week you were over here everyday and takin' my last name in conversation, blowin' up my phone and I was like who is this broad? You were dumb cool the first night you came by the crib but after that you turned clingy real fast and I can't rock like that."

"Why didn't you tell me?"

"OH MY GOD I did. You thought I was playin' but I was bein' dead ass serious."

"Faith said you were only actin' like that because you were still getting over that girl."

"Hell na, she ain't have nothin' to do with it."

"So you still like me?"

"Yeah you cool peoples and we can chill and get to know each other, I just ain't into playin' house na mean? I don't even want to do the whole relationship thing no more feel me?"

"Yeah I feel you. So since that is out the way can I come over?"

"Will you leave in the mornin'?"

"If you want me to."

"Aight, hop on the good foot and com'on."

I had my way with Niki sexually for, no exaggeration, two hours as I plowed her in every position physically possible. I perspired heavily as I tried to bust a nut, as I didn't desire to go at it that long with her. Her blissful moans echoed in my room every time I'd shove it in her as hard as I could and I must admit I love the way she tilts her head back, closes her eyes and slightly open her mouth every time the pleasure hits her spot. I've never really paid that kind of attention to a chick's facial expression during sex but it actually turned me on more.

"Wow. You really didn't want to cum did you?"

"I wanted to but it was too good, I ain't want to stop."

"Wanna do it again?"

"Gimmie twenty-minutes." I sat on the edge of my bed looking at Niki's naked sweaty body while she fanned herself and regretted what I just did. Truth be told I really don't want to be here right now. I looked back at Niki and I made eye contact with Kendra. I stared long examining her curve, her skin tone and her features to ensure I'm not hallucinating again but at the moment I was sure I'm looking at Kendra Niki's face appeared.

"You ready?" She asked.

"Yeah." Niki opened her legs exposing her still wet pleasure center stroking it with her index finger. Every alarm is going off in my body telling me not to climb on top of her but the lust in her eyes overpowered me. My phone rang…saved by the bell.

"Yo."

"Syncere?" I knew by the way she said my name. She stressed the "y" in my name and says it with a hint of country, its Kendra." My heart did cartwheels and my stomach did back flips of exhilaration but my resentment for what she put me through didn't allow me to show any emotion toward her.

"What's good?"

"Nothing, how are you?"

"I'm good."

"Are you busy?"

"Kinda."

"What are you doing?"

"Havin' sex." The very next sounds that came from Kendra's end was a dial tone, I laughed it off and turned back to Niki who is already kneeling in front of me.

"You ready now?"

"Yeah." I responded as my phone rang again.

"Answer it, I'll start with or without you." Niki said placing her warm lips around my sex stick.

"Yo." I said answering the phone again.

"You have some fuckin' nerve you know that?"

"What?"

"You had to have known I'd be calling so why'd you even answer the phone if that is what you are doing?"

"'Cause I wanted to hear you tell me happy birthday."

"You wanted to hear me tell you happy birthday so you stopped having sex to answer my call just to hear that?"

"Yep."

"Do you know what I did on my birthday?"

"What? Have a nice night with your star football player?"

"No, I told you Mulan and I are not dating."

"So what did you do then?"

"I didn't go to class…I screened all my calls and ignored them all just so I wouldn't miss yours. I waited from midnight the night before to midnight on my birthday in my room alone waiting for your call. I only wanted to hear from you and you didn't even call me. And now I try to be a good friend and call you on your birthday and you have the audacity to tell me you're having sex with another girl? Fuck you Syncere." The dial tone again. I painted Niki's face before dialing Kendra's number back. I had no idea she was waiting for me to call her, its ironic I tossed the idea back and forth with myself about calling her and she spent her entire birthday waiting for me. Now I feel like shit.

"What?" she said when I called back?

"What do you want from me Kendra?"

"I don't want anything. I wrote you and tried to make peace with you and keep our friendship in tact but you try to be as sarcastic as you can be and all I get from you is a post card that has "Words" written on it? If I didn't know you well enough to go to Potery.com I probably wouldn't've known what the hell that meant.

"So you read it?"

"Yes I read it and I want to ask you, why do you do that?"

"Do what?"

"You never tell me how you feel verbally. Every single time we get in a fight or we stop talking I have to go to a stupid website to read your true feelings. How can you say you love me the way you do and you can't even express yourself to me?"

"That is how I deal with things and you should know that by now and you should also know I'm not gonna change 'cause that is who I am."

"But what was the point of the postcard?"

"I just wanted to fuck with your head." I confessed

"See that is what I am talking about. Why? What difference did it make? What did it change?"

"Who said it was supposed to change anything? I was feeling sarcastic so I sent it. You knew what to do, you got my response so I don't see why you are so bent out of shape over the whole thing."

"It's your whole way of going about and doing things. You felt that sarcastic with me to do something like that, I mean you really hate me that much."

"I couldn't hate you if I tried. And trust me I've tried."

"Then why?"

"'Cause."

"Because what? 'Cause isn't an answer." She said.

"'Cause all I could think about bein' in that fuckin court room and hearin' how you and Mulan had a relationship and I was the jealous ex-boyfriend that couldn't let you go. I mean you weren't there to confirm or deny the story so I took it as is. I mean if you love me like you say you do then why didn't I hear from you during the entire trial? I'm facin' jail time 'cause I thought I was defendin' you and you weren't even in my corner. If you really loved me or really wanted to prove to me that Mulan was lyin' then you should've been in my corner. Above all else you should've been there for me. Fuck work, fuck school and fuck everything you should've been there. 'Cause realistically I did what I did for you, not because I woke up that day and just had the overwhelming nerve to drive to North Carolina to almost shoot a nigga in the face. If it wasn't for Ben I would've gotten your letter while in jail and we'd be havin' this conversation by collect."

"Do you even know what happened?" she asked after all of that.

"I already know. You was fuckin' wit Mulan, it came out in his testimony."

"No I wasn't fuckin' Mulan. Mulan and I were friends, just friends like I told you before. He started liking me and wanted a relationship with me and he pressured me over and over and over again to break up with you. Then when I didn't he got pissed off and he hit me. That is how it happened and now you know. So go finish doing whatever you were doing. Goodnight." Then it was the dial tone for the third time.

I redialed and redialed and redialed to no avail so for the rest of the night I thought about my whole approach to responding to Kendra's letter and everything that happened leading up to me driving to North Carolina that night. Now that I look back on it I did have a lot of uninvited influence around me. I had Tracy, Wes and Ben in my ear and I had my own past hanging over my head. I remember in college how we used to target freshman girls and it was an added bonus to fuck one that said she had a boyfriend at home or at another school. I guess I thought history would repeat itself with me being on the wrong end and that along with the things everyone were putting in my ear convinced me that Kendra was cheating on me with Mulan. Her calling and complaining about him didn't help it just added fuel to my fire but now I know that I didn't trust Kendra because I didn't trust myself.

"I thought you were going to call me later that day, why didn't you?" Kendra asked.

"Because you didn't answer my calls all night so I figured you'd call when you wanted to talk to me. I just didn't know it was gonna take three weeks."

"So if I didn't call you then you weren't gonna call me?"

"No. I thought you didn't want to talk." There is silence on the phone and I know why. We both have been dying to talk to one another and now we have the chance to but we don't know what to say. Every time Kendra and I take long periods from talking to one another the first two or three phone calls breaking our absence are always the hardest and I just can't wait until we are back on the same track again.

"So…"

"So…"

"So are you dating anyone now?" I thought to myself, I could answer this question honestly but I want to see where she and I stand at this point.

"Yeah."

"Oh." She said sounding surprised. "What's her name?"

"Diane."

"Sounds like a white girls name."

"Actually she is white. She's from Mystic Connecticut. Remember she called when you were here last summer?"

"God I'm so sick of black men jumping over to white girls."

"Lemme guess, Mulan?"

"Yes. Every time I look he has one chasing him around or he's chasing one of them around and driving their cars. Black men who date white women disgust me. Ya'll act like black women aren't good enough for ya'll no more."

"Why does it always have to be a race thing when a black man dates a white girl? I don't see color, I just see an interesting attractive woman. The world isn't just black and white anymore."

"Oh please. Black men date white women so they can get away with the shit a black woman won't tolerate."

"You don't even know what you are talkin' 'bout. The only difference between a black woman and a white woman is pigmentation. I know black girls who stay with their man even after they cheat on them, beat on them or treat them like shit and I know white girls that do the same thing. All women are the same black or white it just all depends on who the man and who the woman is that is all."

"Nice explanation but it's deeper than that."

"You just want it to go deeper than that. But that explanation isn't the one you were looking for that's all."

"I still don't like it and now that I think about it more I don't think I can date a guy that has dated a white girl."

Four months have passed without Kendra and I talking and it gets harder and harder not to call her every time I think about how long it's been. I leave her panties, picture and model cars on display in my room and I look at my tattoo constantly and Ben says I'm torturing myself. I've asked myself over an over again why can't I seem to get Kendra out of my system? We've had this weird circle of falling in and out of contact with each other and getting into relationships that end briefly while we are hundreds of miles from one another. The only reason I have for not being able to erase my feelings for Kendra out of my heart and mind is because I've loved her since I was fifteen. I told myself, my aunt and her Lord that I'm going to marry her and no matter how many girls I fuck or date I still compare them to Kendra in every way possible. On purpose? No. I mean what would be the point of getting emotionally or physically attached to a woman only to compare her to my ex who I know they can't hold a candle to? I'm setting myself and them up for failure every time and that isn't fair to the other women, still I can't help it.

I hear Faith and Ben's laughter from the other room and jealousy sets in. Faith and Ben fist fight each other but they are still together, they didn't call it quits like Kendra and I did. I long to have that kind of love with Kendra the way Ben and Faith does, hell Kendra and I don't hit each other so why can't we work out what we have going against us. You would think we'd be use to it since we have been fighting this uphill battle for five years now.

"Hey man can I come in?" Ben asked.

"You're already in."

"Okay, okay. Why you still dressed man? You got home four hours ago, you goin' somewhere?"

"I don't know."

"What'chu mean? You gotta work tomorrow?"

"Na."

"Then come wit me and Faith."

"Where ya'll goin'."

"Mississippi."

"Mississippi? In the middle of the night? For what?"

"Just to go man and you should come with us. It's a seven hour drive so if we sleep and leave at 2 I'll get to my parents house in time for breakfast."

"Wow you really got it broken down to a science don't'chu?"

"Yeah muhfucka so com'on and come with us."

"Na, I'm peace. Now that you mention it, I should go to North Carolina and visit my aunt and them. I haven't seen them since last summer when me and you went."

"Bullshit. You goin' to see Kendra aint'chu?"

"Kendra? Yeah right, we haven't talked since Christmas."

"Christmas? Didn't you send her a gift and she still ain't call? She cold man."

"Na she called and said thank you but it didn't go much farther than that."

"I still say you goin' to see her. Hey Faith, this muhfucka tryin' to say he goin' to North Carolina to see his aunt, knowin' damn well he goin' to see Kendra." Ben yelled.

"Kendra? When ya'll start talkin' again Syn?" Faith asked sounding excited.

"I told cavemen Ben here that we aren't."

"Oh, I should've known better listening to Ben. I think you should call her though."

"And say what Diggs? Hi it's been four months and we haven't talked but I want'chu back?"

"Is that how you really feel?"

"Yeah. I've been thinkin' about movin' back to North Carolina because that is the only way she and I are gonna be able to be with each other for more than three months. This distance shit is killin' us and we ain't gonna make it."

"Tell me sumthin' Syn."

"Yo?"

"What did the physic tell you?" I got quite as Ben and Faith looked toward me for my response.

"She told me that she isn't the one I'm supposed to marry. Said some shit like the woman for me is a woman that wasn't born in this country."

"Well you know how you be attractin' them foreign girls. Maybe you gonna be wit one of them." Ben suggested.

"I don't want to be with no foreign girl. I want to marry Kendra. I'm tellin' ya'll right now, if I don't marry Kendra then I'm not gettin' married."

"Man you say that now but you gonna meet that girl that's gonna change your mind."

"I already know who she is."

"So what'chu gonna do?"

"I'ma call her."

"When?"

"Right now."

"Aight man, tell us how it goes. We gonna go pack." I haven't been this nervous since the Penn relays when I was in high school. I don't know why I get this nervous every time I call Kendra but here goes nothing.

"Hello."

"Kendra?"

"Syncere?"

"Yeah, are you ok?"

"Are you?"

"Yeah, why."

"'Cause it's kinda late." She said.

"Were you sleep?"

"No."

"You sound like it."

"I'm sick."

"Sick how? It's April."

"I know but I have a cold. How has every thing been?"

"Great. I'm actually 'bout to drive home tonight."

"Drive? You brought a car?"

"Oh yeah, around Valentine's Day."

"What kind?"

"A black Toyota Camry."

"And you're driving to Connecticut?"

"Na, North Carolina. I want to see my cousins and my aunt. Maybe I can bring you some soup tomorrow."

"I'm not in North Carolina, I'm away for spring break helping the homeless."

"Where are you?"

"Georgia." She said.

"Georgia!? And you didn't call me?"

"Well I'm not that close to you."

"Where are you then?"

"Tucker."

"Yo B. how far is Tucker from here?" I hollered.

"About an hour." He hollered back.

"I'm going to be here until next Tuesday but I want to leave now." She expressed.

"Well I'm goin' home tonight if you want me to come get you."

"Really? You'd come get me?"

"Yeah. I would love some company anyway."

"Will you let me drive?"

"Umm, I don't know you sick so I don't want you to sneeze and crash into a railing or somethin'."

"Hee hee, you silly. I'll be fine."

"Ok, then I'm on my way. You're gonna have to have someone give you directions for when I get off my exit."

"Where is I am is literally five minutes down the street from the exit."

"Oh ok, that's wussup."

"Are you sure you don't mind driving to pick me up?"

"Positive." I said trying to contain my enthusiasm.

"Ok, I'll see you in a bit." I hung up my cordless phone and jumped around my room-screaming YES! YES! YES!

"Syn, com'er." I skipped into Ben and Faith's room with a huge kool-aid smile on my face.

"Yeah?"

"So what happened?"

"Guess where she is right now. Like right right now."

"Where?"

"GEORGIA! She's been here since Tuesday."

"So what is she doin' here?"

"Workin' wit tha homeless during her spring break or some shit. It don't matter 'cause how crazy is that. We don't talk for four months then I randomly call her and she's an hour away from me. I'm 'bout to be out. I'll see ya'll on Monday and have fun down in tha delta."

"It ain't like what'chu see on the movies man I'm tellin' you. Mississippi is real nice."

"It is Syn. When Ben took me there I loved it."

"Sounds great but I gotta go."

50 Cent's Get Rich or Die Tryin' pumped threw my speakers as I sped on the highway toward all signs pointed to Tucker Georgia. My heart is happy again at the mere fact that I'm going to see Kendra for the first time since August of last year.

"Aight I'm gettin' off the exit now so where do I go from here?"

"Make a right off the exit and drive about three miles down the road and look for Safe Keeping on your left. That's the name of the facility." I pulled into a dark piece of land with nothing to my left or my right except for what looks like those cabins we use to stay in during summer camp.

"Which cabin are you in?"

"I'm right to your left. Turn your music down it's late."

"Oh my bad." I squinted my eyes and saw a bright light and the silhouette of a woman in the doorway.

"I see you. Pull into the driveway, I'ma get my stuff."

"Aight." I popped the trunk and stood by the back of the car waiting for Kendra thinking about what I'm going to do once I got close to her. Do I hug her? Do I just say hi? Or what. I'ma hug her...na I'm not I'm just gonna say hi. Yeah that's it. Kendra struggled with her bags so I rushed to the doorway and took two of them and put them in the trunk and we were off."

"You look like you put on some weight." She commented.

"You callin' me fat?"

"No, but I can see you haven't ran in a while."

"Yeah I put on a couple of pounds eating that Vietnamese food."

"I like the weight on you though, it looks good."

"You look good." I complimented.

"I'm sick."

"You're the prettiest sick woman I've ever seen."

"Thanks."

Kendra and I stopped just outside of Tucker to gas up and get snacks for the road then we drove in silence while listening to R. Kelly's Chocolate Factory CD. The silence bothered me, a lot. I was so excited to see her tonight and now we aren't even speaking.

"I like this song, listen to the guitar sounds in it." I said turning up the music.

"I want my kids to learn to play an instrument. What do you want your kids to do?"

"I only thought havin' children last summer." I responded.

"Well my kids are gonna be scholastic and musically inclined and they are going to be tutoring your kids."

"Your kids and my kids huh? I thought'chu didn't want to have any kids."

"I don't. I'm going to adopt."

"So we're back to that now?"

"Well I only considered having biological children with you but since we are just friends now I don't have to have any children. I can go back to my original plan."

"If that's what makes you happy then go for it."

"So when are you going to start having some little Syncere's running around."

"I'm not. I've decided not to get married and not to have kids."

"Why?"

"If you don't give birth to them then I don't want any."

"You are going to break some girls heart one day. But when you meet her you might change your mind."

"Ben and Faith said the same thing. You seem confident in saying that. So this is it huh?"

"What do you mean?"

"I mean us."

"Syncere there is no us."

"Well that is what I mean. There is no future for us beyond friendship?"

"I don't think so. I think its better this way don't you?"

"Not really but if I can't have you in my life as my girlfriend then I will take you anyway I can get you so friendship it is."

"Ok."

The distinction of Kendra's kids and my kids is evidence that she has no intentions or desires of being with me romantically anymore and I've fallen back into the dreaded "friend" category. Now this whole ride, this whole trip to NC has turned out to be a waste and now all I want to do is get her to UNC and out of my face. Every minute I'm spend sitting next to her knowing we will probably not get married I feel ourselves growing further and further apart from one another. I can literally feel the gap getting wider with every passing highway sign.

Six hours later with the sun rising behind us I dropped Kendra off three blocks from the official UNC campus in fear of going any further would put me in violation of my probation.

"You have everything?"

"Yeah. Thank you for coming to get me. I really needed to get away from there. What are you going to do in Raleigh?"

"Just chill wit my aunt and my cousins."

"Will you stop by on your way back to Atlanta?"

"I'll try, I might not leave until late and I have to work on Monday."

"Well will you at least call me later?"

"Yeah." I lied. I have no intention of communicating with Kendra any further than today. It's evident that our relationship is over so from this point on as far as I'm concerned she is dead to me.

"Oh my God Syncere." I turned around to see LaTrisha Joyner running toward me with open arms. We hugged as I swung her around in circles.

"How you been?"

"I'm good. What are you doin' in Raleigh?"

"I'm just here for the day visitin' my family."

"You goin' back today?"

"Tonight."

"Stop by my campus." She invited.

"What? You didn't even come down for my birthday like you promised."

"I know, I know and I'm sorry but you gotta drive pass Winston-Salem to get to Georgia anyway so don't act like you don't know."

"I'll think about it."

"Right, you'll come. I know you."

"You think you do."

"No, I do."

After spending the day at the flea market with my aunt, playing football with my two cousins and making a visit to my church family, the Williams' across the street, I jumped back into my Camry and hit the highway. I have a little over an hour to decide where I'm going to go, either to UNC or Winston-Salem State. I know this morning I told myself that Kendra is dead to me but I also wondered why she'd invite me to see her before I leave especially with the lack of conversation and awkwardness we felt toward each other in the car. On the flip side this can be my second chance at fucking Trisha and I can't wait to see her in those boy shorts again with her volleyball toned legs stretching from them. There it is, my mind is made up and I drove clear passed UNC and thirty more minutes to Winston-Salem State University.

Trisha greeted me at the door with a tight hug wearing nothing but a Winston-Salem State t-shirt, which got me, erected before I was in the house good.

"You gonna stay the night here?"

"Na, I'ma leave in a little while so I can be to work on time."

"So you thought you'd come, freak me and leave?"

"Chill it ain't even like that. You said nothin' 'bout me fuckin' you. You asked me to come by on my way home so here I am. I mean I can leave, it's nothin' to me."

"No don't go, stay with me." That reverse psychology always works on Trisha, got her.

"So what's good?"

"You know why I asked you here?"

"No, why is that?"

"I want to finish what we started at Fayetteville State."

"Oh, now you wanna give me your virginity. Why the sudden change of heart?" Trisha's head dropped and she got quite.

"You promise not to get mad if I tell you somethin'?"

"Look if you don't wanna do it then it's ok. I didn't get mad when we were freshmen and I'm not gonna get mad now."

"No it's not that, I do want to do it but it's just…I'm not a virgin anymore."

"WHAT!? Since when?"

"Since December."

"By who?"

"By someone who didn't deserve it. It just happened."

"Are ya'll datin'?"

"No, it was a one night stand."

"What tha fuck have you been gettin' into?"

"Don't judge me. You're not perfect either."

"I'm not sayin' that, I'm just in shock…disappointed a little I guess. I thought you were savin' your virginity for someone special…"

"Like you?" she pointed.

"If you thought I was special enough then yeah. It just caught me off guard because when I met you you were a little innocent gullible church girl. Now you havin' one night stands and shit."

"I only had one. Well it's over and here I am." Trisha took off her over-sized t-shirt and to my shock and stimulation she is wearing the exact same hot pink French laced boy shorts and bra that she wore the night we almost had sex at Fayetteville State.

"Wow, my favorite outfit." She smiled and lay on her back. I undressed her while fighting her to keep her hands from covering her body.

"I'm nervous."

"Trisha, it's me. Why are you nervous?"

"I don't know."

"Well this doesn't work unless I can get to the areas you're covering up."

"Just gimmie a minute." Trisha covered her breasts, pleasure temple and closed her eyes giggling like a schoolgirl. Now here I am naked and losing my erection while she acts stupid. Minute by minute that she's covering herself up my erection lessens and when she finally says put it in I can't get it back up.

"See what you did?"

"Me?"

"Yeah. I've been hard for the past damn hour while you say yes and no and act like this is your first time."

"Well if you want it you better do something." I thought of the freakiest, nastiest sexual things my imagination can conger up but to no avail. While Trisha huffed and puffed as I tried to get my erection back I knew at that moment I should've went to UNC.

I reached Marietta sooner than I thought I would I guess due to being pissed off about last night and the fact I wasn't able to fuck Trisha. *Stupid bitch* I thought to myself. If she wasn't acting dumb I would've beat that pussy up. Fuck it, I guess just like a life with Kendra sex with Trisha wasn't meant to go down. Remembering how Trisha looks naked I drove the entire ride back to Georgia with the longest hard-on, ain't that a bitch?

PART

2

15

After an argument with Kendra about why I didn't go see her the night I left North Carolina everything in my life just seemed to go downhill. I lost my job at the Green Papaya, totaled my car in an accident and started messing around with a thirty-one year old Kenyan woman named Carol. Some good did come out of being unhappy in Atlanta. My mother and I talked out our problems and I promised her if she let's me come back home I'll be out in 6 months. What I didn't know is she went back to the one place I didn't want to go. Now I'm back in Connecticut working at Olympia Sports with Quincy.

In Danbury it's like shooting fish in a barrel when it comes to girls. All day everyday there is one eyeing me or giving me their number and I don't even have to try. I'm fucking with Evelyn again, I naturally called her when I got back to Waterbury and after she asked why I just up and left and didn't keep in touch we were in her mothers living room and I was hitting it from the back like I use to. She's slightly taller, but the same weight and its as if she hasn't aged a second. There is this short and thick black girl named Yvonne that works downstairs at Champs who I flirt with every time she comes upstairs. It's obvious we like each other but I think she got a man. Lastly I have this seventeen-year-old white girl named Jessica who can't get enough of the dick. I smashed her the first night at my moms house, in my car while parked near some woods and even in the dressing room of the store I work in, we broke the bench.

"Syncere wait until you see the girl Quincy is interviewing today." Brad said. Brad is a manager in training like I am and he's worked with Quincy and I at our store in Newtown. Brad is a sarcastic, pimple faced twenty-one year old white guy from Brookfield with a girlfriend only he would be attracted to.

"Why she fine?"

"Wow! She's young but she's hot."

"How old is she?"

"I think she just turned sixteen."

"Oh fuck that she is jail bait."

"I'm not saying you have to date her, I'm just saying she hot."

"Q, what'chu think?"

"I mean I guess she cute. She a white girl, you might like her."

"What's that supposed to mean?"

"He means if you like the white girl you're running around with now you'd love this one."

"Hey, I'm not wifin' her. I'm just fuckin' and all pussy looks the same in the dark." Just as Quincy, Brad and I were conversing this short brown skinned short haired girl walked into the store right up to me.

"Are you Quincy?"

"What do I get if I say yes?"

"Don't mind him, that's Syncere. I'm Quincy."

"Oh, I'm Bianca. I'm here for the interview."

"Oh ok. Come with me when can go in my office."

"You don't have an office. You have tape on the floor around a chair and a desk." Brad laughed at my cheap shot in attempt to humor Bianca. Brad and I watched in amazement as Bianca followed Quincy to the back.

"Wow."

"Yeah, that ass is nice."

After the interview Brad and I included Quincy in on Bianca but we know he is thinking the same thing because when he followed Bianca to the door his eyes didn't leave her ass until she turned around to thank him one last time for interviewing her. I didn't have to ask, I knew he was gonna hire her. We need some dime pieces like that working in our store. Quincy, Brad and I agreed to hire the best-looking girls in Danbury to work in our store and so far we only have one, Emily Nezvesky.

Emily is bad. I mean if bad was a job she'd me making a hundred million dollars a year. Emily is a five foot three Dominican girl with dark brown hair that ran down to the small of her back when she wore it out. Her eyes were that of an Asian girl with the body of a black girl. Matched with the type of personality every guy wants a woman to have she is damn near perfect. Now you know your boy tried to push up and that despite the fact Quincy told me she has a boyfriend. I didn't care whom she was dating until I met him one night when I was still working in Newtown and he told me Emily talks about me a lot. I was so impressed by the way he talked to me like a man and by the confidence he displayed to me that I had no choice but to give him the proper respect by not trying to take his girl. Instead of pursing Emily we have become real good friends.

"Hey Syn look, look. There she is."

"Who."

"The hott girl I was telling you about earlier." I turned to the front of the store to see a medium height white girl walking right passed me.

"She's not that hott B."

"What are you blind?"

"She aight."

"Can I tell you something and you promise not to get mad?" I looked at Evelyn out the corner of my eye while I sat in the car in front of her house wondering what she is about to tell me.

"What's good?"

"I'm pregnant." My heart sank into the depths of my body and I had to roll down my window manually to get some fresh air.

"How many weeks are you?"

"I'm a month."

"I've only been home for a month."

"I'm not sayin' its yours."

"Then whose is it?"

"It's this guy Richard that I broke up with right before you came back."

"Why ya'll break up?"

"Well actually he's in jail, that is why we broke up. I'm not about to sit out here and wait on no nigga to make parole."

"So what'chu gonna do?"

"I don't know. I'm too young to have a baby, I'm only seventeen and I feel like if I have this baby I'ma ruin my life."

"Don't look at it like that. Havin' a baby is a blessin'."

"I know but I'm still in high school and I'm not even with the father. I'm gonna seem like such a hoe."

"No you not. This is the first time you've been pregnant so fuck what everyone else thinks. Plus don't nobody need to be in your business. You will graduate by the time you're due."

"I was pregnant seven months ago." She confessed.

"What? And you had an abortion?"

"Yeah. I'm not ready to be a mother."

"Well didn't you learn from the first time?"

"It was a mistake we just got caught up in the moment."

"Wow, twice? That's crazy. Well check it, whatever you wanna do I'm here for you."

I sat in my 1987 silver Nissan Sentra in front of an abortion clinic while old people and activists protested around my car and to people pulling in. I kept my nose in the book I'm reading and paid them people no mind while I waited for Evelyn to come out. She insisted I didn't come into the clinic with her so I respected her wishes at the same time feeling like this is wrong.

"You good?" I asked when she got in the car.

"I feel like shit. Will you take me to get my prescription?"

"Yeah. How long is it gonna take for you to heal?"

"Are all you thinking about is when you can fuck me again?"

"Whoa, whoa. First off I'm bein' concerned for you, I'm not the one who knocked you up and if I recall I was the one tellin' you not to go through with it. I told you I had your back."

"Yeah right. You would take care of a kid that ain't even yours."

"I'm in a relationship with you aren't I?"

"So what happens when you get tired of me or we get in an argument and we break up? Then what?"

"Why would I get tired of you?"

"Isn't that why you left in the first place? 'Cause you were tired of me?"

"I left because I moved to Georgia to get a deal."

"But you stopped talking to me a month before you left and you kept in touch with Krista but you didn't keep in touch with me."

"Evy, you were fifteen then and you were out here tellin' everybody you were my girl and that we was fuckin'. Ashley Hill came into my job all loud and shit tellin' me that you told her how I worked it. Was you tryin' to get me locked up?"

"No, I loved you just like you claimed you loved me but just like BJ you were just sayin' that so you can fuck me."

"I ain't BJ and you came onto me not the other way around. I treated you then and I do now like royalty so don't say I didn't love you…"

"You never said it. I wrote you that note and told you how I felt about you and you acted like you never read it. I would tell you I loved you over the phone and you would never say it back, why?"

"I didn't think you knew what love was then, you were only fifteen so I thought you were infatuated with me."

"Well I loved you I knew what love was then. You were the only guy that I met that took me to places other than the mall and to the movies and you didn't make me leave after sex, I thought you cared about me."

"Evy I do care."

"Then why ain't my initials tattooed on your shoulder?"

"Is this what this is about, my tattoo? I told you that is a situation that was developed before you and after you."

"I know who she is. I saw a picture of her."

"How? I never told you about Kendra."

"You didn't but Trevor did but I didn't want to believe him and I didn't until you just dropped off the face of the earth. I figured she came down for Thanksgiving and you didn't love me anymore. You're the reason why I am like this."

"How you figure that?"

"'Cause you are."

"'Cause is not an answer, explain yourself."

"'Cause you just are."

After spending every free minute I had with Evelyn while she recovered and going all out on her birthday last week she repays me with a text message at work breaking up with me.

"You know you gotta buy somethin' to go with these shoes right?"

"Why."

"That's the rule here. We make people buy two things and anyone that works here has to buy two things as well. We have numbers to keep up."

"Quincy didn't tell me that, this is my first purchase."

"You're right and you get forty percent off so get somethin' else."

"I don't want anything."

"Well I want some Jordan socks, the red and black ones right there."

"Nice try." Kenya said laughing with her mother, little brother and younger sister.

"Aight I got'chu, wait until you work for me. I'ma have you doin' all the hard stuff watch."

"Like what?" She said challenging me with her body language."

"Just wait, just wait. When's your official first day? You know I do all the training right. It's a wrap for you."

"We'll see." She said smiling sending me a wink before walking away.

"Hear that cut."

"Negative. She just turned sixteen and I just got this blazin Asian girls number a few days ago. I'm good."

"Yeah Brad was tellin' me 'bout that. You call her yet?"

"Na, I think I spent that twenty on gas this mornin'."

"You wrote her number on a twenty?" Quincy asked laughing.

"Yeah. I ain't have no paper."

"Yo see if she got some friends."

"Nigga you married."

"I ain't married and what she don't know can't hurt me. I'm tired of sittin' back watchin' you have all the fun nigga I want in."

"Aight, I gotta find her number first."

I went to the gas station to retrieve the twenty I paid with and surprisingly they still had the bill and I was able to copy Miko's number off it. Yes she's pretty but

I'm more drawn to her wit as our conversations are filled with shot for shot jokes and insults. Miko is a five foot five fair skinned longhaired girl from Cambodia with a chest big enough for a mouthful. She's a senior at Brookline High and fears that her cousins are going to send her back to Pittsburg before the school year is over.

We've hung out plenty of times since we first met doing normal shit like going to the movies, her skipping school to be with me on my days off or me picking her up from school and driving her home. Her cousins are really strict on her so I've never been in her house and she's never come to Waterbury that makes it hard for us to see each other long enough for sex to go down. That is why I've been talking to this double d breasted girl from Danbury High named Monica whose been coming in the store almost everyday since last week and she finally slipped me her number after I helped her buy some air force ones. She's not as cute as Miko but she's loose like Jessica and that is exactly what I am looking for.

Kenya and I have been working together a lot lately and she's a cool girl. Sometimes I find myself looking at her, not because I am attracted to her but just out of habit. Ironically every time I look at her she is looking at me with a cocked eyebrow but I brush it off. Sometimes if I'm not careful I find myself lightly flirting with her on the sales floor and in the stock room. We'll pass each other going down the narrow isles slightly brushing up against our bodies then look back at one another after we pass with smirks on our faces. I'm starting to like the attention despite the fact we haven't had a conversation outside of work.

"So you're going to Pennsylvania for three days huh?"

"Yeah. I really don't wanna go but I'ma do it for all the extra hours I'ma rack in na mean?"

"Yeah…I'ma miss you while you're gone." I looked at Kenya with a strange face because this is news to me. We stood in the middle of the stockroom waiting for the other to say something until we realized we were supposed to be getting shoes for customers. We scrambled to get what we went back for and hurried in the backroom to talk again.

"You gonna miss me for real? Why?"

"I don't know, I just am." She replied cocking her left eyebrow again."

"What's with that eyebrow? Like you tryin' to seduce me or somethin'."

"Maybe…are you paying attention?" We got another shoe, ran it out onto the floor and ran back into the stockroom.

"So you are tryin' to seduce me." I asked.

"I didn't say that."

"Yeah sure."

"You gonna call me while you're there?"

"You want me to call you?"

"If you want."

"I don't have your number." Kenya lifted up my red Olympia uniform shirt and wrote one number on each of my abs putting the last one right beneath my waistline.

"Don't sweat, it might rub off."

"Too late." I said smiling at her. We grabbed more shoes, ran them out and ran back into the stockroom over and over again for the last two hours we worked together.

"What time are you guys getting back babe?" Kenya asked.

"I don't know we are in like stand still traffic and it's pissin' me the hell off." I mumbled.

"Well I asked my mom if we could go to the Waterbury Mall for an outfit I wanted and I talked her into having dinner at Bertuci's but she likes to be home around eight so you need to be there no later than seven thirty." I sat up from the back seat and looked at the car clock that read five forty-two. Shit, that doesn't give us enough time at all and I haven't even seen the welcome to Connecticut sign yet.

"Aight, I'll keep you posted."

The last three days in Pennsylvania is one for the record books. My first night I got a call from Monica wanting to take me out for my birthday that passed last week, then one from Miko saying how she is moving back to Pittsburg the day after Thanksgiving and I wont see her anymore and then the one I was looking forward to all day. The phone call that I anticipated every night around ten o'clock, the call from Kenya. On the first night, the very first night Kenya laid claim to me and I let her do it without putting up any hesitation. There is something about Kenya that drives me wild and it has something to do with the look in her eye when she cocks her eyebrow and puckers her lips.

I've been shifting my position impatiently in the back seat of my District Managers car the whole ride from PA wishing we were going faster in hopes of seeing Kenya before her and her family heads back to Danbury. For the past three days I've only taken the phone calls of one person, Kenya as we talked the night away like Kendra and I use to do in the best stages of our relationship. Talking to Kenya I forget she is sixteen because of the way she converses with me. Her maturity is at the level Kendra's was when she was sixteen, which makes me want to throw out all my omissions about her. I've been dying to set eyes on her ever since the day she wrote her number on my stomach and our calls to each other every night and random text messages throughout the day only makes matters worst. For some peculiar reason I feel like Kenya and I have been dating for months but I haven't seen her in a hundred moons time, I miss her that much. I keep telling myself that a month ago I didn't look at her twice and now she's my girlfriend. I told myself I wouldn't get into any more exclusive relationships after Kendra but my sentiments are gravitating heavily in Kenya's direction and the strength is far too great for me to ignore.

When I look at Kenya time stood still as if everything halted except the two of us. I stared at the entrance of Bertucci's waiting for Kenya to come out and when she did I see her for the first time. I feel her energy but she isn't within ten feet of me and for the first time I see her, really see her. As everything around me seem to be dismal and lifeless her radiance is as bright as the stars. Her eyes have a twinkle in them and her smile made the sun jealous. I saw her for the first time. A beautiful five foot five sandy brown haired Brazilian bombshell. *Oh my God she is gorgeous* I thought to myself as she walked toward me smiling. She wore tight blue jeans, with black heels a white fitted shirt and an open black leather boyfriend jacket. Her brown and highlighted hair is straight but curled at the ends as it hung to the middle of her back. I looked down at my black windbreaker pants and my red Olympia Sports t-shirt and cursed myself for not changing before we left Scranton.

I extended my arms for a hug and Kenya jumped on my waist hugging me as if I just came home from doing a three to five. I'm surprised by her behavior but when we kissed my surprise turned into something different. The funny feeling I got in my stomach whenever I thought about Kendra is present now, my arrogant guard is down and I feel like myself. I looked at Kenya and I'm overjoyed she didn't turn into Kendra.

"What?" Kenya asked while still in my arms.

"You're gorgeous." I replied, with a smile from her a kiss followed. It's like kissing a cloud when our lips meet. Not too hard or aggressive, not wet and just the right amount of tongue.

"I didn't even see you, Alana told me you were out here."

"How did she see me?"

"She went to the bathroom and when she came back to the table she whispered it to me."

"Oh tell her I said thanks."

"I will." A smile is etched on Kenya's face as we stand in front of each other eye gazing and smiling like two little kids on Valentine's Day.

"Miss me?"

"Yep."

"How much."

"This much." She said.

"How much is this much?"

"This much." And she kissed me again. "Baby I have to go, my mom would be wondering where I went. I will see you Friday at work."

"Ok, call me later."

"I will." We kissed again before deciding to let her go back into the restaurant but not before looking back until she was out of sight. I walked the mall feeling like I have a thousand dollar bill in my pocket and I liked the feeling as I haven't felt like this since I was fifteen.

It's great having my family here at Thanksgiving. I haven't seen my cousins from North Carolina since last April. My mother, sisters, my niece, my cousins, aunts and even my grandmother are here. My aunt Buffy brought her Muslim boyfriend Jihad, my mom has her mortician boyfriend Freddy and my Aunt Dimpsey has her high school sweetheart KJ spending Thanksgiving with us. It's a joyous time.

"Oh she cute." I heard my cousin Avery say to a girl he saw on T.V.

"No she not, she ugly." His brother Dominique responded.

"That's right Dom, don't be lookin' at no white girls." My aunt Buffy said butting in.

"Don't tell him that. If she's cute then she's cute it don't matter what race she is." I said.

"You must date white girls huh?" My aunt Rolanda asked looking over her shoulder at us from the table.

"I date all women. Black, white, Asian whatever. I don't discriminate."

"Yeah but at one time in history they discriminated against us so why would you want to be with somebody like that?" My afro-centric grandmother asked.

"Look, I can't help if that is the era that ya'll grew up in but times are different now. It's not that serious anymore."

"It's always serious." She said.

"Syn, is your girlfriend white?" Dimpsey asked.

"She's Brazilian."

"White." About three different people said.

"No she is not white she is Brazilian."

"Oh boy please she white. If you Jamaican you still classified as black, if you French you're classified as white, if her skin ain't like yours then she white." My grandmother explained.

"That's the craziest thing I've ever heard. Ya'll just old, the times have changed." I said defending my position.

"I ain't never date no white boy in my lifetime." My aunt Rolanda said.

"Me either." Agreed my younger female cousins and my mother. The dinner table erupted in talk about race and how bad white people are and all I could do is sit there and listen to it. After a while I thought about Kenya and the image of her smiling at me yesterday is still very much fresh in my mind. I looked around the table and became disgusted with the fact my family, people that I respect and have looked up to all my life are acting like stone cold racists, I lost my appetite.

"Syn nobody's comin' down on you. You know I don't care who you date as long as you like them. All mommy's sayin' is I would rather for you to date a woman in my image."

"Ok, I respect that but what is your image. Is your image just limited to your skin color or everything you are?"

"What do you mean?"

"I mean do you want me to be with a black woman who is all ghetto, not sayin' all black women are ghetto but just hear me out. Would you rather I was with a black woman just 'cause she was black or would you be ok with me being with a Brazilian…"

"White." Someone uttered.

"Ok, white girl who treated me the way you want me to be treated, loved me the way you want someone to love your son and had your same work ethic and everything? Which image do you want, the physical or the complete package? Because the way I see it I want the complete package and I don't care what color she is." I argued.

"You can find a black girl with those same qualities." Aunt Buffy threw out there.

"I'm not sayin' I can't. I'm just sayin' I'm not gonna pass up a nice girl just because she isn't black. I'm not gonna say, yeah well you're everything I want in a girl but you're not the right color sorry. No, that ain't right. This is the exact reason why ya'll say racism is still very much alive today 'cause elder people like ya'll are passin' that shit down to ya'll kids."

"Ooh did he just say shit?" My aunt Buffy joked trying to calm the mood.

"Aight everybody leave my son alone."

"I don't know how my mom would feel about it. I doubt it would be a problem because my last boyfriend was Dominican."

"Yeah but you're Brazilian so it's still kinda along the same lines of your nationality isn't it."

"Yeah and no but Ricky isn't white faced like my dad, he is a little lighter than you."

"Ok then she should be cool about it."

"Yeah. And even if she isn't it doesn't matter because I like you."

"You would defy your mom for me?" I asked surprised.

"It's not about defying her it's about her not being able to tell me who I can and can't be with. I love my mom but I have to do what I feel is best for me."

"Really?"

"Yeah."

"What about you?"

"What about me? My moms is cool wit whatever." I said lying. The store is slow due to snow coming down hard outside and talks of a blizzard circulated throughout the mall. I went to the threshold of the store and looked down the hall and saw no shoppers but only security walking from store to store.

"Anyone out there?" Kenya called.

"Na, just security. I hope they comin' to tell us they closin' the mall."

"Why? You don't like being alone with me?" I turned around and looked at Kenya sitting on the counter with her legs crossed, her hair hanging in one side of her face while she bit her bottom lip and that funny feeling returned. The same funny feeling I got when I am with Kendra. I walked over to her and stood in front of her close enough to smell her lip-gloss.

"I love it. The only thing is I live a half hour away and it's gonna take me forever to get home."

"Oh I know."

"Hey guys we're closing up the mall due to the weather." A strong voice said behind me. Startled we both shot our heads toward the door to see a security guard standing there.

"Is it bad out?" I asked.

"From what I'm told it's pretty bad and the highways aren't any better."

"Fuck. Aight thanks."

"Lemme call my mom and see if she is gonna come pick me up." Kenya grabbed the cordless phone and I started counting down the registers and putting away shoes. Since we've had less than twenty customers walk in all day there was no need for clean up.

"My mom wants to know if you could bring me home?"

"Yeah but how the hell am I gonna get up your steep ass hill?"

"I know another way. It might take a little longer but there isn't a hill."

"Aight, I'll take you. Just as long as I don't have to drive up a hill I'm good." Kenya relayed the message to her mother while I sat in the office chair dreading the ride to her house.

"Hey." She said. I looked up at Kenya standing directly in front of me, my face to her waist.

"What's wrong?"

"Nothin'."

"You ready?"

"In a minute." She sat on my lap with her arms around my neck as we kissed for what seemed like hours getting more and more passionate and touchy with each tongue exchange. I slid my hands under her shirt and felt her smooth skin running my hands up and down her back, stomach and chest all the while Kenya staring me down with her eyebrow cocked and a take-me-now look on her face.

"You scared?" she asked.

"No. I just don't want our first time to be on this dirty stockroom floor. I have more respect for you than that."

"I'm happy to hear that. I was going to see what you were going to do."

"If I just wanted to fuck you I would've but I like you more than that. There is somethin' about you that drives me crazy inside and that doesn't happen to me often."

"Did you feel that same way with Miko and Jessica?"

"Hell no, definitely not with Jessica…"

"Why did you even like her? She was a hoe."

"Sport fuckin' I guess."

"What?"

"My boy Tracy calls it sport fuckin'. It's means just fuckin' for the fun of it you know add some notches on your belt."

"Oh and Miko?"

"Miko was real cool…"

"She's ugly."

"That's messed up. Na she is cute but I am more attracted to her wit than anything. See with me it's not all about the exterior. I look at other things when I decided to mess with a girl or make her my girlfriend. Like Jessica may have been a hoe but she is cool as shit and is down to do anything at the drop of a hat. I'm a real spontaneous person and so is she. Miko didn't back down from anything, a challenge or exchanging insults wit me or anything. Most girls would cry if I said some of the things I say to Miko but she is strong enough to handle that."

"Yeah 'cause you are pretty mean."

"I'm not mean to you."

"I know, why is that?"

"'Cause that is not the aura you give off. With you it's different."

"So why did you decided to date me." She asked.

"What I like most about you is you saw what you wanted and you went after it. You knew I was with Miko and you flirted with me, trapped me back here in between those tight ass isles and just made your agenda known. You're a go getta and I like that a lot."

"Well I know what I want and I always get it."

"Aren't you afraid some girl will come along and do the same thing to you."

"Look at me!" She said with an extremely confident look on her face.
"Yeah, you are sexy as shit."

"No I'm gorgeous." She said pointing at her face and smiling.

"Damn right." I agreed.

I watched as Kenya cautiously trotted down her steep driveway to her house and waited for her to signal she is at her door ok. I looked around the dark neighborhood in between falling snowflakes and it looks as if the clouds fell from the heavens. I tired to pull off but my car won't move. I burned rubber trying to go forward and backward again and again.

"Stuck?"

"Yeah." I said holding my cell phone between my shoulder and ear. I stopped to look down the hill at Kenya's house and saw faces in the window while I heard laughter on the phone.

"My mom says to stay here tonight. She's worried you'll get in an accident on the way home."

"I can't, I have that interview with Finish Line tomorrow."

"I don't think it'll happen because it's supposed to snow like this way into the afternoon."

"Aight so do I leave my car right here?"

"Pull it into the driveway."

"Are ya'll crazy? If I do that I might start sliding and ya'll are gonna have a car in ya livin' room."

"You're right leave it there." I took my overnight bag out of the trunk and busted my ass twice as I ambled down the slippery driveway. I was greeted by Kenya's mother at the front door."

"Nice to see you again Syncere. Thank you for bringing her home. Come in, come in." Her mother said with a strong accent. I honestly can see where Kenya gets her good looks. She and her mother are the same height; they have the same long sandy brown hair and beautiful faces. If this is what Kenya is going to look like in forty years I need to stick around.

"Thank you very much. I really didn't want to drive all the way home. We could barely see on the way here."

"Yeah it's pretty bad out. Give me your things and I'll put them in the living room. Kenya has some friends in the other room so you two go in and have fun. Kenya, keep it down though."

"Ok mom."

"You're moms is nice. Cute as hell too."

"Oh you're checkin' out my mom now?"

"Hey if it doesn't work out with me and you I might have to holla." I said laughing while Kenya hit me with the weakest punch ever. I looked at her and laughed.

"I don't know how to throw a punch."

"You've never been in a fight?"

"No."

"Aight I'ma teach you one day."

"Ok."

Kenya and I sat in their second living room next to the window to look at the snowfall while we talked. Her life isn't as sugar coated as I thought it was, well it isn't entirely. She told me when she was eleven her father was convicted of sexually molesting a neighbor of hers and her mother divorced him. Kenya developed a similar type of hate for her father like I did with my mother a few years ago. She hasn't talked to him in over two years and she has no intention on doing so. Further into our conversation she told me her mother forced her to model when she was young and now she does some print work for a store called Forever 21 as well as doing some stuff for Louis Vuitton catalogs. *I got me a model* I thought to myself.

After describing all the things she's done we switched gears and she listened attentively seeming very interested in my life and what I've done up to this point. I watched as a smile appeared on her face when I talked about me achieving an accomplishment, a sad face when I described my childhood and the relationship I had with my mother prior to me coming back to Connecticut. Most of all she listened to me reminisce about Kendra and the things we went through from start to finish. Her face got soft when she heard about the sweet things we did, sadden when Kendra and I weren't talking and surprised when I described Mulan's ass whooping.

"You have more tattoos other than these." She asked grabbing my wrists.

"Yeah. This one was my first one I got when I was sixteen, it's my stage name Infinate and this is the tattoo Kendra and I got last summer."

"Always K.L" she read aloud. "Why do you still have it?"

"I promised her I wouldn't get it covered no matter what. After all the shit I put her through this is the one commitment to her I'ma keep."

"Even after all that?"

"It was all my fault shit went the way it did not hers. She was just fed up na mean? My karma came back to get me that's all."

"I knew you were a softy."

"A softy?"

"Yeah. Everyone in the store was running around talking like you're this mean ass person and all about work and everything but when you look at me I didn't see that."

"When did you realize this?"

"The day you rang me up for my first purchase. Your face said you are a mean hard ass but I look into your eyes I saw the softness of a teddy bear and I knew deep down you are a sweet guy. That's what attracted me to you."

"What? That you think I'm a softy?"

"No. Not that you're a softy like a punk, but it's your demeanor. You're big, strong and you can be mean as hell but there is another side of you I know most people don't see and you let me in on it that day without even knowing it."

"Wow! How old are you again? You're talkin' like you in ya late thirties."

"I'm young but I'm not stupid. I have a question though."

"What?"

"Why did you tell me you cheated on all your girlfriends except?" I laughed at her question mainly because I wasn't expecting it.

"My boy Tracy says I volunteer too much information but I think it's because I need to face the wrong I've done in order to be right now. See when people meet or start dating for the first time they only talk about how great they are and tell all the great qualities about them. No one ever tells about their flaws but I do so you hear the good about me and the bad about me. Therefore you know exactly what you are gettin' into. So if I didn't scare you away with my violence and infidelity do you still want to be with me?"

"Yes." She said smiling.

16

Kenya and I sat in my white Mitsubishi Diamante in the Park and Ride Lot right off of exit eleven. We do this frequently when there isn't enough time for me to take her to Waterbury and come all the way back to Danbury before her mother gets home.

"Ooh you have a camera back here. Who's is it?"

"Mines crazy, who else would it be?

"I don't know, maybe your mom or one of your sisters. Is there any film left in it?"

"I think it may have two or three shots left."

"Com'on take a picture with me."

"Na, I'm not that photogenic. Lemme take one of you."

"Ok." Kenya rested her head on the palm of her left hand, smiled big and looked at me like she's never looked at me before. It took me a while to snap the picture because while looking through the lenses my heart is melting. The look on her face is indescribable, it's as if she is completely comfortable with me and there is no other place on earth she'd rather be. Click.

"Lemme take another one." I said.

"No take one with me." She snatched the camera out of my hand, wound it and got real close to me, cheek to cheek then click.

"Ok, ok that is enough."

"No one more…do it do it."

"No I'm not doin' it if you're gonna take a picture."

"Oh baby please." She said pouting.

"Ok." I put on a big kool-aid smile and did the bobble head impression she liked so much and she laughed to the point she couldn't keep her head steady enough to take the picture.

"So you know tomorrow I don't have any class."

"Why?"

"Midterms and I took all mine today so I wouldn't have to do any tomorrow. So we have the whole day to ourselves. Do you have it off?"

"No but I can call in sick."

"Babe you just started a week ago, I don't want you to get in trouble."

"Trust me I'm not. My boss Dennis is a bitch. I got it. But what about your mom?"

"She doesn't know."

"What about Blake and Alana?"

"School all day until three and Blake gets home at four."

"Cool. What do you want to do?"

"I wanna go to this place called Guys and Dolls."

"Where is it and what is it?"

"Exit eight, it's a pool hall."

"You shoot pool?"

"A little."

"Ok that's wussup. What time do you want me to come get you?"

"You want breakfast?"

"Sure."

" Leave your house at eight right after my mom leaves."

I pulled up to Kenya's house proceeding with extreme caution not knowing if her mother had left yet and also to be sure her neighbors didn't see me.

"No don't park up front, drive around the side of the house and park near the back." Kenya instructed on her cell phone while she peeked through her window. She greeted me at the side entrance to her house wearing black sweat pants and a white cami. She threw her arms around me when I lifted her up carrying her in the house giving me short kisses over and over.

"Smells good." I complimented.

"Thanks. Bacon, eggs and pancakes."

"Babe I don't eat pork."

"I know…turkey bacon. She said holding up the package. I gave her a big kiss on the cheek.

"That's my girl."

We devoured breakfast then sat on the couch in each other's arms watching the Maury Show and before long we both drifted to sleep.

"Baby, are you sleep?"

"No." I lied.

"Let's go upstairs." I abided without hesitation but when we got the bottom of her stairs I pulled her around to me and planted a long passionate kiss on her soft lips. She lay on the stairs as I gently got on top of her being careful not to drop my hundred and seventy pound body on her ninety-something pound frame. We just kissed and let our hands explore each other's backs, chests, and stomach until she broke the lip lock.

"What?" I asked trying to catch my breath.

"I don't want our first time to be on these steps…maybe it can happen the third or fourth time. Com'on." She instructed again leaping to her feet and running up the stairs.

She pushed me on her twin-sized bed, which I think I am too big to be on, jumping on me resuming our kiss. First went my shirt then hers. I ran my tongue around her A cups then over her perky nipples as Kenya let out a pleasure gasp. She then unbuttoned my jeans slid them off then she stood in front of me, my face to her waist and I took off her black sweat pants. I ran my hands up her thighs before taking off her black-laced boy shorts. Her sex smell is exhilarating as it hit my nostrils and I wanted to get lost in her ambiance as she held my head close to her pleasure lips.

I lay back on Kenya's bed as she climbed on top of me and we kissed again while grinding a little. I looked at her tapping my mouth before I firmly took her by the waist and slid underneath her positioning her sex lips on my face. I wildly swirled my tongue all over and into Kenya's peach flavored mound while keeping my hands planted on her ass and my face buried deep into her. Kenya's sex moans filled the empty house especially when she began to ride my face like a jockey. I orally pleased Kenya until I tasted her peach juices in my mouth.

"Wow! No one has ever made me cum while eating me like that. I want it in me right now." She demanded with a sexy devilish look on her face. She put the condom on and I entered her small tight glove just telling myself *don't cum, don't cum.* I put my all into each thrust and every stroke I delivered. I made sure my pelvis met hers every time she bounced on me as well as making sure we moved as one while she road. This isn't just sex this is a little more than that. It's in between us having sex and making love, whatever it is I put everything physical and emotional into what we are doing until the bed it the floor. We stopped and laughed ourselves silly at what just happened.

"I bet that was a first. It is for me." I said laughing.

"Definitely a first for me babe. Wait, wait I wanna cum again. Do that thing when you hold me."

"Ok." I took hold of Kenya's tiny waist, lifted her body up slightly and delivered short, quick but powerful thrusts as she screamed for me to do it harder, faster.

"OH MY GOD!!" she belted falling on top of me mixing her sweat with mine.

"You like it?"

"Fuck yeah." She replied breathing heavily.

"Good."

"Did you?"

"Hell to tha yeah."

"We broke my bed." She said laughing again.

"I know, I'll fix it."

"Good. I'ma get in the shower."

"Oh what you don't wanna smell like me now?" I joked. She put her hands between her legs and smelled them before licking them off.

"I would love to but eventually my mom will smell and want it all to herself then I'll probably be sent back to Brazil. Now you don't want that do you?"

Kenya got her friend Aaron to drive her to Waterbury today because she promised to give him fifty bucks just because she couldn't wait until tomorrow to see me. For the past two weeks Kenya and I have spent every minute of free time with each other. On my days off I'd go pick her up from school and we'd hang out at Guys and Dolls or at exit eleven or at her house with Blake and Alana. On the weekends she'd lie about having a photo shoot just so I could come to Danbury to pick her up. We have dinner at our new favorite place, Outback Steakhouse we feed each other coconut shrimp in between laughs. I can't go a day without seeing her so bad that I tape the picture she took in my car onto my freshener that hangs from my rear view mirror. Today is no exception, it's Friday and her mother works until 8pm to do paperwork, which gives Kendra and I at least 5 hours to spend with each other.

We locked ourselves in the tiny room I sleep in re-enacting our first sex/lovemaking afternoon when I heard a car pull up.

"I think my mom is here." I froze.

"You said she was at work."

"She's supposed to be." Kenya and I threw on our cloths and ran to the living room where we'd left the television on before my mom got in the house.

"Hey Syn."

"Momadopolis! Hey. Mom this is Kenya the girl I was tellin' you 'bout."

"Oh hi sweetie. You're a cutie. Cutie patuti." She said smiling at Kenya while walking to the kitchen.

"Where you comin' from ma?"

"Work, I forgot to mail off these bills and I gotta make it to the post office before they close."

"Here." I handed my mom three hundred dollars like I do every other week as a symbol of me helping out while I stay here.

"Oh thanks Syn. Well mommy gotta go. Bye Kenya."

"By Ms. Washington."

"You can call me mom."

"Ok mom." Kenya responded sounding excited.

"I think my mom likes you."

"She was just being nice." Kenya said modestly.

"No you don't understand. Normally when I bring a girl home she says hi but she keeps it movin'. She doesn't smile or say call me mom. Normally she shows interest but with you she was real pleasant like she was happy to meet you."

"Aww baby, you talk about me?"

"All the time." Kenya gave me a tight hug and a big kiss on the cheek.

"My mom knows." She said.

"She knows about us sleepin' together?"

"God no! She knows about us dating." She corrected.

"How?"

"Blake talks about you all the time. Syncere has a cool name, Syncere is cool, and hey when's Syncere coming over again. My mom asked him who was he talking about and he said the guy that works with Kenya then she asked Alana but Alana played dumb but she asked me last."

"What did you tell her?"

"I told her we do."

"What did she say?"

"She wants me to come straight home from school and I can only go to work unless I break up with you. But I'm a freakin' model on the weekends I really don't need to sell sneakers. I just do it to pass the time. Besides she doesn't even know you don't work there anymore."

"Why does she want us to break up? I thought she liked me."

"She thinks you're nice but she says I'm too young for you."

"Hold up, didn't you tell me your sister Liz was sixteen when she met Kirk and he was twenty five? And they met off the Internet. What is the difference?"

"I don't think the age is the real reason, I think it's because you are black."

"'Cause I'm black?"

"Yeah. Baby you don't understand. My grandma married this guy who dealt with oil and they moved to Brazil where they built this great big house on this hill and my grandma has servants, black ones. Black people are still looked upon as slaves in Brazil. My mom was raised that way." She explained.

"So what are you gonna do?"

"Do about what?"

"About us, about your mom."

"Where am I right now?"

"Here with me."

"That's what I'm going to do. Be here with you. Now, is your mom coming back or is the coast clear?"

"She's gone."

"I want you to do that thing you do."

As Aaron drove my Kenya away I recapped the last month realizing we have been going hard at our relationship. I began to wonder how long would it really last. She's sixteen and when I was sixteen I would jump in and out of a new relationship bi-monthly. Eleven did the very same thing to me two months ago and we have a longer history than Kenya and I so what is going to stop her? Kenya is a drop dead gorgeous Brazilian girl who can have any man she wants in a hundred yard radius with a mother who disapproves of our relationship. I'm a twenty-year old college drop out, former track star and your average looking guy who is currently living with his mother. I think the odds are stacked against me.

"Cut if her mom don't like you then you need to jump ship now before you start catchin' deep feelin's for this girl for real." Track explained.

"But she don't care what her mom thinks, she wants to be with me regardless."

"Cut I'm ya boy right? I ain't gonna tell you nothin' that'll hurt'chu. Now listen, all that girl is doin' is messin' wit'chu only because her mom told her not too. I know ya'll been together for a month or so and that's cool but now she's doin' it 'cause her mom told her not too. Once her mom find out ya'll still datin' what do you think is gonna happen?"

"Nothin'."

"Do you honestly think this girl is gonna choose you over her own mother? Think about it. She's sixteen, still in high school, no car and she lives at home. She probably still gets an allowance. The time is gonna come when she is tired of sneaking around and lying and she is gonna come to you one day with that face and she's gonna jump ship, I'm tellin' you."

"Na it ain't gonna happen like that."

"Aight cut don't believe me. What do you see in this girl anyway? She's a kid. You need a woman like Kendra."

"Fuck Kendra." I said in the meanest voice possible.

"Aight cut, sorry. So you don't love Kendra anymore?"

"No."

"Then why are you keepin' that tattoo?"

"'Cause I told her I wouldn't get it covered. You wouldn't understand there is a principal behind this. You just wouldn't understand."

"I understand fine. You still love her."

"No I don't."

"Then help me understand then."

"I put her through a lot of shit. I may even be the reason why she did what she did but I made this commitment to her and if I do anything right by her at all I have to live with this."

"Whatever you did when you were younger you have to let go. You can't keep beatin' yourself up and feeling guilty for some shit you did when you were fifteen or sixteen. You fucked up she fucked up and neither one of you owe the other one anything."

"Maybe you right."

"I'm always right cut."

"There go that boss shit again."

"It's tha truth cut."

"Hol' up. Did you just say Kenya is young? Weren't you like twenty-one when you met M.Dot? Wasn't she sixteen too?"

"Yeah but that is different."

"How so? I didn't think so, ya'll have a five-year difference just like Kenya and I do and look you and M.Dot are four years strong."

"True but this is different. You and this girl got so much goin' against ya'll. It's not only the age thing but it's the race thing and she live forty-minutes away. By the time you're ready to settle down she'll just be entering college and really starting her life and where does that leave you?"

"I can say the same thing about M.Dot."

"Man she ain't goin' nowhere unfortunately. But for real for real at the end of the day you have to do what is right for Syncere and not because of what I think. The devil is gonna do him anyway. Just weigh all possibilities if you're thinkin' about gettin' serious with this girl."

"I got'chu cut. Good look." Tracy and I did the Wolf Pak handshake before he left the kitchen to get the door.

"Lisa this is Syncere, Syncere this my home girl Lisa."

"Hey."

"Hi."

"Lisa where KaTasha?"

"She on her way. Does he know KaTasha?"

"Cut you know KaTasha don't'chu?"

"Na, who is she?"

"Launchpad's sister."

"Launch got a sister. I never knew." Lisa and Tracy chopped it up while I shuffled through the cards. I looked at Lisa who is a five-foot eight Dominican woman and the prettiest plus sized woman I've ever seen. In a strange way I am attracted to her. She has long jet-black curly hair, long eyelashes that compliment her beautiful hazel eyes and a smile wider than the Nile. Her voice sounds like God took all the voices of his angels and gave them to her and I just listened from afar wanting to dance to her rhythm. She's articulate, confident and carries herself like a woman and she's sexy while she does it. This is new to me because I have never in my life been attracted to a big woman but Lisa has opened my eyes and even if this thing with Kenya and I don't work out I may have to ask Tre for a hook up.

It's a chilly December night just a week before Christmas but the sky is as clear as a nice summer night in North Carolina. Kendra lied to her mother about working late so we can escape away to New Haven where we are meeting Emily and Mika to hang out.

"Call Em to see where they are." I said as we got off the exit a few blocks from the civic center.

"She said they are waiting outside for us." Kenya and I parked and quickly found Emily and Mika hugged up trying to keep warm.

"Hey guys." Emily said when she saw Kenya and I walk up. The girls hugged while Mika and gave each other pound then we all walked into the civic center hand in hand with our significant other. Touring the low rent flea market Kenya and walk side by side shooting each other smiles and winks every chance we get as I am wondering is this really happening? Just as I swore off women this special beautiful goddess enters my life and is beginning to shake things up.

Tonight Kenya holds my hand a little softer than she normally does and I feel strangely close to her right now. Three times already I've had to stop myself in mid sentence from telling her I love her because it just comes out of no where. I'm afraid if I tell her I'll scare her away due to the fact we haven't been dating long enough for me to say that. Truth be, this is the night I feel in love with her. Every time I look at her my heart does back flips as my soul breaks into song. It's the same feeling I use to get when I was with Kendra but is Kenya ready for love? I wrote Evelyn off when she said it because I thought she was too young, not that Kenya's one year makes a difference. I think the difference is that I want Kenya to love me and I didn't see Evelyn in that way at the time.

"We gotta do it again real soon." Mika suggested as we all walked down the quiet street back to our car.

"What are ya'll doin' for New Years?" I asked.

"We're havin' a party, you guys should come. Mika's coming." Emily invited.

"I have to baby sit 'cause my mom is going out. But babe you can go."

"Can't. I'm throwin' somethin' at my house that is why I asked what ya'll was doin' 'cause I wanted ya'll to stop by and meet the rest of my peoples. Well fuck it we can do somethin' New Year's day."

"Like what?"

"Let's go out of town…New York? You know do a little shoppin', walk around then we can have dinner somewhere in the city."

"Sounds like a plan, you in babe?" Emily asked Mika.

"Hell yeah, I know the city like the back of my hand. We exchanged pounds and hugs again before going in opposite directions.

"I love them." Kenya said locking her fingers with mine.

"Yeah, Mika is cool as hell and I'm so happy you and Em are as cool as ya'll are. When we are all together I feel like we're two married couples. I can see us ten years from now having dinner at their house or at ours talkin' 'bout all the stuff we did when we were young. You holdin' their baby and them holdin' ours na mean?"

"You're thinking that far into the future? You want to have kids with me?" She said and I immediately wish I can take that comment back.

"Not tomorrow but yeah don't'chu think that'll be nice. I mean you're gorgeous and I'm dangerously handsome so it's only right we pass some of these good genes down to someone." I joked.

"Wow, I didn't know you felt like that." She said laughing.

"I don't wanna scare you by talkin' like this na mean? I don't want you to think I'm tryin' to move too fast. I was just thinkin' 'bout the possibilities feel me?"

"I feel the same way."

"What way?" I'm excited and overjoyed to hear her say that.

"Like I could be with you for a long time." Kenya and I stopped walking and we faced each other. I giggled at her little because she has to look up to look at me in the eye. I wrapped my arms around her, hers caressed my back as we just stood in the middle of the side walk gazing in each others eyes trying to see if what we were saying is true. I don't know about her but I have all the conformation I need. After long we kissed and continued walking until Kenya ask if I could carry her to the car. I did and with her in my arms she looked at nothing but my face as she held tight to my neck. Every time I look down there she was smiling at me with her perfect smile and the ever-present twinkle in her eye. A strong feeling swept over me one that is very very familiar.

"Son good look on comin' wit me on Christmas mornin'. I appreciate it." I thanked Jus while I sped on the highway.

"No doubt son. Syn you always on some sweet smooth shit with tha ladies. Where you be comin' up wit this shit from?"

"I don't know. Sometimes it just comes to me when I'm doin' random shit. Seriously I get my best ideas while I'm in the shower. My verses, ideas for my store shit like this. Most of it pops in my head while I'm washin' na mean?"

"I hear that. So do she know you comin'?"

"Na. I just hope her moms let me in na mean?"

"Oh that's right she don't like black people. You darin' as a muhfucka. Syncere don't givva fuck." Jus said laughing.

"Nope. I wanna see her and that's what I'ma do."

"So what you gonna do if her moms don't let you in?"

"I don't even have to come in. I just wanna give Kenya her gifts and just see her face even if it's from the window. That alone is worth the drive."

"Damn son you like her like that?"

"Yeah."

"You know what I noticed? You be wit a different girl like every few months, na hear me out. But when you really like one you <u>like</u> one and I only seen you like this wit Kendra and Krista."

"Yeah I know."

    I crept my car up Kenya's street slowly to be sure they can't see me from the huge living room window. Jus is dressed in all brown with a matching cap resembling a UPS deliveryman. I typed up delivery pages that required Kenya and her mother sign for their gifts. My plan is to have Jus deliver a bouquet of flowers to Kenya's mother first in attempts to soften her up. Ten minutes later I'ma have Jus make a second delivery of Kenya's Christmas gifts, which consists of a personalized Italian charm bracelet that Emily and Mika helped me design, a hundred dollar gift card to Victoria's Secret and a pair of heels I got from Aldo where Kenya's friend Kristina works.

    I watched from my parked car as Jus strolled to the house with the flowers for Kenya's mother. I saw a white guy answer the door that I think is Kirk because Kenya told me her older sister Liz and Kirk were coming in from Canada for the holidays. Shortly after Kenya's mother came to the door to sign for her flowers. She went away from the door but Jus was just standing there then I saw Kirk hand him something.

"Yo they gave me a tip." He said laughing.

"A tip, how much?"

"Ten dollars."

"They fell for it. Aight, aight wait five minutes or so then take Kenya's gift."

"Yo Syn you a muhfuckin' genius."

    Jus repeated the routine again this time with Kenya answering the door with a huge smile on her face. She did the same, signed and Jus ran back to my car.

"Yo that was her? Damn she fine as hell."

"I told you." I said while my phone went off.

"Hey baby. You are so sweet, thank you so much."

"You're welcome. Did your mom like the flowers?"

"Yeah, but Liz destroyed the mood by saying you were trying to bribe my mom."

"Damn."

"Where are you?"

"Waterbury why?"

"Aww, I want to see you so bad. We are about to go to my grandma's house and I wont be able to see you for three more days, this sucks. I wanna give you your gifts."

"Ooh I got gifts as in plural meaning more than one."

"Yes." She said laughing. I walked behind Jus as he made his last delivery. The front door opened before we got to the end of the driveway and Kenya's younger brother Blake is standing there.

"See I told ya Kenya he was coming." Kenya came from the side and met me at the door throwing her arms around me while I picked her up and swung her around.

"Merry Christmas." I said closing my cell phone.

"Merry Christmas baby! Come in."

"You sure that is ok wit'cha mom?"

"Just get in here. You know him?" she said pointing to Jus.

"Yeah this my boy Jus."

"You set this all up?"

"Yeah. UPS don't deliver on Christmas. Hi Ms. Northrop." She waved from the living room. Kenya introduced me to Kirk and Liz and I introduced everyone to Jus while Kenya sat me on the couch and she sent Blake to get my gifts.

"You are amazing. When did you think of this?"

"A couple of days ago actually but I called Jus this mornin' to do it for me. I was afraid he wouldn't answer 'cause he's so hard to get in touch wit. Luckily he my boy and he said yeah without hesitation."

"Well he talks about'chu a lot and he's always been there for me so it was nothin'."

"Open your gifts."

"Which one is your favorite? I'll open that one first."

"This one." I passed Kenya the square shaped box and she tore the paper off it admiring the bracelet as she took it out.

"Baby!"

"Com'er lemme put it on and explain the charms to you. This K is for Kenya, the heart is self-explanatory and the S is for my name. The Taz charm is there 'cause I know you like him and the 1-1-0-3 is for November 2003 the month we started dating. Do you remember the day?"

"The 22nd."

"Here you go Syncere, these are from Kenya."

"Thank you Blake now go away."

"Na my little man can stay." I said gesturing him to sit next to me. I opened the medium sized box and pulled out two bright red Enyce shirts, one long sleeve and one short sleeve.

"Do you like them?" she asked not knowing what to expect.

"I love'em."

"I know your favorite color is Carolina blue but I want to see you in something else."

Jus and I drove back to Waterbury talking about what I just did and where I see myself with Kenya a year or so from now. Some of the things Tracy said to me stuck in the back of my mind especially the part he said by the time she enters college I'll be ready to settle down and her life will really just be beginning. Her mother keeps such a restricted leash on her that I fear once she does "get free" she's going to just wild out.

"You can't think like that Syn. You forgettin' the best part 'bout fuckin' wit a young chick…you get to mold her feel me? You have an influence over how she thinks 'bout certain shit and since you are older she's gonna look at how you act and she's gonna adapt to that. You got a year and a half until she goes to college, that is more than enough time."

"You think so?" I asked Jus. I'm nervous as hell when I think of how things are going to go with Kenya and I don't know why. Normally I'm full of confidence when dealing with a girl but for some reason when it comes to her my confidence turns into uncertainty. It's much too early for me to sit here and say I love her then again who says love has a time minimum? No it isn't love I just feel for her very strongly and its messing with my head.

As I watched television with my niece on my lap I began recapping the last year of my life. This time last year I was broke and lonely in Georgia. I'd sent that classic car book to Kendra and she called me on Christmas day. My insides were overjoyed she'd called me but my pride wouldn't let me tell her how I felt. I acted nonchalant as if her phone call did nothing for me then twenty-minutes later we were off the phone and I was back to feeling lonely again.

I ignored my feelings for Kendra then which resulted in us not speaking for the next four months and by that time anything I hoped to salvage of our on and off relationship was lost so I ask myself, is the feeling I'm feeling right now a feeling I want to feel for the rest of my life? I'm already tormented by the things I did to Keisha, Valarie and Dorcea in high school. Tormented by the guilt of being the reason why Evelyn is as promiscuous as she is now and breaking a young girls heart and I'm tormented at the fact I lost Kendra seemingly forever. The answer, hell no. I remember hearing that for every one man there are three, just three, women that are made especially for that man. Three women made to be the wife of that man but its up to that man to recognize those women.

If that is said to be true then I recognized her when I was fifteen but I pushed it to the side now that one is lost. Is Kenya my second one? I can easily play this like some b.s. relationship and just go day by day allowing myself to feel nothing and for the past few weeks I have convinced myself that I don't feel anything, however, the feeling only lasts until that phone rings and I hear her angelic voice say, "hi baby". After I hear that I'm like putty inside. Kenya and I spend time as if it could be our last moments together because sometimes that's how it feels. Every second we are doing something; talking, shooting pool, sitting in the car just holding each other or exploring our bodies as if it were the first time. The second she gets out my car to leave I feel apart of me leaving and in the depths of my stomach I feel incomplete.

We make love as if we've been married thirty years and we know everything there is to know about each other's bodies. The way Kenya runs her fingertips over my back and stomach to send jolts of stimulation up my spine or the way I hold her up and do the thing she likes. I feel like we've known each other in a past life or something, it's killing me to sit here right now and not be able to be in her presence.

17

"Yo cut where you at?"

"I'm at pullin' into work why what's good?"

"Son my car broke down."

"What? Where?"

"I'm on the side of the highway just an exit away from where Q live. He already halfway in Danbury and Wes ain't answerin' the phone. I ain't got anyone to call."

"Call Deon she lives close to there." Tracy suggested.

Instead of Deon coming to get me she sent Yumeka. I met Yumeka last summer when Deon asked her to sing back up to a song she'd written my cousin Nicole. At the time I thought Yumeka was cute, she's short and dark skinned with shoulder length hair and a nicely proportioned body but I don't think all the lights are on upstairs if you know what I mean.

"Meka thank you very much for comin' to get me you are a life savor."

"It's no problem. Do you need me to pick you up too?"

"Yeah if you don't mind. I'll be ready at ten."

"Ok see you tonight."

I spent most of my day on the phone with Skip at Car World 2, the buy here pay here place I got my car. I traded in my 1993 Lexus for the 1998 Diamante I've been driving for the past two months. I arranged to have it picked up and towed back to the dealership and I told Skip I'd be down in the morning.

"Hey Syncere I got some news for you." My gay boss Dennis said as I slammed the phone back on the receiver.

"What's good?"

"Chris wants you to go over to the Milford store and help out Abbey."

"When and for how long because I don't know when I'ma get my car back."

"It's not until March third. He's promoting Tracy to this store and I'm taking over Palisades Mall."

"A month should be cool. I should have my car back by then." On my break I told Kenya about my car and about the transfer going through in a little under a month.

"Milford? What are you going to do about your car?"

"I won't know anything until I go to the dealership in the mornin' to see what this muhfuckas says."

"Baby how are we gonna see each other? I haven't seen you in a week and now you don't have a car. Valentine's day is next week."

"Babe I know but I'll figure out somethin'. But now I gotta start workin' extra hours and savin' my money 'cause I might just have to buy a new car."

"Why would you have to do that? You haven't even had the car long enough."

"I know but I don't wanna deal wit this dude no more so I'ma go to a real dealership like I should've done in the first place. I'll call you tonight."

Just as she promised Yumeka is sitting outside where she dropped me off this morning. When I got in the car she had a smile on her face as she is dressed in a pair of tight blue jeans and a gray hoodie.

"Hey."

"Hey, how was your day?"

"Stressful."

"What did the car people say?"

"Nothin', I have to go down in the mornin' to see what they talkin' 'bout."

"If you need me to bring you to work and drop you off everyday I will." I looked at Yumeka with a strange look on my face.

"How will you get back and forth to work everyday?"

"I don't go in until ten am and I get out at five then I have class from six to nine by that time you are already done."

"I don't get out at ten every night only three times a week but I can work some overtime so I can save some money. Aight but only if you let me pay your gas every week."

"Deal."

"Can I ask you somethin'?"

"Yeah." She said.

"We haven't talked since August then Deon calls you out of the blue and you come runnin', why?"

"'Cause you a friend and you help friends. I might need you one day you know?"

"Yeah."

"Did you eat yet?"
"Na why?"

"I cooked if you wanna come by and eat with me."

"I'm a picky eater so what did you make?"

"Lasagna."

"What do you put in yours?"

"Meat."

"Nothin' else?"

"Nope."

"Ok let's go."

Yumeka's lives in a housing complex on top of a huge hill that overlooks Waterbury. As we got out the car I just stared at the lights of the city and thought I've never seen Waterbury like this before.

"You can see it better from my balcony."

Yumeka has a nice two bed room one bath apartment with a decent size kitchen and living room. She gave me the dime tour before offering me a seat and serving me a giant plate of lasagna with Italian bread on the side. I ate listening to her tell me about her boyfriend Tyrell who is locked up for dealing coke. Tyrell is five years older than Yumeka and was the only guy she ever loved. My heart kinda went out to her because I know how she is feeling.

"So you waitin' for him to get out?"

"I'm not waiting really because I still need to do me, know what I'm sayin'? A girl does have needs but when he gets out we'll just have to see."

"So you messin' wit anyone now?" I asked.

"No...you."

"No." I answered no because I know Yumeka likes me and I need her to think I'm interested long enough to get these rides back and forth to work everyday.

"Talkin' to anyone?"

"No one special. But a few chicks here and there."

"Any of them cook for you?"

"No."

"See I'm a good woman right? I have my own place, my own car and money and I'm a good cook. What guy wouldn't want me right?" She asked sounding like a personal ad. Before I could answer my phone went off and it's Kenya. I walked out onto the balcony to answer it.

"Why didn't you call me when you got home?"

"'Cause Jus called and told me to stop by the studio so he can get me to spit on this track. I just laid down my verse so I'ma hear it back and go home. I'll call you when I get out of the shower."

"Hurry up I wanna talk to you."

"'Bout what?"

"I wanna tell you about my day. I have some good news."

"Really what is it?"

"Nope. Finish up and call me back." I feel bad when I shut my cell because I've prided myself on the fact that I haven't told Kenya a lie since I've met her four months ago.

"Meka, my mom wants me to help her move somethin', I gotta go." I opened the car door in front of my house and proceeded to get out until Yumeka tapped me on the shoulder.

"What time tomorrow?"

"Eight-thirty. Thanks again and thanks for the lasagna."

"You're welcome. Syncere…can I have a hug?" I hesitated to Yumeka's request with one foot out the door and one foot in the car. Reluctantly I gave her one.

"Thanks again, good night." I shook off the strange vibe I got from Yumeka and walked in the house. I showered and got under the covers on the couch before calling Kenya.

"Well it's about time baby, I was about to go to sleep."

"Can you stay awake long enough to tell me 'bout your day?"

"Of course." She said in an upbeat voice.

"Ok I'm all ears."

"Well first I'ma start with the good news…I got another modeling job today!"

"For real? For who?"

"It's for Forever 21 again. I'm modeling their spring collection@"

"That's big. So I'ma be walkin' the mall and I'ma see you in their store front huh?"

"Yep, and if you go on their website you'll see me then if you get there catalog you'll see me. I may even end up on a billboard!"

"I got me a model, I got me a model! Do you think I'll get arrested if I steal your billboard?"

"Baby! Where will you put a huge billboard of me?" She asked laughing.

"Right outside my bedroom window so whenever I want to feel like you are with me all I have to do is pull back the curtains."

"Aww baby. Well I'll see what I can do to make that happen. I may not be able to do a billboard but I might be able to swing a storefront poster. That way you can put it on the wall in your bedroom."

"Oooh." I said.

"Yeah. That way I can watch you undress."

"Freak." I said chuckling.

"You like it. Maybe I should get a huge poster of you to put in my dorm when I go to college. So when I wake up from a nightmare I can stare at you until I feel safe."

"That'll work."

"Good. You miss me?"

"Yep. You miss me?"

"Yep."

"How much?"

"This much. Can you feel it baby?" She asked laughing

"Yes ma'am." I replied before she suddenly got quite. I looked at my phone to make sure it didn't hang up on her.

"Syncere?"

"Yeah babe?" I answered, as she got silent again.

"I love you." Those three words echoed in my head over and over again for the next few moments and I am speechless.

"I love you too." I responded feeling completely honest about returning the phrase.

"I didn't say it because that is what I want you to say. I said it because I mean it so don't say it if you don't."

"Kenya…I love you too."

"Say it again."

"I love you."

"Again."

"I love you."

"Again, again, again."

"I love you, I love you, love you."

Yumeka drove me to work and picked me up everyday for the next week and even packed me a lunch, since I told her I wasn't spending money to eat at work. On top of that she cooks for me three days out of the week and that is when I realized Yumeka is acting as my girlfriend. She calls me randomly at work to see how my day was going, what I wanted to eat for dinner and I've stayed at her house some nights after falling asleep during a movie. Those nights I feel guilty because I'd once again lied to Kenya about where I am and what I'm doing. I feel extra guilty because Kenya and I have exchanged I love you's just a week ago. My thinking is if spending time with Yumeka is the price I have to pay for the rides everyday then so be it because the day I buy a new car is the day I leave her alone for good which is gonna be in a month I hope.

"Meka, tomorrow I have to meet my DM in the Milford store and I don't know how long I'ma be. I don't want you to drop me off and get all the way back to Waterbury and have to turn around to get me, then again I don't want you to wait either. I guess what I'm trying to say is can I take your car for about two hours tomorrow?"

"Yeah just as long as you are back by six so I can go to school." She replied without a second to think about it.

"Bet. You're the best."

"Thanks. Syn can I ask you somethin'?"

"Yeah, what's good?"

"Why haven't you kissed me yet?"

"Huh?" I said not sure if she said what I think I heard.

"Why haven't you kissed me yet? We have a good time with each other and you said I would make a good girlfriend so why haven't you tried anything with me?"

"That's 'cause we friends Meek just like Deon and I are friends. I would never take it there with Deon 'cause that and we been cool for so long is how I feel about you. We have a good friendship and I don't wanna risk that by doin' anything na mean?"

"You think I'ma look at you different? You think things are gonna get weird between us? All I'm lookin' for is a little affection. Some hugs, a few kisses, someone to suck on my titis and fuck me a little. Like friends with benefits." She explained.

"I can't do that Meek, I respect you too much for that. You are a really sweet girl and you should be with someone who is gonna treat you right."

"You sayin' you won't treat me right?"

"No I'm sayin' I can't cross those lines with you. If you would've told me you felt like that from day one somethin' could've happened but now I've grown to like you as a friend. Besides I'm a real big flirt and a real big cheat I wouldn't want to break your heart. It would just so happen I get my car tomorrow and get so involved with work and my music that I'd go weeks without callin' you and you'd think I hit it and quit it."

"I respect that. See I knew you are a good man…this sucks. You sure you don't wanna try to see what happens?"

"I'm sure hun. Gimmie a hug." I said laughing.

I sat slouched down in Yumeka's green Toyota Camry looking at Kenya's house. I watched Kenya and her mom climb into their black BMW SUV and speed off.

"Syn their gone, where are you?" Alana asked whispering.

"I'm pullin' up right now." Alana opened the house door as I rushed in with balloons and bags. I ran up the stairs into the room Kenya and Alana shared placing roses on Kenya's bed and tying balloons to her headboard.

"Is that all?"

"No I got two more things in the car." I said darting down the stairs and back outside.

"Geez, how much stuff did you buy her?" she laughed. I ran back with a giant plush white teddy year that is almost as big as I am positioning it in the middle of her bed with the roses in the arms of the bear.

"Wow that is big." I said aloud.

"Mom is gonna see that and start asking questions. She thinks Kenya broke up with you months ago. She doesn't like you 'cause you're black."

"I know. Kenya and I came up with that conclusion. So why are you helpin' me?"

"Most of Kenya's guy friends have never paid Blake and I any attention but you're cool and I know my sister likes you a lot."

"You're a doll Alana, thank you. What do we do with this bear?"

"I'll put it in the basement and tell Kenya it's down there."

"The basement?"

"Trust me, no one ever goes down there."

"Ok." I slid the Victoria Secret gift card under Kenya's sheets and placed the roses on her pillow. In her top dresser drawer I put in three pairs of Nike socks that read, *I love you* on one, *Say It* on the other and *Baby!!* On the last one. All the little sayings Kenya and I use with each other.

"I'll keep the door closed. My mom only comes in when one of us is in here. Now get outta here before my she comes back." I ran out the house thanking Alana one last time and sped off dialing Kenya's work number.

"I babyyyy!" she said and I can't help but to smile. She sounds just as excited every time I call.

"Hey. You busy?"

"No. I'm at the mall doing a makeover for someone why? Why do you sound like you're outta breath?"

"I just got finished workin' out."

"Oh. I wish I can see you baby. Tomorrow is Valentine's day and my mom has me babysitting because she is going out. You should come over and let me show you how much I love you." She said moaning a little.

"Damn I would love nothin' more than to come but that asshole Dennis has me workin' all fuckin' day, open to close."

"Are you serious?"

"Yeah, babe I'm so sorry. We can go out this Saturday."

"I have a photo shoot and you know how my mom supervises it."

"Cancel."

"And do what? If I do that my moms is going to wanna sped quality time with me. She already claims to only see me when I'm shooting."

"Ok. Well that sucks. I want to see you sometime this weekend even for five minutes." I stayed on the phone with Kenya until I walked into Merle Norman holding a single red rose. When Kenya saw me her eyes lit up and a smile was instantaneous. She let the receiver fall to the counter as she ran into my arms and I hugged her tight swinging her around two or three times.

"Happy Valentine's Day babe."

"Happy Valentine's Day." She said wiping her eyes.

"Are you cryin'?"

"Tears of job baby. Tears of joy." She said bestowing a fervent kiss on me.

"Wow! I should surprise you more often."

"Maybe you should. How did you get here?"

"I have my moms car and speaking of which, I have to get it back to her by six and I don't wanna get stuck in traffic so I'ma go but I will see you this weekend, hopefully." We kissed again and just as quickly I'm leaving feeling good.

Picking up my used tan 1999 Chevrolet Malibu from Car World 2 despite not wanting to deal with that place ever again I'm texting Kenya telling her I got the car. I haven't seen Kenya in almost a month since I didn't have a steady way to get to Danbury when my Diamante died on me. At first it wasn't that hard not seeing her because we talk constantly whenever I'm not at Yumeka's house but after a while that got old and I yearned to see Kenya more and more which each passing day. It sucked to the point I didn't want to talk to her on the phone because it would remind me that she is so far away. The feeling of not wanting to talk to Kenya made me a little distant to her and if I can feel it I know she can too.

It bothered me a little but not too much because I don't expect us to be together too much longer. I love Kenya but I have to keep things in perspective and think realistically, honestly how long do I expect Kenya to sneak around her mothers back to see me? If not is not enough to worry I have to prepare myself for the day Kenya calls me to tell me there is someone else she is interested in. I'm twenty years old and there is no way I can sit around and get emotionally involved with a sixteen year old girl then mend my broken heart once she leaves me. Everything is telling me to spare Kenya's feelings and break up with her now but there is something in me that is hoping the negative things I am feeling is just paranoia.

"Baby my school is gonna call you so I need for you to act like my father because I want you to come pick me up."

"Why do you wanna leave?"

"I haven't seen you in a month and I have to work this afternoon so I want to see you now so do it." She demanded.

"Wow babe I love the aggressiveness."

"Well you've been tellin' me to have more of a back-bone."

"Yeah just not wit me."

"I gotta start some where." She laughed.

I watched as the security guard stopped Kenya until she showed him a piece of paper that let her leave. Once she out of the school parking lot I backed up so she can get in the car where we clasped each other tightly.

"Miss me?"

"Yes."

"How much?" Kenya hugged me again this time tight enough for me to become short of breath.

"That much."

"Good. Where to?"

"The park." Kenya said then complimented the car as we drove off the campus. The afternoon is clear and sunny but mildly chilly, typical for March. As the wind blew Kenya's sandy brown hair everywhere my hand rests on her lap while she ran her fingers over the top of it. I put my hand between her legs and she looked at me with one eyebrow cocked.

"Hands cold." I claimed.

"They'll be warmer in here." She said sliding it down the front of her tight jeans. Kendra opened her legs wider so my hand can find its way beneath her panties then to her warm pleasure hut then I fingered her while driving. Kenya let out pleasure moans while massaging the bulge in my pants and before we knew it we were at the park.

"Freak." I joked.

"You like it, I'm your freak."

"You better be."

"I am baby." Kenya and I played around with my camera taking pictures with the new used car. She looks so sexy today as everyday wearing black heels, blue jeans, a black t-shirt and her black leather jacket.

"Why do you wear so much black?" I asked curiously.

"Well after Ricky and I broke up all the clothes I brought was black."

"You were mournin'?"

"Kinda. He was my first love and he hurt me like hell so naturally I was a little depressed. I had just gotten over him before working at Olympia."

"Would you ever go back to him? Like date him?"

"No."

"Never?"

"Never. He cheated on me with my best friend well the girl that was my best friend at the time so no, I'll never go back out with Ricky. If you play your cards right I'll never date another guy again."

"How many boyfriends have you had Kenya?"

"Why?"

"I just wanna know. You know about my past but I don't know too much about yours."

"Three." Kenya told me the three boyfriends she had were Terrance, Ricky and myself. She was fifteen when she dated Terrance who was a twenty-one year old black guy who dealt drugs but only dated Kenya so he can have sex with her. She dated Ricky shortly after up until May of last year then me in November.

"Did you love Ricky?"

"Yeah I loved him a lot and my mom loved him too. She would let him come by the house anytime he wanted day or night and sometimes he slept over because she is real good friends with his parents."

"So what would happen if Ricky showed up at your door tomorrow and apologized for what he did and wanted you back, would you take him?"

"Baby you have nothing to worry about. I am with you and I love you now." She said holding my chin.

"How do you know?"

"Because I feel it and I'ma show you. Do you still keep that blanket in your trunk?"

"Yeah I put my winter survival kit in my trunk when I got the car why?"

"Get it."

"Why?" I popped the trunk as Kenya climbed in the back seat kicking off her shoes and peeled off her jeans. We climbed under the covers as Kenya climbed on top of me and began riding.

"Fuck!" I said as fear flooded my body and a vision of a prison cell flashed before my eyes.

"What?" she said stopping and looking at me with worried eyes.

"Cops."

"What!" Kenya hopped off my pleasure stick as we frantically put back on our clothes. By the time the two white officers came up to the window Kenya and I are dressed and had regained composure by making it seem like we are cuddling.

"Young lady can you step out of the car please?" One of the officers said opening the backseat door. Kenya winked at me before climbing out.

"Sir can I see your license and registration please." I climbed over the back seat to get my info out the glove compartment. The whole time my heart is beating a thousand times a second because I am a twenty-one year old black guy in a parking lot with a sixteen-year old white girl and those cops know damn well what we were doing. *I'm going to jail.* I'm sitting in the backseat while the first officer questions Kenya and the second one runs my information for what seemed like forever. I'm praying my conviction in North Carolina don't show up. I looked over at Kenya who didn't seem worried at all and I became more worried.

"Ok sir. Everything checks out. What were you two doing out here?"

"Talkin' sir."

"Under a blanket?"

"It's cold, we were using the blanket to save the gas."

"The park is closed during the winter so you two can't park here. You wanna sit and "talk" in a parking lot I suggest you go to the mall, there is plenty of parking there."

"Thanks." Kenya walked back to the car and once the cops got out of sight we laughed ourselves silly.

"Were you scared?" I asked.

"No. Were you?"

"Hell yeah I thought I was goin' to jail. What did he say to you?"

"He asked to see my I.D. but all I had is my school I.D. I told him I was eighteen and I'm a senior. Then he asked what were we doing out here and I told him talking. I don't think he believed me at first then I told him I my mom would kill me if I even thought about sex. Then let me go."

"That was close as hell. Com'on let's get the hell outta here. Where do you wanna go?"

"It's Friday...you know what that means."

Kenya and I made love on the living room couch, napped for about half hour and made love again before Blake and Alana came home. With Alana in the other room on the computer and Blake running around the house, Kenya went upstairs, changed into a short skirt under a long t-shirt and we inconspicuously made love again while she "sat" on my lap. I slid in and out slowly and easily but when Kenya dug her nails into my knees I knew the mission was accomplished. Afterward we laughed at our sneaky sexual act then lay in each other's arms until seven forty-five when it was time for me to leave. What a day.

"Syncere guess who I saw today?" Mone' asked when I walked into the house.

"Who."

"Charlene, remember her?"

"Yeah. Where'd you see her at?"

"At the mall. She thought you were dead."

"Why would she think that?"

"I don't know she said that is what she heard. When she saw me I was at Arby's and she gave me a hug over the counter and said she was sorry. I was like for what? And she was like 'cause I heard your brother died. I said girl my brother at home probably playin' Madden. She gave me her number, she said call her."

"Where she live?"

"Ives Street."

"Ain't that the next street over?"

"Oh shoot it might be. Call her."

"Hello? Can I speak to Charlene?"

"This is her, who's this?"

"Syncere."

"Mr. Washington! How are you?"

"I'm good Ms. Davis. So you heard I was dead huh?"

"Yeah. I heard somebody say that a few months ago. They said you got shot."

"Na, I was in Georgia a few months ago. I'm surprised niggas still be talkin' 'bout me even though I wasn't here."

"I know it's a shame. So what's good wit'chu?"

"I'm chillin' just got off work. Hey you live on Ives street right?"

"Yeah. Where you at?"

"Irion."

"Are you serious? That's the next street over."

"I thought so."

Charlene sits on the couch talking to Mone' while I'm swiveling in my mothers computer chair thinking that I've been in this situation time and time again. Kenya and I have a phenomenal relationship so why the hell do I have Charlene here? Why am I over reacting were just friends and she's just here to catch up on old times with me. Turning back to the ancient computer as it finally booted up I have an email from KL@unc.edu. *KL? Kendra?*

My eyes ran over the email as swiftly as possible going over the same line twice before moving on to the next. The ever-present weird feeling found it's way into my stomach again and all the feelings I have for Kendra that I've tried to suppress for the past year have resurfaced. Her email started off like one of her normal letters; sweet and subtle then it ran into an apology about blowing up at the fact that I didn't call or go see her the night I left North Carolina and for everything that happened the year before last.

I read the email in its entirety two more times ignoring two of Kenya's phone calls. I told myself *I will tell her I was in the studio* as I continued to read Kendra's email with a huge smile on my face sitting back in the computer chair and exhaling when I was finished. Wow she wrote me...there still might be hope for us after all.

"You gonna stay on that thing all night or are you gonna talk to me punk?" Charlene said walking over to me. I quickly exited out of the email before Charlene put her arms around my neck kissing me on the cheek.

"What was that for?"

"I missed you. You dropped out of site and didn't call nobody. How was I supposed to know you went away to college? Huh punk." She said hitting my head.

"I got'cha punk." I said standing up.

"Oh you don't want none of this." Charlene responded getting into her fighting stance. I put my arm around Charlene's waist and hip tossed her to the floor as she grabbed hold of my neck on her way down. We both crashed to the floor but I'm on top of her and able to pin her wrists down. I stared at Charlene as she stared at me with kiss-me-now eyes. Then without a thought I gently placed my lips on top of hers.

I've cheated on every girlfriend with the exception of Kendra and I made it my business not to cheat on Kenya despite the fear I have that she'd break up with me out of the blue and now I have failed. The words *get up* keep sounding in my head as the longer Charlene and I lay on the floor. After a the words echoed a few more times I got helped Charlene up and I told her I'd be back in a minute. I'm sitting on the couch that I sleep on in with the door closed and my head buried in my hands. For some strange reason I feel awful right now as if Kenya was staring right at me when I kissed Charlene. I picked up the phone to call her when the door to my half of room creaked open.

"What'chu doin' in here punk?"

"Nothin'." I whispered.

"So Mr. Washington."

"So Ms. Davis."

"What's wrong?"

"Nothin' just thinkin'."

"'Bout what?"

"Nothin' in particular."

"Mone' went in her room, you want me to turn the T.V. off?"

"Yeah. Want me to take you home?"

"Not unless it's in the mornin'."

The hot water beat on my shoulders and back like a perfect massage but all I want to do is cry as I am disgusted with myself. Last night I couldn't ignore the history Charlene and I have emotionally and sexually but worse I couldn't ignore the urge to feel Charlene. I punched the shower wall at the images of the pleasure faces Charlene made last night and asked myself *what the hell is wrong with me?*

I ignored Kenya's repeated phone calls during the sexual encounter and now I have to think of another lie to tell her because I can only use the studio excuse but so many times. After Charlene climaxed she curled up like a kitten next to me and fell fast asleep. But wasn't I able to sleep, not until I vision Kenya's face on Charlene's body. I slept like a baby but the smile that was on my face disappeared as I awoke to see that I was sleeping next to Charlene instead of Kenya. Due to having to keep our relationship a secret from her mother and the fact that she is only sixteen Kenya and I have never had the opportunity to spend the night with each other. This feels like Déjà vu.

Over the course of the past five months I have lost myself in Kenya's beauty, company and conversation, which has taken my mind off Kendra to the point that a week ago I was convinced that I am over he. But the email I read last night has me feeling a completely different way and I don't know how to take that. I'm trying to look at the entire spectrum weighing all my options in order to make the right decision for my love life and myself. I am falling fast for Kenya with a part of me wanting to stop myself while the other part wants to keep falling to see where I land. Another part of me is still curious to know if Kendra is in fact the woman I am supposed to marry despite what that stupid psychic told me. Then the last part of me wants to have its cake and eat it too by still having my relationship with Kenya and continue to sleep with Charlene. The elders have always told me if you can't be with the one you love then love the one you're with and if that holds true I should have my fun with Charlene until I can be with Kenya. But I really don't want to do that. I seriously and sincerely want to do right by Kenya because she is an amazing young woman, so what do I do?

I can be the man I wasn't when I was with Kendra and tell Kenya about Charlene and hope she doesn't break up with me. Unfortunately that would just be stupid on her part because I would have to worry about her being able to trust me afterward and that isn't a battle I'm prepared to fight right now. I can really be a man and tell Charlene that last night was great but there can't be another because I have a girlfriend that I am trying to build a relationship. Or, last but not least, I can just do nothing and let things happen as the universe sees it should.

"That's heavy man, I really don't know what to tell you." Mika said after I explained to him and Emily the saga that is Kendra and I.

"Do you love her? Kendra I mean?"

"Yeah…and no. I mean a part of me doesn't want to then again a part does. I mean we have a lot of history with one another and I don't know if I want to just throw all that out the window na mean?"

"I understand you still have strong feelings for her because she was your first love and everything but she almost got'chu locked up for lying about ol' boy."

"Yeah but I almost got her banned from her church too."

"I just don't think you should be trying to hold on to a relationship because of history when you have a gorgeous girl right here in front of you who I know you adore." Mika preached.

"Yeah Syn he's right and I've been talkin' to Kenya and she loves you so much it's not even funny. Have you talked to her about this?"
"Hell no, what are you crazy? She knows the history of Kendra but she doesn't know about the email. I think she feels she has to compete with Kendra but she really doesn't and I want it to stay that way. I don't want her to wonder if I still have feelings for Kendra or if I wanna leave her for?"

"Do you?"

"I don't know."

"In all honesty Syn, Kenya is my friend but you but I were friends first so I'm not gonna tell her what we've talked about tonight but want I am gonna say is that if you are curious about what could've been with Kendra for a fraction of a second you need to call her and try to make it work. I know you care about Kenya and you don't wanna hurt her but if this chick is the woman you feel you should be with deep down inside you have to act on it." Emily explained.

"You really think so Em?"

"Yeah but if you are gonna do that you need to let Kenya know and not let her fall for you any more than what she already has. It won't be fair to her and don't cheat on her by messin' with her and Kendra at the same time."

"Aight."

"So what'chu gonna do Syn?" Mika inquired.

"I don't know. I honestly don't wanna hurt Kenya; I love the relationship we have. Yeah it sucks to have to sneak around because of her mom then have to work around both our schedules but nothin' worth havin' is easy feel me? I'ma just tell Kendra we can't be anything more than just friends." I decided.

"But if you have these feelings for her why brush'em off?" Emily asked seeming confused.

"I'm not brushin' them off I'm just making a conscious decision not to continue the cycle."

"What cycle?"

"The Kendra cycle. I break up with Kendra then I meet a wonderful girl but I compare her to Kendra. Then a few months down the line Kendra pops back into my life and I drop the wonderful girl I was with in hopes of Kendra and I havin' the relationship we both tell each other we want with one another. Before you know it we get into an argument, stop talkin' and I'm back a square one again kickin' myself for letting go that wonderful girl. Kenya is that wonderful girl and I refuse to do that to her…I refuse to do that to myself. Not this time."

"I like that idea. I don't know that Kendra chick so I can't say she isn't the one for you but I do know you and I do know Kenya. I can't see either one of you with anyone else. It's like you two were meant to meet…you two were meant to be together."

I shook my head up and down a few times thankful to have such wonderful friends who can give me unbiased honest advice that is beneficial to me. Emily and Mika a truly wonderful people and the cutest couple next to Kenya and I. Knock….knock…knock. Emily, Mika and I looked at each other wondering who it was because I know I'm not expecting anyone except Charlene a little later but I told her I would come by to pick her up.

"Who is it?" I called to the front door.

"Syncere its Yumeka."

"Who is Yumeka?" Emily asked.

"Oh she is just the chick who drove me to work when I didn't have a car."

"Ohh that's the girl."

"What'chu mean?"

"I remember talkin' to Kenya about it. You told her that this girl likes you right?"

"Yeah. This broad is really nice but seriously I think somethin' is mentally wrong with her. She just talks about random shit. We'd be in the car in mid conversation and she'd come out wit some off the wall shit."

"You gonna let her in?"

"Haven't planned on it."

"Com'on I wanna see what she looks like." At Mika's curiosity I opened the door to let Yumeka in who is followed by a frail looking white girl.

"What's good?" I asked after introducing her to Emily and Mika.

"Nothin' I haven't seen you since you brought your car. I just wanted to stop by and say hi."

"Oh yeah. I've just been crazy busy with the store that's all. I told you that was gonna happen."

"I know and I'm not mad at that. I'm mad because you didn't call and tell me happy birthday."

"When was your birthday?"

"Today. I told you this last week the last time I dropped you off and you promised me dinner for driving you to work and stuff."

"Oh yeah you're right. When you wanna go?"

"How 'bout tonight?"

"Na I can't. I got my friends here na mean."

"Oh no it's ok Syn, Go ahead I have to bring Mika back to Uconn anyway."

"Well why don't ya'll come with us on me?" I said making a weird eye gesture to both of them.

"I would love to but we ate dinner before we got here." Mika said not getting the hint.

"Well I'm really not hungry I would much rather have some ice cream." Yumeka said.

"We could all go to Friendly's. Yumeka follow my car."

"Well I was gonna drop Vanessa off and by that time I thought you and your friends would be done and _we_ could just go."

"Since we are all here let's just all go and get better acquainted." I pressed harder.

"Well why can't Vanessa and I ride with you?"

"'Cause Emily didn't drive her car here and I have to bring them to it so it'll be more convient if ya'll just followed me."

"Damn Syn I thought she was wanna go word for word with you." Mika said as I sped off.

"I told you this girl is nuts. You see she was tryin' everything she could to ride wit me and to go out alone, I told ya'll she likes me. On some real shit the only reason why I'm goin' is because she did bring me back and forth to work for a month and a half so I kinda owe it to her plus it's her birthday. I figured putting up with her for an hour won't kill me. I just didn't wanna go without ya'll so if it feels like I pushed ya'll into goin' wit me I apologize."

"Na it's all good don't even worry about it. I could go for some ice cream anyway." Emily said from the back seat.

I don't know how we all ended up back at my house and in my living room but we are, all sitting down making small talk. Because I don't want Yumeka and her mute friend Vanessa there Emily, Mika and I began talking as if they weren't even in the room.

"So Syn when are you gonna see Kenya again?" Emily asked winking.

"I don't know, maybe after I drop ya'll off. She gets outta work soon and she's supposed to stay the night so hopefully she hasn't changed her mind." I know what Emily is doing as soon as she asked that question so I played along with her.

"Ya'll will be celebrating an anniversary soon huh?"

"Yep six months next month. I got a little sumthin' sumthin' planned na mean? I think she'll like it." I responded smiling from ear to ear, that is when my cell phone rang. Kenya's name popped on the screen and I scurried outside to answer it before she hangs up.

"Hey gorgeous!"

"Hey baby, what are you doin'?"

"Talkin' to Emily and Mika."

"On the other line?"

"No, they in my livin' room."

"What? What are they doin' there?"

"They stopped by 'cause Em was on her way to drop Mika off at UCONN. We just got back from Friendly's."

"Friendly's? You never took me to Friendly's now I'm jealous." Kenya joked.

"You wanna go to Friendly's babe?"

"Yes I do."

"When you wanna go?"

"Tonight."

"Tonight? Aint'chu at work?"

"Yeah but the mall closes in an hour."

"What about ya moms? Isn't she pickin' you up?"

"I told her I'm goin' to hang out with a neighbor of ours another girl named Kenya. She lives like five houses from me."

"Oh ok. You already had this planned before you called me didn't you?"

"Yes sir I did." She said laughing.

"You're a good liar. I'ma have to watch out for you."

"Baby I would never lie to you."

"I know. Okay I'ma see you in an hour…hol' up, are you closin' by yaself?"

"Yeah, Pattie left at five and guess what?"

"What?"

"I'm wearing your Valentine's Day gift, everything down to the cute little socks. So you should come tell me how I look in it."

"Thanks for the visual. I'll see you soon."

"Wait before you hang up lemme speak to Emily." I walked back into the house to hear Yumeka talking while Emily and Mika listened attentively.

"Em, phone. It's Kenya."

"KENYA!!!!" she shouted jumping to her feet and racing to the phone. I stood outside with Emily while she talked and shortly after Mika came out.

"What's good man?"

"Yo that girl has been tellin' me and Emily some crazy shit."

"Like what?"

"Well when you left out she asked us who Kenya is so we were like your girlfriend and she was on some *I'm his best friend and he didn't tell me about a girlfriend* stuff. So Emily and I are like how is he your best friend and we've never met'chu?"

"Really. I told you she nuts. I been told her 'bout Kenya."

"So listen. Then she says, I bet be didn't tell her he fucked me last week."

"What?"

"Yeah." Mika said lowering his voice. "Yeah she was like you fucked her last week and you kept calling her tellin' her how good she was. That is the real reason she came by tonight. So she can fuck you on her birthday."

"WOW!!"

"Yo Syn tell me you didn't fuck that girl." Mika pleaded.

"Hell no! I ain't fuck that crazy bitch. I told you, I told you, and I told you she was crazy."

"Yeah I see. Of course me and Em don't believe a word she sayin' but now I see why you didn't wanna go alone with her."

"Yeah you see? If I did I would say we went and had ice cream but this bitch'll go 'round tellin' muhfuckas I licked the ice cream off her ass or some crazy shit." I said while Mika burst into laughter.

"What's so funny?" Emily asked handing back the phone.

"I was tellin' Syn about ol' girl in the livin' room."

"Yo Syn she is sayin' all types of stuff. I know she helped you out and all but you gotta stop fuckin' with her."

"I know. Mika just told me what she said."

"Well Mr. Man we have to go and I have an hour ride to Storrs and a hour and half ride back and I'm already gettin' tired."

"Aight go grab ya'll stuff and tell them bitches we leavin'."

"What'chu gonna do? You told her you have to take me to get my car."

"Just get in the car wit me, I'ma ride around the block while she goes the opposite way then we'll come back to tha house."

The ride to Danbury is bittersweet. Sweet because I'm over excited about seeing Kenya and every sign that said Danbury on it says Kenya. You know, Kenya 18 miles, Kenya exit 3, Welcome to Kenya. Then it is bitter because the whole ride my thoughts played over the night Yumeka told Emily and Mika about. It's true I had fucked Yumeka but it's not how it sounds. The day after I brought my car Yumeka came by my house looking like I've never seen her before. Instead of her hair being in a ponytail and her dressed in an oversized sweatshirt and jeans she showed up with her hair straightened out and falling to her back. I've never been a big fan of make-up but she had a little on with some lips gloss, which made her look prettier than what she really is. Instead of loose jeans she wore tight fitting ones that displayed her plumped round brown and a blouse half buttoned that told her world how massive her breasts are. When I saw her leaning on her car I was instantly horny.

She told me she cooked baked ziti, knowing full well I never turn down her cooking, so I followed behind her in my car with every intention of eating and leaving using work the next day as a excuse. Well we ate and the ziti put me on my ass and I fell out on her bed. Her warm mango scented body lying next to me made me kiss her big lips, which I didn't like, then unbutton her blouse. She whispered,

"Are you sure you want to do this?"

"Shut up." I whispered back as I shoved my hammer into her hole.

"Ouch Syncere. I haven't had sex in two years I'm tight and I'm small." I ignored her as I thrusted violently causing her to scream loudly. About two minutes into it my phone went off and I knew who it was then something in my head went off. I became fully aware of what I was doing and from that moment on I looked for a way out of it. I faked my orgasm, bolted out of the house returning Kenya's call while in the car telling her I was in Wal-Mart and I haven't seen or spoke to Yumeka since then before today.

"Baby!!" Kenya shouted when she looked up and saw me walking into her store carrying a rose. She literarily hurdled over the counter to hug me and I find it adorable as hell. She makes me feel so good every time I see her and she's always as beautiful as the day before. She's wearing a should be illegal short black shirt with a second skintight sheer black collard shirt in heels. Her hair is in a French bun and as always her right wrist bears the bracelet I got her for Christmas.

"Hey. You almost done?"

"Yep I just gotta put this in the back, com'on." She demanded while locking the gate and turning off the lights then leading me into the tiny backroom area of the store.

"Wow this is small as hell."

"I know but we are only housing make-up so we don't need a huge stock room like Olympia."

"You ain't lyin'." I said looking at all the little pieces of make up everywhere.

"Look at me." Kenya said. I turned around to see Kenya unbuttoning her collard shirt exposing the black French laced bra.

"You're doin' this here?" I asked.

"Shhh. No one is coming, the lights are off and the gate is locked and all you have to do is try not to make me get too loud." She said while letting her black shirt hit the floor.

"Ok." I agreed while proceeding to get undressed.

"Stop…let me do it." Kenya slowly lifted my shirt over my head kissing my neck and chest while in the process of unbuttoning my pant. We made it work in the tiny stock room as Kenya bent over in front of me while keeping her legs completely straight as I took her from behind. Before long Kenya wrapped her legs around my waist and bent herself backwards placing her palms flat on the floors as if doing a handstand while I firmly held her waist sliding in and out.

"I wish we didn't have to sneak around like this." Kenya said while getting dressed.

"Me too. For once I'd like to lay with you or even fall asleep like we did the first time."

"What did we just do?" Kenya asked.

"What do you mean?"

"This…what do you call this?"

"I call it makin' love. We don't fuck and we don't have sex, we make love."

"You love me?" She said sounding as surprised as Kendra use to.

"Yes."

"Say it again."

"I love you."

"Again, again, again."

"I love you, I love you, and I love you."

18

Notwithstanding the conversation I had with Emily and Mika a week ago I finally responded to Kendra's email telling her I still love her and I still want us to try to be together. Kendra asked me once how can I be in love with two people at the same time and I didn't have an answer until now. I am in love with Kendra but I love

Kenya. Right at this very second if Kendra were to walk in on Kenya and I making love I'd stop to leave with Kendra, that is what being in love is. I'm not saying it is right but it is what it is. Kenya's five months stacked against Kendra's five years and everything we've overcome doesn't hold much weight. Can I see myself spending the next 100 years with Kendra? Definitely. Can I see myself spending the next 100 years with Kenya? It would be nice but with her age and her mother I really don't know how much of a reality that could be.

On top of this, in spite of the fact I felt like shit the morning after, I'm still sleeping with Charlene. With recording, work and seeing Kenya every free chance I get I only see Charlene at night when I'm done with everything else and all we do is have sex. We haven't exchanged titles of boyfriend and girlfriend and unless she does I choose not to cross that bridge. Sex isn't making me cheat on Kenya because making love to her is enough, but it's the companionship Charlene is able to provide. The cuddling on the couch watching a movie, the cooking dinner, the hanging out with all my friends having a good time. More importantly it's the ability to wake up next to a beautiful face and to have someone to lay next to at night. That is what made the time with Kendra in Georgia so special. She was the first thing I saw when I opened my eyes and the last thing I saw before they closed. It was her sitting next to me on the bus while I searched for a new job; it's just her presence. The same presence I wish Kenya could offer. Now I can't act like I didn't know the circumstances pertaining a relationship with Kenya and I actually thought I could put that selfishness to the side because I liked her so much, for five months I did brush the selfishness off and I honestly don't know what happened.

I don't like p just to talk to Kenya when she calls in the middle of the night so lying to Kenya about why I didn't answer her calls or tip toeing out I so I can talk her to sleep after she had a nightmare. I didn't mind the lying and running around when I was with Rita, Melissa, Lisa or Diane because I really didn't care about them like that. But I made it a priority not to do it to Kendra and I want to give Kenya that same respect but I just don't know how.

"So how is Jamaica?" I asked Kendra.

"It's wonderful, I just can't eat a lot of the food because of how spicy it is and I don't like eating goat but it's beautiful. I go to the local market to buy my own food but it's so expensive down here. A loaf of break is like ten dollars."

'Why is it so much?"

"I don't know. But the best part is the family I'm staying with lives on the steep hill and you can see the sun set from here every evening. It's the best spot on the entire island. The sun is huge and bright orange as it goes down then at night the stars appear looking so big I sometimes think I can touch them, it's great!"

"That's wussup. How long are you gone for?"

"Until August."

"Do you need me to send you anything?"

"Thank you but no, Mulan sent me a care package." Just the sound of his name makes me angry and the fact that Kendra still deals with this dude makes my blood boil.

"Oh yeah that guy. How are ya'll?" I asked reluctantly.

"We broke up a week before I left."

"Why? Did he hit you again?"

"No. He jus cheats a lot. He's running around with all these white girls, he's picking me up in their cars and he just lies all the time. He gave me an STD a few months ago."

"Wow! And you stayed with him after that? Why?"

"The same reason I stayed with you after we caught you coming out of the old sanctuary with Jewa."

"I told you about that. But I've never hit or given you an STD. That shit is crazy."

"I thought about that a few times." She admitted.

"What?"

"You and how you never raised your hand to me even in the middle of the heated arguments we had when I was in Atlanta. You've never called me out my name and you've always shown me nothing but respect. I keep checking Poetry.com to see if you've written any new poems but I see you haven't."

"Yea. I'm done writin' poetry. Words was my last one."

"Do you remember the one you wrote called *Today*?"

"What about it?"

"The last line said, *today I give up on the only woman I want to give my last name to.* Do you still feel like that?"

"Like what? Like I gave up on you?"

"No, on wanting to give me your last name?"

"A part of me still does. Why?"

"I had a dream about you last week. Would you like to hear about it?"

"Yeah." I said leaning back in my office chair.

"We were in Atlanta and you were dressed in all white with your hair in dreads. You were sitting on the banister on our porch watching Nature play in our front yard and I was standing right next to you also dressed in all white holding your hand. We weren't talking we were just standing there watching our son play."

"That's wussup. So what are you sayin'?"

"I'm saying that when I get back to the states in August I want to try again. I want us to be together like we planned. I want us to watch our son play in the front yard of our house in Atlanta."

"How are we supposed to do this with you in North Carolina and me in Connecticut? I'm at a job where I can't just pick up and move like I use to."

"I've been thinking about transferring to a school in Connecticut. How far is UCONN from you?"

"About forty-minutes to an hour. But that's crazy. I don't want you to transfer schools and loose credits and have to be in school longer than you're supposed to be."

"I'm earning extra credits just by being here…"

"Ok, when you get back let's do the damn thing."

"Really? You really mean it?"

"Five years ago I told my aunt and uncle I was gonna marry you and if I'm gonna do one thing right in my life it's gonna be that."

"You never told me you told them that."

"I know. Ask my aunt Dimpsey she'll tell you. I told them that then ten minutes after the first time I called you."

"How did you know I was the one for you?"

"I just knew…God told me."

"Can I tell you something and you promise not to get upset with me?"

"What?"

"Promise me first?" she insisted.

"I'm not gonna make a promise not to get mad but I'll promise not to yell or curse."

"I got your tattoo covered." Dead silence on my end. I feel like someone has just told me my mother died. I lifted up the sleeve on my t-shirt and stared at the tattoo as emptiness fills my gut.

"It's ok." I sputtered out.

"Are you upset?"

"Yeah and no. I'm kinda upset because that is the last thing I would expect you to do but then again I can't blame you. If you were with Mulan I couldn't blame him not wanting to see my damn splattered on your shoulder. Kenya has been askin' me to cover mine for two months now. What did you cover it with?"

"A rose. Who is Kenya?"

"She's my girlfriend."

"I'm not surprised."

"Why do you say it like that?"

"Because you always have a girlfriend. I've been telling you that for years."

"What do you expect? I didn't think I'd ever hear from you again and I needed someone to help me get over you."

"Did it work?"

"We're talkin' 'bout makin' plans to be together when you get back into the states so you tell me if it worked."

"Do you still have my tattoo?"

"Of course. I told you I'd never get it covered and I meant it."

"So what would've happened if down the line you got married and your wife wanted you to cover it then what would you do."

"I made a decision a long time ago that if I didn't marry you or have kids by you then I'm not gonna to do either with any other woman."

"What if I come up there and we discover we weren't meant to be the way we want it to be and we decided not to get married?"

"I don't know."

"Make me a promise?"

"Anything."

"Promise me that if by any chance we don't end up married but decided to marry someone else we'd send each other a dozen roses and on the card just write "it happened" that way we'll know."

"Aight, I can do that."

"Will you come to my wedding?"

"Hell no."

"Why not?"

"Because I'll probably ruin it. Even though it didn't work out between you and I in my heart you will always be my wife and I wouldn't be able to sit there and let some man take the woman I love. I couldn't even sit in church that day and watch you smile a Quami and you want me to watch a guy take your hand in marriage? So out of respect for you and your husband I'll just send a gift with my best wishes but I wouldn't show up."

"Not even for me?"

"Kendra you know that I'll do anything for you just as long as you ask, I'll walk through the gates of hell but goin' to ya wedding is outta the question."

"Hey stranger." A voice said.

"What's good wit'chu?"

"Nothin' but what's good wit'chu stranger?"

"Why you say that?" Evelyn, when I didn't speak to her for a while she'd always say I'd become a stranger to her.

"'Cause you haven't called me in months."

"You were the one who broke up wit me and decided not to answer my calls when I needed my hair braided. So I just stopped callin'. I hope you didn't think I was gonna chase you?" I said lightly laughing at the thought.

"Oh."

"Oh? Did you want somthin' in particular or are you callin' just 'cause?"

"No. I just wanted to see how you were doin'."

"I'm good and you?"

"Fine. Who is doin' ya hair now?"

"Random people. My cousin does it sometimes or I got this chick that I work with. Why you offerin'?"

"Maybe?"

"Why the sudden pop out of hidin'?"

"Nothin'! Why there gotta be a reason? You didn't miss me?"

"I'm not sayin' all that but I just wanted to know why you call me now after all this time?"

"The same reason you didn't call me when you were in Atlanta but called me when you moved back."

"'Cause you missed me?"

"Maybe."

"I don't have time for riddles and maybes. You gon' do my hair or what?"

"Oh that's all I can do for you is braid ya hair?"

"What do you want then Evelyn?"

"Nothin'." She said sounding depressed.

"Don't do that, just tell me what you want."

"I wanna see you. Come pick me up."

"How you know I ain't busy or 'bout to go out right now?"

"Where you gotta go besides work? You goin' to see ya girl?"

"While you askin' me all the questions where ya "man" at?"

"Who says I have one?"

"You had to have one or have one on deck to break up wit me outta the blue."

"It wasn't outta tha blue either."

"Well I must be crazy 'cause as I recall it you sent me a text message breakin' up wit me after I had just seen you two days prior so you tell me what it is."

"I thought you didn't like me anymore after I got the abortion."

"What are you talkin' 'bout? I'm the one that took you."

"I know but after that you acted like you didn't want to touch me or talk to me. Remember on my birthday we didn't even do anything."

"Evy, oh my God! You were feelin' sick when you came outta tha abortion place. You kept throwin' up and sleepin' a lot but I was right there the whole time. And on ya birthday I had a day planned but you're tha one that wanted to baby-sit ya

258

cousin's son. I could've told you to call me when you were done but I stayed there with you and all we did was watch a movie 'cause you fell asleep on me. I thought you were still feelin' sick from the abortion."

"But you acted like you ain't wanna fuck me no more."

"Evy! You were healin'. Don't it take two weeks to heal from an abortion."

"Yeah."

"Alright then. What was I supposed to do? Try to fuck you even though I knew you were obviously in pain? I was tryin' to be there for you and show you that I wasn't there just to fuck you like you said the rest of ya ex-boyfriends were."

"I didn't know."

"You didn't ask either. You just did what you always do and drop off the face of the earth."

"Well you couldn't've missed me that much you didn't call."

"You broke up with me! I wasn't gonna call. What I look like chasin' after you?"

"Well I'm sorry but you know I'm young, I'm still a teenager."

"You'll be starting college this year, you are no longer a teenager."

"Yes I am until I'm 20."

"Whateva. I'm on my way."

"You comin' to get me?"

"Isn't that what I'm on my way means?"

"Don't get smart."

"Too late."

"I don't live where I used to. I live wit my grandparents now?"

"Why?"

"My mom got evicted."

"Well where is she stayin'."

"At her boyfriend's apartment."

"Damn and she just pawned you off to ya grandparents like that? That's fucked up."

"Yeah, I was mad at first but I like it better over here anyway. My grandma and aunt cook a lot of Trini food. What'chu know 'bout that?"

"Absolutely nothin'." I said as Evelyn laughed washing away all the animosity I had for her.

"Aight. I live up the street from Montel Park."

"Aight. I'll call this number when I'm close."

"Ok 'cause it gets confusin'."

Evelyn ran to my car when I honked the horn. I'm surprisingly happy to see her remembering hands down she is the best I've ever had. I don't know why I agreed to come up here to get her because I don't even know were we are going but more importantly what am I hoping to get out of this? My pleasure tool grew when Evelyn flopped down in my car demanding a hug. She smells like strawberry vanilla body spray as she is dressed in a V cut short sleeve t-shirt that showed off her nicely firm breasts and her jeans are as tight as ever.

"You need some new sneakers bad." I said as I pulled off.

"Leave my sneakers alone. I know I need some new ones but I don't work. You should get me a pair."

"You want some sketchers?" I asked laughing.

"No. I want a pair of those." She said pointing to my Carolina blue and white Retro Jordan 12.

"I don't know if we still these. These came out like four months ago. I should've got two pair 'cause I dogged these."

"Well get me a nice pair then."

"I'll think about it. Where are we goin'?"

"I don't know. Ohh you do need your hair done. You should let me perm it first though 'cause you know ya shit is course as hell." She said chuckling.

"Na, I'm not permin' my hair. That shit is for pimps and faggots, I'm good."

"Oh com'on its gonna be fine. It'll be easier to comb through…It'll be easier to braid… it'll look neater and last longer." She convinced.

"You better know what you are doin'."

Evelyn and I conversed as she washed, permed, dried and braided my hair the way we used to before the break up at the end of last summer. I admitted to her I miss the nights I came home from work and she was there. I miss falling asleep with her and hearing her laugh. I couldn't see but I knew when I told her those things she'd smile but try to hide it as if it doesn't affect her when it does.

For some reason this feels wrong. Sure she's just braiding my hair but something in me is sending off alarms the way my body acted when I was in the presence of Charlene. Maybe because I know what will happen by the end of night. Kenya and I make love, which is great because of the passion that is present but sex with Evelyn is…something different. There isn't any emotion present but it feels like her lock is made specifically for my key. It feels like her lips hug my shaft as if they missed it, as if they've waited all day or all month for it and that makes the sex feel that much better. Not to mention that Evelyn, like Kenya is starting to learn my body and knows what excites me further. I've been aroused and horny ever since I smelled her strawberry vanilla body wash and I know Evelyn, she'll wanna have sex when we're done. Either she is a nympho or we just have this crazy sexual energy for one another because when it comes to sex our minds think alike.

I stared at my hair in the bathroom mirror while Evelyn stood behind me on her tiptoes to look over my shoulder. She has on a huge kool-aid smile I turned my head to look at the intricate designs with approvement on my face.

"She I told you the perm would make them look neater."

"Will I have to perm it every time I get it done?"

"Not unless you want your hair to fall out. I'll have to do it like every other month but the next time I do your hair I have to clip your ends. I should've did it today but you can go two more weeks. You like it?"

"Do a bear shit in the woods and wipe his ass wit a white rabbit?"

"What tha fuck?" she said exploding into uncontrollable laughter."

"It's just my way of sayin' yeah."

"Ok you big ass monster."

"You use to call me that when you were lotionin' me down or washin' my back."

"That's 'cause you are a monster, you're huge compared to me. Look at me! I'm tiny standin' next to you. You get any new tattoos?" she asked examining my arms.

"Na. I been thinkin' 'bout gettin' more."

"More? Like more than one?"

"Yeah. I really been thinkin' 'bout gettin' full sleeves."

"What's that?"

"Thas when you completely cover ya arms."

"Wow you're crazy. Where's ya mom and Mone'?"

"Both of'em at work. I gotta pick Mone' up at ten and I think my moms is workin' 3rd shift. I don't know she was already gone by the time I got home. Why?"

"I don't know." She said smiling.

"You gonna stay wit me tonight?" I asked.

"I don't know. You want me to?" she asked bashfully.

"I wouldn't've asked if I didn't."

"Shut up.

While Evelyn and Mone' chatted in the kitchen blasting music I dipped out to call Charlene to tell her I'm too tired to see her tonight.

"Yo I'm in Middlebury with my brother and my aunt. I'ma be back tomorrow, I was gonna call you but I got caught up." She said over the loud commotion in the background.

"Aight." Then I called Kenya because surprisingly she hasn't called all day and I'm missing her like crazy despite having Evelyn in the house. I may dip around with Charlene and now Evelyn but I would much rather be with Kenya hands down. But the harsh reality is it would take a consistent month of seeing Charlene or Evelyn to equal an hour with Kenya; it's just that real.

"Hey baby! I've been waiting for you to call."

"Were you at work today?"

"Yeah at Merle."

"So why didn't you call me? It's not like you get more than ten customers in at a time anyway."

"Shut up. No I had seven makeovers today."

"Damn, it's that many ugly women in Danbury? Your eyes must hurt." Kenya and I shared a laugh and my stomach felt like it was full of a thousand feathers.

"You are so wrong."

"I know but you like it. I need to stop though because my kids are gonna turn out ugly if I keep talkin' 'bout people."

"Our kids are gonna be gorgeous."

"You think so?"

"Com'on seriously, who can make prettier babies than you and I?"

"No one I know." I said laughing. "When are we gonna get started?"

"Whenever you want baby."

"I miss you."

"I miss you too. You know I work at Merle again tomorrow and I'm closing by myself. Think you can make it up here?"

"Na I gotta close tomorrow but I'm off Sunday."

"Good because I close Sunday too."

"But I don't wanna wait until Sunday."

"Baby I know and neither to do I."

"I'ma only see you for what half an hour? Then I'm not gonna see you again for like another week. This sucks."

"Baby I know but I'm trying to see you as often as I can, I'm sorry." She apologized.

"It's not your fault I just miss you is all. But aight I'ma see you Sunday."

"No wait talk to me."

"I can't I'm to go out wit Tracy and Wes."

"Where? To a strip club?"

"Only if you're gonna be there. Sike na we are goin' to tha casino." I lied.

"Don't loose too much. If you put me on the table how many chips would you get?"

"I don't think they make that many." I responded.

"Good answer now go and have fun. I know Tracy is bitchin' right now.

"Aight, I'll call you if I win big and I might take you to Outback Sunday if you can think of somethin' to tell ya mom."

"I'm pretty sure I can think of somethin'."

"Aight babe."

"Say it."

"Say what?"
"Syncere, say it!"

"I love you." I said snickering.

"I love you too."

I uttered those three words again under my breath as I sat on the chilly stoop of our apartment and thought. Seven months into our relationship afraid. I'm happy because it seems as if Kenya is thinking about a long-term future with me then again it's kind of early for her to be thinking about that which makes me believe that she is going through that young girl thing where every six months she's thinking like that with every new boyfriend.

Then I have Kendra coming home in August so do I really want to string this girl along just incase things don't work out between Kendra and me or should I just say fuck it and do it now? Why is this so hard? I love Kendra but I'm falling for Kenya-that is why. I still want to fuck Charlene and Evelyn so that is why. I'm too weak to stay faithful and ultimately that is why.

"Hey punk, what'chu doin' out here? Talkin' to some girl aint'chu?"

"The only girl I wanna talk to is you."

"Yeah right. Com'on it's gettin' cold."

Evelyn and I went hard just like we used to and she's as tight at the first time I entered her. She whispered dirty words in my ear while I pounded her from the back, missionary and every other way we ended up as we used the half of room to our advantage. Good sex good enough to make the wisest man dumb.

"Stop playin', are you serious?"

"Yeah son. It's gonna be on the website so people can vote on it for a week and if we win they gonna play it on the radio durin' Spank Buddha's show. So tell everybody you know to vote on it." Jus explained as I moved another inch in the super long line at Dominic's & Pia's Pizza.

"Bet. You already know what it is. Who is it under? Jus Infinate or Wolf Pak?"

"Wolf Pak."

"I ain't too mad 'cause it's our song but we all one conglomerate so fuck it. I'm actually goin' to see Kenya tonight so I'ma get her and all her friends to vote on it since they like our music anyway, then I'ma call Emily so she can lock Newtown down. We got this." I said with confidence.

"Aight my dude. Get at me later."

"Aight."

"Syncere?" A female voice said from behind me. I turned to see who it is and it's none other than Stacy Rogers, a girl I dated briefly in high school.

"Stacy? Hey." I said as we hugged like old friends.

"Wow I'm surprised to see you. I heard you were dead."

"Yeah, there is a lot of that goin' 'round."

"Where have you been?"

"North Carolina for a year and Atlanta for the last three. I was in school."

"Oh ok. So how have you been? On my God your hair is long, can I touch it?"

"Yeah." I said smiling." As Stacy felt the back of my head I looked at her reflection in the mirror behind her and checked out her body. She has filled out very nicely since I last saw her three years ago. We chatted over pizza slices and soda, which took me back to our first "date" when we met at Park Pizza across the street from Fulton Park. If I look for it I may still have the picture we took that day.

"So you rap now?" I asked in disbelief.

"Yeah but it's none of that gangsta stuff you do. Mine is more party-like and it has a message. My first song is called shake ya fanny."

"And what is the message in shakin' ya fanny?" I asked laughing.

"That one is more party like but the other ones are positive, yeah positive rap. So how is your music career going?"

"It's chillin'. I'm not pursing a deal right now. I'm just doin' it to have fun na mean? Actually Jus and I have a song called Witness that is on Power 104.2 website for their street beat battle so you should go on the site and vote for us."

"Ok, ok. Doin' big things I see."

"Na it ain't nothin' like that. I didn't even know it was up there. It was on a list of songs and that is the one they picked but I can live with that."

"Ok, I will tell everyone to vote. Where you headed now?"

I rode back to Waterbury feeling like I've just won the lottery, a feeling I get every time I leave Kenya. It is so refreshing to actually sit face to face and talk to Kenya, even though making love to her is mind blowing, I'd much rather take things slow and actually savor our time together instead leaving as if it was a booty call. I know our time is limited but I don't want Kenya to ever think I only drive out to Danbury to make love to her, I drive all the way out there to see that smile and to hear that laugh. To watch her watch me and just to feel her body close to mine when we hug. Since I turned my phone off before I went in Kenya's house I have four missed calls. Kendra...Stacy...Evelyn and Charlene. I haven't seen or talked to Charlene in almost a week because I have been trying to juggle seeing Evelyn, Stacy and Kenya but Kendra is the most important of the four missed calls.

"Hey."

"Hey. I called you an hour ago."

"I know I was at work."

"Isn't it Sunday?"

"Yeah, inventory."

"Ok. You're driving back home now?"

"Yeah so I got about thirty minutes, wussup?"

"I just wanted to call because I was thinking about you?"

"Thas wussup. How's Jamaica?"

"Wonderful but I am ready to come back home though."

"Why?"

"I miss my family and I don't have too many friends down here. All of the guys are older or young but just want to have sex. There are a lot of raping that happen here."

"Damn for real? I ain't think it was like that."

"Well I'm not in the area they advertise on television. I'm in the heart of the island where poverty is stricken everywhere. I have to have someone walk me home from campus when I have night classes." She explained.

"Wow. Well you need to be careful. Now you're gonna make me worry 'bout'chu."

"Please don't, I'll be alright. So what's going on with you?"

"Chillin', workin' hard."

"How's the music?"

"Everyone has been askin' me 'bout my music lately. Actually can you get to a computer down there?"

"Yeah there is one at school, why?"

"'Cause I need you to go to this radio station's website and vote on our song so we can get it played on the radio. But you gotta vote like everyday for the next week."

"Ok. What else is new? How's the girlfriend?"

"You mean ex-girlfriend."

"You two broke up?"

"Yep. I figured since you're comin' here in a couple of months I needed to let her go now instead of stringin' her along na mean?"

"Syncere you didn't have to do that."

"Yes I did. I can wait for you."

"Thank you. Actually I cut everything off with Mulan as well. I told him that we can be friends and nothing more."

"Why."

"The same reason as you. Like I told you before, I am much happier with you. Mulan is a nice guy and all but I just can't see myself with him after college you know?"

"Yep I do. How'd he take it?"

"He's upset. Keeps calling me names and blowing up my phone but I just ignore his calls and emails at this point. He thinks it's because of you."
"Did you tell him that?"

"Yeah."

"Well of course he would. Look, I don't want you to get back to UNC and have a problem wit this muhfucka na mean? 'Cause I have no problem violatin' my probation to beat his ass again. You would think he'd leave you alone after an ass whoppin' like that."

"He's just like you, he goes after what he wants relentlessly." She said comparing us.

"We're nothin' alike. That bitch ass nigga hits women." I'm nothin' like him so compare me to any other dude. Specially that muhfucka."

"I'm not I'm just saying that you guys are alike in a lot of ways. For instance Quami reminds me of you and so does Mulan. I see a little of them in each of you and you do the same thing."

"With the girls I date?"

"Yes. When you are describing them they all sound the same…the all sound like me. Whether it's the way they look or they have an accent like I do. I've seen pictures of some of the girls you dated when I was in Atlanta and all the girls look similar to each other even me."

"It's not on purpose it's just what I am attracted to."

"So when did you start dating white girls?"

"Are you still on that?" I asked about to get annoyed.

"No, I'm just asking. Because it sounds like Kenya is white."

"She's actually Brazilian but it's not like I woke up in the morning and said I'ma start dating white girls. I never seen it like white or black, I just date women. If she is attractive and we click then I'll date her regardless of color."

"I see. Can I ask you something?" she said softening her voice as she always does.

"Of course."

"Do you ever wonder why we continue to do this? Keep trying to be together?"

"All the time." I answered.

"What have you come up with?"

"Absolutely nothin'. If I had to say something I would have to say fate."

"Why fate."

"Because most women I know would not date a guy after he dated a family member na mean? But you didn't acknowledge that. We talked and that very first phone call something clicked. Something we weren't expecting but it's been clicking ever since. No matter how hard I try I can't get you out of my system, it's like my soul craves you."

"Sometimes I feel the same way. I acknowledged the fact you messed with Tausha and I almost wrote you off the day you called me."

"So why didn't you?"

"I felt something extremely special when I spoke to you. Underneath your arrogance…"

"I'm not arrogant, I'm confident."

"Oh no you are arrogant. But underneath it all lies a special person and I wanted to get to know that person and not the person who paraded around the church as a mack."

"Do you still think I'm special?" I asked.

"Yes, I think you are wonderful. But what makes me so special that you are willing to drop whoever you are with just to be with me? I'm not a model like Kenya. I'm just your everyday average college student."

"And I'm just your everyday average blue collard worker."

"Who wants to be a rapper."

"And you want to be a judge. So when you think about it we are really not as average as we think we are. Point is this feels right. Us, we feel right. I've known wrong my entire life but you, you are right. Right for me." I continued.

"You know what I've noticed?" she asked.

"What's that?"

"You love me more than you love yourself."

"You think so?"

"Yes, I do."

"Why do you say that?"

"Because I hear it in your voice and I also read between the lines when you talk to me. You try so hard not to express yourself but you actually tell me more than you think you do."

"You say it like it's a bad thing that I love you more than I love myself."

"It is Syncere."

"Why?"

"Because you can't truly love me or anyone until you love Syncere, flaws and all. You can't love yourself threw me."

19

"I got somethin' for you." I turned and said to Evelyn as I put my car in park in front of her house.

"What?"

"Close your eyes."

"Don't hit me." She said laughing.

"I'm not." I said returning the laugh. I reached in the back under Evelyn's seat and pulled out a Finish Line bag placing it on her lap.

"What is this?"

"Open it and find out."

"Oh my God you got me the Jordan's! The ones like yours. I thought you said you couldn't find them."

"I found them in our stockroom and it was the last pair too."

"They better fit." Excited Evelyn kicked off her beat up New Balance sneakers and put on the Jordan's all the while keeping the biggest smile on her face. I watched on like an excited father at Christmas.

"Why are you puttin' them on now when you're only gonna go in the house?"

"'Cause I want to, shut up." She said giving me a light push on the arm.

"Stay wit me tonight." I asked.

"I would but my grandmother be trippin' 'bout me stayin' out all the time. I'm not grown yet you know and she's not like my mom. She wants to know when I come and go."

"I know. Aight I'ma holla at'chu later." Evelyn gave me a big kiss on the cheek before hoping out of the car. I'd resisted having sex with Evelyn after she did my hair this time and my other half of me is screaming his head off but I don't care. Kendra's accusation of me loving her more than I love myself echo's in my head all the time now as I wonder if it is true? Maybe she's given the answer to why I'm so hell bent over being with her. I'm loving myself threw her. Maybe I don't love anyone, I mean think about it. I'm lying to Kendra about Kenya and I'm lying to Kenya about Evelyn and Charlene. So do I really love anyone? Do I even love Syncere?

When I got back in the house Charlene was sitting on my couch talking to Mone'.

"Brother!" Mone' said.

"Brother!" I replied playfully.

"Aight girl I'll talk to you later. Syncere mommy is workin' third shift again and she said she needs some help payin' the rent so leave some money on the table before you go to work in the mornin'." She instructed.

"What's good wit'chu?" Charlene asked folding her arms and staring me down.

"Nothin', just dropping Evelyn off from doin' my hair."

"Yeah Mone' told me. I didn't know ya'll use to mess. Why didn't you tell me?"

"I didn't know I had to tell you...why you lookin' at me like that?"

"'Cause I was just wonderin' if you fuckin' her too? I heard she a little hot ass."

"I'm not fuckin' her Charlene. Wanna call and ask her?"

"No. Well who are you fuckin'?"

"What? Where is this comin' from? Why I gotta be fuckin' somebody?"

"'Cause you don't spend no time with me during the day so obviously I'm the other woman."

"You know what I am fuckin' somebody else…I'm fuckin' Finish Line ok."

"Don't get smart."

"Well that's were I am all the time Charlene and you know that. Whenever you see me don't I have on this tacky ass uniform?"

"That don't mean shit."

"You know what? You're right…fuck it." I said turning on my Xbox.

"When are we gonna go out?" she asked standing in front of the television.

"What? Go out where?" I asked irritated.

"Out like on a real date. All I do is come over here at night, you fuck me then we go to sleep and you drop me off in the mornin'. We barley talk durin' the day unless its you sayin' come over or me sayin' I wanna come over. I wanna go on a real date Syncere because this thing we're doin' has me feelin' like a hoe."

"Where do you wanna go Charlene?" I asked beginning to wonder if ass worth the headache?

"Out to eat maybe. A movie, the park or somewhere outta town just somewhere."

"You know I'm always at work and it's hard for me to get days off then when I do get a day off they end up callin' me in 'cause somethin' happened."

"Mone' says you have Sunday off."

"Ok…I was plannin' on sleepin' in then goin' to the studio."

"The damn studio. If it isn't work it's the damn studio. Why can't we go out Sunday, just this once for me?"

"Sunday night?"

"No, all day. I wanna go to breakfast, then I wanna go to the flea market in New Haven then I want dinner and a movie Sunday night. I want you for twenty-four hours. I wanna just walk around holdin' ya hand and talkin' 'bout whatever."

"Aight we can do that."

"Don't bullshit me Syncere and I wanna eat at Outback Steakhouse."

"Outback? Na we can't do Outback."

"Why not?"

"I got food poisionin' from there a couple weeks ago."

"Who the fuck you go to Outback with?"

"We went there for Quincy's goin' away party. Our whole staff from Olympia went, calm down." I explained lying threw my teeth.

"Look at that, you even take your staff out before me. Well I wanna go somewhere just as nice."

I dropped Charlene off at her house so she can get changed for dinner. I figured I can take her out to Carmen Anthony's Steakhouse for a number of reasons. One I'm tired of driving and two I don't have to risk running into Kenya while being in her vicinity by going to Outback. All day I've been missing Kenya, as we haven't talked since I saw your yesterday.

"Hey baby!"

"What's good?"

"Nothing. Talking to Chrissy."

"Oh tell her I said what's good." I heard her relay the message.

"Look, Chrissy's birthday is Tuesday but we all have to work so tonight we're going to have dinner at Uno's after the mall closes."

"Who's we?"

"Me, Chrissy, Megan, Marcus, Derrick and I want you to come."

"Really? I get to see you two days in a row?"

"Oh yeah! I told my mom Chrissy is driving me home so she said to be home by ten thirty and I figured after dinner we could go to our favorite spot. Oh yeah, oh yeah, oh yeah!"

"The park?"

"Oh yeah!" she said again making me laugh because she's so damn cute.

"Remember what happened last time? Do you really wanna do that again?"

"Are you afraid?" she teased.

"Please, neva that."

"So you coming?"

"Do you really have to ask me twice?"

"Close your eyes first." Kenya demanded as we sat in my car at our favorite park while my suspicion turned into anticipation.

"Why?"

"Because it isn't a surprise if you see it coming and you better like it because it took a lot of phone calls to get this. Now close your eyes!" I abided then I feel something sitting on my lap.

"Can I open them now?"

"Yeah." To my surprise there is a Jordan box sitting in my lap.

"What are these?"

"I know you said you wanted another pair so I called a bunch of stores and one of them sent them to me." I opened the box to find a fresh pair of Carolina blue and white Retro Jordan 12's before my eyes.

"Babe, oh my God...and they my size but what did I tell you 'bout us buyin' each other shoes?"

"Baby, I know you love your aunt and all but that is a silly thing. I'm not going to walk out of your life just because I brought you a pair of sneakers. Hey, you weren't saying that when I brought you those Michael Vick edition Air Force 1's did you? Nope. Look at me...I'm not going anywhere and do you know why?"

"Yeah."

"You better know why because I love you."

"I know, I just need to hear it sometimes."

"Why?"

"It feels nice to hear it na mean?"

"Yeah. It does...say it."

Surprisingly Charlene hasn't blown up my phone today like she's done for the past week after I basically stood her up for dinner when I went to be with Kenya last Sunday. It wasn't planned but I cut her off. Not because being with her is cheating on Kenya but because I just got bored.

"Yo you madd messed up Syn." Mone's attacked as soon as I walked into the house.

"What I do now?"

"You stood Charlene up and now you dodging her calls. She's pissed. She threatened to break your car windows but I talked her out of it."

"Thanks." I said laughing.

"It ain't funny. You liked her in high school so what is so different now? I know you ain't stop messin' with Charlene to mess with Evy?"

"Why you say it like that?"

"Syncere everybody know how nasty Evy is com'on now. I been tellin' you 'bout Evy ever since you got home. She madd cool but she fucked madd niggas and had like four abortions. Everybody knows 'cause she be tellin' everybody her business. I really like Kenya but you need to leave Evy alone."

"I know."

"I don't even know why you cheatin' on Kenya like that. She real nice, you a dog. Then I heard that you talkin' to Stacy Rogers?"

"How my own sister gonna call me a dog like that? You supposed to be on my side."

"'Cause you are man. I am on your side, I'm not sayin' I'ma go tell Kenya or nothin' like that, I'm sayin' you came home almost cryin' to mommy when you found out Krista was cheatin' on you. Now here you are cheatin' on Kenya and for what? She ain't never did anything to you."

"I know fudge, I know." I really can't say anything because my adorable chocolate little sister is right in every sense of the word.

"Stacy! Stacy! Stacy!" Anija said as she ran into the arms of Kenya.

"No Anija. Kenya remember?"

"Oh yeah. Hi Kenya." She said looking at me then back at Kenya.

"Hi sweetie. You look cute today." Kenya said keeping a smile on her face.

"I know. Uncle Syncere you comin' to my mommy's house?"

"Nope. Ya mommy is still at work. You wanna hang out wit me and Kenya today?" She nodded her head yes and we jumped into the car.

"Baby I'm hungry." Kenya said. I looked at the car clock, which read three o'clock, and I wondered where the time had gone? I picked Kenya up from her house this morning because she doesn't have any exams and we came back to my mother's house, made love, slept and cuddled on the couch until Nyri called to ask me to pick up Anija.

"Uncle Syncere, I'm lovin' it." Kenya and I exploded into laughter as we passed a McDonalds and Anija began singing the theme song.

"Where you wanna eat?" I asked

"Anywhere but McDonalds."

"I'm lovin' it." Anija repeated again.

"There is an Applebee's right here, how 'bout there?"

"Ok."

Anija entertained Kenya and I with her random cute comments and childish antics and occasionally calling Kenya Stacy again. Anija almost knocked over Kenya's cup when she reached across the table for a napkin and as Kenya caught the cup Anija said, "my bad" and we all shared a laugh again. When Kenya took Anija to the bathroom to get cleaned off I watched Kenya pick Anija up in her arms and carry her off but not before the both of them turned to wave to me. At that moment I see a future with Kenya. From an outsider looking in Anija, Kenya and I looked like a happy family. While we ate I sat back and observed Kenya interacting with Anija and imagined Anija is our own daughter. The images give me a view into the future five or so years from now if Kenya and I were to start a family and it is confirmed then that I want a life with Kenya.

"Why does she keep calling me Stacy?" Kenya asked when we dropped Anija off.

"She sees Stacy a lot."

"Who is she?"

"She's a friend of mine that works at the day care where Anija goes."

"So how does she confuse me with her. I'm guessing Stacy is black. How often do you pick Anija up?"

"Like twice a week. Ok, like two weeks ago I brought Anija some Jordan's and I had to bring them to Nyri's house. First I went to Stacy's Miss Waterbury pageant and then she rode with me to go see Anija."

"So you and Stacy hang out? Is that what you are saying?"

"Yeah basically. We just hang out. We don't like each other or anything like that she's just cool peoples." I lied knowing full well that I'm trying to have sex with Stacy.

"Why haven't you said anything about her before? I know about Evelyn who does your hair so why haven't you told me about Stacy? Are you hiding something?"

"I don't want you to think I'm fuckin' around on you that's all."

"But when your niece who's seen me I don't know how many times calls me Stacy over and over again then what am I supposed to think?"

"You're right…I apologize I should've told you. But it's not like I told you any lies either. You always know where I am, what I'm doin' and who I'm with so I'm not keepin' anything from you."

"Except the fact you hang out with Stacy."

"Oh my God babe I hung out wit Stacy probably twice. Remember that I asked you if you could come to Waterbury 'cause I was takin' Anija to the carnival?"

"Yes."

"Well when you told me you couldn't come…"

"You called Stacy!?"

"No listen. Only Anija and I went but we saw Stacy there wit her little brother so we all hung out together."

"And the other time?"

"I met Nyri at Dominic's wit Anija and Stacy walked in and we all had pizza together. Nothin' really major and I told you I was at both of those places."

"But you didn't tell me you were wit her is the point I'm gettin' at."

"Do you trust me?"

"Baby I'm not sayin' I don't believe you it's just that…Well what if you came to my house and Blake called you Ricky? Would you be upset?"

"What? Hell yeah."

"So you see my point then. Listen, we don't see each other as much as we want to and I'm afraid that you're gonna meet someone older and don't have a racist mother to hide from. So when I hear Anija calling me her name it makes me think you've been around Anija with Stacy enough for her to make that connection."

"Babe. The drive to Danbury is thirty-five minuets one way. Do you know how many women are in that vicinity? Hundreds. I drive all the way out here once, twice or four times a week because I love you and I want to be with you. What would be the point of cheating?"

"You really love me?"

"Yeah. Why do you sound surprised?"

"'Cause you haven't said it in weeks. I thought you changed your mind. I guess that is why I'm making a bid deal about Stacy."

"I didn't notice. Why didn't you say anything?"

"Because I don't want to be the type of girlfriend that has to hear you say I love you every time we get off the phone. I just noticed you had stopped is all."

"Trust me babe it isn't on purpose. You know I've been workin' like crazy and I just had the show at the Webster Theatre plus I'm trying to find an apartment, I'm sorry."

"It's ok. I understand. I guess I'm a little paranoid."

"About what?"

"Are you kidding? Syncere every girl in my school wanted to date you when you started working at Olympia, every girl. So when I think of that then our situation and I think about you being all the way in Waterbury where everyone knows you I just worry you'll get tired of sneaking around and barley seeing me you know?"

"Yeah. But if you can lie to your mom on a daily basis to see me then I can deal with this. As long as you are with me we will get threw this." I assured.

"Do you mean that? I mean really mean that?"

"Yeah."

"Good. Just do me a favor baby? I understand you have friends that were before me so could you just tell me who you're hanging out with? That way if Anija calls me her name or anything it won't look like you're cheating."

"Will do."

20

"Mr. & Mrs. Washington how are you today?" Mr. Lansky said as he extended his hand.

"Mr. Washington and Ms. Roberts. We're not married."

"Well is the apartment for the both of you or just you Mr. Washington?"

"Just me. We've just started dating and we're not at that level yet." I said as Stacy lightly hit me in the stomach.

"All the same. I'm sure a pretty young lady like this will be around often enough."

"You bet she will."

Stacy and I walked around the one bedroom apartment checking out every inch of it in detail. I loved the newly remodeled stand in shower and the medium sized kitchen but the selling point is the two walk in closets.

"I'm so glad you like this one. Finally one we agree on." Stacy said failing to whisper.

"You two have seen a lot?"

"Almost twenty around Waterbury, Wolcott and Naugatuck." I wrote Mr. Lansky a check for the first months rent and told him I'll be back with the deposit in two weeks when I am ready to move in.

Since our discussion about Stacy I have told Kendra about every time Stacy and I hang out and how Stacy has gone with me to a number of apartments to help me pick out the right one. I would much rather have Kenya here with me on my apartment search but she can't be here every time I go see a place so Stacy has been the substitute offering a woman's opinion on what I should get.

"Why can't you do that on your own? Why does she have to come with you?" "Babe you know I hate doin' things on my own. I won't even go to the movies by myself. She is only givin' me a woman's opinion that is all. I'm serious…you do believe me right?" I explained to Kenya as we walk around Ikea picking out things for he new apartment.

"Yeah baby I believe you. When do you move in?"

"In two weeks."

"I'ma get you a housewarming gift. What do you need?"

"Shit, everything. But I really want that bed I showed you at the Futon place next to Olympia when I was there. You remember?"

"I think so but do you think they still have it? That was a long time ago."

"They should. It's not like they sell those things like hot cakes anyway. Can you go check it out for me and tell me how much it is 'cause I don't remember."

"Of course and I'll pay for it too."

"Thanks babe. You gonna help me break it in too?" I asked winking.

"Oh yeah!"

"So in between now and Friday will I be able to see you?"

"I don't know baby. I have to actually work at Merle Norman and model at a car show on Saturday. My weekend is pretty full."

"Oh." I said sounding disappointed and letting go of Kenya's hand.

"Syncere? Don't act like that, you know I am trying."

"Seein' you once or twice a week ain't enough for me. I need to see you more often."

"Baby I'm trying but it isn't easy working around both our schedules plus trying to come up with new lies to tell my mom. You know I'm running out here."

"Can't you call out of work on Wednesday or somethin'?"

"Baby I'm trying to save up enough money so I can buy a car. Don't you want me to be able to drive to Waterbury instead of you coming to Danbury all the time?"

"I guess. Well can't you tell your mom you're stayin' at Chrissy or Tati's house on Friday?"

"She'll call their mothers to confirm and I don't know if their parents will lie for me like that." I huffed harder at her lack of corporation.

"You sound like you don't even want to see me."

"Syncere how can you say that?"

"'Cause you shootin' down everything I say but you ain't comin up wit no suggestions."

"I can't believe you're acting like this! I lie to my mother on a regular basis just to see you. I call out of work on top of skipping school and you are acting like I do anything for this relationship."

"I didn't say all that."

"Yes you did. While I'm day dreaming about you during class and work I have to wonder if you are with Stacy looking at apartments or doing whatever."

"So you think I'm cheatin' on you with Stacy?"

"I don't know Syncere I'm not in Waterbury."

"So you gotta be here in order to know if I'm cheatin' on you or not? Like I don't tell you everything."

"All I know is what you tell me but I don't know if it's the truth or not. I don't know if you and Stacy are doing what you say you are. You did tell me she is your ex isn't she? I thought you cut off all communication with your ex's."

"I normally do but only if we broke up on bad terms but Stacy and I are cool just friends." I said lying.

"So why did it have to take for your niece to call me Stacy a hundred times for you to tell me that you two use to date but now you just hung out?"

"I didn't want you to think I was tryin' to play you as stupid. What was I supposed to say? Oh babe by the way I hang out with my ex girlfriend Stacy but we are just cool. When I told you 'bout Stacy I could've easily left out the fact she is my ex-girlfriend but I didn't. I told you everything 'cause I didn't wanna keep anything from you." I explained.

"Oh lucky me but how do I know if what you are telling me is the truth. I'm way down here and I don't know any of your friends well enough to just call to see how everything is going but I shouldn't have to. I should be able to trust you."

"You don't trust me? Oh you don't trust me now?"

"Syncere what would you do if I was around all my ex's all the time?"

"I'm not."

"You are around Stacy and Evelyn all the time. You're either with Evelyn because she's doing your hair or you're just hanging out with Stacy so what's to stop you from doing what ever you want to do with either of them, huh?"

"I already told you 'bout this. She's celibate and you know I don't do those so it's not even like that."

"Again I don't know."

"Oh so you don't know now? You think I'm fuckin' Evelyn and Stacy? Is that what you think?"

"You're the one who can't go too long without sex and its not like we see each other on a regular basis so no I don't know what to think. You use to put it on me like no other but lately we don't do it half the time."

"What? You don't know what to think? That's fucked up. Sometimes I just like to be in your presence babe. I don't have to have sex all the time. But I could be sayin' the same thing 'bout you."

"Whatever. You know where I am always and tell me when do I have the time to mess with someone else."

"You know what? I don't need this shit. Got me drivin' up and now tha fuckin' highway every chance I get and you don't believe me? Fuck it."

"Fuck it then." Kenya responded as she walked ahead of me.

Standing in the kitchen section of Ikea I'm amazed that Kenya actually walked away from me. She's never done that before but now that I think about it I really can't blame Kenya for thinking what she's thinking especially since she does know about my past relationships. I know very well I'm cheating on Kenya with Evelyn and Stacy but I don't want Kenya to know she's right.

"Em?"

"Hold on Syn I'm on the other line with Kenya."

"Aight but don't tell her you're talkin to me tho."

"Ok." As I waited for Emily to come back to the line I thought that this has been the only "fight" Kenya and I have had since we've started dating. I've always told her that if we ever did get in a fight it would result in us breaking because it would have to be something major to get us mad at each other. The closet we've ever been in an argument is fighting over who's turn it is to pay the check at Outback.

"Em?"

"Yeah I'm back. What happened?"

"I don't know. One minute we're picking out furniture in Ikea and the next thing I know we're sayin' fuck it and she's walkin' away. I don't know where she went."

"She called me right before you did crying."

"She's cryin'?"

"Yeah, she thinks you want to break up…Do you?"

"No. I don't wanna break up. I'm just a little frustrated that I can't see her when I want to na mean? You can Mika don't have to sneak around ya'll parents to see each other or to stay at each other's houses like we have to. Sometimes it gets to me fell me?"

"Yeah but hanging out with other girls is not the answer Syncere. You knew all this before you two got serious so why is it bothering you now?"

"Em it's bothered me since the day we started, I was just able to control it but the more and more I'm gettin' into her the more I need to see her."

"Now do you really need to see her or do you want to see her because of the sex?"

"Na chill the sex ain't even the reason. I want her…for more than thirty minutes or an hour. I wanna fall asleep with my arms wrapped around her with my face buried into her fruit smelled hair. Feel me? I wanna wake up to her without her havin' make up on so I can see how naturally beautiful she is in the mornin' or just to sit down and watch a movie on the couch together. Quality time. The kinds of time quality relationships are built with it."

"So if you feel like that then why were you with that girl at the show and not with Kenya? And don't lie."

"'Cause all the things I wanna do with Kenya I do with Stacy minus the sex."

"You mean to tell me you haven't fucked her?"
"Na she's not havin' sex and I just like her company."

"So you've never thought about it?"

"Of course I've thought about it Stacy's a pretty girl. She ain't Kenya pretty but she's still pretty and her body is crazy but she's not havin' sex and I respect that."

"But if she offered it you'd do it?"

"Maybe. But it's not a sex thing 'cause if it was I have plenty of women to choose from here plus all the chicks she goes to school with are always callin' me so don't think it's about sex."

"Well I haven't told her about Stacy but that is the last time I keep something like that from Kenya 'cause she is my friend too and the only reason why I haven't is 'cause I met you first and you've always looked out for me. If you really wanna be with Kenya you have to cut this things with Stacy off 'cause Kenya says you are distant to her."

"Like how?"

"She says you use to call her three to four times a day just to say hi but when she calls you she always gets your voice mail. Then she said when you two talk you always seem like your mind is somewhere else."

"Wow I didn't even think she noticed hell I didn't even notice."

"She's a girl Syncere of course she notices things like that."

"Aight Em I got'chu."

"So go find her now."

"Aight, bye…thanks again Em."

"I don't wanna break up." Kenya said sniffling when I found her in the children's section o Ikea.

"I don't either baby."

"I just feel like I can't be the girlfriend you want and need."

"Na don't say that 'cause it ain't true. You are everything I want in a girlfriend, I just neglected to see all that you do to be with me. I got a little selfish and I apologize. For real for real."

"It's ok baby. Believe me, I want to see you as much as you want to see me and one day next year when I graduate we will be able to see each other like we want to but right now we have to make this work in order to get to that point." She explained while stroking my hand.

"I know, I know. I just really miss you."

"Is that so?"

"It is"

"Ya'll hungry?" Tracy asked meeting back up with us at the register.

"You always hungry hamburgerler."

"Here we go wit the fuckin' jokes. Look Quizno's is right there and me and Michane want a sub."

"You wanna eat at Quizno's babe? Mmm mmm toasty." I said moving my eyebrows up and down.

"I don't like their food. Can we get something to eat in Danbury? We have to get back soon."

"Like what?"

"The Olive Garden."

"Aight we can do that." As Kenya and I got into my car my cell phone rang.

"Who is it baby?" She said looking as surprised as I am.

"It's my boss. He never calls my cell phone. Am I in trouble? I don't wanna answer it.

"Go ahead it could be important."

"What's up Chris?"

"Hey buddy you got a minute?"

"Yeah, what'chu need?"

"You told Johnny D. you were relocate able anywhere on the east coast remember?"

"Yeah…"

"Well we need a store manager in a store in Virginia. When can you be ready?"

"Virginia? I don't know I would have to talk to my girlfriend about that." I said looking at Kenya whose face grew increasingly curious.

"Well I need to know now because I have to tell John on Monday."

"Aight I'll go." I answered without thinking and in the same breath I wish I hadn't because I could see the tears begin to form in Kenya's eyes.

"Great buddy. I'll relay this to John and we'll talk to you on Monday because he has a couple other people in mind so this isn't definite yet. Have a good night."

"Thanks."

The drive to Danbury is a silent one, as I didn't know what to say to Kenya. She's obviously upset with my decision and I have to say I am surprised at what I agreed to without thinking. I have half a mind to call Tracy but that can wait until the ride home when I'm alone.

"Do you still wanna go to the Olive Garden?" she nodded her head yes but remained silent. Instead of sitting next to each other and talking Kenya and I sat across from another not saying a word and trying not to make eye contact.

"Babe. I don't want the next half hour to be quiet can you please tell me what's on your mind?" I pleaded.

"I wanna go to school in California."

"California! Why?"

"Because that will be a great place to start my career after college."

"What school is in California?"

"Johnson & Wales."

"There is a Johnson & Wales in Rhode Island at least if you go there we would still be in the same time zone. I thought you were goin' to school in Connecticut or Atlanta like we talked about."

"I know but after I thought about it I think I would like California better."

"Then what about us? What's gonna happen to us?"

"Well still be together. We could see each other on the weekends. You could fly me out."

That's not gonna work. You'll be too far, when will we see each other?"

"So how often do you think we'll see each other after you move to Virginia? 'Cause wasn't that the plan you were gonna feed me? Seeing each other on the weekends and such?"

"First of all the move isn't definite and second Virginia is a lot closer than California."

"We'd still hardly see each other."

"Oh my God. If I move to Virginia I could fly you down on a weekday, we could chill all day and I can have you back home by 8pm but we can't do that if you move all the way to freakin' California."

"So why is it ok for you to move? Why can't I move and you do all the flying back and forth, huh?"

"Why don't you come with me?" I suggested.

"You know I can't."

"I'm not talkin' 'bout now I'm talkin' 'bout when you graduate. Fuck California. Let me get established in VA and when you graduate move to Virginia to go to school."

"Why do you wanna leave me?" She said while giving me the puppy dog eyes and poked out quivering lip that she know is my kryptonite.

"Baby you know damn well I don't wanna leave you but I'm tryin' to be a DM. I didn't finish school and Finish Line is all I have so I gotta go as far as possible. You can go to school anywhere for hotel management so come with me."

"How about you go to Virginia, do well there then ask them to transfer you to California when I start school?"

"That might can work. Look at that beauty and brains."

"Can you do that?"

"Hell yeah. If it means I'ma be with you then hell yeah I'm all for it."

"How are you gonna handle that if you can't handle us not seeing each other and we're in the same state?"

"I can handle it. You know when I told you to start speakin' your mind to people? I don't like it when you do it to me."

"Well I have to start somewhere."

21

I hung up with Kenya as I pulled into Stacy's driveway as I saw her peaking through her kitchen window. *Alright Syncere time to put in work* I said to myself. My strategy is to use reverse psychology on Stacy and make her jealous by bringing up sexual things with Kenya to force her into giving in. Well here goes nothing.

"Hey baby." Stacy said greeting me with a kiss as I stepped into the door.

"What' good?"

"Nothin'. You hungry?"

"Na I already ate."

"Who were you on the phone with?"

"Huh?"

"Who were you on the phone with?" she repeated.

"Oh that? It was just Kenya."

"She still calls you?"

"Every now and again."

"Well what did she want?"

"Nothin'." I said purposely-avoiding eye contact with Stacy.

"Syncere tell me what she wanted." Stacy demanded standing in front of me with her arms folded.

"She just wanted to know if the bed was delivered today."

"What bed?"

"The bed she brought me for my new apartment."

"How'd she know about the new apartment?"

"I told her a few weeks ago when I was up in Danbury with Tracy."
"So she brought you a bed? Did you ask for it?"

"Not really. She asked me what I needed 'cause she wanted to get me a house warming gift and I may have mentioned somethin' about needin' a bed."

"So she brought you bed just like that?"

"Yeah I guess so."
"So is that all she said?"

"Na she was like I need to stop trippin' and let her come over so we can break it in 'cause I know that you can't do it like she do. But I told her you and aren't havin' sex and she was like then that is more the reason for me to let her come over."

"Call her! Call her right now!"

"What?"

"Call her, I wanna talk to her."

"For what?"

"Just because I do, she is disrespectin'. Does she know about us?"

"Yeah but don't worry 'bout it. Where am I right now? I'm here with you and not with her."

"Yeah but you're not gonna be here all night."

"I will be if you want me to be."

"Ok. But I'm not sleeping over your house in that bed if she brought it."

"Why not?"

"'Cause I'm not."

"Yeah but you and I are the only ones to sleep in it. The laugh is on her 'cause she brought me a bed with her money that I'ma sleep in with another girl. We should go back to my house and break it in then call her and tell her we did it."

"No! I'm not havin' sex until I'm married and when we get married we are throwing that bed out."

"Whoa, whoa, whoa! When we get married?" I asked with a complex look on my face.

"Yeah. I figure this time next year you'd get another promotion and you'd propose and…"

"Stacy, Stacy I'm not gettin' married hun I'm sorry."

"What? Then why are you even with me?"

"I'm wit'chu 'cause I like you and we have a good time together and we're tryin' to build a relationship together but I'm not gettin' married."

"I'm not gonna be someone's girlfriend for the rest of my life and I'm not gonna be shacked up playing house either. Why are you playing games with me Syncere?"

"Who's playin' games? I'm not even thinkin' that far into the future we just havin' fun right now."

"So you're not gettin' married ever?"

"Na."

"Why do I have to pay for the mistakes Kendra made?"

"Who said this has anything to do with Kendra?"

"Oh com'on Syncere. I remember what'chu said. You said Kendra broke your heart and now you're not gonna marry anyone."

"If you remember that then why are you acting like this is such a surprise to you?"

"'Cause I thought you were a little bitter about the situation but we've been together five months now and you drop this shit on me. Why do you even get in relationships if you're not gonna get married?"

"That is not the reason people date Stacy."

"Yes it is. You date to find the person you're gonna marry."

"Stacy even if I wanted to marry you we couldn't it wouldn't work 'cause we have a lot of different views on things."

"Like what?"

"First of all the whole sex thing."

"Why does everything have to do with sex? Every conversation we have deals with sex. You told me you're not here for that."

"I'm not but sex is a huge part of any relationship and I can't get married to a woman I haven't already had sex wit. Fifty percent of divorces are due to someone cheating because the sex was bad. Because people wait years until they get married to have sex and when it happens it sucks and now their stuck in a marriage." I explained throwing out a non-documented statistic.

"What are the other reasons?"

"Stacy I could go all night but one more is I can't marry someone I haven't lived with for a at least a year. Again a lot of marriages end because people wait until they get married to move in and when they don they find out all these little things about the other person that they didn't already know which annoys the other person to the point they can't take it anymore. Doin' shit like waitin' until marriage to have sex or move it is walkin' into a situation blind."

"Well I'm not doin' either. I'm not having sex wit'chu and I'm not movin' in wit'chu until we get married. So where do we go from here?"

"I don't know 'cause it's evident you're not changin' how you feel and I most certainly am not either so I guess we call it a wrap."

"Just like that?"

"Hey you're the one who said you date to find the person you want to marry and quite frankly I don't wanna get married so it's up to you."

"Fine."

"Fine what?"

"Fine, go call Kenya and tell her you'll be home in ten minutes."

"I'm not goin' home. I'm stayin' here wit'chu."

"I don't know why…we ain't havin' sex."

"Who said anything about us havin' sex? I just wanna sleep next to you."

I lay in Stacy's bed while she began drifting asleep and I thought that I'll stay the night here so Stacy won't think that fight was about us not having sex but tomorrow I'm cutting her off. There's no need for me to fuck with Stacy if we're not fuckin' 'cause I still have Evelyn for that. In mid thought my phone rang.

"Hello."

"Hey Syn guess what?"

"What?"

"I'm home! I'm back in the states! I wanna come to Connecticut before I start school again in two weeks." Kendra said sounding super excited. It's obvious she hasn't forgotten about the decision we made to try our relationship one more time. In the mist of moving to Virginia, dealing with Kenya, Evelyn and Stacy I had forgotten about it.

"Aight. Lemme call you later I can't talk right now."

"Why not. What are you doing? Are you whispering?"

"Na. I'm in the middle of somethin' so lemme call you back."

"Why? What are you in the middle of?" she pressed.

"I'll tell you later."

"Syncere something is wrong. Why can't you tell me now?"

"'Cause I'll tell her later." I insisted.

"Why can't you tell me now?"
"'Cause I can't tell you now. I'll tell you later." Those are the only words I could give Kendra at the moment as my brain searches for a believable lie to tell as to why I can't talk right now. Kendra isn't stupid. She knows that when she calls I will stop healing the world just to talk to her so me not being able to talk right now is peaking her curiosity.

"Syncere I'm not hanging up until you tell me what is going on. I've counted down the days until I get home so I can see you. So if you've changed your mind please let me know now."

"No I haven't but I'll tell you later."

"No tell her right now!" Stacy said waking out of her sleep and sitting up in the bed.

"Syncere who is that?" Kendra asked.

"That's my friend Stacy."

"Friend! I'm your friend now? Tell her…tell her right now why you can't talk. You can't talk because you're in bed with me." Stacy persisted this time getting in my face and more than close to the phone so she knew her voice is being heard.

"Syncere tell me what is going on."

"Look Kendra lemme deal wit this and I'ma call you right back."

"But…" I couldn't make out what she is about to say because I hung the phone up to tend to an out of control Stacy.

"What is your problem? You're actin' like a real hood chick right now doin' all that yellin' in the phone."

"Was it her? Was it that bitch Kenya?"

"No and what if it was my mother on the phone."

"You didn't wanna tell her you're over here do you?"

"You're buggin'."

"Tell me who she was. Tell me!"

"Be quite, you're gonna wake up JD and your grandparents."

"Then tell me who she was then. Tell me!"

"You know what? I ain't gotta deal wit this shit. Explaining myself to you and we ain't fuckin'. I'm gone."

"Oh so you leavin' now? 'Cause I wont have sex with you you're leaving now?" I didn't respond to Stacy as I slipped back on my jeans ad my white and orange Air Force 1 sneakers. Stacy followed me all the way to the back door yelling in my ear and tugging on my shirt but I managed to get her off me without doing anything drastic. Before I even got out of the driveway I'm dialing Kendra's number.

"Hey."

"What the hell was that all about?" she snapped.

"Nothin'."

"Who was that Syn?"

"This crazy girl Stacy." I replied.

"What were you doin' with her? Do you need me to call you back? Was I interrupting anything?"

"It ain't even like that? She asked for a ride home 'cause she works with Mone'. So we get in the car and she starts talkin' like she wanna get with me and can she come by my house and shit like that."

"So why was she acting all crazy?"

"'Cause I told her I had a girlfriend and I didn't wanna fuck wit her. She was like what would my girlfriend think if you knew we were in the car together right now and I was like nothin' 'cause you ain't the jealous type then that is when you called."

"But you hung up with me to deal with her?"

"I had to. How was I 'possed to talk with this bitch in my hear riffin'?"

"I don't know but I come first and you just hung up on me do deal with her."

"What? I didn't have a choice. It was either talk to you with her riffin' in my ear until we got to her house or just hang up wit'chu and call you back." You takin' this too serious."

"No I'm not. If I'm the woman you love and the woman you want to be with then you put everyone else after me. Just hearing that makes me not want to come to Connecticut now."

"Why?"

"Because Syncere, you always have a bunch of girls either around you or flocking toward you and that reminds me of Shiloh and Saint Aug again. We are getting too old to be going back and forth like this so you need to figure out if you really want to be with me or not. But if I'm have situations like the one that just happened then I don't want to go through it."

"I do want to be wit'chu."

"I don't know if you are ready. You know that if we try this again and it doesn't work and we are gonna just have to be friends right?"

"Yep."

"So make sure you're sure." She said before hanging up. I thought about calling her back but I dialed Kenya instead.

"Hey were you sleeping?"

"A little."

"I'm sorry babe."

"It's ok. What's up?"

"They offered me Virginia Beach and I have to leave by Friday."

"That soon? Why?"

"'Cause they need someone how."
"So I guess you're really going to go huh?"

"I turned them down."

"Why?" She asked trying not to sound so enthusiastic.

"For real for real I thought 'bout it and I'm really tryin' to build a solid relationship wit'chu. And I noticed that the night my boss called I had already made the decision to leave without even askin' you or discussion it wit'chu and that isn't how a relationship works. It's 'posed to be fifty-fifty."

"So you turned it down for me?"

"Yes ma'am."

"Aww baby that was sweet but I don't want you to put your career on hold for me."

"You were gonna go to a college you didn't wanna go to for me and I'm workin' on the whole not bein' selfish thing it just take me a little longer to get it na mean? But yes I'm stayin' 'cause I don't wanna be anywhere with out'chu."
"Good." Kenya and talked briefly until she told me she wanted to get back to sleep. We exchanged I love you's and I then dialed Evelyn.

"What'chu doin'?"

"Playin' wit myself."

"I'm on my way."

"Hurry up I'ma 'bout to cum."

The sun shone rays of light into our half empty living room as I looked between the blinds. What? Kenya's car is here. I ran to my room to get my cell phone, which was vibrating when I picked it up and Kenya's name was displayed.

"Hello?"

"Where are you?"

"Home. You parked right behind my car."
"Open the door." She ordered. Upon opening the door it was visible that Kenya has been crying and a wave of concern overwhelmed me.

"What happen?" I asked. For a few moments Kenya just starred at me with hate and disgust in her eyes as tears and mascara began sliding down her face.

"Are you fuckin' Stacy?" she finally said.

"Babe I told you 'bout that already, no."

"Are you fuckin' Evelyn?"

"No."

"Then tell me how I got FUCKING Chlamydia Syncere??" The very next breath was stolen along with the rest of the air in my lungs and my mind can't comprehend what my ears just heard.

"What?"

"I have fuckin' Chlamydia! ARE YOU DEAF?"

"I don't."

"I was just tested Syncere, twice and you're the only person I'm having unprotected sex with so tell me how the fuck I got this shit."

"I don't have any symptoms of no STD."

"The nurse said it doesn't show up in men like it does women so you could have it and not even know it. Please…please Syncere just tell me the truth. Who are you fuckin'?"

"No one. I swear."

"Then how did I get this?"

"I don't know."

"I didn't give it to myself…I thought you love me."

"I do."

"Fuck you." Kenya yelled as she stormed out of my apartment. I stood my half empty living room not knowing what to do or say, I think I just lost my girlfriend because I wasn't smart enough to put on a condom with Evelyn. Ok, this shit is getting out of control and it's gone too far. Now I'm jeopardizing the life and well being of Kenya and that ain't cool at all, this has to stop.

"Nute."

"What's up cousin?"

"Yo I think this bitch gave me somethin'."

"Who Evy?"

"Yeah."

"How you know?" I told my little cousin Charm what Kenya had told me as she rode with me to Waterbury Hospital so I could get a full blown STD and AIDS test. The minutes passed like days while I waited, got tested and waited again. I worried sick the entire time, pacing back and forth or getting pissed off at the fact I could have endangered Kenya's life. To tell you the truth if I do have and STD or possibly even AIDS I really wouldn't care just as long as I didn't give those things to Kenya because she doesn't deserve them…I do. I made my bed so now I must lay in it.

"You ok Syn?"

"Na Nute. I'm tellin' you if I got somethin' I'm fuckin' this bitch up for real that's my word." I said trying to fight back tears.

"We all told you how Evy get down. I don't wanna say I told you so 'cause that isn't what you need right now but I met Kenya and Evy has nothin' on her. I know you want to be in your girlfriends company and all but you already know it can't always be that way but that don't mean you go out and find someone else to fill that void. You gotta man up and just deal with it or let the girl go 'cause I know you and you must get tired of lyin'. You told me yourself you hate lyin'."

"I do. Well either way these test results come back I'm cuttin' everyone off 'cause I can't do this shit anymore. I'ma just have to be lonely until I can see Kenya." Kenya called to see where I was because she had came back to my house so I gave her directions to Waterbury Hospital and just as she was walking in the doctor is coming out.

"Are you ready to hear these?"

"Hold on." Charm clenched my arm and I opened my hand for Kenya's who didn't accept it so at this point I'm like fuck it.

"For Chlamydia, gonorrhea, syphilis and any other sexual transmitted disease you are negative. But as far as the AIDS test we wouldn't know anything for seventy-two hours so I'm afraid you will have to think about it until then." Charm and I hugged and the weight of the world just lifted off my shoulders.

"Hold on. I am his girlfriend and when I went to my doctor this afternoon she tested me twice and told me I have Chlamydia and he is the only person I am sleeping with so how does he not have it and I do?"

"Well I'll tell you what. Come in the back and I'll test you." Charm waited with me until Kenya came out and forty minutes later the doctor came out to deliver the news that Kenya doesn't have Chlamydia but instead has a urinary track infection. I kindly shook the doctor's hand thanking him repeatedly before dropping Charm off at home and meeting Kenya at my apartment. Upon arrival she is still sitting in her new Jeep Liberty that her mother got her two weeks ago. I looked at my cell and saw it is going on nine o'clock and she would be leaving soon.

"Hey." I said tapping on her window. She opened the door but didn't look at me. She stared straight ahead why tears trickled down her face.

"You hate me don't you?"

"Babe I could never hate you. Why would you think that?"

"Look at everything I put you through today. I accused you of doing something you kept telling me you weren't. I yelled at you, I cursed at you and I even said I wish I'd never met you." She said as more tears started coming down. Looking at Kenya cry and hearing mad she is with her self I can't stop a few tears from coming down my face.

"Babe it's not your fault. If the doctor had told me some shit like that I would've driven to Danbury and did the same thing you did to me today. You have to protect your body and your life and that is all you were doing. If I wasn't out here hanging out with Stacy or having Evelyn doin' my hair you wouldn't have had those thoughts in your head. So don't think you did anything wrong today because I don't think you did. Despite our relationship Kenya has to watch out for Kenya first."

"I love you so much Syncere."

"I love you too babe."

"You better." We hugged long and tight as if I was about to go to war but I don't mind at all. With her fruit smelling hair in my nostrils and her arms around me I wouldn't rather be anywhere else in the world right now. Right now nothing at all matters to me except this moment right here.

"Look it's gettin' late so you better be gettin' home."

"Fuck it, I'll make up somethin'. I'll tell my mom the agency called me in for a last minute photo shoot."

"Wanna come up with me?"

"Yeah."

"How long do you plan on stayin'?"

"Until eleven maybe. But the doctor said I can't have sex for three days."

"That's fine by me. Wanna order some food and watch a movie?"

"I'd love to."

Brazil is beautiful I thought looking out my little window on the airplane as we flew into Recife Brazil about eighty miles from Joao Pessoa Brazil where Kenya is from. Kenya held my hand tight as she is excited as I am to be here. For her birthday I told her I'd take her anywhere she wanted to go and she chose Brazil, lucky me I had a couple thousand saved up for a new car that I used for the trip. We were greeted in the tiny airport by her three cousins one being Yelena, who is almost as beautiful as Kenya. The other cousin is another girl who looks as if she could be older than me by the name of Querida then a male cousin Amaro. They hugged and danced around the airport speaking in Portuguese and I was able to make out bits and pieces from what Kenya has taught me over the months.

As we rode in a yellow jeep my eyes can't just focused on one thing because this country is so beautiful yet the residents live so poor. Before leaving the states Kenya instructed me not to wear any of my expensive sneakers, clothing or bring my cell phone so I pack wife beaters, shorts and sandals for the weekend trip.

"Baby I can't believe it! Brazil! You and I are in Brazil!" Kenya shouted.

"I know I can't believe it myself!" We never thought it'd work.

It's six p.m. when we arrived at the house where Kenya and I would be staying and despite being extremely tired from traveling Kenya showed me around Joao Pessoa. I'm smiling so much my face hurts but I've never ever seen Kenya so happy and I am too. We have little less than a day and have to spend with each other but it'll feel like weeks because we don't have to rush to get her home or anything. Periodically we'd have to get to a phone to call Emily so Kenya could call her mom but it's a small price to pay for a time like this.

"It worked baby."

"Yeah I know. Emily and her mom are the truth, we have to bring them somethin' back."

"Ok. Tomorrow we are gonna see my grandma and my grandfather."

"You sure that is a good idea. I mean you want me to meet your mother's mom and yours doesn't even know where here."

"They don't even talk anymore because my mom quit her modeling career for my dad. They haven't talked in seventeen years so I don't think it'll be a problem."

"But is your grandma a racist like your mom?"

"I have to tell you that black people are still kinda like slaves here to Brazilians. Not like they work in fields but they don't have the same rights as us and they are considered below us."

"I don't know if I can do that."

"Com'on baby do it for me pleeease! I met your grandmother."

"Yeah and you see how that turned out."

"But you're still with me and I will still be with you no matter what anyone says. Haven't you realized that by now?"

"Yeah but you never know."

"Why don't you ever tell me exactly what you are thinking?"

"I don't know."

"You know what you got me for my birthday?" she said turning to me.

"I want you to keep it and tell me what you feel about me and our situation. I mean honestly break it down for me."

"You want specifics?"

"Yes. I wanna know what you love about me, what you hate about me and what are your fears about us."

"Are you sure you wanna hear this?"

"Yes." She said as we stopped walking and sat on the edge of a fountain. With the sun completely gone the temperature is still in the seventies making it a beautiful night I hesitated for a minute. Instead of coming right out answering Kenya's question I looked at the stars that are in no comparison to Kenya's eyes as I just gazed at them for a minute, which made her smile.

"I honestly do not hate anything about'chu. I can't even find anything I don't like about'chu. I love your beauty, like seriously I have never been with a woman who makes men wish they were in my shoes and women wish they were you. That shit still amazes me when women stare, wow. I love the way you look at me, smile at me, moan my name, hold my hand I mean everything you do I love it and I crave it all the time. But my fears are this isn't gonna last that long."

"Baby you said that when we first started dating and look we're nine months in."

"Yeah but I'm thinkin' long term na mean? I'm thinkin' 'bout what is gonna happen after you graduate. You're gonna move to California and we're gonna try to stay together but the distance is gonna get the best of us. You'll call me one day and say you met some guy but ya'll are just friends and I'ma be sittin' here goin' crazy wonderin' what you are doin' until my jealousy is gonna get the best of me and ultimately push you away. That is even if we make it to graduation. My other fear is that your mom is gonna find out and she's gonna move you back here just so we're not together or that you'll realize that you are still young and you wanna have fun and not be tied down to me na mean? So I am afraid to put my heart into it fully na mean?"

"Baby, where ever I am in this world I will never choose another man over you. Syncere you have shown me things none of my boyfriends have ever shown me and you treat me like the woman I am and you don't use my age as an reason for the mistakes I make. Even though she doesn't want us dating you still respect my mother to the point that you feel bad when I lie to her. Baby that tells me you love me and you care about my mother as well. You treat me with a level of respect that I have never felt in my life by anyone."

"Really?"

"Yes. Baby you are the first and last thing on my mind everyday. Do I worry about me going to college? No because I know you'll do what you have to in order for us to be together. I trust you that much and I know undoubtedly you love me and want to be with me."

"So you're not worried about if I can't move to Cali when you go?"

"No. Baby I am not Kendra and I am not going to do the things she did to you. I wouldn't be able to live with myself if I inflicted that much pain on you. If you want to be with me as much as I wanna be with you then we can't loose."

"Even if I never get the tattoo covered?"

"Fuck that tattoo. I was mad at first, well a lot and all my friends said that if you're keeping that tattoo then in some way you are holding on to her. Then I thought about the promise you made to her and for you to keep it after what she's done just further tell me how wonderful you are. So you don't have to cover it."

"You really don't mind?"

"No. What we can do is name our first daughter Kenya Lane' Washington and we'll just go add a W on the end."

"How'd I get so lucky?"

"No, how did I get so lucky?"

Kenya's grandmother lives on a huge hill at the end of Joao Pessoa that we can only get to by car. The house sits on the very top of the hill with a God's eye view of the entire city with the clouds seem to just hover above our heads. Her grandfather who to my surprise is an American white male greeted us. He is taller than I am, slim, and clean shaven with a head full of brown and white hair.

"How are you doing young man?" He asked giving me a firm handshake. "Nice grip you got there. You must be a man of great character."

"Poppito!!" Kenya said throwing her arms around her grandfather.

"Easy, easy. I'm old." He said even though he doesn't look or sound a day over forty.

"How old are your grandparents?" I whispered.

"Seventy."

"Damn, ya grandpa move like he our age."

"It's Brazil baby, there's something in the water." She said laughing. We ate lunch in their football field sized back yard as Kenya and her grandmother chatted as if her grandfather and I aren't at the table. Kenya was right about black people being below Brazilian's because her grandmother didn't even make eye contact with me once and anytime she wanted so know something about me she asked Kenya in Portuguese.

"So young man, how do you like Brazil?" her grandfather asked.

"It's beautiful, absolutely beautiful and I love your home. You have an amazing view of Joao Pessoa from up here. I wish I can live like this one day."

"Well I'll give you a tip. Work hard and save up a minimum ten thousands dollars and you could. One U.S. dollar is thirty dollars here and everything is cheap. If you really want to live in Brazil that is how to do it. And let me tell you another thing, I've been all around the world but no place is like Brazil." I hugged Kenya from behind as we stand in the front of the house looking at the sun disappear behind Joao Pessoa.

"You know we could see this every night?"

"What?"

"You heard your grandfather, only ten thousand dollars…minimum."

"Baby you want to live in Atlanta. That is all you talk about, moving back to Atlanta."

"That was until we came here and you're the one every time I said somethin' 'bout Atlanta said no place is like Brazil and you ain't told no lie. I'm with it."

"What will we do for money once we get here and run out?"

"I'll think of somethin'. But by the time you graduate college I'll have ten thousand dollars. That's a mere twenty-five hundred a year, four hundred a month."

"You got it all broken down huh?"

"Yeah, that is what I've been thinkin' 'bout all this time."

"You're so spontaneous and I love it."

22

Upon our return from Brazil I made a decision not to cheat on Kenya any further, at all. No hanging out with other females, no sleeping in the same bed as them and no sex. Anytime I miss Kenya I stare at her picture while we talk on the phone. On the other side Kenya is doing her part to keep me from missing her too much. Since she got her new car she drives to Waterbury every chance she gets or she'll drive to my store in Milford to see me after school whenever I can't make it out to Danbury. Even though making love to Kenya isn't as important to me seeing her we still do it every change we get. The backroom at Merle Norman has become our new spot to sexually express our love for each other. The night I flew back from being in Indianapolis for a week Kenya begged me to drive out to Danbury at two o'clock in the morning where she snuck me into her garage to make love to me.

Just like in any relationship you have to find ways to make it work and instead of me finding excuses to be with other women I accepted the situation for what it is and chose to make it work. The best thing is Kenya has taken my mind off Kendra all together and I think I am in the process of finally getting over her, this time. I haven't spoken to Kendra since the Stacy incident almost two months ago.

"Son I don't get'chu." Tracy said as he fried chicken while I sat at our kitchen table waiting for KaTasha and Lisa to come over and play a few games of spades.

"Why?"

"'Cause you and this white girl."

"Brazilian." I corrected.

"Whatever. I don't even know why you messin' with her still. You know what happened to Kendra when she went to college just imagine what is gonna happen with Kenya when she moves all the way out to California. She gonna be around young, rich muhfuckas who are gonna be on her ass everyday. You see how many dudes try to fuck with her right here at home. You are not gonna be around her all the time so do you really wanna put'cha self through that again?"

"She told me she doesn't want to be with anyone else but me. I mean we snuck away to Brazil, what else does she have to do 'cause she has me convinced? So if she can have any guy she wants what is she gettin' out of stringing me alone?"

"I don't givva fuck. That girl all the way in Danbury and just like she didn't know 'bout all the hoes you was fuckin' with you don't know which niggas she fuckin' with."

"Why are you so intense about me bein' with Kenya?"

"'Cause dude I know you and you still want Kendra."

"Who?"

"Ok, play stupid. You and I both know you only goin' hard with Kenya because you want to be over Kendra but you can't be 'cause you still love her. Admit it, nigga just admit it. Be real wit'cha boy…be real wit'cha self."

"Na. I love Kendra. I mean Kenya."

"Look see you said it right there."

"Their names are almost identical, I made a mistake. Shut the fuck up." I snapped.

"Don't get mad at me 'cause the truth is comin' out."

"Just look at the pros and cons cut. Kendra is in her last year of college and you're ready to settle down. I don't know why you wanna settle down but that's neither here nor there. You can move back to North Carolina and ya'll can start ya'll life and live happily ever after and all that dumb shit." He explained.

"Or?"

"Or you can wait four more years for this "Brazilian" young chick to go through college and have all her fun while you sit at home prayin' she ain't got some dick in her."

"Cut…"

"Son I'm just bein' real wit'chu. You my nigg and I don't want you to make a bad decision like I did."

"What?"

"Yeah man with D. Dot. I was just like you are right now. On that cocky shit 'cause I had madd bitches and whatever but at the end of the day I wanted her and now that I realized that it's too late. A woman will put up wit'cha shit until they just say fuck it. All hope ain't lost wit'chu and Kendra all you gotta do is call her."

"It's been like two months man." I protested.

"So when was that ever a problem? You've called her outta the blue after nine months? But hey it's all up to you. But I have never seen you happier with anyone like you are with Kendra."

"That's 'cause you don't see me with Kenya."

"I mean you don't have to convince me. If you feel as though Kenya is the one for you then we can end the conversation. But I think Kendra is ya rib."

"My rib?"

"Yeah. You know how God took the rib from Adam and used it to make Eve? That is what I'm talkin' 'bout. God took your rib and made Kendra with it."

"Man you know I don't believe in that God shit no more."

"Maybe you need to start believing in that God shit. Don't be stubborn and hot headed like I was. You need to just sit down and figure it out man."

Tracy's words last night stuck out like a sore thumb and I can't them out of my mind. Just as I'm getting committed to Kenya he says some shit like this to have me second-guessing myself. I seriously don't know what kind of hold Kendra has over me or what it is that makes me believe so greatly that she, and no one else, is the woman for me but I need to find out.

"Hey long time no hear from." I said to Kendra when she picked up the phone.

"Yeah three months. Is everything ok?"

"Why does somethin' have to be wrong?" I asked.

"No reason. I see you haven't forgotten the number so what's up?"

"Nothin'. I couldn't forget your number or address if I tried but I just wanted to call to see how you were doin'."

"I'm good and you? How's Finish Line?"

"Great. I was promoted to store manager around the same time you came back from Jamaica and my store is ranked number 5 or 6 right now." I boasted.

"That's wonderful Syncere. I'm so proud of you."

"Thanks. So what about you?"

"Nothing much. I moved off campus and I'm living with my momma again but other than that I'm just getting ready to graduate and get outta here."

"I hear that, finally huh?"

"Yeah and I am so ready to be finished. I'm tired of school."

"What? I can't believe my ears. Kendra Lewis is tired of school? Wow, the devil is eatin' an ice cream sandwich right now."

"You're silly." She said laughing and her laugh is still like angels singing.

"But I can understand how you feel though."
"Have you been to North Carolina lately?"

"No, actually I'm takin' a vacation and I'll be down there in two weeks."

"You'll be here for my birthday?"

"Yeah and I want to see you."

"You want to see me?"

"Why else would I be commin' to North Carolina?"

"To see your aunt and cousins…"

"Well yeah I'll see them too but I wanted to see you on your birthday."

"Why? What do you have planned? You know I don't like surprises Syncere."

"Would you be easy it ain't even that serious. But can I see you though?"

"Yes."

"I knew you'd say yes."

"Then I take it back." She joked.

"Too late."

"Can I ask you a question?"

"No." I joked back.

"Thanks. Why do we do this?"

"Do what?"

"Talk, stop talking…talk and stop talking again. What are we trying to do?"

"Be together."

"You still want to be with me?"

"For a while I thought I didn't but it's painfully evident that I do."

"Why do you love me so much?"

"I knew you were goin' to ask me that."

"How?"

"'Cause I know you."

"Ok so why?"

"I don't know."

"You say you love me but you can never tell me why, why is that?"

"I don't know. I know I love you because of the feelin' I get inside, the feelin' I have in my stomach and my heart right at this very moment. It's only present wit'chu. I can name a million things I love 'bout'chu so if you add those million things up it equals why I love you." I explained.

"That doesn't make any sense."

"Who says anything 'bout love makes sense? Each person's definition of love is different but the feelin' and knowin' love is universal so my theory may not make sense to you but it does to me but should that really matter. All that should matter is that I love you."

"But you love Kenya too. How can you love two people at the same time?"

"Why are you so convinced that love is based on these rules and boundaries? Who says you can't love two people? Who says love has to make sense? I don't know how I can love two people at the same time but I just do. The difference is I'm actin' on one person and that person is you." I said getting irritated but trying to mask it. "Why me?"

"Is this gonna be twenty questions? Does it really matter why you? Look Kendra, if you're not feelin' the same way about me as I am you then that is fine just let me know and we can keep it strictly friends na mean?"

"It's not that."

"Then what is it?'

"Syncere every time we decide to try one more time something drastic happens and we end up not speaking for months on end. I don't want that to happen again. Maybe the only way we could save our friendship is if we don't try to be together."

"What are you sayin'?"

"I don't know. My mind is saying one thing but my heart is saying another."

"Say what you feel." I advised.

"This will never work unless we are in the same state and you know it."

"Ok where do you wanna go?"

"Virginia." As soon as Kendra said Virginia I thought about Chris offering me to move there three months ago.

"Fuck!" I shouted.

"What?"

"Three months ago my district manager asked me to go to Virginia Beach to run a store and I turned him down."

"You turned him down to be with Kenya?"

"No. I was afraid to go somewhere alone where I don't know anyone."

"Afraid? All the places you've been and you were afraid?"

"Yeah. What can I say? I'm not the same guy I used to be. I grew up and toned down the arrogance level just a tad."

"See that is what I mean. I'm not the same girl I used to be either."

"Are you the same girl that dreamt of us sittin' on a porch in North Carolina while our son played in the yard? Does this girl now feel the same way that girl felt?"

"Yes."

"Then as far as I'm concerned you are the same girl."

"We'll talk about it when you come to North Carolina." Tracy knocked on the door causing me to jump a little.

"Damn cut I just wanna know how it's goin'? You talkin' to her?"

"Yeah."

"Who's that?"

"Tracy."

"Do you mind if I speak to him please?"

"Why?"

"Because I want to ask him a question."

"So tell me and I will ask him."

"If I wanted you to know I would just ask you. Please give him the phone."

"Here." I handed Tracy the phone as he coped a squat on my neatly made-up bed but before long he got up and left the room.

While Tracy spoke to Kendra I sat on the edge of my bed staring at one of Kenya's modeling pictures. She's done up in make up wearing fire engine red lipstick and a black mink coat. She's so beautiful, next to perfect. There is no doubt in my mind Kenya and I will give birth to gorgeous children and live an unimaginable happy life in Brazil but something in me so powerful won't let me pull away from Kendra once and for all. Something that strong has to be entertained.

"Syncere, what's good homie? Recorded anything new lately?" Lajuan asked as he gave me pound.

"Na man I told you I don't do music anymore."

"And I told you you're crazy. Witness is a hit and you should've ran wit that. What'chu doin' up here? You on break?"

"Na I'm off today but I need ya help wit somethin'."

"What'chu need? Need me to come back to Finish Line?"

"Oh hell no, please do me a favor and stay right here. But seriously I need your discount."

"You know I get sixty-percent so what'chu need?"

"An engagement ring."

"Ahh shit, when you need it by?"

"This afternoon. I'm flyin' to North Carolina in the mornin'. I got cash."

"Now you talkin' my language."

As usual the airport lost one of my bags, the one with the Jordan's in it of course. But not even the thought of loosing a bag containing a collection of sneakers that are nearly impossible to obtain can bring me down as I sit in the passenger seat of Kendra's car. The Tuesday afternoon is a warm one with the sun high in the sky while we sped down the highway with the sunroof open and a smile on my face. Kendra and I have said little to one another during the drive, which frustrates me because I had so much to say to her when I was on the plane but now I'm drawing a blank.

"You wanna go to your aunts house first?"

"Can we go get some Bojangels? I haven't eaten all mornin'." I asked.

"There is one near Saint Aug, wanna stop there?"

"We can." The trip is bitter sweet because I lied to Kenya telling her I am coming down here to visit my aunt and cousins but if Kendra accepts my proposal then I will have to tell Kenya the truth. Right now I won't worry about that because I'll cross that bridge when I come to it.

"I love it here?" I said trying to break the silence.

"Since when? You hated when you were here. You purposely got in trouble so your aunt would send you back."

"I was young and I didn't know until I went back to Connecticut that I'd rather be here na mean?"

"I love when you say that. I read your letters and hear you saying "na mean" in my head. Have you ever been to Virginia?"

"Yeah. I visited Old Dominion and Norfolk State University when I was looking for grad schools. Oh yeah I was thinkin' 'bout goin' to grad school, once."

"So why don't you go back to school?"

"'Cause school is some bullshit just like religion."

"How can you say that when you met me in the church. You got baptized in the church."

"Again I was young but I have matured and I don't believe in silly stuff like God's and devils and shit like that." I explained.

"Syncere you do know that I am religious right? What do you believe in if you don't believe in God or the devil?"

"Nothin'. I don't believe in anything."

"So where do you go when you die?"

"No where, its just lights out."

"I can't believe you just said that. Are you being for real or are you testing me?"

"Yeah. I told you I changed. I left my religion in the Chapel Hill court room."

"You stopped believing in God when you went to trial?"

"It's a long story. It's not just because of that but a collection of things that I don't want to get into right now."

"So what do you think about Jehovah's Witnesses?"

"That religion is the worst. My mom made us is Jehovah's Witnesses when we were younger. I hate them muhfuckas. I understand you're supposed to go out and preach the gospel but them muhfuckas are pushy and inconsiderate."

"Syncere I'm a Jehovah's Witness."

"Since when?" I said in disbelief.

"Since Jamaica."

"You didn't tell me that."

"I didn't get the chance to. So you're an atheist?"

"No!"

"If you don't believe in God Syncere then you are an atheist."

"Damn I guess so then." I agreed.

"How would that work? I'm at the Kingdom Hall on Sunday and Thursday while my husband stays at home."

"Hey I don't have to be religious to be married to you."

"How will we raise our kids then if one of us in the church and the other one isn't?"

"Wait until the kids get older then let them decide on what religion they want to take, if any."

"Syncere a family that prays together stays together."

"That is nothin' but a catchy phrase."

When we arrived in Garner we discovered no one is at my aunt's house so we had to drive over to my aunt Rolanda's house where my Aunt Dimpsey is. I don't know if my Aunt Dimpsey is happier when she saw me or when she saw Kendra but she hugged us just as tight.

"I am glad to see you two together. How's school Kendra?"

"It's going well. I'll be graduating in May."

"That is excellent. Maybe you can talk to Syncere about goin' back. I have the strange feelin' he'll only listen to you."

"You think so?"

"Yeah. You're the reason he stopped fuckin' up in high school and even made it to college."

"Is that right?"

"Hello! I'm standin' right here." I said interrupting the two. In the house I sat on the arm of my aunt Rolanda's chair next to Kendra and I glanced over to her left shoulder.

"Lemme see your arm."

"No." she said pulling down her sleeve further.

"Kendra, you already told me you covered it so you might as well let me see it." Reluctantly Kendra pulled up her short sleeve exposing a huge red, black and green rose that covers her entire shoulder. I searched within the lines and colors trying to find where my initials use to be but to no avail.

"He did a good job."

"Yeah I see."

"That is why I didn't want to show you because I knew you'd get upset."

"I'm not upset. It's nice." I said in a low voice. I know Kendra isn't the lying type but when she told me in February she covered my initials I thought she was trying to make me feel bad but I see she was dead serious. Seeing the tat hurt a little because I never thought she would cover something we got together after we committed to keeping them. If anyone I thought I'd be the one to break the bond.

"You still have mine?" she asked. I didn't verbally respond I just rolled up sleeve showing her that I still have her initials on my shoulder.

"See."

"Don't say you never thought about it." She said looking at me with sadden eyes.

"Nope. Not even after everyone told me I should."

"It is that important to you."

"Yep."

"Why?"

"'Cause it is. These were gestures of us committing to one another that we promised would never get covered and you broke your promise."

"Who broke somethin'?" My Aunt Dimpsey asked interrupting us.

"Nobody, chill."

Kendra and I bounced all around Raleigh but didn't stay in one spot long. One minute we are at Wal-mart then the next minute we are at the dollar store and now we're picking Tausha up from some guys house.

"What are you doin' here?" Tausha asked with an attitude when she got in the backseat. Tasha looks away different then I last saw her which was at Kenya's graduation party. Last time I saw her I thought she was big but now she is huge. She has a huge ass, huge legs, huge waist and huge titis and a fat face. She just gets uglier with time.

"I came to visit Kendra for her birthday and hi to you too." I responded not making eye contact in fear of going blind.

"Kendra where are we goin' 'cause I'm hungry."

"Syncere and I want to go to Barnes & Noble for a minute."

"A book store? How boring."

"Well I can take ya ass home if you wanna complain but I didn't have to pick you up. I was trying to be nice."

"Dang calm down. I'll just sit in the car and talk on my phone."

After Barnes & Noble Kendra and I got hungry so we all drove over to this steakhouse that is in the same shopping complex as Barnes & Noble for dinner. I want Kendra to sit next to me but she sat on the same side as Tausha instead. This is a little awkward for me because I know Tasha still has some resentment for me after what I did so I'm not comfortable having her sit across from me. To be as frank as possible I don't want her here at all but I'm not going to tell Kendra that.

"So is this why Kendra offered to pick me up so she can rub you in my face?" Tausha asked when Kendra got up to use the bathroom.

"What? Actually she didn't even want to go pick you up but me bein' the nice guy that I am told her to. I can't believe you think your cousin is that petty to have to bring me around you to make you jealous. She can make you jealous in so many other ways without using me, trust me."

"What ever. You know you're fucked up for what'chu did."

"Tausha that was like six years ago so let that shit go. We messed around; it wasn't that serious so get over it. I don't think a two-week-old "thing" is worth six years of hostility. Do you?"

"I liked you and you knew I did. How could you fall in love with my cousin? Both yaw'll ain't shit, you or my so-called blood."

"I want you to tell her that when she comes back to the table if that is how you really feel."

"Do it and I'ma tell her what you said."

"I didn't say anything."

"You said that you wish you would've had the chance to fuck me and you still think about me."

"She'll never believe you."

"Oh please. You're the liar remember? The whole church knows you're a liar so who do you think she's gonna believe? Her own cousin or a lair? She hasn't forgot what'chu did and she knows you're capable of doing it again so there."

"What do you want Tausha?"

"I wanna know why. Why'd you choose her over me?"

"'Cause she's everything you are not. Beautiful, smart, she has ambition and she makes me a better person."

"You callin' me dumb and unmotivated?"

"I didn't say that so don't put words in my mouth."

"Yes you did."

"Yes he did what?" Kendra asked on her return to the table.

"Yes he did say we can order what ever we want."

"I said Kendra could order what ever she want. I don't even know you but she can have anything in the world."

"Why can she get anything she wants?"

"'Cause I love her." I expected Kendra to return the comment but she keeps reading the menu as if she didn't hear me. Tausha got up to go to the bathroom and she stood behind Kendra signaling for me to follow. When I shook my head no she gestured she would tell Kendra what I supposedly said which leaves me no choice.

"Must be this damn soda 'cause I have to go to the bathroom too." I said before getting up.

"I don't think you're in the position to be tellin' me no right now." Tausha whispered as we walked to the bathroom.

"What the fuck do you want Tausha?"

"Christina and Carla told me you fucked them outside the church."

"So."

"So does Kendra know?"

"She don't need to 'cause it happened before her."

"That's not what I'ma tell her."

"Then cut the shit and tell me what do you want."

"I want you to fuck me in the bathroom."

"You're outta your fuckin' mind." I turned to walk away but got stopped by Tausha's grip on my package.

"You don't listen. This is what I want or I'm tellin' Kendra everything and I don't care if it's true or not. How 'bout I tell her you signaled me to come to the bathroom and tried to pull me in with you?"

"Fuck you and you can tell her what ever you want. Get the fuck off me."

"What's this?" before I could react Tasha already has her hands in my pocket.

"Cut the shit you crazy bitch."

"Ahh what do we have here? An engagement ring. Now Syncere you wouldn't be planning on proposing to my cousin would you?"

"Yeah now gimmie the fuckin' ring." I said adding more bass to my voice.

"Wait until I tell her this." Tausha tried to walk away but I grabbed her by the neck and pinned her against the wall not caring who sees me at this point.

"Listen fuck face. Close the box and put it back in my pocket and keep ya fuckin' mouth shut."

"How much is my silence worth to you?"

"What? I ain't givin' you shit."

"Ok then I'ma tell her. By the way I like being chocked, it adds to the excitement and adrenaline during sex. But you might not wanna hold on too tight. You wouldn't want me to tell Kendra you put a suck mark on my neck now would you?"
"Alright. Twenty dollars."

"Twenty dollars ain't shit. I got twenty dollars. A hundred." I released Tausha's neck and handed her a crisp hundred-dollar bill.

"No you wait here. I'm goin' back to the table first."

Just like yesterday Kendra's bouncing me around Raleigh as if she is running from something or someone. As we shopped in the mall we walked at least five feet away from each other and made small talk.

"You know that I set aside four-hundred dollars for you to shop?" I asked trying to get some conversation out of her.

"You're gonna spend that much on me?"

"Yeah. I told you I was takin' you shoppin' today but we've been to seven places and you haven't picked out one thing."

"Syncere you know I can buy my own clothes right?"

"No one said you couldn't. What is the matter wit'chu? This is your birthday present. You know a gift from me to you so pick out what ever you want."

"Did I tell you I'm celibate now?"

"Ok…that came outta left field. I'm talkin' 'bout shoppin' and you're talkin' 'bout celibacy. How does that work?" Kenya didn't answer. "Yo for real for real, what's good wit'chu? You've been actin' weird ever since you came to pick me up yesterday. Is there some where else you rather be right now?"

"No. I was up studying late and I have midterms this next week that I am not ready for."

"Worry 'bout midterms next week. Today is your birthday and I flew all the way down here to spend it wit'chu so relax."

"My birthday…it's just another day. We as Jehovah's Witnesses don't celebrate birthday's or any other holiday for that matter."

"Ok, for one day can you make an exception for me? Can you be Christian Kendra today and a Jehovah's Witness tomorrow?"

"No I can't. This is my religion and I wish you'd take it seriously."

"Ok, fine." I said growing frustrated.

"Can we leave now? I have class in an hour."

"Sure, what ever you want. Can I at least see you tonight? Maybe take you out to dinner?" I asked searching for a yes.

"I'll call you and let you know. I don't know what my family has planned for me."

"I thought you don't celebrate your birthday?"

"If they planned something for me I can't stop them."

"You stopped me."

   I drove around Raleigh aimlessly trying to sort things out. Suddenly I don't feel the same way about Kendra as I did before I got here. What the hell is her problem? She is acting as if she doesn't want to be with me, be seen with me or anything. I feel like a tagalong, like I'm annoying her and I don't like that feeling.

"Hey baby! It's about time you called." Kenya said answering the phone before it rang twice.

"My bad. I was runnin' 'round with my aunt all mornin' and now I'm in the car with my cousins."

"They are awfully quiet."

"That's 'cause I'm on the phone."

"What's wrong? You sound a little down."

"Nothin', just a little tired and I miss you. I just wanted to hear your voice."

"You're so sweet."

"Guess what?"

"What?"

"It'll be a year in a week and a half. Can you believe it?"

"Wow! It doesn't even feel like a year."

"I know."

"Well it's been the best year of my life."

"Aww baby. Hurry up and come back home. When are you comin' back anyway?"

"In two days. You gonna pick me up from the airport?"

"Of course. I brought this cute outfit and these boots I'ma wear when I come get you."

"Ohh I can't wait."

"I know and guess what?"

"What?"

"I'm naked." She said giggling.

"Nice, thanks for the visual babe."

"Anytime. When are you gonna bring me to North Carolina? Your aunt invited me so I wanna go."

"When we can come up with another good lie to fool ya mom with."

"I'll work on it while you're gone."

"Ok." I said smiling from ear to ear.

"Call me tonight. I'm getting dressed to go do s shoot. Oh I knew I forgot to tell you something. I may be going to London next summer to for Louis Vuitton!"

"That's definitely what's up but now that creates a big problem."

"What's that baby?"

"I already have to fight the guys off you here at home now I have to take on Europe too Damn!" I said joking.

"You're gonna give me a tooth ache. Bye baby."

After talking to Kenya I suddenly feel better than I did before and I know this may sound like a broken record but I know who I want to be with and it isn't Kendra. Just these past two days has shown me just how much Kendra and I have grown apart so I have to call it like it is. It's time to let go. I'll see her tonight, maybe and then I'm spending the rest of my vacation with my family like I intended. Maybe I should call Trisha, then again thinking about that dumb shit she pulled at Winston-Salem State I rather not.

Around eight Kendra called and asked me to drive out to her aunt's house in Morrisville because that is where she will be for the night. I talked to Kenya during the forty-five minute drive making plans for our anniversary. We've decided to keep it simple. She'll skip school and we'll make love a couple times at my apartment in between watching a movie or two. We'll probably a nap with each other then shower and change for dinner at Outback before we hit our favorite park then call it a night. The more and more I talk to Kenya while I am gone is making me miss her uncontrollably and now I can't wait for my United Airline's flight to land.

"Why you stayin' here tonight?"

"'Cause Al, Chris and Tausha are coming over to hang out with me. That reminds me, what was Tausha really talking about when I left the table?"

"About me payin' for her dinner." I lied not knowing why am I protecting Tausha.

"I'm sorry about her. I told you I didn't want to pick her up in the first place. She's still upset with you."

"Really? I hadn't noticed."

"My momma told me that her momma says Tausha's jealous of me for being with you after all this time."

"Why? Don't she have a new guy like every five minutes?"

"I think that's the problem. Tausha uses sex to get guys then after they get it they only call her for it or they don't call her at all. I think she really wants a real relationship but she is going about it the wrong way."

"Tell me about it."

"I don't care anyway. It's not my fault."

"What isn't?"

"The way she is."
"Can I ask you somethin' personal?"

"Depends." She replied.

"I'm not tryin' to put'cha family down 'cause I came from a background like this. But no one from your aunts to your cousins has the desire to better themselves, no one but you. Where do you get the aspiration from?"

"Where do you get yours? When I met you all you did was fight, skip school and run around with a bunch of girls. I remember you saying you're never going to college, never getting married or anything. When I first met you I thought you were going to end up like Quami. So where did you get it from?"

"I'll tell you if you tell me."

"Do you remember telling you about my daddy?"

"Actually no. I've talked 'bout my home life but you kinda stay away from those convos."

"Well my momma and daddy use to fight often, almost three nights a week. He'd hit her, curse at her then she'd come in my room to beat me just because she was mad. We had this forest behind our house in Morrisville so one night I hear them and I just knew she was going to come in my room. So before he could I jumped out of the window wearing only my night clothes, no shoes on and I ran through the forest to my aunts house here."

"Didn't you cut your feet and legs up?"

"A little. See I still have some of the marks on my legs and the top of my feet."

"I've never noticed them."

"I never really pointed them out. So anyway, I stayed here with my aunt who even back then was a big crack user. So I watched different people come in and out of the house all the time. She was sleeping with a lot of older men I guess for money but we never had food in the house and there were roaches everywhere. It kinda looks like it does right now."

"Ok." I nodded as I looked around the room we are in. The room has holes in the wall, is painted three different colors, the carpet is torn and it wrecks of urine, plus the roaches are still present. The smell of crack is in the air but not as heavy as an actual crack house but it is starting to make my stomach turn.

"I just didn't want to live my entire life like everyone in Morrisville you know. In the same house I grew up in, around the same people who had no desire to leave or do better. I didn't want to get married to some local guy I grew up with, birth his children and live in the same house that I did and that be the end of it. All I'll be doing is repeating the cycle. I love my momma and my family, I just don't want to turn out like them."

"I had no idea."

"See, you don't know me as well as you think you do. Your turn."

"Well you already know my story but honestly the thing that made me change was you."

"How?"

"When I got to North Carolina I was livin' out in the country, you see how far I am from everything livin' in Garner and I was pulled straight out of the city where I can walk to a corner store of a bag of chips at anytime na mean? For years my mom and her husband told me I wasn't gonna be shit and after a while I started to believe it. I was miss-treated so badly that by the time I got to my Aunt Dimpsey I didn't know how to act and I was fuckin' up even down here. All I wanted to do was get back to Connecticut, back to my friends and back to doin' music."

"I remember. You use to say Connecticut this and Connecticut that. You would think you were running for mayor the way you talked about it." She said as we shared a little laugh.

"I had prayed to God for years beggin' him to end my mothers marriage so that we could be the family we were before Wallace came into the picture but to no avail and that made my faith start to lessen more and more. So on the very day I met you or saw you rather I knew that there was somethin' different 'bout'chu. I saw it in your face but it was confirmed in our conversations. You had your whole life planned out at fifteen and you were so confident about it. At first I wanted to be apart of it so I figured if you and I were even gonna be together I had to get my shit together. The more and more I started to improve myself the more and more things started to fall into place. Then I noticed whenever you and I weren't talkin' thing fell apart." I explained.

"So I'm the reason?"

"Yeah. Like I've been with madd girls and none of them were on your level. Like most girls I was with didn't wanna attend college, had no desire to move outta Waterbury or do anything special with their life. I did but I didn't feel like that until I met you and I saw how my life could be. No one in my family went to college, all the kids were born outta wedlock and my family worked their asses off but got nowhere. I wanted more and you made me want more."

"I think you're giving me too much credit." She responded walking away from me.

"Kendra, do you know that the only reason I went to college was because I knew you were goin' and I didn't want to be the dumb, uneducated boyfriend. And I only went to school in North Carolina because I knew you were goin' to school here. I work so diligently now 'cause yes I want more but I want to be able to provide you and our son with the life neither of us had. No one has ever made me feel like that."

"Do you remember when I said God puts people in your life for a reason? Sometimes it's short term and sometimes it's long term."

"Yeah. You sayin' that "God" put'chu in my life for the sole reason of makin' me better?"

"Maybe. Have you ever thought me not being the woman for you?"
"No, not even after you said it to me before we got our tattoos." I said lying. Right now I feel Kenya is the woman for me but if I don't put my all into Kendra right now I'll be wondering all my life is she really the one and that wouldn't be fair to Kenya.

"I don't think I am."

"How could you say somethin' like that?"

"I don't know. Syncere you're expectations of me are so high and I don't think I can meet them."

"What are you talkin' 'bout?"

"I really listen to how you talk about your store, your staff and even your sisters and your expectations for the people in your life or you deal with are very high. Then I listen to how you talk about me and those expectations are double what they are for everyone else. You're making me out to be someone I'm really not." She explained sounding disappointed.

"Kendra, the only I expect from you is to love me the way you've always loved me that's all. I don't expect anything more or less from you." Just then we heard the door opening and closing then Tausha appeared in the doorway.

"Oh you're here. I thought that was your car outside."

"Hello to you too."

"Kendra I have to talk to you…alone." She said rolling her eyes at me.

"Syn can you step out for a minute?" I abided by sitting on the torn duck-tapped black sofa in the living that looks like an extension on the room I was just in. I took the ring out of my pocketed and stared at it for a minute tossing back the idea of proposing to Kendra tonight. I feel my phone vibrate in the other pocket and it read

Kenya on the screen but I'm not gonna answer it. The ring in one hand and Kenya calling in the other hand, what do I do? I hit ignore on the phone…I put the ring back in my pocket.

"Com'on let me walk you to the car." Kendra said coming out of the room.

"I'm leavin'?"

"Yeah."

"I thought Chris and Al were comin' by? I haven't seen them since I stopped comin' to church."

"They're not the same people they were when you knew them. Al deals drugs and Chris smokes a lot of weed. That is all their going to do when they get here, Chris, Al and Tausha."

"I don't care. I want to spend your birthday wit'chu."

"It's not a good idea. Tausha is having these two white boys she knows coming over too and you all will not mix. Thank you for the flowers, it was really sweet. I remember you use to bring me flowers to church every Sunday."

"What's good wit'chu? I feel like you hidin' somethin' from me." I suspected.

"No." I stared at Kendra searching for a hint that she's lying but stopped after a few seconds thinking if she is hiding something from me I rather not know it. I hugged Kendra tight and long because I know this is the last time I'll see her. It's obvious she doesn't see a future with me and it's time I face the reality of it all and take the loss.

"Goodnight, happy birthday."

"Syncere…"

"Yeah."

"What's the worse thing I could do to you?"

"You know that one already. Stop lovin' me."

As my Aunt Dimpsey drove me to the airport I didn't want to stop the tears from falling down my face. For some odd reason I cry every time I leave North Carolina but this time it's a combination of that and the fact that it's really over with Kendra and I. She didn't call me all day today knowing that I am leaving but I didn't call her either. It's better I don't see her before I left it would only hurt more.

23

"Hey."

"Hey Baby!"

"I just landed. Where are you?"

"Sitting at the baggage claim and some white guy keeps looking at me so you better hurry up before she tries to wisk me away."

"I'll kill'em."

"You know I'm not going anywhere. I missed you so much baby."

"I missed you too." The hour and forty-five minute flight was long enough for me to get all cried out and my head back on straight, I went to North Carolina looking for an answer and I got it. It wasn't the one I wanted but I'm not going to dwell on it anymore. It's over, finally over.

As the escalator descended I first saw a pair of brown boots then a beautiful set of crossed legs. My heart began to jump as I got close enough to see a short brown skirt, a flat stomach, and hair resting just above her breasts then the smile that made stars jealous. Kenya's sitting right in front of the escalator then rose to her feet when I walked closer to her. We shared a kiss that is long overdue and at that moment I know what happened in North Carolina happened for a reason. Kenya is that reason.

I drove Kenya and I back to Waterbury in her Jeep Liberty while she clenched my hand and kissed my cheeks over and over for the entire ride. Kenya really knows how to make me seem like I'm the most important person in her live and I have to admit I really like the feeling.

"I can't stay long. I told my mom I was going to Emily's house for a little while." Kenya said as she flopped on my bed. I tossed my Adidas duffle bag on the floor next to the bed and joined her.

"How much did you miss me?" I asked her.

"Lemme show you." She said pulling my face to hers and kissing me. I tried to pull Kenya on top of me but she resisted and I think she is playing hard to get. I tried again but she resisted a second time.

"What's wrong?" Kenya pulled her shirt down and sat on the edge of my bed with her back turned to me. I repeated the question but she didn't answer again so I got up and sat beside her then I notice her crying.

"I have to tell you something."

"Are you pregnant?" I asked as a laugh managed to escape her cries.

"Baby if I were pregnant these would be tears of joy."

"Then what's wrong?"

"I went to the doctor again yesterday…"
"What?"

"I can't have kids."

"Why not?"

"I have cancer…cervical cancer. That's why I kept getting all those urinary track infections." Kenya buried her face in my chest sobbing and I've never felt so powerless in my life. The only thing I can think to do is cradle her until she stops crying.

"Is it treatable? Will it kill you?" I worried.

"No, it won't kill me because we caught it early and I have to take pills to treat it. If it spreads to my ovaries and uterus kids will definitely be out of the question."

"So it's not definite we won't be able to have kids. Babe it's ok. If we can't then it's ok."

"You don't want to have kids with me?"

"No I'm not sayin' that. I would love to have kids wit'chu but I want you to be ok wit this. A lot of things could go wrong durin' a pregnancy…I could loss you while givin' birth na mean? We'll worry 'bout havin' kids when you graduate college. Right now don't worry anything."

"I love you."
"I love you too. Kenya lay in my arms for a while long enough for me to drift to sleep and be awakening by her kissing me.

"You leavin' me now?"

"Aww baby I don't want to but I have to get home. Carry me to the car?" she asked smiling.

"Of course."

"Call me when you get home."

"Are you gonna be awake?"

"Yeah. I feel like I haven't talked to you for weeks."

"I know, I thought I was the only one that felt like that." As soon as I got back into the house and into my room Tracy is sitting on my bed with an intrigued look on his face.

"So cut what happened?"

"Nothin'."

"You didn't do it did you?"

"Nope."

"Oh my God cut why? Is it 'cause of Kenya?"

"Na it had nothin' to do with Kenya but I've realized that Kenya is the one for me."

"Tell me what happened cut?"

"Nothin'. All I know is that wasn't the Kendra from Georgia."

"So what'chu do with the ring?"

"It's right here." I showed Tracy.

"Michane com'er?"

"M. Dot is here?"

"Yeah."

"Look at the ring Syncere got for Kendra."

"Oh my God! Tracy told me you got her a ring. This is nice." Michane said as she stared in awe at the platinum band two-carat diamond engagement ring that Lajuan gave me at a steal.

"See Tracy, if Syncere is ready to get married then what the hell is your problem?"

"Oh God here we go." He sighed.

"Cut you should've known better showin' a weddin' ring to a woman."
"Yeah I know. So what'chu gonna do now?"

"I'ma put all my heart and energy into Kenya. I really do love her plus she's put up with my up and down mood swings for almost a year."
"I don't like her." M.Dot reveled.

"M.Dot you don't even know her."

"I know but when she is here she acts like she's better than everybody."

"You hardly interact with her. When you here you in the room with Tracy and she's in the room too."

"I don't know cut I think Michane is right. She does come off a little Paris Hiltonish."

"Whatever. She's not crazy like Michane is so you don't know how what a normal woman acts like."

"True statement." Tracy agreed.

"Oh so now I'm crazy?" Michane asked as Tracy and I looked at her with the you-already-know-this face.

"See what'chu done did cut. I'll holla." Tracy said leaving.

"Aight, go get'cha lama." I joked.

Kenya and I celebrated our anniversary just as we had planned it with plans to celebrate next year in the Virgin Islands. I can't help but to think about Kenya having cervical cancer and how she's dealing with it. Since the night she reveled it to me we haven't made love as frequently because with her medication she says it hurts a lot more. I'm trying to be there for her as she is dealing with it but she's more concerned about me being upset at the fact we can't make love the way we use to. Seriously if I didn't have genuine feelings for Kenya us not making love might be a problem for me but in our case it isn't. I get drunk off her smile, high off her laugh and hallucinate off her beauty which all is more than enough for me to get by on.

Christmas time in a retail store is hectic as hell especially with it being Christmas Eve. You'd think people would be at home with their families and such but it amazes me at how many last minute shoppers there are in the mall.

"Yo Wes I'ma take a break real quick so I'ma be in the office if you need me."

"Aight homie. Me and D got it out here." As I sat in the office with my head in my hands I thought about another Christmas about to come and go without me even caring less about it. My mom is going to be at work as usual which doesn't surprise me. I'm more surprised at the fact it still bothers me not to spend holidays with my mom or my sisters like a regular family does. To add insult to injury Kenya is going to be in a whole other country for the next week leaving me with more than enough time to miss the hell out of her.

It kills me to see Kenya in the state she was in last night and not able to do a thing about it, funny, she is even beautiful when she's not feeling well. Usually when she knows I'm coming by she'll get all dressed up with her hair done but last night was when she was at her sexiest. No make-up, her hair in a ponytail and snuggled under a blanket. Just the sight of her last night made me want to jump on top of her and tear her cloths off, if she wasn't sick I'd would've done it.

"Yo Syn. Some white girl out here to see you." My sales associate Derek said knocking on the door.

"Is she a customer?"

"I think so."

"Tell Wes to handle it."

"Aight." I thought about New York last year then got excited about us spending the day in Boston. Just as my eyes got heavy wanting to put my head down another knock came to my office door.

"Yeah." I said to no answer. I turned my chair around to see Kenya's gorgeous, smiling face behind and half inch of glass. As she stood there smiling I looked at her confused while I tried to figure out if I'm dreaming or not.

"You gonna let me in or not? If not gimmie my face back." She said laughing.

"What are you doin' here?" I said opening the door and embracing her with a hug.

"Well we don't leave for Canada for another five hours so while my mom took Alana and Blake shopping I snuck away to see my baby." We kissed then I noticed something in her hand.

"You went shoppin' didn't you?"

"Yes but this time it is for you, here. Merry Christmas baby."

"I'ma open in tomorrow."

"No open it now. I opened yours last night. Oh the coat does fit, thank you. I just wish you didn't get white. I almost wore it today but I got make-up on it."

"Damn babe."
"I'm sorry."

"It's ok. I'll get'chu a black one."

"I want to keep the white one.

"But you'll never wear it."

"Yes I will, promise. Now open it." I opened the little box first and in it was a Burberry Brit cologne collection equipped with aftershave, lotion and cologne.

"This is kinda hot, thanks."

"I know you don't wear cologne but the lady said this shouldn't irritate your skin. Here open the big one."

"Lemme guess. A red Enyce shirt."

"Did Alana and Blake tell you? I wanted it to be a surprise."

"No. All I wear is Enyce and for some odd reason you keep me draped in red so I just put two and two together."

"Baby you look so cute in red."

"Are you feelin' any better? 'Cause last night you were dyin'.."

"Shut up. I'm feeling fine…if you come into the bathroom I'll show you."

"Or we can do it right here on my desk." I suggested throwing everything on the floor.

"Won't they see us when they come back here?"

"Yeah but I like an audience." I said as we both shared a laugh.

"Well I don't, now put something over the window." Kenya demanded while she unbuttoned her shirt.

Kenya and I spent our second New Years in each other's arms while we watched the ball drop on television as we sipped on green apple Smirnoff's. I can hear Mook letting off shots in the air outside but I won't leave Kenya to act stupid in the middle of the street.

"What's your resolution?" she asked me after we rang in the New Year with a kiss.

"I have a few. Some for work, some personal."

"Tell me."

"Well the one for work is…"

"No tell me the personal one."
"To keep you happy, that's the main one."

"Aww baby, really?"

"Yeah. There's another one but that one has to be kept to myself na mean?"

"Ok."

"You're turn."

"I don't make resolutions."

"Why not?"

"I'm perfect so I don't have anything to improve on."

"Wow! Love the modesty babe."

"I'm playing. You really wanna know?"

"Yeah."

"My resolution is to love you and love you hard enough to make you forget all about Kendra and to get that tattoo covered."
"Wow, really though?"

"Yeah. We should check some tattoo shops out while we're in Boston. Maybe Amber knows of some."

"Strongly doubt it. I thought we had the talk 'bout the tattoo."

"You're seriously not getting it covered? I thought by now you'd want to."

"Why would you think that?"

"Uh 'cause you love me and we've been together for a year and we don't seem to be slowing this down. We plan on moving to Brazil and having kids so I thought my assumption was a pretty accurate one." I didn't respond to Kenya's comments. I merely got up, went into the bathroom and stared at the tattoo in the mirror. It's been a month and a half since I last spoke or seen Kendra, which certifies everything is over and done with. When I'm with Kenya Kendra doesn't exist in my mind but occasionally I do find myself staring at her picture and wondering. I think about the dream she told me she had while she was in Jamaica and how happy she sounded as she put the images in my mind. *What are you going to do Syncere?* I asked myself.

"Quincy is on the phone." Kenya said when I walked back in the room.

"You answered my phone?"

"Yeah…and."

"What's good?" I asked taking the phone from Kenya.

"Happy New Year sassmo."

"You too Mr. Muffins."

"Yo I got that beat you want if you wanna come get it."

"Now?"
"Yeah if you ain't busy."

"Aight I'm on my way."

"Aight call me when you're outside."

"Babe I'ma run to Q's house real quick. I've been waitin' on this beat for a month now so I need to go get it now."

"You're leaving me in your house alone? I thought you don't do that?"

"I trust you."

I burned up the streets trying to get to Quincy's house then back to Kenya as soon as I could. When I got back to the house there wasn't a sound coming from my room. I cautiously walked in to find it Kenya less. I walked around the corner to the bathroom and she isn't there either then it dawned on me, I didn't see her car outside when I pulled up. I went back to my room to get my cell when I discovered a note on my bed saying, *I can't do this anymore.* What? I thought. I sat on the bed to try to make sense of this when I saw the letter I'd gotten from Miko in the mail last week. Fuck! She found the letter. I dialed Kenya's cell phone five times and got no answer until the sixth time.

"What!" she shouted.

"Come back."

"Fuck you. You're still fuckin' with Miko. I hate you!!"

"No I'm not."

"Then why are there pictures of her in her bra and panties?"

"She sent them to me. If you read the entire letter you'd see that she is the one tryin' to get back wit me, not the other way around."

"What did you write back to her?"

"I didn't write anything. I just laughed it off and tossed the letter to the side. The damn pictures are still in the envelope."

"Then why didn't you throw it away?"

"I wasn't thinkin'."

"Bullshit, you never think Syncere. So she wrote you outta the blue huh? Just for nothin'. You had to have been talkin' to her."

"Yeah, we're still friends."

"For someone who cuts off communication with ex-girlfriends you sure do still talk to a lot of them. Stacy, Evelyn, Kendra and now Miko. You must think I'm stupid."

"You're blowin' this way out of proportion. What were you doin' goin' through my shit anyway? Just when I trust you to leave you in my house you go and pull some shit like this."

"I wasn't going through anything. I was looking for my slippers under the bed and there it was. You should hide your dirty laundry a little better."

"Trust me. If I wanted to hide it you wouldn't've found it. And if I didn't want you to know 'bout Stacy you wouldn't've know 'bout her either."

"You're right. All I have to do is ask Anija right?"

"Where are you? Let's talk 'bout this face to face."

"I'm on the highway going home and I don't wanna talk to you face to face."

"Why?"

"'Cause you always talk your way outta stuff like this that's why."

"I'm not talkin' my way outta anything. I'm just tellin' you how it is." I explained as my Chevrolet Malibu reached ninety miles per hour on the highway.

"Do you see me?" I asked flashing my headlights. I caught up to Kenya by exit 11 just fifteen minutes away from Waterbury and Danbury in each direction.

"You're crazy! What are you doing?"

"If you wont talk to me face to face then I'll stick my head outta the window and you'll have to talk to me." I put the car on cruise, rolled the window down and sat on the window steering with one hand and holding the phone with the other.

"Syncere stop it! You're gonna crash. Stop it!" she screamed

"Turn around then."

"No."

"Then I'm not stoppin'." I proceeded to explain the contents of the letter and why I had it tossed under my bed but I think Kenya is worried more about me crashing than she is anything else.

"Get off exit 8."

"You comin' back to my house?"

"Yes now get back in the car and drive right before you don't make it." We both got off exit 8 but instead of turning around Kenya got out of her jeep and ran over to my car. I got out expecting a hug instead I got a slap to the face. The slap surprised me to the point I looked at Kenya as if I was about to slap her back but the fear in her eyes was instantly replaced with anger.

"Don't you ever scare me like that again. You almost killed yourself, what the hell is wrong with you?"

"It worked."

"Unbelievable." She said trying to fight back a smile.

"I'm sorry."

"I hate you."

"Then why'd you stop?"

"'Cause I didn't want to tell your mom your body is spread all over I-84 East."

"Nope not it. 'Cause you love me." Before Kenya could reply the sky ripped open a loud sound of thunder and rain fell from the heavens.

"Call her right now!"

"Who?"

"Miko. Call her right now." Kendra said being drowned out but sound of thunder.

"Babe it's pouring can we do this at my house."

"No. Before I go I want you to call her right now and tell her you don't want to be with her that you are with me and we don't appreciate her letters and indecent pictures. Do it Syncere or I'm going back to Danbury."

"We're gonna get sick out here. You hair is gettin' messed up."

"I don't care. Do it right now." Staring at Kenya as the rain soaks her body and the lighting illuminates the world behind her I picked up my cell phone and dialed Miko. I could've dialed anyone and pretended to call her but I didn't. Luckily for me Miko didn't answer so I left a voice message loud enough for Kenya to hear over the sound of raindrops hammering our cars.

"Can we go now?"

"Drive right. I'll follow you."

"Ok but if you try to go the other way I'ma do it again. This time I'ma stand on top of the car."

"Crazy ass, I believe you too."

24

"Syncere?"

"Kendra?"

"Yeah. Are you busy?"

"Na I'm drivin' home. Why what's good?"

"Nothing I just wanted to say hi."

"After three months? Why?" I asked voicing the animosity I still have for what she did last November.

"I was just thinking about you and I wanted to say hi."

"Great...hi." Kendra and I sat on the phone not saying a word to one another and for some strange reason I feel slightly happy to be not talking to her.

"So..."
"So..."

"How are things? I take it you and Kenya are back together?"

"Why would you say that?"

"I don't know. You seemed into her so I figured you two worked things out since you and I decided just to be friends."

"Well we're not." I don't know why I just told that lie but I'm curious to get to the real reason she's calling.

"Oh. So who are you with now?"

"Why do I have to be wit somebody?"

"You're right. So how is work?"
"Cool. I won a couple of contests and I love my staff so everything is going well."

"Are you mad at me?"

"Should I be?"

"You're not acting like yourself."

"What's myself? Excited and talkative?"

"Syncere if you have something to say then why don't you just say it. I mean we are friends right so we can talk about what is on your mind."

"What happened when I was in North Carolina? And don't say nothin' 'cause I know somethin' was up. You ran me around for three days; I think I deserve an explanation. I used my vacation time and my money and in hopes of spending time with you and that is how you do me?"

"I don't know if you can handle it."

"Don't insult my intelligence. If you're not gonna talk to me then why did you call me?"

"I didn't call to talk about that. I called to see how you were doing."

"I'd be doin' a lot better if I can have a three month old question answered."

"I didn't want you to run into Mulan." She said so quick that I have to wait for my mind to process it.

"What? You ran me around Raleigh because you didn't want me to run into Mulan. Fuck Mulan! Why in the hell would we run into Mulan? I thought you weren't messin' with him anymore."

"I'm not but he won't leave me alone. He's always calling me, showing up at my momma's house and just be everywhere."

"Why didn't you tell me that then? I thought that it was really over between us and that was just your way of sayin' it."

"No. Mulan is still upset that you beat him up and I'm afraid of what would happen if you two ran into each other."

"He'll get his ass whooped again that's what'll happen. Wait, wait how do I know you're tellin' me the truth?"

"What?"

"Yeah, how do I know if you're tellin' me the truth?"

"You think I'd lie to you?"

"I don't know. I've been thinkin' 'bout this ever since you were in Jamaica. When you first started tutoring Mulan you insisted you didn't like him right? So how did ya'll end up a couple? Why would you date someone you don't like?"

"It's complicated."

"You're makin' it complicated and it's really quite simple."

"That's not important. I just didn't want you two to go at it where ever we would have ran into each other. I was just trying to avoid confrontation."

"If that was the case you should've told me that from the gate instead of runnin' me around and have me thinkin' you didn't want me there."

"I know I just didn't know how you would react to me telling you. I thought if hid it we could still go on as normal."

"I would've just said fuck that nigga and that's it. But you made me ruin my vacation by not tellin' me. Remember that night you called and I said I had that girl in the car and she was yellin'? I told you I would call you back so I could handle her and you were upset that I hung up wit'chu to tend to her but isn't this the same thing?"

"I guess you're right. I apologize Syncere, really. Is that the reason you haven't called me?"

"That and the fact you haven't called me either. I was just like fuck it, it's a wrap na mean?"

"What's a wrap?"

"Me and you, tryin' to make somethin' work that obviously ain't workin'."

"Do you want it to work?"

"What kinda question is that? Do I want to make what work? There's nothin' to work at."
"You and I? We can't work on that?"

"Aren't you the one who said you were tired of us doin' this? Goin' back and forth months at a time?"

"No I asked why do we do this not that I was tired of us it."

"Well aren't you? Kendra where is this comin' from?" I asked not comprehending what she's trying to say.

"You know how I teach for Summerbridge every year?"

"Yeah."

"Well this year a site opened up in Connecticut."

"What part?"

"West Haven. How far is that from you?"

"'Bout thirty minutes up 69 north."

"I was thinking about spending the summer in Connecticut with you to really give us one last solid try."

"Why?"

"I remember the first time I came to visit you in Georgia and how happy we were? The only time I felt like that was the second time I came to visit you even after all the arguing and I just wonder did we try hard enough or did we both say...fuck it."

"Is that what you did?"

"I try to all the time but I can't. The only way we are going to be together is if we are in the general vicinity of each other and since your career at Finish Line has started I could move to start my career in Connecticut." She explained.

"Seriously? You want to move to Connecticut? How long have you been thinkin' 'bout this?"

"Since you left North Carolina. I don't want to move but I will if that is what it takes for us to get a fair shot at seeing if what we've been wanting for the past five years is actually going to be. I can go to grad school at Yale and work afterward while we live together. I think the thing that almost killed us in Georgia is that we weren't around each other enough to know how we would react to certain things and I have to tell you the truth, I got a little scared because I knew I wasn't the same girl you met when we were fifteen, I was afraid you wouldn't like the woman I've become."

"I could never not like the woman you've become. Not as long as you love me the way you've always loved me, unconditionally."

"Syncere?"

"Yeah."

"Why do we want this so badly?

"I don't know but just the fact you told me means you feel the same way I do; I know this is real."

"So you want to give this another try?"

"Do you have to ask me twice?"

"I don't hope so." I thought long and hard for a minute about the next words to escape my lips. Memories ran about in my head of Kenya and I in Boston then Kendra and I in Atlanta then back to Kenya and I in Brazil. As the images ping-ponged back and forth the words just sort of slipped out without warning.

"Yeah."

"Do you really mean it?"

"Yeah I really mean it. What about'cha boy?"

"Who Mulan? What about him?"

"I don't know. It don't seem like you were able to shake him in North Carolina so how you gonna tell him you're spendin' the summer with me?"

"It doesn't matter and he doesn't have to know. I'm not worried about Mulan at this point in my life. I'm about to graduate college and I need to be with someone who is going to love me for me and not run around all the time. Can you be that person Syncere?"

"I was always that person wit'chu except when we were younger but I drop everyone I'm dealin' with when it comes to you and I was that person you dragged around Raleigh to keep me away from your "boyfriend".

"Ok. Are you ready for me to come up there? I'm not the same girl that came to visit you in Georgia." She warned.

"Why do you keep sayin' that?"

"'Cause Syncere I'm not the same girl. I'm a Jehovah's Witness now…"

"Yeah I know and we gotta talk 'bout that."

"Why?"

"'Cause I don't believe in God or Jehovah anymore." I confessed.

"Since when? Last time we talked you weren't into church anymore. Now you don't believe in him at all. When did this change?"

"This changed years ago, I just never told you. But I figure if we're gonna be together we have to talk this religion thing out. I mean if you were a Christian I would go to church wit'chu on Sunday's with no problem but I have a big problem with Jehovah's Witnesses. I don't like them muhfuckas."

"Well I had a real problem with Christians, you see how Shiloh was being run. Gossip, lies, jealousy and sex; I didn't want to be around that."

"Yeah so you change churches not religions. You're gonna find those things in any ghetto black church. It sucks to say that but it's the nature of the beast. Look at the people that went to Shiloh. You're crack head aunt, deadbeat fathers, a crooked pastor, all those fast ass girls, Tausha and so on. I think the only people there for the Lord was Don and Mrs. Renee, oh and you 'cause I was surly only goin' for you."

"What about before you met me? Why were you going?"

"At first it was 'cause I had just moved here and I was deep into church in Connecticut. That changed when I started gettin' all that attention at Shiloh and after a couple weeks I was just goin' to see who I could mess with."

"Syncere, I have to know the truth about something before I come up there and I hope you'd trust me enough to be honest with me."

"Always."

"Did you have sex with Carla, Christina and Jewa?"

"Carla and Christina were months before you but Jewa no."

"Did you want to have sex with Jewa?"

"No. I don't know why I got in that conversation with her or why we ended up in the old sanctuary but no I didn't. I didn't have the urge to wanna fuck her like I do Gabrielle Union but what guy turns down ass whether the girl is cute or not. Plus I was young and overwhelmed by it all. All the girls with the exception of Erica and Toya chased me around week after week."

"Do you still feel like that now?"

"Like what?"

"Like having sex with a girl even if you really don't think she's cute or even if you don't like her?"

"If I'm single and I want it yeah. I have at least five or six girls I could call up if I wanted sex. But If I'm in a relationship then no I don't do that. Seriously sex isn't that serious if I really like someone. Like Kenya lives thirty minutes away from me and we hardly saw each other but when we did we made love. After while I just wanted to enjoy quality time with her na mean?"

"So tell me something else. Truthfully, why did ya'll break up?"

"Her mom. Her mom is a racist and she kept Kenya at home all the time or busy with photo shoots. If it wasn't school or modeling she had to lie to get out. We had exhausted lies to get her out until we just threw in the towel. We agreed to take a break until she goes to college but who's to say she won't meet someone like you did."

"Syncere you know that wasn't my intention. But you said it yourself, you can't help who you like."

"I do believe it was you who said that."

"Do you still love her?"

"Yeah. I'ma always love her just like I've always loved you and always loved Trisha."

"How can you do that? I still don't understand how you can tell me you love me and in the same breath tell me you love two other women."

"It's a different type of love. Their love isn't romantic is more along the lines of if they need me I'm there no question. I'm still a little protective, I care about their well-being, I think about them on occasion na mean? Not that I love them and wanna be with them 'cause if I wanted to you and I wouldn't be on the phone."

"One more question. If Kenya's mother wasn't a racist would ya'll still be together instead of you talking to me?"

"I seriously can't answer that 'cause I can say no but every time you call me everyone else becomes non existent. So I don't know. My love and need to be wit'chu is as strong as it was the day you called. It just won't go away."

"I feel the same way. God refuses to let us go our separate ways no matter how hard we try to change things up."

"Yeah it seems like that huh? Well not the God part but there is obviously somethin' that is tryin' to keep us together. So why are we fightin' it?"

"I don't know."

"Hey let's change the subject. Ben and Faith are gettin' married."

"Oh my God that is wonderful. When is the wedding?"

"March 22 in Atlanta and guess what? He asked me to be the best man."
"That is great Syn. Did he ask Tracy and Wes to be in the wedding too?"

"Yeah, they are groomsmen. So since I'm goin' to be in Atlanta for a week I was wonderin' if you could be my date to the weddin'."

"Really?"
"Yeah. Why do you sound so surprised all the time?"

"I don't know. That would be great because I haven't seen Faith and Ben in two years. How is Lyric?"

"Big from what I hear. So is that a yes?"

"I'll have to let you know. March 22 is three weeks away and I don't know if I'll be able to do it."

"Let me know ASAP and if you need me to I'll fly you down."

"I may have to take you up on that offer."

"Aight."

"I'll pay you back though. I know I have a huge debt but I'll get it covered." She joked.

"Don't worry 'bout it." Kendra and I talked more as I sit in my car parked outside my house. The night grew old and my car grew cold but the conversation continued, as I didn't want to move from that spot for anything. Kendra does that to me. I could be walking barefoot on hot coal and stop in my tracks to hold a conversation with her. That is until my phone beeped and Kenya's name appeared.

"Hello." I said in a sleepy voice.

"Baby, why didn't you call me when you got home?"

"I thought you were at work plus I was madd tired. I came home and got in bed. I still have my clothes on."

"Aww baby. Ok go back to sleep I'll just talk to you tomorrow."

"Na what's up I haven't talked to you all day?"

"Nothin', miss you."

"I miss you too."

"How much?"

"This much." I said making her laugh. "Say it."

"Say what?"

"You wanna ask me somethin'."

"No I don't." she said.

"Kenya I know you so just tell me."

"I want you to come to Danbury."

"When tomorrow?"

"No, tonight."

"Your mom isn't home?"

"No she is but she goes to sleep at like eleven so I want you to leave Waterbury at midnight. I'll sneak you in my basement again."

"Aight."

"Call me at midnight."

As all signs stated Kenya 8 miles away my mind isn't completely on seeing her. My mind is thinking about Kendra and what I committed to a few hours ago. Why? Why? Why? Kenya is everything I want in a woman and we've made this thing work for a year and a half and we can't be happier. So why did I just run back to Kendra without fail? *Curiosity killed the cat Syncere* I reminded myself. That's it, that's what it is. It's my curiosity that keeps me running to Kendra but is Kenya enough to erase that from my thoughts?

Kenya greeted me at her basement door dressed only in nothing except the Italian charm bracelet that I've never seen off her wrist, her green bra and panties set I got her for Valentine's day last month and that smile that looks like she has a mouth full of stars.

"You're goin' to freeze." I said trying to act unaffected by the mere sight of her body. I quietly thanked Aphrodite for what my eyes are beholding right now.

"Well get your butt in here and keep me warm." She said pulling my body close to hers and kissing me deep.

For the next hour nothing to me mattered except making Kenya have an orgasm. Her pleasure faces and sounds are like music to my ears but the I love you's that came in between sweetened the experience. I kissed Kenya wiping sweat from her eyebrows while she smiled down at me saying she loves me over and over.

"I'm not ready to leave."

"You want to do it again?" she asked.

"No...I mean yeah we could but what I really mean I want to lay here wit'chu for a little while and hold you."

"What's on your mind baby?" she asked lying her head on my chest and wrapping her arms around me, her hair smelling like strawberries.

"Nothin'. I just miss you."

"Babyyyy, tell me. I know you too you know."

"Do you really think we'll be together when you go off to college?"

"Syncere we had this talk. Why are you so worried?"

"Remember I said sometimes I just need to hear it? This is one of those times."

"You're so cute. Yes baby we will. Then I'll graduate and we'll move to Brazil where I'll have your handsome son and your gorgeous daughter." She said laughing.

"Kenya I'm serious." I said while I pictured Kenya and I at the alter then Kendra and I.

"Baby I'm serious. What's wrong? Where is this coming from?" She asked pushing herself up to look into my eyes.

"No where. I just love you so much and I've been thinkin' 'bout it lately. I've loved you for the pass year but recently that love has elevated and I don't know if you love me as much as I love you."

"I don't love you as much as you love me. I love you more and I'm not just saying that. I really do love you more."

"Cool. Hey guess what?"

"What?"

"Ben and Faith are gettin' married and I'm the best man."

"That's great baby."

"So you know what that means…you're finally comin' with me to Atlanta."

"I can't do that, I have school."

"Nope. The weddin' is on March 22, that week is your spring break."
"Wow you got it all planned out. But what are we gonna do about my mom?"

"Isn't Deon in Atlanta? Ask your mom if you can spend your spring break with Deon in Atlanta. Talk to Deon and her mom then all you guys talk to your mom, I think it'll work."

"You think so baby?"

"Yeah. I'm confident."

"That's one of the many things that I love about you. Kiss me."

"Just one?" I said after the kiss.

"No there's more but I don't want your head to get any bigger. By the way what are you doing on May 13? It's a Friday."

"Spending it wit'chu?"

"Wanna go to prom with me since you missed my Junior prom? This is important to me."

"Yeah. That's more than enough notice so I'll put the request in when I go to work tomorrow."

"Baby you told me that last year and you ended up having to work. You hardly take time out for yourself so please be able to take me this year"

"What'll happen if I can't?"

"I'll cry." She said giving me the puppy dog eyes and poked out lip that she knows I can't resist.

"How can I disappoint that face? I'll go if you promise to call Deon tomorrow."

"I will. You and I in Atlanta? I'm there, it won't be as nice as Brazil but as long as I'm with you I'm sure it's gonna be great." She said lying back down on my chest.

   I wish I could have someone tell me which girl to be with. When I talk to Kendra my heart tells me Kendra and when I'm with Kenya my hearts screams her name but when I'm alone I'm split right down the middle. I could've told Kendra I'm still with

Kenya and I could've told Kenya that Kendra wants to spend the summer with me but I know if I do that I would loose Kenya instantly. What would happen if things don't work out between Kendra and I? Then I'm out two girlfriends. Kenya will not go for Kendra spending the summer with me no matter how great of a lie I'll be able to come up with just like If I tell Kendra I'm still with Kenya she wouldn't come up here in June. Kendra's not the type of girl to step on another woman's playing field so if I tell her I'm still in a relationship she'd probably wish me best of luck and just step off as well.

"I don't know man you in a tough spot. I never met Kenya but I did meet Kendra and me and Faith thinks she's good for you, but what about what the Psychic said?" Ben asked.

"How many times do I gotta tell you I don't believe in that shit?"

"You don't believe in psychics and you don't believe in God, man you better start beleivin' in somethin'." Ben explained.

"That fake ass physic told you you'd be rich in a year. It's been two years and you still broke. I guess it's safe to say she lied."

"Fuck you man. I'ma be rich."

"Aight B. How's the weddin' comin'."

"A lot of fuckin' money man. You know you gotta give a speech at the reception right?"

"Yeah and I'm workin' on it."

"Tracy bringin' Michane?"

"Yeah and Q bringin' Dorian. I don't know who Wes bringin' though. But we all already took the time off work so don't worry 'bout us not comin' 'cause we are."

"Aight nigga. This my weddin', don't show up and I'ma drive to Connecticut and put my foot up ya ass."

"B. You're the only one who likes things up their ass so don't confuse me with your late nights." I hung up the phone laughing hysterically at my joke as Evelyn jerked my head back to were it was while she braided.

"Stay still. Before I mess it up. I'm on the last one."

"My bad."

"Done. Go look in the mirror and tell me if you like it." When I came back to the room I found Evelyn lying on my bed.

"You ready to go?"

"Not right now."

"Ok…what you wanna watch a movie or somethin'?"

"How come you don't fuck me like you use to after I finish doin' your hair? It's been like almost a year and I see you three times a month. You don't like me anymore? You gonna throw me away like you did when I was fifteen?"

"Na, I got a girl and you know that."

"You had the same girl a year ago and you were fuckin' me then and without a condom. So what's changed?"

"I love her and I don't wanna cheat on her anymore. I'm growin' up."

"Please. You probably got some other little bitch on the side that you're not tellin' me about. Who is it Krista?"

"Who? No!"

"So fuck me then. Kenya is all the way in Danbury, she's never found out and she never will." Evelyn said as she pulled her t-shirt over her head and began to unzip her jeans. She smiled when she saw the bulge in my jeans but as my smaller head screamed, fuck the shit out of Evelyn, I looked to my left at Kenya's modeling picture and it was kryptonite for my smaller head.

"Na I'm good." By that time Evelyn is completely naked with her perky nipples harden from the cool air and her pleasure center moist from her licking her fingers and touching herself.

"You said it yourself, I'm the best you ever had. You loved me at one point and I loved you. Love like that just don't just disappear."

"I didn't love you Evy. I loved having sex with you and yes hands down you're the best sex I've ever had but Kenya is better at making love." I said grabbing Kenya's picture and holding it in front of Evelyn's face, which made her stop unbuckling my belt.

"So all those nights you came by my grandparents house meant nothing? Who was the first bitch you fucked in this bed that your "girlfriend" brought for you? ME! Who do you call when you can't see your "girlfriend"? ME! Now you're standin' here while I'm naked and your honestly gonna tell me to put my clothes back on?"

"Look at this face. I'm serious. Get dressed and let's go." Evelyn stormed into the bathroom with her clothes and came out ten minutes later by walking right out of my house and to my car.

"So I've always been the other woman huh?" she said, as we got closer to her dorm at Briarwood College.

"Yep."

"Why couldn't I ever be number one? I've loved you since I was fifteen. You treated me differently like I was your age and you showed me things that no one else has. Why wasn't I enough?"

"It's complicated Evy. Back at my house when I said I didn't love you it wasn't entirely true. I care about you a lot but face it you like to jump from guy to guy too much. I had to drive up here last year with Mook and them and beat some niggas ass 'cause he was fuckin' wit'chu while you were fuckin' with me and it's always been like that."

"Like what?"

"You're inconsistent. You are all into me for a few weeks until you meet someone else then you're into him. You only want me when you want me, you're sporadic."

332

"When I was all yours you left me here and moved to Atlanta without tellin' me then you didn't have the decency to keep in touch with me when you got there but you kept in touch with Krista. I told you I loved you in that letter and you said nothin' about it. Acted like you never read it. Why?"

"'Cause…"

"Don't say it was because of my age 'cause I know it wasn't. Is it 'cause of all the shit you heard about me while you were in Atlanta?"

"Your age was the biggest thing. It's not like I could've taken you to Atlanta with me na mean? I should've kept in touch wit'chu I admit that. But as far as the shit I heard 'bout'chu I really don't listen to gossip and rumors na mean? 'Cause I never saw that side of you first hand, when you were with me you were on the up and up. However I do keep it in the back of my mind and that night I drove to your dorm I went up there on a feelin' I got that woke me out of my sleep. Then it turns out I was right. At that moment I as like I can't be doin' this. What I'ma do? Fight every dude you decided to sleep with 'cause I can't beat your ass for cheatin'? Na, I'm good."

"But you were cheatin too."

"You didn't know that until now. Point is I decided to man up and even though I have strong feelin's for you I love Kenya."

"So I guess she's the one you're taken to Atlanta?"

"Yep."

"You could'a asked me you know?"

"You have school and plus how would I explain that to my girlfriend?"

"So what. You still could'a asked even if it was just to be nice. WATCH OUT FOR THAT DEER!!"

25

Maybe I have convinced myself of something that really isn't. Maybe I've allowed myself to actually believe I love Kendra when I really don't and maybe I'm fighting against the feelings I have for Kenya because I'm afraid to let go of Kendra. Kendra's the only real love I've ever known my entire life and I think If I dead it I'd be wasting six years with all the women I've hurt in the past while trying to be with Kendra will be in vain. I honestly don't want Kenya to be among the women I hurt because I'm chasing a six-year relationship that doesn't seem like it wants to be caught. I'm screwed up so many ways it's scary. I don't want another man to be with Kendra because she's my first love but in the same breath I don't think I want to be with her anymore. Part of me wants to find out if what I'm going through is real but the other part of me says fuck it and be with Kenya because at the end of the day that is who my heart dances for every time I think about her. Sometimes I feel like I'm incapable of making a smart decision. I think my head is fucked up and so is my heart but all I want to do is find the woman I am going to grow old with.

Personally I know it will be on of these two women as I can't imagine anyone else out there who could match their beauty, ambition, personalities just everything Kenya and Kendra brings to the table. My mom says I'm only 22 and I will fall in and out of love a couple more times but I think she's wrong. I don't want to fall in and out of love a couple more times. I'm already in love, I just want to be in love with the right woman and who is that? Is it Kendra or is it Kenya? Somebody help me.

Ben and Faiths wedding was beautiful but it was the time I spent with Kenya that made that week so special. Despite us getting into a little spat about a text message Kenya and I cherished the opportunity we created. I gave Kenya a tour of Atlanta pointing out places we'd live if she ever changed her mind about moving. Kenya and I made love the first and as she slept I sat up just staring her amazed that for the past year and a half this seventeen year old girl has lied to her mother countless times to be with me. Remembering some of the things Tracy told me still lingers in my mind but I don't see any of it happening. I know without a doubt Kenya loves me and if she says she's going to be faithful in college then that's what it is.

On the drive back home I got a call from my new district manager Mark promoting me to the Trumbull store effective the Monday I return. The drive from Trumbull is about the same distance from my house to Milford and usually I'd get a phone call from either Kenya or Kendra. Since Georgia I've erased my call list whenever I know I'm going to be with Kenya to avoid confrontation. I still haven't told her Kendra is coming up here in less than a month and I'm still not sure at which one I'm going to choose to be with but I am leaning more toward Kenya despite her change in attitude she's had since we came back from Atlanta.

Our conversations are shorter most times and we haven't made love not once out of the last five visits she's made to my house or me going to Danbury. The first couple of times didn't bother me because I was just as satisfied at being in her company but the fifth time made me think that maybe it's because she doesn't want to. Kendra on the other hand has called me almost every other day since I agreed to try our relationship one more time. Confused I'm stopping by my mother's house before I go home to talk to her about it.

"Ohh Syn that is a nice suit, who picked it out?"

"Me but Kenya picked out the shirt."

"So when is her prom?"

"Next Friday."

"What are you gonna do about Kendra?"

"I don't know that's why I stopped by 'cause I wanna talk to you."

"What do you want me to say?"

"I don't know. I'm not lookin' for you to tell me what to do but…I don't know what I'm lookin' for."

"You want me to tell you what you're feelin' is ok?"

"Yeah. Is it?"

"Syncere I've always told you I can't help who you like and you can't help who you love. But you can't sit around and play wit both dem girls like this, you have to pick one and stick to your decision. I don't know the other girl but I do know Kenya and even though she's not black I still like that girl. She comes by and talks with me, she's not afraid to open her mouth and I have heard nothin' but good things about her for the past, what has it been? A year and a half now. I know my son and I know when my son is happy with someone and right now you're happy. But if this other girl makes you happier than Kenya or if you feel you'll be happier with her then let Kenya know. Don't do to them what Evelyn and Krista did to you."

"Aight, I got it. That was all I needed to hear."

"So what are you gonna do?"

"I don't know yet ma."

"Oh Lord." My mom said rolling her eyes.

"Na I heard what you said. I just have to think on it long and hard."

"Take your time and chose right but if that other girl Kenya…"

"Kendra ma."
"Well their names sound so much alike I don't know how you don't mix them up. If Kendra is comin' up here you need to tell her so she can find an alternate place to stay before she gets here. If that is the one you're gonna let go, you need to do at least that much."

"Aight."

I stood over my bed with Kenya's picture to my left and Kendra's picture to my right thinking this decision is harder than choosing which college I was going to go to. I heard Tracy go into the kitchen but he came to my room and stood next to me.

"I'd hate to be you right now."

"Tell me 'bout it."

"What if I choose the wrong one cut?"

"Live with it, bounce back then learn from it."

"Can I ask you a question? But on some real shit no jokes 'cause this is my life right here. Forget the fact Kenya isn't black and forget her age. Who would you choose?"

"Why you askin' me?"

"'Cause you ain't never told me nothin' wrong since I've known you na mean? It may've not been what I wanted to hear all the time but it ain't been wrong. Sometimes you are a little close minded so that's why I said forget Kenya's race and age 'cause that'll even out the playin' field plus you know both of them na mean?"

"Honestly and don't tell M.Dot I said it but for real for real I think you're better with Kenya. I know we have the white boy jokes but I know she's down for you 100%."

"How you know that?"

"Look at all she goes through to see you. She lies to her mom, sneaks to Waterbury, sneaks you to her house and she madd cool with everyone now. I thought she would've gotten tired of lying to her mom and sneakin' 'round but she still does it and every time I see her with you it's cool. She reminds me of M.Dot."

"How? She ain't short and crazy." I picked.

"Ok think 'bout this. Say Kendra is in North Carolina and Kenya is in California right? Say you got in a bad accident and I called them both, who do you think will come? Kenya or Kendra?"

"Ok, who will come eventually or who will drop what she is doin' and come?"

"Who will drop what she's doin'. 'Cause you would drop what you're doin' for the both of them but I get the feelin' only one would do it for you."

"Aight, I got it."

"Don't tell me who you think, you take that person and you be wit that person. Good luck cut."

"Thanks." I said as Tracy left the room. I took his advice and I thought about who would drop what she's doing to come to me and now I know what I have to do but I won't do it until after prom.

Kenya's dress is equivalent to the shirt she brought for me and with the snow-white suit I brought we looked like two Hollywood couples on the red carpet. Kenya's bright lime green jewel studded dress reached the floor covering her matching shoes looks incredible on her, tonight she is more beautiful than I've ever seen her which makes my decision that much harder. We opted to leave the prom early due to the lack of decent music and the fact Kenya looked like she was being forced to stay there. We sat in the car in our favorite park just looking at the stars from my back seat cuddled up with each other. I know I have something to get off my chest but I sense she does to.

"Say it." Kenya looked at me with surprise in her eyes before she dropped her head and that notion started to frighten me.

"I got into Johnson & Wales. I leave August 17th."

"Congrats babes, that was your first choice right?"

"Yeah."

"Well hey we both knew this time was comin' so don't be sad we should be celebratin' right now. Wanna go get some ice cream from Friendly's?"

"Ok! But before we go I wanna tell you that I'm not moving to California...I'm movin' to Rhode Island." At the sound of that I want to shout out for joy because instead of Kenya moving across the country she'll only be two and a half hours away but I contained my excitement because disappoint is on her face.

"I know you really wanted to move to Cali. How 'bout we go to visit over the summer?"

"Yeah I would love that baby. I'm not too disappointed but my mom doesn't want me to go that far."

"I'm actually surprised. She does realize that I'd me thousands of miles from you? You know I'll never tell you to defy your moms but you'll be eighteen this year. If you wanna go to school in Cali then go to school in Cali."

"What about us? I thought you'd be just as happy as my mom that I wasn't going to California."

"Babe, I'm only happy if you are happy. As far as us the plan stays the same but now that you'll be closer we can see each other more."

"Promise me something?"

"Anything." I agreed before I heard the terms.

"Promise me that no matter what you will come to Rhode Island at least once a month and I promise to come to Connecticut once a month."

"Promise."

"Good now let's go to Friendly's."

"Babe I have somethin' to tell you." I said changing my demeanor and letting her hand go.

"Can you tell me over a nice hot fudge Sunday with M & M's over it and whipped crème?"

"I gotta tell you now. You know I want to always be honest wit'chu so that is why I am tellin' you this 'cause I don't wanna keep any secrets from you."

"Baby you're scaring me. You know what? Let's not ruin a perfect night, tell me tomorrow?"

"Ok." Kenya and I never made it to Friendly's. Instead we made love in the park.

"So are you as excited as I am? I'm going to be there in less than ten days!"

"Yeah."

"Syncere you don't sound like it, what's wrong?"

"I lied to you."

"About what?"

"I was still with Kenya when I agreed to give us another try but I just broke up with her and now I don't know if I'm makin' the right choice."

"Oh. You sounded so confident a week ago. Can I asked what changed?"

"Me thinkin' that's all. I don't know I'm madd confused right now."

"Syncere if you don't want me to come then say so. The program will put me with a family in Connecticut close to the school."

"No I don't want you to stay with anyone in West Haven. I told you we are gonna try this and put our all into it and that is what we are gonna do."

"What did she say when you told her?"

"Nothin'. She just hung up the phone."

"You didn't tell her to her face?"

"Na, I thought the phone would be easier."

"I'm going to ask you this again. Are you sure you want to do this. 'Cause I don't want to drive all the way up there and have to deal with a crazy girl."

"Kenya isn't even like that. She barely raises her voice. I do want you two to meet though. What ever goes down both of you will still be a big part of my life."

"You want me to meet her?" Kendra asked sounding surprised.

"Yeah, just like you wanted me to meet Quami and Mulan."

"You never met Mulan."

"Yes I did, just not the way you wanted me to meet him."

"Ok, I'll meet her."

"Aight, I gotta get up early so lemme shower and I'll call you tomorrow."

"Bye." As soon as I heard the dial tone I called Kenya.

"Hey baby! I was just about to call you, what's up, what's up, what's up?" She said sounding like she's just drank five cups of coffee.

"Wow you sound real excited. You got some good news?"

"Yep. I'm going to London next week for a photo shoot for Louis Vuitton's spring magazine."

"Wow, that's big. Congratulations."

"Thank you, thank you. And do you know what the best part is?"

"What?"

"My mom can't take off from work to go so that means its you and I in London England!!" she said cheering.

"Babe. Remember last week after prom I told you I had somethin' to tell you and you told me to tell you the next day."

"Yeah but you never did. What was it?"

"Ok here goes."

"Kendra got a job in Connecticut for the summer in West Haven."

"Ok, so your ex-girlfriend will be in the same state as you for the entire summer. Ok, I'm ok with that."

"There's more. Tracy and Michane invited her to stay with us because they don't want her in West Haven by herself."

"So… your ex-girlfriend is going to be living with you for the entire summer and I have no say so in this?"

"Not really. She's already been invited and she's gonna be here the day after you leave for London."
"A day after we leave for London." She corrected.

"Baby me and Tracy just moved into this new apartment, I don't have the money to go to London."

"They are paying for me and a guest and putting us up in a hotel for the week. Everything is paid for Syncere. You are going to London.

"But I don't think I can get the time off from work like that. I would have to talk to Mark."

"Wait a minute, what is this? Are you trying to break up with me? Is this what this is?"

"No, babe if I wanted to break up wit'chu I wouldn't be tellin' you this. But I didn't invite her and she doesn't know anyone up here. Don't think of her as my ex-girlfriend think of her as a friend of mine."

"So if I told you Ricky was going to stay at my house for the summer because his parents are going out of the country you would be ok with that?"

"If that was the case and you don't wanna have anything to do with him then yeah."

"Bullshit Syncere! You can't stand for another guy to look at me let alone let my ex stay in my house. I'm just as jealous as you are I just don't show it like you do."

"Do you trust me?"

"That is besides the point Syncere. Your ex-girlfriend who you still have a tattoo of will be under the same roof with you for the whole summer while I'm stuck in Danbury wondering if you are going to call me up one day and say you don't want to be with me anymore. Just tell me now and let's not ruin each other's summer."

"You're just willin' to give me up like that? Just like that?"

"Syncere I can't compete with Kendra, she's your first love. You said it didn't work because you two were never in the same state long enough but now you will be so how you can sit here and tell me something is not going to happen?"

"'Cause it's not. First of all I love you and that is why I'm tellin' you this, I don't want anything kept from you. Second Kendra and I are two different people now. She is a celibate Jehovah's Witness that's two strikes right there. Listen if it makes you feel any better I can stay at my moms house na mean?"
"What would that do? It's not like you're still not gonna see her."

"I'll go to my apartment once a week to get enough clothes and I'm out. You always know where I am at all times anyway. Nothin' will change. We'll still talk daily; still go out you can still come to the house. You still have a key and all your clothes are still in the closet and dresser. Trust me when I tell you nothin' is gonna happen."

I couldn't sleep so I got in the car and rode around Waterbury like I normally do until I get tired when out of the blue my phone rang. I looked at my car clock that said one thirty a.m. and the name read Emily.
"Em?"

"Syncere did I wake you?"

"Na, somethin' wrong?'

"Yeah, you. Where do you get off letting your ex-girlfriend stay at your house for the summer? I just got off the phone with Kenya who cried her eyes out on the phone for two hours saying you're gonna leave her."

"I'm not gonna leave her Em."

"Then what the hell are you doing 'cause when Kenya comes by your house before she leaves for London she's breaking up with you."

"She told you that?"

"Yeah and I think she's serious. No I know she is. She thinks you are passing up London because Kendra is coming. Don't tell her I told you but I'm only telling you 'cause you've been like a brother to me and damn good friend and I love you both. So you need to do what you can to keep her with you."

"Thanks Em. But I can't get the time off from work!"

"Don't thank me until it's fixed. I am so disappointed in you. Does Mika know?"

"I didn't tell him 'cause I didn't want to involve ya'll until I told Kenya na mean?"

"Yeah. Syncere you have a great girl. I listened to you at Olympia talk about how all these girls did you wrong and how you wanted someone to love you for you and stick by you always. Well Kenya is that girl and you're about to loose her knowing full well half the guys in Connecticut are just waiting for you to do so, including Ricky."

"Ricky?"

"Yes Ricky. Kenya told me how he came to her house the night of prom and apologized for cheating on her two years ago."

"She forgave him?"

"Sure did and they've been hanging out a few times since then."

"What the fuck!!"

"Don't tell her I told you. Matter of fact don't tell her a thing because you had that one coming for not telling her about you hanging out with Stacy last year. Fix it Syncere because if you don't Ricky is gonna get her back. But don't do it because you don't want him to have her do it because you love her, I know you do."

"I do and I will."

Thinking about Kenya breaking up with me has me disoriented at work and even worse at home. I haven't spoken to her for more than ten minutes in the last five days as she is running around getting things ready for London. Ironically Mark did give me the time off to go but called the next day and told me our Regional Vice President is coming to my store and it's a good thing I didn't tell Kenya I would be able to go because I would've hated calling her back to say I can't. Two more days before Kenya leaves and one before Kendra gets here and I think my choice has been made for me, *stupid boy* I said to myself.

At ten o'clock a.m. I got a knock at my front door and I already know Kenya would be on the other side when open it. I'm only in a pair of Jordan shorts and a wife beater while Kenya is dressed good enough to hit the runway at any moment. We hugged and even when she went to let go I held her tighter not knowing if this would be our last one.

"I'm on my period." She said stopping me from leading her to my bedroom.

"I just wanna lay wit'chu that's all babe."

"I can't stay long and I don't wanna wrinkle my cloths. We can just sit in the living room." Kenya sat on the sofa and I sat in the armchair with this being the first time ever anywhere we've sat separate from each other and in silence.

"So when are you gonna do it? Now or before you leave?" I asked.

"Do what?"

"You came here to break up with me didn't you?" Instantaneously tears fell from her eyes and she dropped her head.

"I don't want to but I have to."

"Why Kenya?" I asked on one knee in front of her."

"I don't think I can stand for you and her to be under the same roof for two months and I'm not here. You two will be like you an I want to be."

"But I don't want her like that. Like I said she is only here 'cause Tracy and Michane invited her."

"Why would they do that without asking you first?"

"'Cause they want me and her together."

"That's what I mean. Syncere I love you and because I love you I've taken some shit from you. I've put up with your mood swings, you're always working and pushing me to the side, your friendship with girls like Stacy and Evelyn but this is enough. You're asking me to be ok with your first love staying in the same house as you…just a room away."

"Like is said I'll stay at my moms house if that will put your mind at ease but I don't want her, I want you. What do you want me to do?"

"What should I do Syncere?"

"Tell me you trust me and mean it when you say it. Tell me you love me enough to get passed this. Two months just two months is all I'm asking for and she'll be out of my life forever. I will stay at my mothers house or I'll sleep in the car, I'll do whatever you want me to just please don't leave me. I can't get pass this without you." I pleaded.

"Everyone says I'm stupid if I let this go down. That you're gonna leave me for her."

"Fuck everybody else, what do you think?"

"I think you and her have each other's initials still tattooed on your shoulder's so what would you think?"

"Only I still have the tattoo…she covered hers."

"How do you know?" My mind thought at this moment I can tell her a lie and say she told me or I can take the high road and tell the truth.

"I saw it."
"When?"

"Last November."

"You saw her when you were in North Carolina! Why didn't you tell me?"

"'Cause I didn't want you to think she is the reason I went down there in the first place."

"How did you see her? Did you call her up or did you conviently run into her some where?"

"My church mother Mrs. Williams lives across the street and she just so happened to be there when I went to see Mrs. Williams. Neither one of them knew I was comin'."

"Yeah right. All this time and you didn't tell me you saw her?"

"'Cause I saw her and it didn't mean anything. I felt nothin'. I didn't feel sparks or that fire I'm feelin' right now."

"Maybe you were right you know. Maybe this wasn't meant to last this long. Why don't we end it right now." I took Kenya's hand and I put in on my chest as I put my hand on hers.

"My heart is yours…your heart is mine. No one has my heart but you and if it's ok wit'chu I'd like it to stay that way for the next eighty years."

"Only eighty? You don't wanna be with me for a hundred?" She said cracking a smile behind her tears."

"A hundred. Babe just tell me you trust me, please. All I need to hear is that you trust me, you love me and you're gonna ride this out wit me. Just tell me those three things and nothin' will stop us from spendin' the rest of our life in Brazil together. Please tell me you trust me."

"I trust you."

"You're not gonna break up with me?"

"No. I'm gonna ride this out with you because I love you too much to just give you away. I'll be right here the whole step of the way. But if you so much as to look at her with any intentions of being together, if you even think it I'll kill you and I'm so serious. You better not hurt me Syncere." I wiped Kenya's tears and we lay on the couch holding each other until it was time for her to leave.

26

I got the call at eight o'clock in the morning that Kendra had gotten to Waterbury late last night and now she wants me to drive her mother to the airport. Yesterday was like hell for me after I talked to Kenya about this situation. I asked her to ride out with me and it feels damn good to know that she'll be waiting for this all to end. I told Kenya and Kendra both about the situation thinking one of them wouldn't go for it and say fuck it which would allow me to make an easy decision but they both accepted it leaving me to go to plan B. Too bad I don't have a plan B. I slept long and hard on the idea of choosing Kendra but the truth is no matter how wonderful and perfect I feel Kenya is for me Kendra and I have a crazy history. I just need to be sure that it wasn't going to work or if it is supposed to work.

I sat in my car outside the Holiday Inn next to Saint Mary's Hospital waiting for Kendra and her mother to come downstairs. I spotted Kendra's hunter green Saturn because of the first in flight tags in the back. With every second that passed I grew more and more nervous but I don't know why. I still have to think of a way to get away from the house for an hour or so when I have to meet Kenya for lunch at Outback before she leaves for London. Then there she is. With her hair braided and her mother not too far behind her Kendra came out of the automatic doors and I got out to greet her.

"Hey."

"Hey."

"Hi Ms. Lewis. Nice to see you." I said trying not to smile too big.

"Hi Syncere." She said giving me a hug. "Now you gonna take care of my punkin this summer right?"

"Yes ma'am. You all set to go?"

"Yeah. I never been on plane before so I'm a little excited and a little afraid."

"Momma you gonna be fine." I put Ms. Lewis' bag in the trunk and walked around the passenger side to let Kendra in. Everything in me wants to grab and hug her but I fought the urge. I changed my hardcore rap CD and slid in the Lyfe Jennings CD then we hit the highway.

Most of the forty-five minute drive was driven without a word out of Kendra, her mother or myself. Occasionally Ms. Lewis could comment on something she saw on the outside but Kendra sat on the far side of the passenger seat staring at the window.

"You ok?" I asked. She nodded her head but didn't speak a word and that is when I realized she's crying but I didn't ask her why. When we arrived at the terminal Kendra kissed and hugged her mother before hopping in the car still sobbing.

"You gonna miss her huh?"

"Yeah. I cried when I went to Jamaica too. I don't like being too far away from her you know?"

"Yeah."

"Are things with your mom still good?"

"As a matter of fact yeah. She's cookin' for us a little later when I bring you by to meet her and my sisters."

"All of them?"

"Probably Mone' since she's the only one who still stays at home, the rest of them you'll probably meet throughout the summer."

"Ok. Can you put some different music on?"

"You want rap or R&B?"

"You have any Mike Jones?"

"Who?"

"Mike Jones."

"Who?"

"Mike Jones."

"No. I hate Mike Jones."

"What! You hate Mike Jones? Mike Jones is that dude."

"Not up here he's not. I got some Luda."

"He sucks."

"Wow! Get out right now." I pretended like I was pulling the car over.

"Boy you better keep driving this car to wherever you're supposed to be taking me. Don't be trying to leave me out in the middle of nowhere."

"So what'chu think 'bout Connecticut so far?" I asked.

"It's ok I guess. Yaw'll have a lot of land."

"Land?"

"Yeah you know grass? Just land everywhere with cows and stuff. I feel like I'm back in New Hampshire when I look at them cows."

"You ever go cow tippin'?"

"Cow tippin'? No but them white boys at school talk about doing it all the time. They get a big kick out of it too."

"'Cause that shit is so funny."

"No it isn't. You know that when you tip them cows over the owner has to kill'em?"

"Why?"

"I don't know exactly but cows are hardly off their feet and they are too heavy to pick up I guess."

"Oops. I've tipped a lot of cows in my day."

"I bet you have."

"So you followin' me straight to my house or you goin' back to the hotel?"

"I'm still a little tired so I'ma go back to the hotel to lay down for a while, you?"

"Once I'm up I'm up."

"So what are you gonna do?"

"Probably go for a run and get my clothes out."

"For what?"

"Ben hooked me up with a Master Mason up here and I have to go meet with him at noon."

"You want to become a Mason? You never told me that. When did you make that decision?"

"Ben has been talkin' to me and talkin' to me 'bout it ever since we lived together but I never really paid him too much mind. But one day I drove by a temple we have in Waterbury and I talked to one."

"I heard bad things about Masons." She said.

"Like what 'cause I've only heard good things."

"They practice black magic and are sacrilegious."

"Get outta here, no they not!"

"My granddaddy is a Mason."
"The one I met?"

"Yeah."

"And he practices black magic?"

"No but he says some temples do. What kind of Mason are you gonna be."

"A Prince Hall Mason."

"Oh."

"Aight here we are. Just call me when you are ready to come over and I'll come get'chu."

"Can you just give me directions? I need to learn my way around here if I'ma be here all summer."
"Aight."

I drove back to my place feeling a little uneasy about the vibes I'm getting from Kendra. She didn't act the way I expected she would then again she's never been visually excited to see me. When we see each other the encounter is as if we just saw each other yesterday like there's no big deal. I don't know about her but my insides have been jumping since she got in the car.

"Cut where is she?" Tracy asked when I got in the house.

"She back at the hotel. She said she was tired and wanted to lay back down."

"So what are you doin' here then?"

"'Cause she wanted to go back to sleep."

"Yeah wit'chu dumb ass!"

"What?"

"That was an invitation for you to come and sleep with her."

"She's celibate cut."

"No not fuck her but really sleep with her."

"You think so?"

"Cut who do you think you're talkin' to? I know these things. You're stupid."

"I had no idea."

"So you goin' back?"

"Na, I gotta shower and shit."

"Why?"

"I gotta meet with Kenya at one so I gotta be outta here by like noon."

"Cut you wilin'. I thought you chose Kendra. You waited all this time to get her back wit'chu and you're goin' to see some young ass white girl."

"BRAZILIAN!"

"Damn cut sorry. She Brazilian my bad. Damn you got both their pictures on your dresser. Are you tryin' to make this girl say fuck it?"

"No why?"

"Dude you got both their pictures up."

"So, Kenya never said nothin' 'bout it."

"And Kenya is dumb. Kendra isn't gonna go for that. If I was you I'd take it down. Here I'll do it for you."

"Cut chill. Kendra is not jealous like that." I said snatching Kenya's picture out of Tracy's hand.

"It's not 'bout jealousy. It's 'bout respect. M.Dot would NEVER let me leave D.Dot or I.Dot's pictures up in my room nowhere. You see I gotta keep the photo albums on the livin' room, they can't even be in my closet. And believe it or not M.Dot and K.Dot are the same woman."

"First of all no they are not. Kendra isn't a psycho and secondly don't dot my girl."

"If she's ya girl then why are you goin' to see Kenya."

"Fuck you."

"Here we go with the sassy shit. I hope you know what you're doin'."

"I do. Kenya is on her way to London for the week plus she is still in school until the 20th. She has a bunch of modelin' shit to do this summer so on my days off while Kendra is teaching I can be with Kenya."

"What about if Kenya wants to go somewhere at night?"

"Inventory, shakedowns. I got mad excuses; Kendra doesn't know how our stores operate. I'll deal with Kendra at home and Kenya outside. They will never meet each other unless I set it up."

"Why are you gonna live a double life instead of just pickin' one?"
"I don't fold without seeing the rest of the cards."

"Don't try to act like you're this expert poker player, nigga you play blackjack."

After showering and putting on my black slacks with the devil red collard shirt Kenya got for me I made closet space for Kendra's clothes then placed three roses on the bed. One red, one pink and one yellow as I waited for her to call.

"Syncere?"

"You outside?"

"No I'm lost."

"Ok tell me what you see." I said laughing.

"I see run down buildings, a lot of them."

"Well you can be anywhere in Waterbury. What is the closest street to you?"

"Green Street."

"Green Street? Where the hell are you? Drive straight and tell me when you get to a cross street."

"Walnut."

"Shit I know where you are, you're in the hood."
"The hood!"
"Yeah but it's still day light out so you'll be aight. Put your hazards on and I'll be right there. Lock your doors and don't say anything to anyone." I met Kendra and showed her two alternate routes to my house from different parts of the city before bringing her back to my apartment.

"Where is everyone?" she asked as we entered an empty apartment.

"At work. Tracy should be home at five and Michane should be here at like six."

"Are you gonna be gone long?"

"No. I have to drive to Brookfield which is thirty minutes away but I think the meeting should be no longer than an hour."

"Will you take me the way I would need to go to get to work on Monday?"

"Aight, we can go Sunday night."

"I want to go today so I can drive it tomorrow and Sunday."

"Aight. I made you some closet space so you can hang everything up and you can have the two top drawers."

"Where you keeping your stuff?"

"In the bottom ones, see."

"So that is her?" She said looking at Kenya's picture.

"Yeah."

"You leave her picture up?"

"Just like I leave yours up. Remember these?" I said pulling out her red French laces boy shorts she'd given me almost two years ago.

"I can't believe you still have these. Syncere throw these away."

"No! Why? I told you I was gonna keep them."

"They're supposed to be attached to your blinds."

"You're right."

"Stop, don't do that."

"Aight. I'ma head out now so if you need anything you have my number and I think Wes has the day off so if you need him I have his number on the dresser. I'll see you a little later."

"Ok."

"You gonna be aight?"

"Yeah. Thank you for the flowers. Why do you always have flowers for me?"

"I don't know. I wanted to get'chu balloons and a banner but I had to work late all this week."

"Do you know I didn't like roses until you started giving them to me?"

"For real for real?"

"Yeah."

"That's what's up. Aight lemme go so I can hurry up back." Before I left out of the house I went back into the room to find Kendra sitting Indian style on my bed looking down at the Carolina Tar Heels throw blanket I laid out for her. "I'm happy you came." She responded with a nod and I left.

"You're gonna be late aren't you? You know my plane leaves at four?"

"I'm not gonna be late I'm on my way."

"On my way means twenty-minutes."

"On my way means I'm like right there."

"Well I'm here and I don't see you."

"Ah but I see you." I said pulling into the parking lot. When Kenya saw my car she hung her phone up and began walking in my direction with a big smile on her face. She seems unaffected by yesterday and this whole Kendra thing, which makes me ecstatic. She's look beautiful as usual wearing the Coach heels I got her for Valentine's Day with a super short black mini shirt and a pure white collard shirt that is unbuttoned down far enough to see the crease at the top of her breasts. To top if off she's wearing minimal make-up, her hair is down and she smells like the Burberry Brit perfume I also got her on Valentine's Day.

"You smell good."

"So do you."

"And you said you couldn't wear cologne."

"Yes babe you proved me wrong yet again."

"I know."

Kenya and I sat closer than Siamese twins in our booth while we laughed; exchanged love taps and kisses in between our conversation and coconut shrimp. The time seemed to be moving sluggish so I enjoyed every moment without worry.

"So are you gonna miss me while I'm gone?" Kenya asked feeding me a shrimp.

"Yes ma'am."

"How much?"

"From here to London and back twice." I said.

"Wow that's a lot." She said giving me a kiss."

"If you multiply that by a hundred you'll get how much love you."

"I love you more, trust me."
"I love you more than you think I do."

"You say that but I'm tellin' you I love you more. I have your love beat."

"How 'bout we say we love each other as much as the other does."

"I can live with that… I trust you Syncere." She said out of nowhere but I know why she said it.

"That's all I needed to hear."

"And I'll call to tell you everyday if I have to. Just if the thought of being with your arises while I'm gone or during the summer just know that *she* is not the woman for you, *I* am dammit." She ended with a smile.

As the sun went down we all sat in white lawn chairs outside of Sean's condominium sipping on juice exchanging stories from Georgia with Sean and Natalie while Tracy ran around the yard with his nephew Tre'Shawn.

"We better get goin', I told my mom we'd be other there by seven."

"I'm kinda not in the mood to go. Can we go another day?"

"She's expectin' us to come tonight. What's wrong?"

"I drove all day yesterday and we've been running around all day, I'm just a little tired is all."

"Can we just go for five minutes? I just want you to meet my mom. I've talked about you to her for years but ya'll have never met. Just five minutes." I begged.

"Syncere I don't want to. We can go tomorrow, I want to lay down."

Extremely disappointed I drove Kendra back to my apartment and headed back out to see my mother. A part of me wants to call and say I got held up or the store needed me but I decided not to, plus I didn't want to miss my mom's food.

"Where is she?" my mother asked when I walked into the kitchen.

"At the apartment."

"Why?"

"She said she is tired."

"Too tired to meet your mother. What kind of girl say's she's too tired to meet a guy's mother."

"But ma she drove from North Carolina last night, then we had to go all the way to the airport to drop her mother off, then to West Haven, Trumbull and back here. I'm tired too."

"I'm tired just imagining it." My younger sister Mone' said.

"I don't care if she drove from California. I bet if you went down there and said you were too tired to meet her mother it'll be a problem wouldn't it?"

"I don't know."

"Yes it would. I don't like her and you need to leave her alone."

"Ma you didn't even meet her."

"I don't need to and now I don't want to. Too tired to meet your mother, what kind of shit is that?" she said under breath as she walked back into her room. I sat with my mom and talked to her one more time at what I was doing as she expressed her dislike toward Kenya. I figured she is only acting like that toward Kendra because of the stunt she pulled today but I know once my mom meets Kendra her attitude toward her will change.

When I got back to the house Tracy and M.Dot are in the room talking and laughing with Kendra but stopped when I walked in, possibly because of the mean look I have on my face. Tracy jumped off my bed because he knows I don't like people sitting on it but M.Dot stayed there.

"Why'd you leave her here by herself?" M.Dot asked.

"'Cause she didn't wanna come."

"Was your momma upset?" Kendra asked.

"Uh yeah." I said sarcastically

"What did she say?"

"She is pissed that you didn't come by to meet her."
"But I was tired."

"Yeah, you seem real tired now. That is my mother and she see it as disrespect to her and to me. I would never say I am too tired to meet your mother if it was for the first,"

"Aight I'll get up wit'cha later. I'm 'bout to go make some food." Tracy said.

"I'm not surprised." As Tracy and M.Dot left the room I saw the closet door is left open with her exposed side still empty and her suitcase is on the floor still up opened.

"Why didn't you unpack?"

"I don't want to. I'll just get what I need out of my suitcase when I need it."

"I don't want you living outta a suitcase all summer that isn't comfortable trust me I know. I lived outta mine when we first moved to Atlanta."

"I didn't know you were into heels and Baby Phat." She said gesturing into the closet.

"Oh that is Kenya's. She never came by to get her stuff and I guess I just forgot them being in here."

"Didn't you just move in?" Kendra asked with a mean look on her face.

"Yeah like three weeks ago."

"So you put them there or did she come visit?"

"She came by to see the new apartment 'cause it's better than the last one. We still talk na mean? Where not total enemies."

"I don't know how I feel about that."

"Why not? You and I talked when Kenya and I dated but she was aight with it."

"I'm not Kenya."

"I see. Kenya met my mother."

"Why did you invite me to come up here if you're not over her?"

"Who says I'm not over Kenya?"

"You have her clothes still in your closet, shoes and her picture is up right across from mine."

"So I can't be over her 'cause her picture is up? What am I supposed to do throw her clothes in a trash bag and put'em outside my door? She is in London so when she gets back I'll give'em to her." I explained.

"If you knew I was coming you should've given them to her when you moved in. What am I supposed to think when I walk into your room and I see all this. When I look at your Olympia name tag and it says *Property of Kenya* on the back of it? I mean why do you still have that?"

"When someone gives me somethin' I don't just throw it away 'cause we broke up. I held on to your panties for two years just like I told you I would. I didn't cover my tattoo like I said I would never do unlike you."

"I wish you would."

"You wish I would what?"

"Cover the tattoo." I can't believe my ears and what Kendra just let escape from her mouth.

"How can you say somethin' like that? This was a commitment we made to each other. We had this talk already."

"Syncere I'm not the woman for you. You need to just call Kenya and get her back because she is the one you need. Look at her, she's beautiful." She said picking up her picture.

"If you felt like that why'd you come up here? Why didn't you tell me that before you came?"

"Why did you switch up on me?"

"When?" I asked confused.

"Last month. You called sounding so down and confused and I asked you what was wrong and you told me you didn't know if you were making the right decision. You remember that? What was that about? You were so excited and confident about me coming then one day you tell me you don't know if you're making the right decision. I always knew I wanted to be with you but when you told me that I stopped expecting this visit to evolve into anything."

"I felt like that then but I don't feel like that now."

"And when did that change. Today?"

"It changed when I saw you this mornin'. I knew when I saw your face you were the one I wanted."

"You can't just switch like that. You tell me one thing then you act another way."

"Oh this is comin' from a woman who went outta her way to dodge her "ex" boyfriend while I was in town then waited three months to tell me the reason."

"Contrary to what you may believe I didn't start dating Mulan until the year before last and he is my ex. I didn't want you two to collide with each other and you possibly going to jail and Mulan ending up dead this time."

"You care about him more than you do me?"

"No I don't."
"THEN WHY WEREN'T YOU AT THE TRAIL!!! Why weren't you there? I almost threw away my life, na fuck that I almost killed this muhfucka over you and you didn't have the decency to be in my corner when the shit it the fan."

"You didn't almost kill him over me. You almost killed Mulan over your jealousy and feeding into all the shit Wes, Ben and Tracy were telling you. I'm not the cheater you are, I'm not the liar you are." She said pointing.

"When did I lie to you?"

"You took Kenya with you to Atlanta and you didn't tell me. I saw the pictures."

"You went through my stuff?"

"It was out so I looked in them."

"I took Kenya to Atlanta...so."

"So? What do you mean so? You ask me and since I couldn't go you ask her? You told me you didn't go with anyone therefore you lied."

"I didn't have to tell you shit. You weren't my girlfriend then..."

"So was she?"

"It don't matter. If I didn't wanna tell you somethin' I'm not entitled to. Did I have to tell you I took her to Boston, New York and Brazil too? No and that's why I didn't. I wasn't obligated to."

"So we keep things from each other now? Is that what we do?" she asked.

"I'm keepin' things from you? Me? What about you and Mulan? You kept that from me. Tell me, how long was it exactly you waited until you got the tattoo covered? One week maybe two?"

"I covered it before I left for Jamaica."

"So was it your idea or his?"

"This isn't about Mulan this is about you."

"And you."

"There is no me and you. There is Kendra Lewis and there is Syncere and Kenya because you obviously love her so why don't I get my shit and let you get back to your relationship. I'll even call her up and wish her all the best with ya'll future."

"You know what do what ever the hell you wanna do. I'm tired of this shit. I wipe my hands wit'chu." I said before grabbing my car keys and slamming the door behind me.

The first night Kendra and I slept in the same bed in two years was one of silence, awkward feelings and tension. I drove around for two hours trying to clear my head and fighting the urge to call up some girl I knew and fuck her real quick. I did speak to Kenya when she landed in London and she sounded so excited, which made me feel miserable. I played back the argument Kendra and I had last night wishing I could take back some of the things I said but now I can't. I tried to work at my normal level of productivity then when that didn't work I went next door to Rave Girl and flirted with Jamie for a while. But when I sensed my terrible mood was getting worse I stayed in the stock room to run some shoes up. I looked at my blue-black fossil watch and the time said seven o'clock. I was only scheduled to work today until five o'clock but I don't want to go home. As I sat on the boxes contemplating whether or not I should go home a weird feeling hit me and I know Kendra left. I tried to ignore it for the past twenty minutes but it just got worse and worse. I didn't call Tracy to see if she was there I just got in my car and sped home.

I walked right passed M.Dot, who is sitting on the couch, right down the hallway to my room. The door is closed and before I opened it I stopped not knowing what I'm waiting for but I just stopped for a minute wishing she'll be sitting on my bed Indian style staring down at her laptop. I opened the door and just like the pit o my stomach told me at work she isn't here. I looked on the floor to see her suitcase gone and her picture taken off my dresser. Nothing but a letter sat on top of my North Carolina throw blanket. I held it in my hand just staring at it for what seemed like hours until I actually unfolded and read it.

"She's gone M." I said flopping in the armchair in the living room.

"I know. She left an hour ago."

"Where'd she go?"

"She doesn't want me to tell her but she is ok."

"What type of shit is that? She don't want me to know where she is."

"She doesn't want you to know what do you want me to say?" M.Dot said shrugging her shoulders.

"This is some bullshit!" I shouted.

"You call Kenya yet?"

"No. Why would I be callin' Kenya."

"I mean Tracy said you had a tough time tryin' to decide who to choose now Kendra left only leavin' Kenya."

"This isn't how I wanted it to be. I wanted us to break up 'cause we realized we weren't right for each other not 'cause we got in a fight."

"She feels like ya'll aren't right for each other that's why she left."

"What do you think M.?"

"I think you fucked up." She said which sounds like a punch to the face.

"I fucked up?"

"Syncere you told her you don't know if you're makin' the right choice. You left Kenya's pictures and her clothes in the room and you let her find the pictures from Atlanta? I would'a left too."

"I didn't let her find anything. She went through my shit. I didn't know I'd have to Kendra proof my room prior to her comin' here." I explained.

"You sent her a lot of mixed signals Syncere, what did you expect her to do?

"Talk it out, work it out. I mean ain't that why she's here in the first place so we can work things out? Instead she leaves after the first day without tellin' me?"

"No you left. You do want you always do when you're in an argument you leave. You left her standing in the middle of the hallway while you left the house. Me and Tracy talked to her for two hours last night when you left. She loves you so much but you keep doin' dumb shit." At that moment Tracy walked in the house still dressed in his Finish Line uniform shaking his head.

"What?" I asked with an attitude.

"Nigga you fucked up. I told you to take Kenya's shit outta your room."

"She left 'cause of that?"
"You still don't get it dude. Yo she came up here with every intention of doin' this wit'chu and in less than 24 hours you changed her mind."

"Changed her mind? Do you know what I had to risk for her to be here?"

"Do you know what she risked?"

"Not her life, not her freedom like I did two years ago."

"Yo don't blame her for that. You drove all the way to North Carolina without knowin' the whole story." Tracy defended.

"Oh and you know the whole story?"
"Yeah she told us last night. Mulan liked her but got so tired of hearin' her talk

about'chu he just went off on her."

"Ok he still hit her and he still deserved to get is ass whooped. So she didn't risk anything like I did."

"What about her education?"

"Huh?"

"Did you know UNC wasn't even on Kendra's list of schools to go to but she went there 'cause you promised her you were gonna be in North Carolina. She got into Stamford but she passed it up for you. She hates UNC and she is miserable but worst of all she just spent three years at a school she didn't want to go to, for you."

"Why didn't she tell me this? Why did she tell ya'll?"

"I don't know you'll have to ask her. Now I hope you'll listen to me now when I saw call her."

"I'll wait until tomorrow."

"Tomorrow she's gonna think you don't care. Call her right now." I dialed Kendra's number three times and three times I went straight to her voicemail.

27

Kendra and I sat across from each other at Outback Steakhouse in Southington, while we waited for our food to come not saying a word to each other. It's been two days since the fight and two days that I've slept alone wondering where she is and if she is ok. I finally called last night to apologize and Kendra agreed to have dinner with me but I get the feeling she doesn't want to be here. As she look around avoiding eye contact I fiddled with my new cell phone storing numbers and answering an occasional call or two wishing someone break the silence.

"Why'd you ask me here?" she finally said.

"I wanted to see you and apologize to you in person."

"For what?"

"For the things I said the other night."

"Don't apologize unless you mean it."
"I do. Where are you stayin'?"

"With a family who has a son in the program. They're nice people." Kendra and I engaged in some consistent dialog and when the food came we talked in between bites and I'm starting to feel good about being here with her. After dinner I drove Kenya back to her parked car the mall in Waterbury where we met and we went separate ways.

"How'd it go cut?" Tracy asked when I walked in.

"I guess it went ok. We talked and laughed a little so yeah it was aight."
"So is she comin' back?"

"I don't know I didn't ask."

"You didn't ask? Isn't that why you went in the first place?"

"Yeah. I just didn't know how to ask her. Maybe it really is a wrap. Maybe this is what was supposed to happen. I'm supposed to be wit Kenya."

"It's only a wrap if you say it's a wrap. Can you honestly say you can be with Kenya and not worry if you did everything you could with Kendra?" he asked.

"No."

"Then it's not a wrap. You gotta get her here and show her that ya'll do belong together…that is if that's what you really want. At this point you should stop takin' advice from us and do what is right for Syncere."

"I don't know what that is. I never know what that is."

"You better figure it out soon."

I thought about what Tracy had told me and I'm still as confused as I was before Kendra even got here. Nevertheless I picked up my phone and sent Kendra a text message saying; *it was great seeing you tonight & just so you know it wasn't supposed to be like this*. Not even five minutes later Ginuwine's Differences played as my ring tone.

"Why did you send me that text?" she asked.

"'Cause that is what I was thinkin' so I sent it to you."

"Why didn't you call me and tell me that?"

"I don't know."

"At the table when I kept asking what was wrong and you kept tellin' me nothing what was really going through your mind?"

"That I want you to come back home."

"Then why didn't you say that Syncere? You waited until I got all the way back to West Haven to send me a text saying something you could've said earlier tonight. You had me all that time and you said nothing. You still do that."

"Do what?"

"Instead of verbally telling me how you feel or what you're thinking you'd rather send me a text message or a poem or a letter. How can you love me when you can't verbally express yourself to me even after all this time?"

"That is just how I am Kendra and you know that."

"So is that what we're gonna do when we're married? Send text messages, emails and letters to communicate with each other?"

"No. Listen. You were right about everything and I should've taken Kenya's things out of the room of which I did. I would really like it if you came back and spent the summer with me and really give this thing the shot we talked about."

"Are you sure you're making the right choice this time?"

"Yeah."

"Syncere if I come back I don't want any bullshit between us."

"And there won't be any. Everything that happened the other night is over, done with forgotten."

"I'm already outside."

In bed with Kendra lying beside me clenching her legless teddy bear I thought about our first night in Georgia and this feels nothing like that night. With her back to me I'm not sure if it's ok to put my arm around her or how close I should get to her so instead I stayed on my side of the bed and silently wished her sweet dreams. I thought to myself I don't even know what I'm doing anymore then as I looked up into the darkness I resisted from asking "God" for help.

Throughout the week I updated my interested manager in training Noe about the things going on between Kendra and I as well as speaking to Kenya every afternoon trying to make things appear normal. For the whole week Kendra and I slept in the same bed without touching each other or saying much. The two and three hour long conversations we'd have on the phone when she was in North Carolina are replaced with two and three hour phone calls from her cell phone to someone else as she sits in her car every night. When she does that I feel nothing but pure anger and I'm convinced she's talking to Mulan. I take advantage of the opportunity to call Kenya especially as it grew closer to her graduation day.

"I wish you can be there so bad baby."

"Why can't I go?"

"Because my mom is going to be there."

"Just give me a ticket and I'll sit somewhere she can't see me. I wanna see you walk across the stage."

"I want you to see me too but I don't know."

"Aight well I'll take you out afterward."

"No can do, my mom is taking me and Christina to dinner."

"Ok so I'll see you this weekend then?"

"No can do either. I have another photo shoot with Forever 21."

"Will I be able to see you before you leave for college damn?"

"Baby don't act like that. Now you know how I was feeling when you were working so much."

"I'm workin' so much so we can live in Brazil."

"I now but you still didn't make the kind of time I wanted you to. You use to change your entire schedule to fit me but now it's work, work, work first."

"Is this your way of avoiding me? Are you tryin' to distance yourself from me?" I asked fearful at the thought of her trying to avoid me.

"No, why would I do that?"

"I don't know but I have this strange feelin' you are gonna break up with me either before you get to college or once you get there."

"Syncere, how many times did we talk about this? I said we are gonna work it out so we are gonna work it out. Stop being so paranoid you're starting to piss me off."

"I just don't wanna loose you."

"I know I know. I gotta go."

"Say it."

"I love you Syncere and yes I trust you. Bye." Kenya hung up before I could return the I love you and that doesn't fit well with me. I don't know what to make of it. She's been back in the states for three weeks and I haven't seen her yet. Photo shots here, car shows there, work, school I hope this isn't a sign as to what's to come when she goes to college. I know what she said the day before she left for London but I feel otherwise. I tried to change my train of thought because I'm a firm believer of thinking something into existence.

As I do everyday I race home from work anticipating seeing Kendra hoping things between us would be different despite the fact we talk to Tracy and M.Dot about each other more than we actually talk to one other. But today is different I'm feelin' really good. I just got paid with a huge bonus at work which allowed me to buy the new Retro Jordan 10 in white and red and I also picked up the Reebok TNG Jets Kendra saw when I took her to my store. I saw her car in the spot next to mine and I got excited.

"Hey!"

"Hey Syncere. You seem like you're in a good mood. Tracy is here already." Kendra said as she sat Indian style on the floor in front of her suitcase.

"I know he never works on paydays. Close your eyes." I said.

"Why?"

"I have a surprise for you."

"Syncere you know I don't like surprises."

"I know but just close your eyes."

"No. Can you just show me please?"

"You killin' me." I pulled the Reebok out of the Finish Line bag and handed it to her.

"You didn't get the those sneakers did you?"

"Yep."

"Syncere I told you not to."

"I know but you're like my mom. You see somethin' you like but you won't buy it 'cause you think you don't need it. So like a good son and boyfriend I get it for you."

"You didn't have to."

"I know but I wanted to so please accept them."

"Thank you."

"You're very welcome."

"Smell this." She said spraying perfume in the air.
"I like. Smell this one I just got it today."

"What's it called?"

"Burberry London. I have the Britt on the dresser."

"I know I smelled it already. I like the Britt better than the London. Since when did you get into cologne?"

"Evelyn brought me Burberry Touch a while ago and it was the only cologne that didn't irritate my skin. But Kenya introduced Burberry Britt to me a year or so ago and it's been my favorite cologne since." For a while I sat on the floor next to Kendra smelling her different perfumes and body washes picking out my favorite ones but just cherishing the time spent with her. It feels like Georgia again.

"So what are your plans for the night?" she asked.

"Actually nothin'. I was just gonna make it a blockbuster night, order some Zeng Zeng and chill."

"What is Zeng Zeng?"

"This Chinese place we love to eat at, it's the only place you can get beef rolls."

"Do they have other things?"

"Yeah the food is good. We keep a menu in the kitchen. Cut you want Zeng Zeng tonight?" I hollered at Tracy.

"Hell yeah!" Tracy bellowed from his room as Kendra and I laughed at the sound of enthusiasm in his voice.

"What are you gonna get from blockbuster?"

"I don't know. I was gonna see they have, why is there something specific you wanted to see?"

"Can you get Amistad and Rosewood?"

"Never heard of Rosewood, what is that about?"

"Rosewood? Ya'll 'bout to watch that?" Tracy asked coming into the room.

"Na she wants me to get it. Why is it good?"

"Syncere I don't think you should watch a movie like that. It might make you wanna go out and kill white people."

"Why is it a slavery movie?"

"Kinda. I can't believe you never heard of Rosewood before. Do you know what Amistad is?"

"Yeah it's that slave movie right."

"Do you know what the Amistad is?"

"One of the slave names?"

"La Amistad, it is the name of the ship that carried the slaves to New Haven Connecticut."

"Here?"

"Yes. Did you know the ship is still docked in New Haven and you can get a tour of it?"

"What? Na I didn't know that."

"How do you live here and you don't know anything about your state?"

"'Cause I hate this place."

"Well you need to go see it." She said.

"Will you go wit me?"

"Of course." Kendra said making me smile.

"Aight Cut you order the food and me and Kendra are gonna run to blockbuster."

Excited like two kids in a candy store Kendra and I jumped in the car and sped to Blockbuster, Hollywood video and best buy looking for Amistad and Rosewood until I found them.

"Oh Syncere can you get me this CD. I've been looking for this for months and I haven't got paid from the school yet but I'll pay you the money back." Kendra asked.

"Yeah, go ahead."

"You don't even know how much it costs."

"It don't matter. You can have anything you want."

"Syncere?"

"Yeah. Remember that summer I came to visit you in Georgia and you lost your job and you had such a hard time finding another one?"

"Yeah, I don't wanna remember but I do."

"Looking at you now I'm so proud of you and everything you've done for yourself. I knew that you'd find what you're good at and you seem like you love working at Finish Line."

"Thank you. That means so much comin' from you but I owe it all to you."

"No you don't. You don't owe me a thing."

"I owe you my life. When you met me I was on the path of destruction but you showed me something special and I changed. With the help of Mr. & Mrs. Williams, My Aunt Dimpsey and you I'm the man I am today. And once I get this market leader position the next stop is District Manager. I'd say another three or four years."

"I love how you stayed dedicated over the years. Dedicated to your music now this makes me really happy for you."

"You forgot dedicated to us too."
"Yeah." She said dropping her head. "Can we go get some push pops?"

"Anything you want."

　　Back at the house Tracy, Kendra and I downloaded old soul songs similar to the ones on the Soul CD I brought Kendra. We ate, joked and Kendra and I even play fought in the living room while Tracy and M.Dot looked on. In the mist of it all I am completely happy. Tracy said it would take some time for Kendra to come around and maybe she is now. Now maybe we can start having the relationship we talked about having prior to her coming.

"On July 1st I'm going home for the weekend and I'll be back on the third."

"Ok. You flyin' right?"

"Yeah. Syncere can I ask you for a favor? Can I borrow two hundred dollars for the plane ticket and I'll give it back to you when I get paid next week." Kendra asked as we got into bed.

"Yeah. Hey how 'bout Sunday I cook you breakfast."

"You still think you can cook? What are you gonna make?"

"Eggs, bacon, pancakes you know. Whatever you want."

"Just as long as you don't make grits again."
"Got'cha."

"Who does your hair? I see them done over but I never see when you have time to get it done."

"Oh I go to Evelyn's dorm up at Briarwood College to get it done. She's been doin' my hair before I went to Georgia and since I've been back home."

"Why do I remember that name?"

"You hear me yellin' at her when she's doin' my hair while we're on the phone."

"Isn't she the girl Trevor said you were going out with?" I played dumb for a minute pretending like I'm trying to remember that incident knowing full well I remember it like it was yesterday.

"Yeah, that is her."

"Did you two ever date?"

"Briefly when I moved back home, before I met Kenya. I've actually been thinkin' 'bout cuttin' it."

"Oh can I cut it please?"
"What? You wanna cut my hair? I thought you loved my hair?"

"I did when we were younger but you're getting older now and you're doing great in your career so since you want to move up you need to cut this and look like a young business man."

"I thought 'bout that too but why do you wanna cut it?"

"Because I do. So I can keep a little piece of one of your braids."

"Aight. Before you leave we'll do it."

"Really!"

"Yeah."

"Goodnight Syncere."

I left work early leaving Noe in charge so I can drive to Danbury and surprise Kenya at work while she's at Merle Norman. With flowers in hand her face lit up when she saw me stroll into her store in the middle of her finishing up a makeover.

"What are you doing here baby?" she asked before giving me a kiss.

"Just thought I'd surprise you."

"Well I'm glad you did. It feels like forever and a day since I saw you last."

"I know. You're the one with the rock star schedule." I teased.

"I know." She said laughing trying not to mess up her client's makeover.

"Miss me?"

"Yes, yes, yes."

"How much?"

"This much." She said then jumping into my arms allowing me to deliver twenty short kisses on her cheeks, lips and neck.

"Aw man baby. I wish you would've came later."

"Why?"

"You know why." She said cocking her eyebrow.

"Well I can stay. I'm in no rush to get home."

"How's everything going with Kendra?"

"It's aight I guess. Most of the time I'm at work and since I get home later than she does I shower, talk to you then might watch a little T.V. then I go to sleep on the couch. We don't talk that much, she tries to but I think she got the hint and she talks to Tracy and Michane more."

"Does Michane live there now?"

"Yeah. Her and Tracy got engaged."

"Wow, he's crazy."

"Well what do you expect? Crazy girl, crazy decision so guess how the weddin' is gonna be na mean?" I ordered Kenya and I some food from Uno's downstairs in the mall and we fed each other while no customers entered her shop for the remainder of the night. I then helped her close the store and we made love in the stockroom.

"Baby what are you doing on the 9th?"

"Nothin' why?"

"I told my mom I had to work but I really don't. I want us to go out you know something simple like a dinner and a movie?"

"Ok we can do that."

"Then afterwards who knows?" she said cocking her eyebrow again and biting her bottom lip.

"That's cool. Kendra will be gone so that's cool."

"You're only saying yes 'cause Kendra is gonna be gone?"

"No. I'm just sayin' she'll be gone."

"So if she was here you would'a said no?"

"Babe she's here now and where am I? I'm right here."

"So if I said I wanna go back to your house right now and make love to you you'd be down for it?"

"Yeah. I never said you couldn't come to the house you just don't come. I gave you a key for a reason so if you wanna come by then come by I welcome it. Shit let's go I miss making love to my baby."

"You're lucky I'm gonna respect her enough not to throw our relationship up in her face like that."

"Ok but like I said if you wanna come by then come by."

I lay half asleep on one side of the bed and Kendra on the other like it's been for the past month thinking to myself this doesn't feel like a relationship trying to blossom. It feels like two longtime friends sharing a room and a bed nothing more.

Faintly I heard Usher's Seduction playing on my cell phone then I realized it's Kenya's ring tone. I looked over at Kendra who is still asleep and I crept out of bed, grabbed my phone and snuck quietly out of the room.

"Hey babe, what's wrong?"

"Why are you whispering?"

"I'm not, I was sleep."

"Come to Danbury."

"Now."

"Yes. I had a nightmare now I can't get back to sleep so I need you to tire me out."
"You're a freak." I said laughing.

"Yeah but you love it."

"I sure do. I'm on my way."

I looked at Kendra as she looked at me while still in bed not saying a word to each other for a while. I examined her lips, the arch in her eyebrows and every other feature of her face the same way I did when we were in Georgia and she's beautiful.

"What are you looking at?" she asked.

"Nothin'."

"You lie."

"No I'm not. You hungry?"

"Yeah."

"I'ma get up and cook aight."

"Where can I go to wash my clothes?"

"There is a place down the street I'll show you were it is."

"No I'll find it."

"Hey wanna go to the park with me later?"

"What's at the park?"

"A park. There is a nice one near Meriden. I thought we could go and just chill. You know get outta the house for a while it's a nice day outside."

"Ok." As promised I cooked breakfast; sausage, eggs, bacon and pancakes all while cleaning up the room as I waited for Kendra to come back from the laundry mat. I looked at the clock when my stomach started rumbling and it just turned one' clock meaning Kendra has been gone for the past three hours and I'm pissed. The food is cold and the orange juice is warm and I'm hungry as hell.

"You can't get too mad she told you she was goin' to wash her clothes." M.Dot said.

"M. Three hours though. She doesn't have that many clothes to wash. She knew I was cookin' breakfast so why would she stay this late or why couldn't she wait until I was done?"

"I don't know you'd have to ask her."

"Fuck that I'm not." I sat in the living room staring at the television getting mad at every passing second until I heard the door open. Kendra casually walked in the house and went straight to the room to put her clothes down before she came back into the living room.

"Did you eat yet?"

"Um no I was waitin' for you."

"Oh you could've ate without me."

"The whole point was for us to have breakfast together like I told you last night."

"Sorry."

"You're not gonna eat?"

"I'm not hungry, I ate while I was waiting for my clothes to finish."

"Are you serious?"

"Yeah but I think it was sweet you waited." Inside I am going bananas right how at the fact Kendra knew I was cooking for her and she ate out anyway while I stayed here starving waiting on her. Sweet? Who the fuck cares about sweet? That was just plain downright disrespect. I ended up eating the entire breakfast myself pissed off.

"I'm sorry Syn."
"It ain't'cha fault M. but thanks." I walked in my room to my closet bypassing Kendra folding her clothes on my bed. I picked out an outfit and sat it in the kitchen to iron it.

"Michane said her and Tracy are going to an amusement park. Lake…Lake something."

"Lake Campounce."

"Yeah, you wanna go with them?"

"Not really I thought we were goin' to the park."

"Syncere why do you really want to go to the park?"

"So you and I can have some alone time so we can talk."

"Talk about what? We can talk right here. What do you want to talk about?"

"You're missin' the point. I wanna chill wit'chu only you. Know what we can go to Lake Campounce."

"Syncere if I wasn't here would you have gone to a park?"
"Uh yeah."

"Really. So Tracy can vouch for you just going to a park."

"Tracy doesn't know every little thing I do in my spare time. I remember the night we went to that park and we laid on the jungle gym and just talked na mean? Just me and you so I thought that would be something nice for us to do together since everything we've done up to this point as included Tracy and Michane and everyone else."

"Fine we can go to the park."

"Na I'm good. Don't go 'cause you wanna make me happy, I want you to go 'cause you want to. You wanna go to the amusement park so that is where we are goin'." I said walking out of the room.

"Why do you always do that?" Kendra asked chasing behind me.

"What did I do this time?"

"You walk away from me every time we disagree or you don't get your way."

"No I don't."

"Yes you do. You did it when we were in Georgia and you did it when I first got here. You always talk about talking and working things out so let's work things out."

"There is nothin' to work out. You wanna go to the amusement park so that is where we're goin'. We're doin' what'chu wanna do." I said flopping on the couch.

"Here."

"What is this?" I asked taking the pen and paper she handed me.

"Write down what you honestly want to do and I'll write down what I want to do."

"I already know what you wanna do Kendra."

"I want to go to the park with you."

"No you don't. You're sayin' that so we can "work this out". I changed my mind, I wanna go to the amusement park."

" You're lying. If that is true then write it down." I took the piece of paper and scribbled down *the park* and handed it to her. Kendra got up and threw the pieced of paper in the trash.

"What did you wanna do?"

"The same thing as you so we're goin' to the park."

"Now you're lying." I reached in the trash and picked out Kendra's piece of paper that read *whatever you want to do*. Before I could say anything Kendra left out of the house. I watched as her car door opened but she never closed it so I went out there.

"You lied."

"I didn't lie. I said the same thing you wanted to do and you wrote the park so that's what I said. I thought you wanted to go to the amusement park?"

"I lied."

"I knew you were that's why I had you write it down."
"What did that accomplish?"

"Syncere you never come out and say what it is that you want. You always change things to accommodate me, for once I wanted you to tell me what Syncere wanted to do. So the only way I can get you to admit what it really was you wanted to do was to trick you like I just did."

"Why do you have to go through all that?"

"'Cause you never tell me how you really feel."

"I told you I wanted to go to the park from the jump so that wasn't really called for. You want me to tell you how pissed off I was that you ate knowin' that I was cookin'?"

"Why were you mad?"

"Are you serious? You knew when we woke up I was cookin', I told you last night. If you were gonna be that long washin' cloths you should'a called and told me. Then you stroll in and you tell me you already ate, that was fucked up."

"I'm sorry."

"I'm over it now."

"So what did you want to talk to me about when we got to the park?"

"Nothin', it don't even matter anymore."

"Tell me."

"Na."

"Syncere…tell me." She said searching my face for an answer.

"I wanted to talk 'bout us, me and you."

"What about us?"

"What's goin' on between us. We don't act like we're tryin' to be a couple. We sleep on opposite sides of the bed, we barley talk and I get the feelin' you really don't wanna be here but you have to be 'cause you have nowhere else to go. So what's good?"

"Syncere we have to get to know each other before we can try to be a couple."

"Kendra we've known each other goin' on six years now."

"Yes but we know nothing about each other. You're not the same man I knew back in Georgia and I'm not the same woman. I mean I'm a Jehovha's witness and you're an atheist, I bet you don't even know why I am the way I am because I know I don't know why you lost faith. We don't know anything about each other. A telephone relationship is not enough to say yes we are going to try to be together for the rest of our lives. So right now we are just friends."

"Why didn't you say all this before you left? It's like you're a totally different person now that you are here. You talk 'bout me switchin' up, you switched up big time."

"I owe that to you. You said you didn't know if you were making the right choice and that made me think if I was making the right choice."

"Between who? Me and Mulan?"

"No, my life in general. I had to ask myself if you are the man I'm supposed to be with or are you the man I want to be with. If you look at it they're two different things."

"And...?"

"And I don't know. I don't know what I want and it's hard to figure that out when you walk around with an attitude all the time." She accused.

"I be tryin' to talk and make things pleasant but you don't respond. Shit we don't even sleep together. If the bed wasn't so big just maybe I can get close to you."

"I told you I'm celibate and as a Jehovah's witness I'm not supposed to be that close to you. My granddaddy always told me not to lay in the same bed with a man unless you're married."

"What the fuck? Since when did you follow that? To my knowledge we did that in Atlanta and I didn't hear anything about your granddaddy then. And I'm not sayin' I wanna be close to you so we can have sex I just wanna hold you the way I use to."

"I only did it in Atlanta because I was trying to please you, I thought that is what you wanted."

"You only made love to me 'cause you thought that is what I wanted?"
"Yes."

"You're right. You don't know shit about me 'cause if you did you wouldn't've thought that. All I wanted all I've ever wanted from you was your heart; it was never about sex, never. I didn't even call what we did sex...I called it makin' love. Come to think of it I wouldn't even bring it up unless you did and if it wasn't for you sayin' anything about it that mornin' we'd probably be virgins to each other to this day. I bet that would fair well with your Jehovah's witnesses huh? How long have you been a Jehovah's witness?"
"Two years."

"What did Mulan say 'bout that when you told him? Exactly 'cause I know you laid down with him."

"How do you know that?"

"'Cause if a nigga like that ain't gettin' no ass he'll find it somewhere else and you've been jealous of the bitches he ran around with since freshman year. So if you made love to me 'cause you thought that is what I wanted then I know you fucked him to keep him around."

"If you knew me like you say you do you wouldn't've said that."

"I guess the ever so intelligent Kendra is right again. Neither one of us knows shit about each other. Thanks." I said walking away.

28

The rest of the week I slept on the couch and let Kendra have the bed to herself out of respect to her and her "religion". The thought of us not knowing each other like I thought we did wrecked my mind all week putting me in a pissed off mood every single day. I took my anger out on my staff, talked Noe and Derricks ears off about the situation and performed poorly as a manager but I don't give a fuck. The only light at the end of the tunnel is tonight when I get to see Kenya now that Kendra flew back to North Carolina for the weekend. Since Kenya expressed her like for me when I get dressed up I get cleaned up nice every time we go out just like she is always. I put on my black dress pants and lavender dress shirt with my black fossil watch and checked myself out in the mirror. I made it a priority to get my hair redone and a shape up today before she comes over.

"Goin' out wit Kenya huh?" Sharell asked. Sharell is Michane's twin sister who's been hanging out around the house everyday since our forth of July cook out, the same girl Tracy has been trying to hook me up with for the past year.

"Yep."

"What about Kendra?" Michane asked.

"You heard her, we're just friends. I sleep in the living room, she sleeps in my bed and in three more weeks she goes back to North Carolina and we're good."

"That's not what you want is it?" Sharell said.
"What I want is beeping right now so I have to go." As always Kenya is dressed to perfection, hair down, short skirt in heels and a tight sleeveless shirt.

"You drive." She said hoping over into the passenger seat of her silver SUV. We drove with her hand locked with mine to Plainfield to catch a showing of Jarhead but the next showing is after eleven so we decided to drive around to find a restaurant we haven't eaten at yet. Then the rain came down so hard that the drops were the size of water balloons.

"How 'bout that place?"

"You ever eat there?"

"It looks nice, it says Italian food. Wanna go in?"

"Sure baby." I parked as close to the crib as possible since neither Kenya or I have a coat or umbrella. When Kenya and I opened the car doors where was a huge puddle of water on each of our side so I ran around the car to Kenya and lifted her out of the car and carried her to the threshold of the restaurant. There is a couple sitting by the window that smiled when they saw me.

The mom and pop Italian place has a nice homey feel to it. It is small consisting of no more than fifteen tables that have pictures of Italy tastefully placed on the walls while Sinatra plays in the background.

"This place is nice." I complimented.

"Yeah I know."

"Good choice baby."

"Thank you." Our server must be the owner because she is an older woman dressed in regular clothes but she is pleasant nevertheless. She complimented us as a beautiful couple then gave us a brief history of the restaurant and its cuisine. We ordered appetizers and engaged in conversation.

"Baby I didn't get my period."

"How late are you?"

"A week. I should've gotten it after the night you came to Danbury but I haven't yet."

"Don't worry 'bout it you will. You know how your cycle gets messed up with all those pills you gotta take for your cancer. By the way how are you feelin'."

"I'm fine baby. It is sweet that you call me everyday and ask me how I'm feelin' but I'm not gonna die so don't worry."
"You're my baby I'm supposed to worry so you can focus on what you have to do."

"Who's gonna do your worrying?" she asked.

"I can handle that too."

"Let me help you."

"Not tonight. I'll worry for the both of us, you have the night off." Kenya smiled and kissed me and my stomach did back flips.

"What if I do get pregnant?"

"I'll be the happiest man in the universe. I'm already ready to have a family."

"You'd make a great father but I don't think I' ready to be a mom yet. What about school and modeling?"

"Let's just say hypothetically that you do get pregnant before college or while you're in college. Let's do this summer you find our you're pregnant we'll do this. Take the first year off and work a little so we can save up some money then when the baby comes you start school next semester. By that time I'll be a market leader and I'll ask to get transferred to Rhode Island or in that general vicinity so I can still work and you can still go to school."

"What about the baby?"

"Day care. Don't take any night classes that way you can be home at least by three or four and I will be home with you both at night."

"So you got it all worked out huh? What about if I get pregnant while in school?"

"Same thing really except you'll finish out the semester while I still transfer up their get an apartment so you can finish."

"You've thought this out huh?"

"I think about it a lot."

"Oh really? You trying to get me knocked up?"

"If I say yes would you get mad?"

"I'll kill you." She said smiling.

"I'm not tryin' to get'chu pregnant but if you are I'll be happy as hell."

"You would want me to have the baby?"
"Hell yeah. I don't believe in abortion but more importantly how can I tell you to get rid of something our love created?"

"I don't know."

"I wouldn't. Can you imagine how beautiful our child will be? The doctor is gonna have to put our baby in a room by his or herself because all the other parents will be jealous."

"That's right baby! You're so good to me, I'm so lucky."

"Yes you are."

"Oh I love the modesty baby."

"I'm playin'. Truthfully I'm the lucky one. When this does happen whether its now or after you graduate, what are you gonna do about your mother? You know she despises the fact we're together."

"Oh did I tell you she found the prom pictures under my pillow last week?"

"Under your pillow?"

"Yes baby I sleep with a picture of you under my pillow every night. Anyway she found them and asked Alana if we're still together."

"What did Alana say?"

"She said she didn't know."

"I love Alana she's the dream little sister."

"I know. My mom didn't say anything to me though."

"You think she will?"

"No. It's been almost two years I think she is accepting it. She won't say it but I know she is."

"So answer my question."

"I love my mother but she always talks about sending me back to Brazil and disowning me. So if she was to disown me because I had your baby then I'm better off without her in my life."

"You would throw away your relationship with your mom for me and our child?"

"Wouldn't you?"

"Yeah but it'll be easier for me."

"Why?"

"'Cause I hated my mom for eight years but you and yours have had a wonderful relationship until me. I feel guilty about the way things are now."

"Don't. She thinks she can tell me how to run my life and who I can and can't be with. She can't do that."

"I love you."

"I love you too. Do you think before we move to Brazil we can spend a couple years in California?" She asked.

"You really wanna go to California don't'chu?"

"Yes."

"Why didn't you go to school there?"

"Because my uncle is paying for me to go to school just as long as I stay on the east coast."

"Got'cha. Do this. Get a scholarship and then move to Cali and I'll be right behind you."

"You mean that?"

"Yes. I want you to have everything you want. As long as you're with me I wanna do what it takes to keep you happy."

Kenya and I stumbled into my apartment like two drunken people fresh out of a bar after a night out on the town. We held each other up as we walk pass Sharrell and Michane sitting on the couch in the living room. They shot dirty looks and smacked their teeth at the sight of Kenya and I but we don't care it only made us laugh harder. Kenya lay on my bed staring at me as I stood over her enjoying the view. We took a couple of pictures on my new camera phone then made love as if it was our first time. Just like that I'm watching her get dressed as we made plans for the next time we'd see each other.

"Fuckin' Kenya while Kendra isn't here. I wonder what she'd think about that?" Michane asked as I sat down in the living room.

"Ask me if I care."

"You care."

"If you say so." I responded.

"So that's it with you and Kendra?"

"She said we're just friends so that is what we are just friends."

"So what is Kenya?"

"My girlfriend."

"Does Kendra know you have a girlfriend?"

"She says as far as she knows I always have a girlfriend so it doesn't matter either way."

"Umm. I never thought I'd see ya'll like this." Michane said shaking her head.

"Me either. For all this she could'a stayed her ass in West Haven where she went the day she left."

"What are you gonna do?"

"I ain't gonna do shit. I'ma be her friend and wait until she leaves. It was a mistake agreeing to let her come here in the first place. It almost cost me Kenya."

"If I were you I'd pray on it."

"Do what? I gave that religion shit up a long time ago."
"What happened? Kenya told us that you use to be into the whole church thing and now you're an atheist."

"To make a long story short before I met Kenya I was loosing my faith 'cause the church I was goin' to was so corrupted. I told ya'll 'bout the two girls I fucked outside the church right?"

"No!" they said surprised.

"Oh that's another story. Anyway Kendra helped me get my faith in God back na mean? I got baptized 'cause of her na mean I got my shit straight 'cause of her. So after talkin' to her 'bout the relationship with my mom and how my life was goin' she encouraged me to pray and have faith. Then after a while I turned to God and began to pray that our relationship grows strong and that he'd make her my wife. But when all that shit happened two years ago it made me believe that all my faith was in vain. There is no God and therefore I was prayin' to air 'cause nothin' I ever said got answered."

"Just 'cause your relationship with Kendra didn't work don't mean there is no God."

"I met her in a church and I changed my thinkin', my way of life because she believed in God so much. She made me believe. But it isn't just the situation with her it's even the shit that happened with my mom and her husband when I was younger. I've been takin' shit my whole life and the entire time I was prayin' to some "God" to make shit better. Kendra has taught me a bunch of important things, one she isn't for me and two there is no God. I make the choices that define my life not some imaginary figure the world is fooled into beleivin'."

"I think you're takin' this a little further than it has to go." Sharell said

"Think what'chu want but for the past six years of my life I've pushed away and hurt countless women who could'a potentially been the woman for me. I'm not loosin' another one, I'm not loosin' Kenya."

"If that's who you think you should be with then go ahead but I think you need to try harder with Kendra."

"I'm good. I'm not 'bout chasin' no girl and I've been chasin' this one too long."

"Syncere, telephone."

"Take a message. I'm countin'."

"She said it's important."

"Is it Kenya?"

"I don't think so. Just stop askin' questions and answer the phone." My assistant Mary demanded.

"Yo."

"Syncere its Sharell."
"What's good?"

" She didn't want me to but I called to tell you Kendra's in the hospital."

"What? What's wrong?" I asked as my heartbeat sped up and the room seemed to close in around me.

"Remember how she's been complaining about her side hurtin'? Well she as an absist on her kidney."
"What the hell is an absist?"

"It's like a little bump but if it gets bigger or if it bursts it can be bad so she has to stay in the hospital for a few days."

"Aight I'm on my way."

"No, no, no. Stay there and let her call you. I wasn't supposed to tell you stupid."

"She's not gonna call." I said.

"Well if she doesn't then she doesn't. I thought you didn't care anymore."

"Shut up. Keep me posted. Go to the house and get her some clothes."

"Already did that. Calm down me and Michane are rotating our shifts here so we can keep an eye on her. We got this."

"Aight." I hung up the phone with this strange feeling of concern in my stomach that I know is going to pick at me all day, I have to get out of here.

"Everything aight?" Noe asked.

"Na."

"What happened?"

"Kendra's in the hospital."

"Damn dude this saga with you and her never ends does it? What you do black her eye? Throw her down some stairs?"

"Na, it's somethin' 'bout her liver."

"Well go to the hospital and check on her and me and Mary will hold it down if Mark calls."
"Na I'm not supposed to know."

"Why?"

"She didn't want me to know."

"Yo I'm tellin' you somethin' ain't right with that girl. Why wouldn't she want you to know that she is in the hospital?" Noe asked.

"I wish I knew. But considerin' all the shit that has been goin' on I think she thought I wouldn't come."

"What else has been goin' on?"

"Well you already know we barley talk and every night she goes out to her car to talk on the phone for hours na mean? But I walk in the house yesterday and I see a Finish Line employee folder on the couch with her name on it. Tracy hired her at his store and nobody told me."

"You think Tracy and her messin' around?"

"Hell no, Michane will kill'em both. Shit she'd kill Tracy twice."

"But how do you know? He hired her without tellin' you and she goes to him for everything. How do you know Tracy ain't tellin' her what you tell him? He could be playin' both sides. You never know, he could want her and instead of him tryin' to help you he could be helpin' himself." Noe said painting a very likely scenario.

"Please, don't nobody want Tracy expect for his crazy girlfriend." Mary said butting in.

"How's everything with you and Kenya?" she asked.

"Man she really a ride or die chick for real for real. She's been so understandin', so patient with everything and the wild part is I thought she'd flip out and break up with me over this."

"I would've."

"Nobody asked you fuckin' Asian. But she really holdin' it down for me. She don't be callin' all crazy like what'chu doin', where you at. It's like she's not worried."

"Should she be?" Noe asked.

"Nope. I got three more weeks until this bitch is gone and I can't wait."

"So now she's a bitch?"

"I just call it how I see it."

"I told you when I met her I didn't like her, you definitely should stay with Kenya."

"M. you don't like any chick when you meet them."

"That's a lie. I liked Kenya when I first met her and I still do."

"Yo if stuff don't work out with you and Kenya can I have her?" Noe joked but I didn't find it in the least funny.

"I'll fuckin' kill you."

I resisted the urge to go by the hospital last night so for the first time in a month and a half I slept in my bed and enjoyed it. I tossed a little thinking about Kendra laid up in a hospital bed but I thought more about Kenya and how mature she's handling the situation. Kenya's every man's dream girl and she really doesn't have to sit around waiting for me to stop chasing my past.

"Good mornin'." Michane said while I walked in the kitchen to raid the refrigerator.

"What's good M.? How is Kendra doin'?"

"She aight but she talkin' crazy."

"What do you mean?"

"Don't tell her I told you but you know she still talks to Mulan right?"

"I kinda figured it."

"Yeah. So Sharell says that she talks to Mulan all the time but the crazy part is Kendra and Sharrell had a conversation last night."

"'Bout what?"

"'Bout'chu. You know my sister likes you right?" Michane reveled.

"No. Is that why she's been hangin' 'round the house all the time?"

"Yeah. Well apparently Kendra told Sharell that she can have you after Kendra leaves."

"What!"

"Don't say nothin' to either of them."

"Na I'm not but what kinda shit it that? Who is she to give someone else permission to "have" me when she leaves. See I told ya'll she didn't come up here to be wit me 'cause if she did she wouldn't be doin' stupid shit like this. Who the fuck does she think she is?"

"I know Tracy was sayin' the same thing. I guess you were right, call it a wrap dude."

"Na it been a wrap but I got somethin' for her ass when she gets back."

"Don't hit her."

"Why does everyone think I'ma hit her for?"

"'Cause we all know you and you a violent dude Syncere. I've seen you pissed off and it gets me scared." Michane said trembling.

Two days ago, right before Kenya and I were about to give each other a work out, Kendra called telling me that she was admitted to the hospital. I seemed a little concerned but it was only to get her off the phone so I could enjoy what little time I have with Kenya as I have been in a salty mood since Michane told me what Kendra and Sharell has in store. Today Kendra came back to my apartment to welcome arms on the behalf of Tracy, Michane and Sharrell but I'm less enthusiastic. However I am excited at what I have in store for Kendra. She wants Sharrell to be with me so I'm going to make is seem that way. For the next three weeks I'm going to make it seem like Sharrell and I are the cutest couple alive unbeknown to either of them, not even Tracy or Michane.

"Cut we ordered pizza so go get it." Tracy said.

"Who's comin' with me?" Everyone looked around but no one said a word. I noticed Sharrell looking directly at the television so I asked her.

"Me?"

"Yeah you. You the only one in here named Sharell ain't it? Com'on." I nudged by locking my arm with Sharell's as we walked out of the house. Since she's been hanging around the house Sharell hasn't said more than three words to me at once so I want to see if there is any truth to what Michane was saying.

"So things aren't workin' like you planned huh?" She said before I even turned the car on.

"You'd know. You, Tracy and Michane talk to her more than I do."

"Trust me I know what you're goin' through. I just got out of a serious relationship myself." By the time Sharell and I reached Pizza Hut in Watertown I had explained the Kendra saga as if she is oblivious to the situation. In between the conversation Sharell repeated the words *you singing' my song right now* and by the time we were on our way back I knew what Michane told me is true. Sharrell and I walked into the house laughing loud as if we are in our own little world to Tracy, Michane and Kendra sitting in the living room.

"Damn cut! What took ya'll so long?"

"Sharell and I were talkin' 'bout runnin' away and eloping." I joked.

"Hear that!"

"Hear that!" I mocked. I didn't have to glance out the corner of my eye to know Kendra is making a mean face, I can feel the negative energy coming from behind me. Instead of eating in the living room with everyone else Kendra took her pizza in my room and stayed in there while we watched Coming to America. I sat on the couch with Tracy on one side of me and Sharell on the other purposely laughing a little louder and harder at the funny parts. Ironically Sharell laughed just as hard at the things I did. Each time we laughed Sharell got a little closer then a little closer and a little closer until we were almost joined at the shoulders. Kendra stomped her way in and out of the kitchen, living room and bathroom a couple of times cutting her eyes at me whenever I looked at her. I'm laughing in my head at how upset she is becoming so I continued with what I am doing.

"Cut, what are you doin'?" Tracy whispered.

"Nothin'. What are you talkin' 'bout?"

"You and Sharell. First ya'll go out for pizza and ya'll come back inseparable. What's goin' on?"

"Nothin'. Sharell good peoples."

"All of a sudden she good peoples? She been here everyday for two months and now she cool peoples?"

"Why you trippin'? Before Kendra got here you been tryin' to get me to hook up wit her so when Kendra leave I might just do the damn thing."

"What about the white…I mean Brazilian chick?"

"Two years and you don't know her name yet? She goin' to school so it's whatever na mean?" I lied.

"Hear that! Cut finally listenin' to the boss."

"Yeah. I might be late but I listen."

"'Bout time. Know what that means right?"

"What?"

"Twin weddin'!"

"Whoa, whoa. I ain't sayin' all that. I told you if I didn't marry Kendra or Kenya then I'm not gettin' married at all. I'm not gonna fall in love, fuck love."

"We'll see you can't stop what God has in store."

"I really wish ya'll get off this God shit…fuck God."

"Wow. I'm goin' to sit over here on that note. I don't want to get hit my the lighting' that is intended for you."

"If there's really a God then I welcome the bolt." I said looking up in the air.

"Somethin' is really wrong wit'chu."

"No. For the first time in my life I know who and what I want. I know what is real and what isn't real. I'm in control now."

"Syncere can I talk to you in the room for a minute?" Kendra asked interrupting our whispering.

"Yeah, I'll be there in a minute."

"Now please."

"Ohh cut you better go now."

"Please. I ain't scared."

"Syncere!"

"Comin'." I strolled into my room as Kendra is standing with her back to the door.

"Shut the door please."

"Aight what's good?"

"Do you like Sharell?"

"What?" I said sounding surprised.

"Do you like Sharell?"

"No."

"You sure act like you do. You two look like best friends."

"Why 'cause we're laughin' at a movie?"

"Ya'll haven't stopped laughing since ya'll came back from Pizza Hut. What did ya'll talk about in the car?"

"Nothin' really."

"Are you sure you don't like her?"

"I'm sure. I'm tryin' to make shit right wit'chu so tell me how I can like Sharell. For real for real she ain't even my type like that. Are you jealous?"

"No. If you like her just say you like her but don't be throwing it up in my face."
"Well I don't like her aight?"

"Syncere what's going on between us?"

"What do you mean?"

"You didn't even come see me at the hospital when I called and now you're acting like you don't want me around. If you don't want me around just say so 'cause I have somewhere I can go."
"If I didn't want you here then I would tell you but don't use Sharell as an excuse to leave or the excuse to get into an argument. If you'd pay me any attention I wouldn't be on the couch laughin' it up wit Sharell I'll be laughin' it up wit'chu."

"What does that mean?"

"It means you're the one talkin' 'bout us bein' friends and gettin' to know each other but you're the one barricaded in the room all the time or you sit so far away from me as if you really dislike me. We were supposed to be tryin' to make this work so what happened? I apologized about Kenya's picture being up and I took her clothes out of the closet so what more do you want?"

"I don't want anything Syncere. I don't understand you, I don't understand what goes on in your head."

"What? Where is this comin' from?"

"You are so confident and passionate and you know exactly where you want your career to go but when it comes to your love life you don't know which way is up."

"And how did you come to that conclusion?"

"One minute you don't know if you're making the right choice and the next you want to be with me. I don't know if that is going to change from day to day."

"Well what 'bout'chu?"

"What about me?"

"One minute you wanna be with me, the next minute you don't think you're the women for me then the next you wanna be friends so we can get to know each other. What's up with that?" I said.

"Syncere I would love for us to be friends but I seriously don't think I'm the woman you need or want, Kenya is."

"And how do you know that and you don't even know her? Never even held a conversation with the girl. You're making blanket statements."

"I just do. After this summer nothing else between us will happen. You'll go off and become wildly successful at Finish Line, become a District Manager and one day I'll get those flowers. Me? The same will happen, I'll achieve what I've been working for and just maybe I'll send you the flowers but in between we'll talk and keep in touch but we will only remain friends, nothing more."

"So that's it huh? Just like that? We throw away six years just like that?"

"Syncere we are not throwing away anything. Face it we just grew apart and we both have changed too much. But over the past six years you have taught me so much, you've been there for me like no other guy I've ever been with and I really appreciate it. But the type of woman I am now doesn't fit the type of man you are. Two years ago we were ok but too much has happened and I don't want us to drag this out longer than it has to be." Kendra stood firm with her comments, as she looked at me emotionless, cold and unaffected by her own words unlike me as I am dying inside.

"Remember when you asked me what's the worst thing you can do to me?"

"Yes."

"You remember what that thing was?"

"Yes…stop loving you."

"Yep. Now I know how that feels and I don't have to wonder anymore."

"Syncere I didn't say I don't love you, I…"

"You don't love me the way I love you and love goes two ways. Goodnight Kendra."

"Where are you going?"

"For a drive."

"Why do you always leave when a conversation doesn't go your way?"

"What do you care?"

"I care about you very much. I don't have to be your girlfriend to care about you."
"If you're not my girlfriend it really doesn't mean anything to me. I want you the way I want you and if I can't have you the way I want you then I don't want you at all."

"You use to say if you couldn't have me the way you wanted you'd take me anyway you can get me."
"You put it best when you said we have changed too much. I use to pray, I use to do a lot of things."

"When you stopped praying everything got worse."

"Everything was already worse when I was praying, I just acted like it wasn't."

Driving around Waterbury aimlessly in circles thinking and thinking and thinking trying to grasp on the inevitable but more importantly try to figure out why I'm so miserable inside. I still have Kenya who's been right by my side through all of this so I have every reason in the world to be happy. I can finally give my love and myself to Kenya one hundred percent without having any doubts or what if's in my mind about Kendra but this doesn't feel right. Now that I know where Kendra and I stand indefinitely I know inside she'll become dead to me. When she leaves she'll be out of sight out of mind and I can move on with my life but for some oddly reason I feel like my mother just died. The fire and the fight is hard to escape but I always told myself that if Kendra ever said it'll never go down again I'll let the ball go, the only problem is I can't. I can't just accept that she won't be Mrs. Syncere Washington or the fact that one day the woman I've loved since fifteen will forever be in the arms of another man, one who will never possibly love her as much as I do.

I walked into a house full of people when I got home from work forgetting that today is Sunday and we normally have everyone over for dinner. I walked right passed Tracy, Michane, Quincy, Dorian, Sharell, Kendra, Sean, Natalie, Wes, Mook and all the kids and headed right to my room without returning the greeting from everyone. Since Kendra and I talked the other night I haven't been in a sociable mood so I kicked off my shoes and flopped on my bed. Through my closed door I could still hear laughter but it was hearing Kendra's laughter that upset me the most and made me pull out my cell until I remembered Kendra is in London again. I popped in the old school R&B Kendra and I had made then took out a picture of her when she was in high school. Her hair was braided long and she wore a beautiful black dress with a content smile on her face, one of my favorite pictures. I lay on my bed staring at it listening to Wyclef's 911 remembering how hearing that song makes feel. I didn't fight back the tears falling but I did fight back the urge to get on my knees and pray to a God I know isn't there.

I awoke in complete darkness and silence yet I can still hear laughter coming from the living room. I looked at my watch, eight fifteen and decided I've been anti-social enough. I went to put Kendra's picture back in my album but it isn't there. I look under the pillow, on the side of the bed, under the bed but it is gone. I don't remember hearing anyone come in my room but maybe Kendra took it.

"Cut 'bout time you came out. We thought you were dead. You make the day today?" Tracy asked when I walked into the living room squinting my eyes from the light.

"Hell yeah."

"What's wrong then?" Quincy asked."

"Just doin' some thinkin'. You leavin'?"

"Yeah man I gotta work in the mornin'. Yo did I tell you Nadege is gettin' married?"

"Are you serious?"

"Yep."

"To Amistad?" Everyone started laughing.

"Yeah to that nigga." Dorian confirmed.

"See I should'a fucked her when I had the chance. That's what I get for tryin' to be a fuckin' gentleman."

"Yea. I don't know why you didn't. But I'll get at'chu cut."

"Aight." Quincy and I did our Wolf Pak handshake and he and Dorian carried little Quincy out. Everyone already left leaving only the people who live with me in the living room. I sat down in my blue office chair next to Kendra who then got off the floor, walked to the room and closed the door. I huffed and rolled my eyes growing more and more agitated with how she is acting.

"You can't get mad at nobody but yourself cut."

"What?"

"Michane, you and Sharell go in the room while I talk to Syncere."

"Aight so how am I fuckin' up?"

"Dude all this today was for you and you stayed in your room listening to Ereyka Badu all night."

"This was for me?"

"Yeah. I was talkin' to Kendra 'bout what to make tonight and since you like that Italian shit her and Michane made chicken Parmesan and a cake and madd shit that you like and you acted like a bitch on her period. You always talk 'bout Kendra not payin' you attention and actin' like you don't exist and you do some dumb shit like this. Now you pissin' me off."

"Fuck that. For the past four days we haven't said two words to each other so today I'm 'pposed to magically know she wants to be sociable wit me? I ain't got time for all the games she playin'."

"Nigga she ain't playin' no games you are. You're so wishy-washy with everything. She ain't gonna sit back and wait 'til you figure out what it is that you want."

"I know what I want!" I said standing up. "I know exactly want I want. I want a woman who doesn't want to be with me, a woman who passed me off to your sister in law after she leaves. A woman whose picture I go to sleep with. I wanna move to North Carolina, get married, have a son and live happily ever after with the bitch in my room right now."

"That shit looked suspect."

"What did?"

"You sleepin' wit her picture. She told me 'bout it and for real for real that shit looked like it was staged."

"Fuck you and fuck her 'cause it wasn't it just so happened like that. I was lookin' at it and I fell asleep. Now I know who took it."

"Yeah she took it, she said it freaked her out."

"Again she tells you everything and me nothin'."

"That's 'cause you always walk away. Aight know what? I'ma call her out here so ya'll can talk and I'ma make sure nobody walks away. Kendra!" Tracy yelled.

"Yes." She said from the hallway.

"Com'er please. You and this nigga gotta talk 'cause both ya'll walkin' 'round here miserable as fuck. He tells me shit, you tell me what you feel but ya'll ain't talkin' to each other so we gon' to this right now." Kendra sat Indian style on the floor while I swiveled back and forth in my office chair but no one said a word so I broke the silence.

"Why do you talk to Tracy more than you talk to me?"

"He listens and doesn't try to dominate the conversation like you do. Plus you walk around with an attitude all the time and that makes it hard for me to approach you."

"Bullshit I'm fine when I walk in here, my attitude come from you. I only get that way when I'm tryin' to be cordial wit'chu and you don't respond."

"That's your problem Syncere, you want people to respond the way you want, do what you want, think what you want and it doesn't work that way." She explained.

"It ain't even like that. I expect the woman who says she loves me to act like it."

"What do you want Syncere? You want me to hang onto your arm, giggle at your jokes, tell you I love you before we go to sleep and leave for work in the morning? What do you want?"

"You're missin' the fuckin' point...fuck it."

"Na cut you wanna talk so talk, don't say fuck it." Tracy said trying to keep me talking.

"I want us to be the way we were in Georgia."

"So you want to have sex with me? Because all the arguing we do now we did in Georgia, the only thing we don't do now is have sex."

"There you go again. If I wanted sex I have a plethora of bitches to call so it ain't even like that. In Georgia we spent ninety percent of our time together. Yeah we argued but every night we lay in the bed and talked it out 'cause we never wanted to go to sleep mad at each other. The next day we got up as if nothin' happened, the slate was wiped clean and we went on with enjoyin' each other."

"I told you I'm different now and Georgia was a mistake."

"What? A mistake? Fuck does that mean?"

"I mean just what I said it was a mistake. We should've never had sex and I should've never come down there. I did a lot of things that summer that I should've. I should've gotten the tattoo, I should've gone to school at UNC or even consider transferring to Emory. 'Cause when I did all that it wasn't enough for you and it wasn't going to keep me with you."

"What are you talkin' 'bout?"

"I talked to my advisors to transfer my credits to Emory just so I could be closer to you. I passed up going to Stamford so I'd be in North Carolina where you said you were going to be. Then we had the argument on the phone and when I went to call you back you were already gone. I told Wes to tell you I called and you never did? Then I hear from you months later on your birthday and you have the audacity to tell me you just got finished fucking some girl. Syncere I put up with a lot of shit from you but I've loved you the same. But me being here and seeing Kenya's stuff all over the room and the pictures from Atlanta I had to think what is best for Kendra and you're not it."

"Mulan is?"
"No one said anything about Mulan."
"But that is who you talk to every night though, you must think I'm stupid."
"You don't know who I talk to. Why do you love me so much? You've never given me a straight answer."

"What does it matter now? It's not gonna change anything."

"If I told you it would change everything instantaneously would you answer me truthfully? 'Cause truthfully I think you only say you love me because you feel like you have to, like you owe me something. Kenya you love and I can see it all over your face, I know because you looked like that in Georgia. Tell me why you love me so much."

"I can't put it into words I just do. I just feel like you complete me and I can do anything when I know I have you."

"That isn't enough."

"It's the truth."
"It still isn't enough. I think you are holding onto memories of us when we were younger and you've convinced yourself just like you mentioned in your poem on poetry.com. What happens in ten years when you wake up and realize Kenya was the woman for you but you're married to me? Then what?"
"That isn't gonna happen."

"Yes it is. If not by you then by me. Syncere I don't want to be with you romantically but I would love your friendship."

"If that is the case then why'd you tell me we need to get to know each other in person like we do over the phone? If you don't want to be with me then why'd you lie?"
"To make the summer go by as smooth as possible."

"You lied. This whole time you lied. Why'd you come back after that day you left then?"

"Because you wanted me to."

"But you knew you felt this way why didn't you just stay where you were?"

"I didn't know then. Over the past month and a half I've learned more about you than I thought I knew and more about myself but honestly Syncere this will not work. Face it; you're an atheist for heaven's sake. How does that look? I'm a Jehovah's Witness and my husband is an atheist? There are so many things I love about you Syn. I love your relentlessness, your determination, your ability to overcome adversity, work ethic, creativity, the love and loyalty to have for your friends but there are other things about you I know I can't deal with."

"Like what?"

"What did the physic tell you?"

"We agreed not to speak on that."

"Would you tell me please?"

"She said you weren't the one for me."

"She told me the same thing and all this time I've been questioning if she was right all along. Maybe this isn't what God has planned for us."

"There is no God. We determine what happens in our life and if we want it bad enough we can make it happen."

"But I don't want it anymore…I'm sorry."

29

I walked in my apartment for the first time in two weeks to get dress up clothes of which I didn't take with me when I decided to spend the remainder of Kendra's visit at my mother's house. I've talked to my aunt Kim and Mrs. Williams for most of the summer and they keep telling me the same thing, to go to church and put it in God's hands. Aunt Kim and Mrs. Williams have never told me anything wrong so in order to get my "faith" back I'm going to church with Aunt Kim tonight and I'm going to put God to the test. I got dressed wearing the lime green shirt Kenya got for me long with the white slacks I wore at her prom then lightly sprinkled some of my Burberry Britt cologne before checking my hair and face.

"Hear that! Where you goin'?" Sharell asked as I headed to the fridge for a bottle of water. I walked into the living room and all eyes were on me, Tracy's, Michane's, Sharell's and Kendra's.

"What?" I asked.

"Where you goin' cut?" Tracy asked.
"Church."

"Is that the name of a new club or somethin'?" He joked.

"Na, I'm really goin' to church right now." If one word could describe the look on everyone's face it would be wow!

"Why? I mean I'm happy for you I just wanna know why all of sudden you're goin' to church?"

"I'm goin' to get my faith back." I said leaving out of the apartment before anyone could ask me any more questions.

I'm feeling nervous as hell as Aunt Kim and I drove to Meriden where her church is but I'm also feeling confident I'd find the answers I am looking for.

"Syncere I'm so glad you've decided to give the Lord a second chance 'cause you know he gives you second chances everyday."

"I'm only going 'cause I want to know what I'm supposed to do."

"It doesn't matter the reason. I told you God is working on you and when he is done you're gonna see that it was him all along and all this happened to set you up for the end result. But if at anytime you feel the need to leave just go right ahead. I have a friend who lives not too far from me and she'll drive me home."

"Aight."

My body got hot the minute I stepped out of the car and onto church ground. My palms are sweating, I felt the beads of sweat on my forehead and I'm becoming dizzy almost immediately entering the sanctuary. I thought to myself I don't belong here but despite everything in my head saying turn back now I fought through it and sat next to Aunt Kim while the service got underway. One thing I loved about going to church was the music. Even after I swore off religion and became an atheist ironically I still loved listening to gospel music. While the church enjoyed the music Aunt Kim stood clenching my hand with a big smile on her face. I looked over at her and Aunt Kim turned into Kendra, the church turned into Shiloh Missionary Baptist Church and I am fifteen again.

Memories ran wild in my mind as I remembered all the Sunday's Kendra and I sat next to each other writing notes, whispering, biting each others hands and running around outside afterwards. I remembered my baptism and how Kendra was there when I was done, I remember the two of us surrounded by all the kids at church just everything good about those times I remembered. Despite clapping, dancing along to the gospel and sweet memories that hot feeling stayed with me through the entire service.

"At the time if you have anything on your chest or anything you want to say to God, brothers and sisters join us at the alter. If you don't know who God is and haven't accepted him as your Lord and savior please find the faith and strength to make your way to the alter and join us in prayer and salvation." The preacher announced.

As many of the congregation began to crowd the alter I made my way up there also to do what I'd come to do. I got down on both knees, bowed my head, closed my eyes and spoke to God for the first time in two years. As I spoke the heated feeling I had over my entire body slowly faded away and I can hear nothing but my own whispers…then I opened my eyes and got up. To my amazement the entire church is on their knees or standing up behind me. Many of the women are crying uncontrollably while some are shaking and fainting. This is too much for me I thought as I made my way to the back of the church trying not to step on anyone.

Almost away from the sea of church members filled with the Holy Ghost I stood face to face with an elder African American man who is speaking in tongues with his eyes closed. I stopped to look at him for a second wondering why don't I have the feeling this entire church has. While everyone is filled with the spirit the only thing I could think about is getting the hell out of here. As I proceeded to walk by the elder man from the corner of my eye I saw his body gave out and he began falling to the floor. Without hesitation I grabbed his arm to keep him from falling.

Once he balanced again the elder man opened his eyes with tears falling out of them as he looked at me as if I were God himself. He kept his hand on my wrist then he put is left hand on my right shoulder and nodded in gratitude.

"God is with you young man." he said. I looked back at the alter and watched Kendra turn back into Aunt Kim. We met eyes and she nodded her head as well, I nodded back then left the church.

Once Kenya returned from London a second time we talked every night even after I started staying back in my own apartment after the night I went to church. Not much has changed between Kendra and I since my talk with God and this time I know I have the answer I was looking for. I accepted the inevitable and let Kendra go. We walk passed each other in the hallway or whenever I go into the room but I no longer feel that need to want to say something to her, just as I'd hoped she's grown dead to me inside and that has opened me up to give one hundred percent to Kenya.

"When does she leave?"

"Tomorrow and it can't come soon enough."

"Are you gonna be sad?" Kenya asked.

"Hell no. I'm good. Look babe I wanna tell you, if I haven't already, that you've been the best girlfriend ever for handling this situation with pure maturity and trust in me. If I've learned anything this summer it's that I only want to be wit'chu."

"Good 'cause I only want to be with you too. When am I gonna see you again?"

"For your birthday this Thursday."

"Oh really? What do you have planned for me?"

"Can't tell you, it's a surprise."

"Whatever it is can we eat at Red Lobster?"

"Oh course."

"Call me later when I get off work. I love you."

"I love you too." Knock, knock. I looked up to see Tracy standing in the doorway of my room with Michane behind him.

"Cut. We was thinkin' that since Kendra is leavin' tomorrow that we'd have everyone over and throw her a goin' away slash congratulations party. And we wanna know if you wanna chip in."

"Nope!"

While Michane cleaned up, Tracy cooked dinner until everyone started to arrive for the party. Music played, laughter filled the room and I bounced little Tre'Shawn on my lap as Sharell and Kendra walked in the house while everyone shouted SURPRISE!!

"All this for me? Ya'll didn't have to do that."

"But we wanted to." Michane said. Kendra worked the room giving hugs and kisses to everyone before we all finally ate and joked around with one another. I didn't say too much to Kendra and she didn't say too much to me except thank you of which I returned with a nod of my head. It is a fun night that carried on until almost midnight before people started clearing out.

I rushed home from work today hoping to at least to see Kendra leave for the airport to pick her mother up but when I got home at six Tracy told me her mother's plane doesn't arrive until nine o'clock tonight. Michane and Kendra spent the evening in my room talking and Sharell sat on the couch watching while I whooped on Tracy in Madden as the time drew later and later. 2 games later Kendra brought out a gift bag to Sharell and thanked her for the fun she's had this summer then doing the same for Michane and Tracy. I sat in my office chair acting as if she isn't in the room while she hugged Michane and Sharell then as he jumped on Tracy, almost knocking him to the ground, giving him the biggest tightest hug possible.

"Tracy will you please give these bags to Wes, Quincy, and Dorian. I thought they were coming by but it's getting late and I have to go."

"Aight." Kendra made two trips to load up her car with the help of Michane and Sharell then with only her duffle bag on her shoulder she said good-bye once more to Tracy, Michane and Sharell before walking out of the apartment not saying two words to me. I listened for her car to turn on; lights to appear then disappear before I threw the controller on the floor.

"She had the fuckin' audacity to walk outta my house and not say good-bye to me?"

"Cut you didn't exactly make an effort to say anything to her either."
"Neither did you but that didn't stop her from jumping on you. That's some bullshit...fuck that bitch." I said picking up the controller while everyone else didn't say a thing. Tracy and I played another game of Madden but I'm too pissed off to concentrate which allowed Tracy to pick up his first win over me in a year.

I threw the controller down again pissed off that I lost, pissed off that this broad left my house without parting her lips in my direction and I stormed into my room slamming the door behind me. As I paced around my room I notice something on my bed. I looked and saw a small candle attached to a card with my name on it. I sat on the edge of my bed and read it.

Syncere,

I have learned so much about myself this summer and I want to thank you for everything you've done for me. I wish you the best of luck at Finish line because I know you will be successful with anything you choose to do. Since you pretty much have the money to buy whatever you want I didn't know what to get you but I hope you like the candle. Thank you and best of luck with the rest of your life. Take care and thank you again.

Kendra Lewis.

I read over the card two or three more times before taking it into the living room for Tracy and Sharell to read. I sat on the couch still pissed off while Tracy and Sharell didn't know what to do or say to me. Tracy and I played another game of Madden of which I beat his ass again but I'm still furious and I must do something.

"I need to get out and fuck somebody up." I finally said.

"What?" Tracy asked as he and Sharell looked puzzled.

"I need to get out and inflict as much pain on someone else as I feel right now."

"Nigga you crazy, what'chu need is some pussy." Tracy said winking at Sharell.

"No...I need to beat somebody's ass." I went to the front door and slipped on my running shoes and grabbed a hoodie out of the closet.

"Nigga where you goin'?"

"I already told you."

"Well I'm goin' wit'chu 'cause it just be your luck that'chu go out and get your ass whooped."

"Yeah right, me? Nigga I'm tha fuckin' devil."
"Aight nigga you can't beat everybody. Look lemme call Mook and we can go out and do somethin' else."

"Na I need to find a hooker and beat the fuck outta her."

"Why a hooker?" Sharell asked.

"'Cause a woman hurt me like this so I gotta punish a woman."

"Somethin' is really wrong wit'chu. I don't think you need to be goin' out anywhere."

"Na fuck that."

After two hours of driving around splashing spoiled milk and throwing eggs at innocent bystanders I feel a hundred times better. I really wanted to smash my fists against human flesh but Tracy, Mook and Sharell convinced me to do otherwise. I paced around my room thinking and thinking about where my life would be in the next five years when I got to thinking that a year itself is a long time. I don't know where my life will be in the next five weeks or in the next five days when Kenya leaves for college; this is beginning to be too much.

"Cut?" Tracy said sticking his head into my room.

"Yo?"

"Yo why you got Sharell sleepin' on the couch? Let her sleep in here wit'chu."

"Na I'm good."

"Cut, for real for real. I know you like her so just com'on. She madd lonely in there and you slept on that couch so you know how uncomfortable it is."

"I ain't ask her to stay here and she's been sleepin' on it all this time. Kendra is gone but Kenya is still my girlfriend. I'm in no position romantically, or psychologically to be in bed wit another broad."

"Why she gotta be all that? Look I'm just sayin', you mad as hell and she madd lonely so ya'll should just lay next to each other and talk or somethin'."

"Na I'm good. Close my door on your way out."

Tomorrow is the day, the day Kenya leaves for Rhode Island and we haven't seen each other for a week. I'm anxiously waiting to see her sliver Jeep Liberty pull up in front of my apartment so we can drive to the car dealership together and pick out a new car. Dressed in my black slacks, black shoes, red collard shirt and topped with Burberry Brit cologne, I double-checked my braids again when I heard the horn. I gave Kenya a tight hug lifting her up off the ground as she giggled in my ear.

"Miss me?"

"Oh yeah. You ready?"

"Yeah but I can't stay long I still have a ton of things to do today."

"You got me on a time limit? Me? I thought we'd have the whole day together."

"I'm sorry baby but you only have me for a couple of hours. Don't pout." She said kissing me. Just the thought of being with Kendra is enough for me so I pushed aside the short amount of time we have together in order to cherish the time we do have.

Kenya sat pretty beside me while I talked to Phil and finalized the paperwork for the new 2005 Saturn Ion 3 I am purchasing. Whenever I looked around the dealership I saw guys trying to catch a look at the diamond on my arm and it make me smile and each time I did I clenched Kenya's hand a little tighter than before.

"Mr. Johnson you have purchased yourself an excellent vehicle and I believe you will be happy with it. We're going to put the vehicle through our 127 point inspection and by that time the plates should be at that time I'll personally give you a call to come pick it up. Roughly three days." Phil explained.

"Alright. Thank you very much. I'll see you then.

"You're leaving without your car? Oh yeah it has to get inspected, duh." Kenya reminded herself.

"You like it?" I asked walking back to the car.

"Yeah I like the color and the OnStar you have in it. That's something you need 'cause you're always gettin' lost."

"I do not. I only get lost when you're givin' directions so now when I drive to Rhode Island I have accurate ones. You hungry?"

"Yeah but I'm supposed to have dinner with my dad so I can hit him up for some money before I leave."

"What do you need money for?"

"I don't, I have all I need but why spend mine when I can spend his? Besides he owes me for ruining our family."

"Oh ok since you put it that way. Wanna lay down with me?"

"I can't have sex Syncere, I'm on my period."

"Why every time I wanna lay wit'chu you assume I wanna have sex?"

"'Cause I know you and you can't go without sex that long and the last time we've done it have been a while ago."

"Well answer me this. You've been here four times since the last time we made love and every time you tell me you're on your period. Is that true or you just don't wanna make love to me?"

"That ridiculous. If I didn't wanna do it I'd just tell you."

"Would you really?" I asked why sitting on the edge of my bed watching her get articles of clothing out of my closet and dressers.

"Yes I would. Can I use your Burberry overnight bag? I'll bring it back to you when I come home."

"Yeah, you brought it. Why can't you look at me when you say that?"

"Say what?"

"That if you didn't want you you'd tell me."

"I'm packing Syncere. Are you trying to start a fight with me?"

"Why would I wanna do that knowin' that tomorrow every guy on the campus is gonna try to fuck you. The last thing I wanna do is make you leave mad at me."

"We have to talk."

"'Bout what?" Kenya dropped my Burberry overnight bad containing all her belongings on the floor beside her and took my hand in hers.

"I think we need a break."

"A break from what?"

"A break from each other."

"What for?"

"For the past almost two years you have been my life and all I've known. I just wanna go to college and focus on getting adjusted and getting the most out of it."

"So you wanna see other people?"

"No of course not. I just don't want to get there and cheat on you."

"What? You don't wanna get there and cheat on me? What the fuck does that mean? If you don't wanna cheat on me then don't."

"I can't promise you that. I don't want you sitting here worrying about what I'm doing. Baby you just made market leader and you're gonna have a lot on your plate and I don't wanna add to the burden."

"Kenya you're not a burden. Tell me what's really good and stop makin' up excuses. I don't think you've lied to me in two years so please don't start now. Tell me the truth."

"You want me to tell you the truth?"

"Yes, just tell me what it is 'cause to me a break means a break up."

"It's not a break up. It's just a break. To see if moving to California or Brazil is what the both of us want to do. To see if we want to spend the rest of our life together like we keep talking about. But you wanna know the truth? Ok. Do you know why kind of emotional stress I've been under for the past year dealing with you Syncere?"

"Emotional stress?"

"Yes, emotional stress. I've had to listen to how you were parading around Waterbury with Stacy; I've had to deal with you accidentally calling me Kendra in the middle of a conversation. I've had to endure my summer before college without my boyfriend because he was sleeping under the same roof with his first love. Syncere I've had to compete with that woman since day one and I shouldn't have to. When everyone said I was stupid for being with you while she stayed here I believed in you. I've had to stare at her initials on your arm every time I watched you get dressed or undress. The nights you didn't call I cried myself to sleep wondering what you were doing, wondering if you still love me…"

"Kenya I do love you."

"Ha, you love me? You love me? Well if you love me so much then why didn't I have a say so in her coming here?"

"I told you Tracy and Michane already told her she could come. I even told you that she."

That's just it Syncere, you told me but you didn't ask me. You didn't give me the option of saying yes or no. You just dropped that on me and left me to deal with it and as your girlfriend as the love of your life you were supposed to include me in this more than what you did. And you know what the worst part of all is? You justified it all summer."

"Kenya how could you say that? I called you every chance I got, you knew where I was at all times, hell for the last three and a half weeks I stayed at my moms house. I did everything I could to make sure our relationship stayed the same."

"Then why didn't you tell me that she left the first night she was here and that you asked her to come back? Why didn't you tell me about the day at the amusement park? Why didn't you tell me the reason you stayed at your mothers house was because she told you she wasn't the woman for you? Why'd you leave all that out?"

"Who told you all that?"

"Don't worry about it. Is it true or not? You know what? It doesn't even matter anymore because look at me. I'm gorgeous! What guy wouldn't want me and hold on to me when he gets me? I gave you my heart for the past two years and all you've done is lie to me, cheat on me and made me believe you're someone you're not and I hate you for it. I sincerely hate you for it."

"So this whole break shit was a lie? We lie to each other now?"

"As much as I hate you right now I still have feelings for you because I love you. I knew you were cheating but I loved you and I knew what Kendra coming here meant but I still loved you, loved you harder and I just can't do that anymore. You don't deserve me." She said crying.

"And Ricky does?"

"This had nothing to do with Ricky."

"How many lies are you gonna tell me today. You're already breakin' up with me so why don't we get it all out in the open."

"Ok, yes Ricky does. Ricky and I have started hanging out again like I told you before and things kinda escalated."

"Escalated? Into what?"

"Something more than friendship."

"You fucked him?"

"No but we are talking about getting back together. He's even moving to Rhode Island."

"So you already had this whole thing planned out? All day you've been waiting to break up with me. You hugged me, kissed, smiled in my face all day knowin' you were gonna do this. That's fucked up."

"No you're fucked up for doing me the way you did. I would've done anything for you Syncere and I did and this is how you do me? You were perfect to me especially when you came back from your trip in North Carolina but then I found out you went to propose to Kendra only to have her turn you down. But you love me right? Look at me, I'M FUCKIN' GORGEOUS!! I'M PERFECT!! Men will kill to have me by their side. I'm destined for greatness and you just lost the best thing you will ever have in your life. Take care."

I can't say a word, not one single word. As the tears rolled down my face and as Kenya wiped hers I watched in helplessness as she picked up my Burberry overnight bag, walk out of my apartment and out of my life. A million pleas and apologies crowed my head but I can't utter a single one. My heart said run after her but my legs said *get real she's gone*. I can't bring myself to watch her Jeep Liberty drive away; I can't bring myself to pick up my cell phone to call her only to hear the phone ring a thousand times knowing she will no answer. Just let her go. I sat on my bed like a defeated animal crying my heart out as this feels like something I've never ever felt before. My heart hurts, my soul hurts and it feels like my life was just taken from me.

It's hard to breath yet I keep inhaling the last of her Burberry Brit for women perfume lingering in the atmosphere. I don't know what to do yet; my mind has so many things going through it. I reached for the picture of us together in Atlanta knocking over my penholder. A razorblade fell out so as I went to put it back I stared at it for a while. Then I slid it open and pressed it hard against my wrists and closed my eyes. The cold steel on my warm skin sent chills up my spine, as I pressed harder, then my cell phone rang. I tossed the blade to the floor as I scurried to my feet searching for my phone.

"Kenya?"

"Syncere."

"Kenya?"

"No dummy its Mary."

"Oh, what do you want?"

"Mark wants you to do a shakedown tomorrow at store 618 so he told me to call you."

"Aight." I said trying not to sound sad.

"You ok?"

"Yeah."

"You sound like you've been cryin'. What happened? Did Tracy sit on your head?" She said laughin'.

"Na I just woke up."

"What? It's four-thirty in the afternoon."

"I know. I'm tired."

"Doesn't Kenya leave today?"

"Yeah. I'm goin' to see her later."

"Tell her I said hi."

"I will."

The razor blade had landed on my red and black notebook and the reality of Kenya walking out on me set in again and I seriously want to die. I looked down at my wrist and saw a thin red line from me pressing the blade on my skin and thought I have to leave something for whoever find me, something that justifies my passing and something that tells my final thoughts. I began to write and I could only write to one person. Not my mother, not my Aunt Dimpsey, not Tracy and not Kendra…but Kenya.

Kenya,

   If you would just bare with me for these few minutes I want to tell you a couple of things. You are the omega of my heart and the understanding for my idea of love. But I was afraid to fall in love with you in the beginning but I felt it when I saw you walk out of Bertucci's that day. You were more of a woman at that time than I was a man but I couldn't see that because our age difference and our obstacles blinded me. From day one you put 100% into our relationship and you loved me unconditionally even with my numerous flaws, all the times I took you for granted and you did that without compliant. Over the past two years I have fought the urge to commit my entire self to our relationship because I thought there was someone else better for me not seeing that you were perfect in every shape, way and form. You complimented me, you inspired me and you made me, in some ways, a better man. Most of all you taught me what love really is and how to love someone. You showed me that making love is just as much mental as it is physical and I want you to know that when we made love it meant so much more to me. Yes you are gorgeous, even more gorgeous when you're naked but it was your eye contact that got me aroused and with one look you brought me to climax without even touching me. The conversation, the good vibrations that made me want to express myself physically with you so much. I know I never told you enough but thoughts of you consume ninety-percent of my day and every song reminds me of you. When I miss you I stare at your pictures and listen to songs that compliments the memorable times we've shared together. You may think you are with your soul mate, but regardless of how things turned out, he and no other man are capable of loving you as much as I do. It took for the summer to happen the way it did for me to man up and commit to how I feel about you and the only thing I wish is that I would've manned up months ago. All the plans we made, Brazil, California and a life together I just want you to know I meant every single word of it despite of my actions. My intentions were never ever to hurt you in any way only to love you like I do. The words sorry aren't enough and I know that but that is all I can say right now. I didn't deserve you but I'm thankful for having you for the time I did, as the times are the memories that keep me from crying. Picturing you with Ricky burns me to the soul, not because I'm jealous but because I want to be the one to make you smile the way you do and as happy as you can be. I'm going to leave you with one more thing because I know everything from here on will start to repeat itself so here goes. Kenya, I would give my sight just to see you smile at me again. I will also give up my sense of sound only to hear you tell me you love me one last time. Touch and smell? They can be taken away as well if it means I get to feel your body against mine. The smell of your hair, your petite frame pressed up against me as the softness of your lips grace mine. And if there is a devil I hope he's reading because I would sell my soul to him if he'd allow us to grow old together and if there is a God, like they say there is, he'd allow it to happen because he knows how much I love you. I guess that's it. I want you to know, whether you believe it or not, I love you with all my heart and despite of how you may feel now I hope that one day you find it in your heart, find it in that love you had for me to give us another chance. If the way If feel right now is a fraction of how I made you feel then I hope I feel like this for a long time as I want to take back the pain I inflicted on you. Words will never define how I feel for you or how miserable I'm certain my life will be without you so just know every time my phone rings I pray your name pop up. I'll be right here waiting because you were right, you can have me back if you wanted to. You are my soul mate and I love you.

Good-bye,

Syncere.

   With that written and after reading it over I took the razor and put it in the pages of my red notebook and sat the notebook beside my bed deciding to wait for Kenya to take me back. I'll apologize until I'm blue in the face, once that has run it's course I'll send her roses until she develops an allergy to them then when that runs its course I'll visit her until she puts a restraining order out on me. I have to show her I'm here for her and I'm the one she's supposed to have in her life. Most of all I'll be her friend when she needs one, be a friend and wait for my time.

30

The days passed like years, the hours passed liked months and the minutes never seemed to pass at all. My depression grows by the day but everyday I fight the desire to open my red book up to the page of Kenya's letter and leaving it on the kitchen table next to my lifeless body for Tracy, Michane or Sharell to find. As I walk pass other stores in the mall to get to mine I stopped to look at myself in the mirror, hideous. I haven't shaved in two months nor have I gotten my braids re-done; I just don't care about my appearance anymore. Honestly if I didn't work with the general public everyday I'd probably wouldn't shower either.

"Dude what the hell has happened to you?" A mid-western voice said causing me to look up. Shit, my district manager is here.

"Hey Mark, what's up?"

"Dude what's up with you? It looks like you've been through hell. Mary told me you haven't been yourself and I can hear it Mondays on our conference calls but dude what is going on?"

"I...I..."

"Look, just go open your store, clock in and we'll talk about it over breakfast." And we did just that. Mark and I sat in the food court eating Dunkin Donuts bagels while I told him how hellish the last two months of my life has been. I told him how I trot around the store until it's time for me to go home and when I go home I retreat to my room where I watch the film of Kenya and I in Atlanta just so I can hear her laugh and call me baby. I explained that my whole source of motivation, inspiration and willingness to take care of myself physically is not there anymore...I straight came out and told him I feel like dying.

"I know I'm supposed to leave my problems at home Mark but she is the only thing I can think about. When I think about selling an insole I think about the first time I put one in Kenya's Air Force 1's, when I think about coming to work I think about her meeting me here and having breakfast with me and now it's starting to snow which is killing me."

"Why?"

"'Cause the first night I stayed in her house was because her mom didn't want me to drive home in the storm. So we sat by the window in each others arms and talked all night."

"Dude I'm not gonna lie to you. You got it bad but I know how you feel. Do you still talk to her?"

"She calls the store every Monday at three o'clock like clockwork."

"That gotta be torture to hear from her every week knowing she's with someone else. I feel for you man."

"So you're not mad?"
"Not mad now that I know why your 41 reports, accessories, multiples and training looks like crap. I don't even want to walk into the store because I'm afraid of how it looks. But now I know what's going on with you so I can fix it. So Syncere how do we fix it? 'Cause right now I have every intention of firing you right now."

"Get me Kenya back."

"Realistically you or I have no control over that. Syncere I just made you market leader two months ago and you go and start performing like this. I've never seen your face full of hair or your braids looking like a pile of tumble weed. You need to pull yourself together and get back on track. You think if Kenya were to walk in your store right now and saw you like this she'd want you back? Dude you look like you haven't even showered."

"I showered." I said sharing a laugh with Mark.

"Or what if she were to walk in with that other guy right now? Would you want them to see you at your worst or your best? The next time you see this girl you would want her to look at you and say, damn I want Syncere back. But right now you're scaring her away. I know you love her, I met her and she's an amazing young woman but you can't let it affect you like this. Take the rest of the day off and I'll do your visit tomorrow."

"Thanks Mark."

"No problem."

On the way home I made a two o'clock appointment with Mel to get a much-needed shape up before calling Evelyn and begging her to do my hair. She put up a fight but I won. Once back at home I watched the tape of Kenya and I in Atlanta while I sat on my bed taking my braids out thinking of a way to get Kenya back. As I stood in my mirror looking at my jet black blow-dried hair sit on my shoulders and the top of my back I looked at my left shoulder for the first time in months. Kendra's initials stick out like a sore thump...then it hit me. I looked at my hair then back at the tattoo, back at my hair then back at the tattoo two more times before throwing on some clothes and going to the barber shop.

"What's good Syn? Long time no see. I thought somethin' happened to you cousin."

"Na Mel I'm good man just been goin' threw a lot of shit na mean?"

"I feel that. So you want the regular?"

"Na cut it all off."

"No beard, no goatee? Just clean shaven?"

"Na I mean everything...all this." I said grabbing my hair.

"YOUR HAIR?" he said causing everyone in the shop to stop in mid conversation and direct his or her attention to us.

"Yeah. All of it."

"Are you sure?"

"Yeah."

"Aight. How you want it?"

"Bald fade."

"Bald fade? What?"

"I guess. That was the last type of haircut I got before I started growin' my hair. Well shit, do it like yours. What's that?"

"It's just a cut down to a one and a half."

"Aight do mine like yours then."

"Are you sure you wanna cut it all off?" Mel asked again turning on the clippers.

"Mel just do it."

"Aight." Then without warning a foot of my hair landed in my lap followed by a tear. Normally there hardly any women in the shop but today the seven that just so happened to be there all stood around gasping every time Mel cut off another chunk of hair. Forty minutes later I'm staring at a man I've never seen before. With a low haircut, ice picked side burns and a sharp goatee I picked my cut hair off the barber shop floor and stuffed it in a plastic Stop & Shop bag. I paid Mel and exited without further conversation ignoring the women complimenting me.

The cool October air hit my head sending chills throughout my body making me regret not bringing a jacket with me. I rubbed my shoulders trying to think of what I'm going to do next when I eyes looked upon Dogg E Style tattoo shop across the street. I looked down at Kendra's initials and thought the next time I see Kenya I'd be able to show her I finally let the last piece of Kendra go by having her initials covered.

"What can I do for you today?" A heavyset heavily tattooed and pierced white guy said looking up from tattooing a young white girl.

"I wanna know if you can cover a tattoo for me."

"Well sure any tattoo can be covered. It just depends of what you choose to get over it 'cause if you don't like the new one it'll be kinda hard to cover them both with a third one."

"Na that won't happen."

"Come behind here and lemme see it." I rolled up my sleeve and showed the guy, who introduced himself as Dogg.

"I already know what I want. Can you cover it?"

"Yeah. Here sign this and I'll with you in twenty minutes, I'm almost done here."

"Aight."

I chose the theatre masks that represented laughing now and crying later. Instead of getting them both on the same arm I got one big one, the crying one, on my right shoulder and the laughing on my left shoulder covering Kendra's initials. But the laughing one isn't exactly laughing, it's smiling devilishly.

"Why do you want this one different?"

"'Cause I don't cry now and laugh later. I cry now then get even later. So the devilish face is actually my get even face."

"Sounds personal."

"Kinda."

"So who was the girl?"

"Nobody important."

"So I guess you're covering it up because your new girlfriend wants you to huh?"

"That and to close this long chapter of my saga one would call a life."

"Got'cha. Well I'm done. Go in the mirror and check'em out." With my arms burning from the needle scraping my skin over the past hour I stood in front of the mirror satisfied with Dogg's artwork.

"How much do you owe you?"

"Hundred fifty." I gave Dogg one seventy-five.

I couldn't help but looking at the new me in the mirror when I got home, shirtless and hairless I felt my suicidal attitude change for the better. I read over the letter I wrote Kenya two months ago in the kitchen while eating a bowl of cereal when the strangest idea hit me. I grabbed my phone.

"Biggy Ones! What's good cousin it's Syncere?"

"What it look like?"

"Chillin'. Yo what'chu doin' right now?"

"Smokin' this L why?"

"Wanna take a ride with me?"

"To where?"

"Rhode Island."

"Rhode Island? Aight fuck it let's go."

"I'll be there in an hour.

Brand new black Stacy Adams crocodile shoes, black Perry Ellis dress slacks, Sigma blue button down collard shirt, a new hair cut and confident attitude are on their way with a dozen roses and Biggy Ones to Johnson & Wales University in Rhode Island. I repeatedly called Kenya's cell phone and dorm to no avail as I just think she's in her last class of the day until I remembered that on Thursday's she doesn't have any class.

The two and a half hour drive was spend listening to Biggy Ones recite almost every song on my iPod while I rehearsed what I'd say to Kenya when I see her and what I'd do if that bitch ass nigga Ricky gets in my way. Flash backs of Mulan played in my head as I agreed to what the consequences of my actions would be if I took that route. Fuck it...go down fighting. I used map quest and the address that I send her flowers to every week to direct me to her dorm and when we finally got there the sky had changed from sunset to dusk.

"She still not answerin'?" Biggy Ones asked.

"Na son and now we here."

"Don't she know you comin'?"

"Na. I wanted to surprise her."

"She doesn't know you comin'? We drove all the way up here and she ain't know? You wild Syn."

"That's love. Com'on let's see if they let us up. Excuse me, can you tell me what room Kenya Northrop is in?"

"No."

"No? Look I'm her boyfriend and I just drove here from Connecticut to surprise her so can you just page her or something?"

"Call her phone and tell her to come down and sign you in."

"Duh, I did that but she isn't answerin'."

"Doesn't she know you're comin'? She'll answer soon."

"I just told you I'm surprisin' her so she don't know."

"Wow. How smart are you to dive all this way not to know if she is even here for not. Genius."

"What?" I tried to grab the pencil nosed white boy from over the counter but Biggy Ones stopped me.

"Let's just go outside and try callin' her again." While Bruce talked to white girls who entered and exited the dormitory I called Kenya seven more times and still got no answer.

"Hey Mr. Man how are you babes?"

"Not good Em."

"Aww sweetie, still miss Kenya?"

"Yeah that's why I called. Do you know her dorm number 'cause I think I got the wrong one?"

"Why what's wrong?"

"I came to her school to surprise her and she not answerin' the phone."

"Aww sweetie she came home today. She's in Danbury."

"WHAT! She's in DANBURY??"

"Yeah she just called me a second ago. Here lemme connect you to her."

"Hello?"

"Kenya? Its Syncere."

She relucatantly said "Hey. What's up?"

"Umm why haven't you been answerin' ya phone?"

"Mine is dead so I'm on my friends'. What's wrong?"

"I'm in Rhode Island."

"What are you doin' there?"

"I came to surprise you."

"Syncere why did you do that?"

"'Cause you never come see me when you're at home and I miss you so I wanted to see you."

"Syncere when I said I needed space it wasn't my idea of you popping up to surprise me in Rhode Island. You're crazy."

"Well how long are you gonna be home?"

"The weekend."

"Can I see you tonight?"

"I have plans."

"Can I see you tomorrow or Saturday?"

"I'm working at Merle Norman Syncere. Look I'm on my friends' phone so I'll call you later." And just like that she hung up.

"Syn?"

"Yeah Em?"

"Just makin' sure you're still there. I have some stuff to tell you."

"What?" I asked signaling Biggy Ones to get in the car.

"I don't know how to tell you this 'cause it's a lot."

"So start from the beginning."

"Before the summer was over Kenya went by your store to surprise you but you weren't there."

"Nobody told me." I said trying to remember if someone did and I just forgot.

"Listen. Mary and Noe told her that you brought Kendra to the store to meet everyone then went on to say how happy you two looked and everything."

"Oh my God. I just stopped by there 'cause I was showin' her how to get to her job so I figured I'd stop by the check on the staff na mean?"

"Shut up Syn and listen. Who is Jamie?"

"A chick that works at Rave Girl down the hall."

"Do you like her?"

"I mean she cute and we flirt a lot when she come in but she got a man, why?"

"Well Mary and Noe told her you and Jamie were fuckin'. They also told her about the girl from England that you met and a bunch of other girls which upset Kenya a lot."

"Why didn't she say anything to me?"

"She said you'd just talk your way out of everything, she says you always have some kind of logical excuse that makes her think you're not lying when everything in her head says otherwise. But there's more. Around the same time Kenya found out she was pregnant."

"By me?"

"Yeah, she wasn't having sex with anyone else but you. But shut up and stop askin' questions. She wanted to tell you but she was afraid 'cause ya'll talked about havin' kids before so she knew you'd want to keep it."

"She didn't?"

"Syncere! You wanna know or not?"

"Please Em.... just tell me if she wanted to keep it."
"Yes she wanted to we even started picking out baby names the day she found out. Anyway, Kenya's doctor called but Kenya's mom answered the phone and she told her about the baby. So Kenya's mom confronted her about it and they got in this big argument in which Kenya's mom told her she wouldn't pay for her to go to school and she'd kick her out of the house and disown her. The day she went to your store she had most of her things packed up & loaded in her truck because she was gonna tell you. I convinced her you'd take care of everything so she was basically running away. Her mother didn't know, her sisters didn't know 'cause she only trusted me. But when Mary and Noe told her about all those other girls she drove to the park and ride you two go and cried to me on the phone for hours not knowin' what to do."

"So she do?" I asked bracing myself for the worst.

"She felt like she couldn't compete with Kendra. She felt like everything you told her was a lie, everything from the I love you's, the plans for Brazil, havin' kids and everything. She thought keeping the baby wasn't gonna make you change your ways so she asked Ricky to take her to the abortion clinic."

"She aborted it? Ricky took her? Why Em? When...when did she go?"

"Two days before she saw you last. Syn she didn't want to do it. She really wanted to keep it but with Kendra staying with you, all the girls Mary and Noe told her about she felt stupid so she made a decision. It was either have an uncertain life with you or go to school and try to have a normal one. She knew you were cheating but she loved you to the point she convinced herself otherwise but brining Kendra here re-opened the wound."

"Why'd you wait two months to tell me?"

"Because I wasn't. I thought since she broke up with you that you went back to Kendra. Just at the moment you called saying you drove all the way to Rhode Island to surprise her made me change my mind. That is love Syncere I know it is. I didn't tell you for the same reason I didn't tell Kenya about Stacy and Yumeka, because I am your friend. And as her friend I had to keep some secrets from you. I hate being in the middle but I felt guilty for not tellin' her."

"So when she told you what Mary told her why didn't you dime me out and confirm everything."

"I would never do that Syn. I'll never to anything to hurt you or her but I will protect you both."

As raindrops beat on my windshield and tears streaming down my face my heart sank. Just at that instant I wanted to take the gun from under my seat and blow my brains out, I made her kill our child and pushed her into the arms of another man. I can hear Emily saying she's sorry over and over again but I just let the phone drop

and I cried all the way home ignoring Biggy Ones' pleas to tell him what happened. All I can think about is finding Noe and beating his ass and calling all my sisters to fuck Mary up. My two assistant managers and my so-called friends dimmed me out and lied about Jamie in the process, they deserve worse.

Back in Waterbury I dropped Biggy Ones off and jumped back on the highway high tailing to Mary's house since I know Noe would be there also. I took the same gun I beat Mulan with from under my seat and took the clip out myself before stuffing it in my waist. As my car hydroplaned on the highway Nelly & Tim McGraw's song Over & Over played on the radio making every lyric relevant to my current situation I thought to myself I left my notebook in the kitchen on the table open to Kenya's letter but no one has called me so I assume they didn't read it or take it as a suicide note. In my rearview mirror two bright lights appeared nearly blinding me. I switched from the fast lane into the traveling lane to avoid the car thinking as slippery as it is out here they're gonna hit someone. With the light out of my mirror I focused back on the highway.

BOOM! CRASH!! CRUNCH!!! I felt a tremendous force hit my silver Saturn, that Kenya named Bella, from behind. The bright lights are now back in my mirror as I struggled to regain control of the car. BOOM!! Again this time coming from the driver side door delivering excruciating pain to my left side of my body as I felt my car slide into the slow lane. CRASH!! Again from what seemed like another car hitting me on the corner of the passenger side pushing me skidding to the other side of the highway. With red in my eyes, my head pounding and a paralyzed left side everything seemed to calm down and move in slow motion. I barley turned my head to see the barricade slowly coming toward me but I didn't try to grab the wheel. I braced myself for the impact and just as the barricade was close enough to touch...

Kenya's smiling face appeared. The image that appeared is of her smiling and posing for the picture I took of her when I had my white Mitsubishi Diamante the winter afternoon we sat off exit eleven at the park and ride. She wore the white sweater with the white headband while resting her face on her left hand smiling big for me, my favorite picture of her. Not the ones of her half naked but the first picture I ever took of her. I stared at the image managing to smile through all the pain I am feeling and I whispered...I love you Kenya...CRASH!!!